BLACK CREEK
WHITE LIES

Also by Murray Bailey

Map of the Dead
I Dare You

BLACK CREEK WHITE LIES

Murray Bailey

Heritage Books

HB

First published in Great Britain in 2017 by Heritage Books

1

ISBN 978-0-9955108-7-6
e-book ISBN 978-0-9955108-8-3

Printed and bound by Clays Ltd, St Ives plc

Heritage Books, Truro, Cornwall
HB

For Maureen, my mother.
You are the white light.

ONE

Except for a string of street lights by the green, darkness was absolute. There was no moon, and clouds hid the stars. For a few minutes she hid, checking in case anyone was waiting, anyone was hiding in the shadows. She was early so expected no one, but she had to be sure before crossing the green and taking the track by the foreshore. She stepped carefully even though she knew the path well. Twist an ankle on one of the big stones and her plan would be ruined.

Over a hundred yards later she was at the fence by Dan's boatyard. It was buckled to waist height, caused by many years of people climbing over rather than skirting around.

A creamy light seemed to come from the sheds so she made herself comfortable and waited.

Was Dan still up in the middle of the night? As she waited to see if the light would go out, she looked at the dinghies tied up close to the water's edge. Dan had taught her to sail the old Laser two years ago. He was the only one who cared, showed an interest and encouraged her. He even thought she had talent. Maybe she did. If she went as far as Salcombe, she could sail seriously. Perhaps make the Olympics. And if she didn't then never mind. She would have plenty of money.

The pale light didn't go off. She could see the tide was coming in and as she waited it seemed to crawl stealthily towards her.

She checked her watch. High tide was ninety minutes away. Even though there was a light on somewhere, she couldn't wait much longer. She needed that Laser.

Because of the water level, she had to climb the fence rather than go around on the shore. Three paces across the concrete and floodlights burst on.

Despite expecting them, the bright lights still made her freeze momentarily. Then she quickly flung her backpack into the dinghy and waited.

"Jade?" It was Dan's voice.

She looked towards the sheds and saw him on his decking. The creamy light she'd seen was from his art studio.

"Hey," she called up and waved.

"I'll come down."

A minute later he appeared downstairs where she met him halfway.

He said, "What the heck are you doing here at this time of night?"

"Couldn't sleep. You?"

"I was finishing a sculpture. That's the thing when you're an artist—you have to do it when the mood is right."

She could see he was trying to appear relaxed, but there was a crease of concern on his brow.

He said, "Not like you to miss a Saturday sail. Especially since it's been such a lovely day."

"It's been a bit tame today. I prefer it windier."

"Of course you do, but a great sailor can race no matter what the conditions."

"I could take her out now."

"It's much too late."

2

"I've been out in the dark before—many times." As soon as she said it, she regretted letting him know. Funny that when you have a secret you think that the slightest thing gives it away.

Dan shook his head and opened up the office. "Want to talk?"

"OK," she said. She was a bit nervous about this. Killing some time by sailing alone would have been fine. Talking to Dan? Well, she would have to be careful not to say too much. He would dissuade her. He wouldn't understand. And he was an adult with adult worries. He would see risk where she saw opportunity. This was the chance to change her life and she was going to take it.

Dan turned on the lights and she dumped herself on the sofa.

"Let's go over the new course that I've put together to test you." He was over by the whiteboard. The map of the Truro River had buoys marked on it and he traced a route and indicated a wind direction. Then he asked her to talk him through her moves.

She knew she hadn't made any mistakes, but he challenged her and painted scenarios where other boats took her line. Then he switched wind direction and had her go through it again.

"You're distracted," he said.

"Just a bit dull, that's all."

"But important. Your next race—Mount Bay—is only two weeks away and I want you to win."

She faked a smile. How could she tell him she wouldn't be there for that race? She couldn't.

"So talk to me," he said, as though reading her mind.

She shrugged.

"What's up? Has your dad hit you again?"

She shrugged again. Nothing new there. "Got anything to eat?"

3

"Beans on toast, OK?"

"With a Coke?"

"Sure."

There was a small kitchen for the staff in the office, with a kettle, a small fridge, a microwave and a toaster. Dan put the bread in the toaster, some beans in the microwave and boiled the kettle. "Marmite on your toast?" he asked, pulling a jar from a cupboard.

"Yuck."

He laughed and put the brown stuff on his own slices of toast before dumping beans on top.

He made tea for himself and handed her a Diet Coke.

"You should get the real thing."

"Tell Auntie Margaret," he said. "She's the one who buys it."

She nodded. Too late for that now, although she knew Dan's auntie wouldn't buy fully leaded Coke just because she wanted it. Auntie Margaret was OK but she could be a bit suspicious. Not that she had anything to be suspicious about—not really. Jade hadn't ever stolen anything from Dan's place. Just because she had a rep. That was the problem with everyone. Even Tom, who worked there. He had warm eyes but sometimes he made her uncomfortable. The way he watched her. She knew what men were like. She knew what they looked at on their computers. But not Dan. She'd been through his laptop when he'd been away. She knew how to find the files that men hid, but Dan didn't have anything like that. He was nice.

Sometimes she imagined he was her dad—though he was too young, wasn't he? She was sixteen and he was thirty-one. The thought of Dan with her mum made her feel a bit sick. He was much too nice. And good-looking. Fifteen years age gap—was that too much?

4

And then she said it. It came out of her mouth unbidden and didn't fit with the plan at all. She said, "Can I stay?"

He'd been talking, and her sudden question silenced him. Then he looked sad.

"No, Jade—"

"You say you care but you don't." She felt tears prickle her eyes and it made her cross to show him weakness.

"Jade, I—"

He reached out to hug her but she pulled back.

What was she thinking? This wasn't the plan. Get back to the plan. She said, "Let me take the Laser out."

"I told you—"

She pushed past him. "God! You're all the same!"

"What?"

"You don't care about me."

She was at the door and she couldn't look at him in case he saw the tears. Then she knew what would hurt him. She said, "You don't care about anyone. And Karen left you because you didn't care about her either."

She ran out into the dark. Her head was a jumble of thoughts. She needed to think. The plan...

The security lights clicked on and she ran harder towards the fence. To her left she could see the dinghy. That's what she'd do: she'd hide on the path, wait for Dan to go up into his loft and then take the Laser. Even if he saw her, it no longer mattered.

He called out just as she was about to jump the fence. She hesitated, her foot caught in the chains, and by the time she realized she was going over, it was too late.

Her jeans snagged and then tore at the ankle.

She sprawled over the top and lurched sideways. She hit the path awkwardly, banged her head, tried to stand and slipped towards the foreshore. Only, the tide was in of course. Her hands dug into slick mud, water up to her elbows.

She pushed back and scrambled to the path. For a moment she squatted, catching her breath. Adrenaline made her hands shake. Damn! Her head stung. She shook the excess water off and brushed her hands down her jeans to get the muck off. Then she gingerly touched her forehead where it hurt. It was sticky.

She looked at her fingers: black with dirt and blood.

"Jade, are you all right?" Dan was in the middle of the yard.

She stood up.

He sprinted over. "Oh my—" He swallowed the rest and she guessed he didn't want to alarm her. He reached out. "Come on, let's get you cleaned up."

She took his hand and carefully climbed the fence. Once beside him she reached out for a hug. He held her tight and she let the tears flow freely.

TWO

When the sobbing eased, he steered her up the slope to the office. She was cross with herself. The plan was going all wrong. Maybe she wasn't so smart after all. And when he held her she suddenly felt the worries go. Maybe the plan was wrong. She didn't know. She still couldn't think, and the pain in her head made it worse.

In the light over the door she saw him wince at the look of the gash.

"Dan?"

"Yes?"

"Can I use your shower?" He looked uncertain. "Please, Dan. I can't go home looking like this."

He thought for a moment and then shrugged.

"Afterwards, you let me drive you home."

"But…"

"Deal?"

She agreed. He gave her a plaster for the cut and took her up the stairs to his home above the office.

Although Dan didn't know, she'd been up here before. Maybe Margaret had seen her. Maybe that's why she looked at her with suspicion, although she'd never mentioned it.

Dan gave her a towel and showed her the bathroom. Which was funny, because there was just open space and the bathroom. It was obvious where it was.

He left her then and said he'd make another drink. He was sure there was cake in the cupboard too if she wanted some.

Jade showered quickly. She didn't have a great deal of time. It felt good to let the hot water sting her skin and for a moment she relaxed. She watched her watery blood swirl around the plughole and it snapped her attention back to hurrying. After turning off the shower, she tried to clean her jeans with the wet towel. Her favourite pink top had mud on the arms, which the towel just smudged and greyed.

She looked at herself in the mirror. Blood still trickled from her forehead. It was just a nick of less than a centimetre. She used tissue to clean up the wound and then stuck the plaster over it.

Naked in Dan's loft and in front of the mirror, a cheeky thought struck her. Suddenly she relaxed again and felt carefree. She took a white shirt from Dan's wardrobe and put it on without her bra. It smelled clean and fresh like him. Not all smelling of sweat and beer and smoke like most men's clothes. She pulled on her panties, jeans and boots and tied her pink top around her waist. She ran her fingers through her wet hair. Her skin was still damp, and flesh showed through the white cotton. She breathed in his smell again and smiled. He would like her like this.

Jade trotted down his steps and entered the office. He must have heard her coming because he'd started to boil the kettle. He turned as she came in. And then he froze, horror etched on his face.

"What the...?"

She immediately realized she'd made a terrible mistake. He didn't want her like that! He didn't love her.

His jaw was tense as he told her to go back and put her clothes on. He shouted at her. God, he was angry. He made her feel like a foolish little girl. Her head hurt.

"I hate you!" she screamed at him.

The tears came again, but he didn't see those because she was already running out of the office.

He said something but she wasn't listening. He didn't care. He'd screwed up her plan. He was a bastard like everyone else.

The floodlights came on as she tore down to the path. Then she hesitated. Not that way again. She couldn't take the Laser now, Dan would know. Maybe she could go with their plan and return after. She could take the Laser later.

Go the other way.

She spun and headed left, away from the fence she'd fallen over, to the fence on the other side.

She thought Dan called something but she couldn't hear, her blood pounding in her ears. She paused only to clamber over the fence, taking care not to make a fool of herself a second time. Her hands trembled. Her chest burned. She stood on the path and sucked in air to calm her racing heart.

After a few minutes of silence, the security lights went out. Dan's loft and studio lights went out a couple of minutes later. She was alone, on the path towards Plynt, and could hardly see more than a few yards ahead. The tide was high and menacing in its inky blackness. You couldn't reach the other side when the tide was this high.

But that didn't matter. She had the new plan. Not the clever plan, and sure it was more risky, but it would still work. Her eyes started to adjust to the light, because out in the country it's never really dark. The moon wasn't up there. She understood that it was on the opposite side of the Earth, but there was still light.

Jade began to walk slowly along the path. It would go about a hundred yards she reckoned before she'd have to stop. She hadn't paid attention to the time. Was she too early? Was she too late?

And then she froze. He was already here. Waiting. She could see a dark outline ahead. *Be confident. You can do this.*

She straightened her back and walked towards him. He stepped forward now and she thought he looked bigger in the dark. He was still over ten yards away. Then she realized.

She stopped. "You!"

He said nothing.

"The deal was…"

He said, "You want the money or not?"

She said, "Don't try anything."

He said nothing but took a step closer. Then another.

She felt her throat constrict. "I'm not alone," she said.

He moved like he was looking past her.

"He's not far," she said, sounding more confident. "If I scream he'll hear me."

The man took another step forward. He had a bag in his hand.

"Is that the money?"

"Yes," he said, and took a pace forward again.

The bag was almost in touching distance. She stepped closer and reached out. "I won't say anything."

"No. You won't."

She realized his tone was off but it was already too late. A gloved hand clamped over her mouth and muffled her scream.

THREE

DI Angie Melville stood on the path and watched the dive team out in the creek. "What do you think, Gary?" she asked her sergeant.

DS Collick rubbed at his neat beard. "It's odd."

"I know it's odd, that's why I'm asking what you think."

It was four days since Jade had disappeared on Sunday the nineteenth of April. She hadn't been reported missing until the evening even though her parents didn't know where she had been from midday on Saturday. They hadn't worried at first because she was often sneaking out at night, according to her father Steve Bridger. But she'd always been there in the morning before.

Dan Searle had reported seeing her in the early hours of Sunday, and they had watched the grainy black and white video footage from his security system. Each time the security was triggered the camera recorded the action.

From that, they saw her throw something into one of the dinghies, and on Monday they'd found her backpack. It had some snacks, some clothes and a little money, but there was no clue as to why it was there or what she'd been doing.

Melville began to stroll along the path with her sergeant a step behind.

Probably to fill the silence, Collick said, "So according to the recording she arrived at *Bluesky Boatyard* at four minutes past three. She's close to the dinghies on the hard standing when the lights kick in. We see her throw the bag into the Laser and then walk up the slope and meet Searle midway. Then they turn and go up towards the buildings. There are no cameras at the front or side so we don't know for certain but Searle says they went into the office. That's the room below where he lives. We see her again at three-forty. She runs away from the same building—we don't know for sure why—back the way she came, and falls over the fence on the right."

"She was heading for the green."

"Then we see Searle run after her and help her back over the fence." Collick paused before saying, "We see them embrace. Then they both go up towards the shed on that side—the office according to Searle—but of course his home is there too. The security recording jumps forward to four twelve—over half an hour later. We see the girl running away again only this time she heads left towards this path. And this time she's wearing something different."

They stopped as a diver came up beside the dive boat. He looked their way and shook his head.

Collick said, "It must be pretty murky down there."

Melville looked up and down the foreshore. "Why does she come this way?"

"Maybe she doesn't want to fall over the fence again."

"Why doesn't she go back for her bag?"

The sergeant didn't answer.

They were close to the end of the first section of the path now. Ahead were eight large stepping stones that

12

were used to avoid the sludge where a stream met the creek. On the other side was an island known as The Ridge. It stretched another two hundred yards or so to the Plynt promontory.

Melville asked, "Couldn't she have crossed on the stones?"

"It was high tide—five point three metres. The spring tide. Most of the time the stones aren't covered but we reckon they would have been four inches underwater. It was dark. There was no moon and it was cloudy. As far as we know, she didn't have a torch. Trying to cross this stretch in the dark would be hard enough. Not being able to see the stones would have been treacherous. I for one wouldn't want to try and cross them under four inches of water."

"She must have known she couldn't get off this path at high tide," Melville said, looking back. "She knew the area well, knew the creek well. She goes down a path with no way off it except to come back or go into the water. And she didn't go into the water—"

"They've been all along the water's edge here. If she'd gone in, they'd have found some evidence in the mud and the undergrowth on the other side where she came out."

"But if she'd swum?"

"Possible, but still difficult not to put your foot down. Plus this section is really dangerous. If you stand in the silt... well, it's like quicksand. And as you know, we're covering that option with the divers checking in case she miraculously did get into the water without any evidence and then got in trouble."

Melville sighed. "So what other option do we have? She didn't go. We know that from the video footage."

"Searle could have tampered with it. Maybe he went after her? Maybe the tape would have told us what happened but he wiped the evidence?"

"Let's get his tape checked. See if it looks like anything has been deleted since."

Collick moved past her and checked she was following. "Why did she run?" he asked.

"She runs both times."

"But she goes back after the first time."

"Because she hurt herself."

Collick stopped and looked back towards Searle's boatyard. "Maybe she was afraid. The second time, I mean. That would explain her coming this way."

"How?"

"Well, I'm thinking... if she was afraid. If she panicked and just needed to get away..."

"Then she might have forgotten about the tide."

Collick stepped off the path into the narrow strip of undergrowth beside the path. Beyond that, the ground dipped away and became a trench. He was at the narrowest point, although still too far for someone to jump.

Melville said, "We've already agreed she didn't go over the trench. At high tide that would have been full of water. If she stepped in that she might have never come out. What are you looking for?"

"I don't know. Anything would do me. Anything at all."

"If she didn't cross the stones and didn't go into the water—"

"Then she must have gone back."

"OK, let's assume she did." Melville turned and walked back to the edge of the yard. Collick stopped beside her.

14

She said, "Find out how far out you need to go before triggering the lights and security cameras again."

"Already have. The tide was all the way up to here." He pointed to the concrete just a few feet to their left. She would have to have waded quite a way in to avoid the cameras."

Melville shook her head. "Either she did that or it's been erased again. Let's for a moment assume Searle isn't here. Does she go up to the road or continue on the path."

"Searle said he'd locked the gates for the night."

Melville marched across the yard and reached the fence where Jade had fallen the first time. Rather than climb over, she walked around, on to the foreshore and then back to the path. "If she wanted to get away then this is the way she'd run."

"Reasonable," Collick said, keeping up with his boss.

They followed the track towards the green, with the inspector talking the whole way, trying to visualize the scenario.

Collick hesitated.

"Let's go house to house again along the road by the green. Maybe someone saw something. Anything that may give us a clue. We could make sense of it if we knew she'd come back this way."

Collick didn't respond. She turned to look at what he was doing.

He stood to the right of the path and was sweeping the gorse and brambles aside left then right with his boots.

Melville shook her head. "Gary, we've had this area swept."

"Guv…" Collick crouched down and pulled a large clump of weeds and earth out of the way.

When he stood back, Melville saw what had got her sergeant so excited. Half buried by earth and weeds was a pink top. "Unbelievable!" she snapped. "We had the team scour both paths and they found nothing."

"Looks like they trampled it. Or maybe a walker trampled it before the team got here," Collick said. "Whatever, they missed it and it got more buried."

"Unbelievable!" she said again, before procedure kicked in. "Don't touch it, Gary. Let's get forensics down here immediately. Let's examine that top and all the earth around it. If we don't find anything in the creek, this might be the only clue we'll get about what happened to that poor girl."

Two days later, Dan was working on a lathe in the workshop.

He stopped as Tom ducked his head in. "How you feeling now?"

"I'm fine."

Dan waved an admonishing finger. "Don't work too hard. If you aren't well—"

Tom shook his head. "Stop worrying. Seriously, I'm fine now. It was just gastric flu. I'm back now and Margret has told me there's a carpentry job out near Redruth. I'll be heading out to do that unless you need me."

"No, you go and do that."

Tom carried on walking until he stood on the opposite side of the lathe.

"And how are you? This whole thing with Jade Bridger must be pretty unsettling."

Dan nodded. He was worried about her, about what had happened, but the police were on it. They'd stopped searching the creek so he was sure they'd decided she'd just run away. Maybe she'd planned to take the Laser and sail off someplace. He thought about her request to stay there. Should he have let her? Maybe something really awful was going on at home. Maybe she just had to get away and he was the only one who she could turn to and he'd turned her away. He'd let her down.

He shook away the thoughts. They weren't helpful. He could have been in all sorts of trouble if he'd let her stay, and what would Amber, his new girlfriend, think? That would have killed their relationship stone dead. What would it have looked like—a sixteen-year-old girl staying with an older single guy?

A car pulled into the yard and then another.

"You said Margaret is here?" Dan asked.

"Yes. Like I said, she told me about the job."

"Sorry." Dan shook his head to clear it. He hadn't slept well, through worry about what had happened to Jade. It didn't help that the inspector and the sergeant kept coming back—and Collick had a sneer on his face last time.

At least he had Amber to take his mind off things. Would she be back tonight? He expected so, although she'd been quite vague. It was almost as though she wasn't sure, wasn't ready to commit. They should talk about it. He was totally happy with a casual relationship for now.

It sounded like more than two people in the yard heading for the office. Seconds later he heard them approaching the workshop.

"Can I help?" Tom said as a uniformed policewoman appeared at the entrance. A male officer joined her and then Collick appeared behind them.

Collick took the lead and they walked like an arrowhead past Tom and stopped in front of Dan.

"Morning," Dan said with a smile which quickly melted into a frown. "Do you have news of Jade?"

"Dan Searle," Collick said, "I am arresting you on the suspicion of the abduction and murder of Jade Bridger."

Dan shook his head, his eyes wide with disbelief.

Collick continued: "You do not have to say anything, but it may harm your defence if you do not mention when questioned something you later rely on in court. Anything you do say may be given in evidence."

FOUR

Eighteen months later

Dan pulled down the visor against the glare of the mid-September sun as he came up the hill out of Truro on the Falmouth road. At the Passingplace roundabout, he turned off. This route to Trevelyon would pass his father's farm, which stretched about a mile, all the way to the River Fal.

At the north-east end of the farm was Bucker's field, so called because it abutted the old Bucker tin mine. Then came the dairy fields followed by the first driveway that led to the farm manager's house. The main Searles farmhouse was two-thirds of the way along the stretch.

His father also owned two fields on the other side of the road. At the roundabout Dan had half noticed a large sign for Redcastle Estates. As he approached the first of the two fields on the right, another sign made him slow. It announced a new development of thirty affordable homes.

Dan shook his head in disbelief. Although they hadn't properly spoken in years, his father had always claimed he wouldn't sell, not even a section of Searles Farm. "Too much history," he'd say. And yet here it was, plain as day. His father had sold a chunk of land to a property developer; evidence of another contradiction in the old man's life.

After low hedges, Dan approached the trees marking the main farm gate and driveway. Searles farmhouse couldn't be seen from the road but, as Dan passed the main gate, he couldn't help glancing left. He knew that hidden beyond the avenue of oak and beech was the sprawling array of weathered stone and redbrick. The old man would be in there, decaying like the building around him.

Dan breathed deeply to slow the pounding in his chest and flexed his tight fingers. He'd seen a shrink about not being able to sleep, but it hadn't worked. What had she said? *Confront your demons, there's a deep subconscious issue that needs to be addressed.* Dan didn't go a second time. He knew what the issue was and it wasn't subconscious. Now was not the time to address it. Perhaps he half hoped the old man would die before they talked again. Then the demon would be gone for good.

He forced a smile to show he didn't care and then glanced at himself in the rear-view mirror. His eyes betrayed him and the smile faded.

On the opposite side was the entrance to the second field. This was where his mother had started Pick-Your-Own over thirty years ago. The sign was faded and broken and Dan knew it was unlikely that the trade would ever return. He wondered whether this would be the next block of land to be sold.

Next on the left was Lower Field, which dropped away to what locals called the Black Woods, the forest that ran along the eastern edge of the farm all the way to the river. Over the hedge he could see a late crop of sweetcorn, ripe for harvest.

At the bottom of the hill, Dan slowed. The road split: continue following the bend to the right and on to the village, or left down a lane that led to Plynt, a promontory that narrowed the entrance to Trevelyon Creek. There were grand, riverside houses along there with great views of the river, Falmouth and beyond.

Dan's boatyard was less than half a mile to the right, before the public space known as the green and then the main village itself.

He hadn't been back to the boatyard since the day he'd been arrested. Six month's he'd spent first in a Truro police cell and then on remand at Exeter Prison. When their nonsense case collapsed, he couldn't face going home.

Dan took the branch off the main road before cutting left again down a track. Smooth tarmac gave way to the rumble of compressed earth. Another month and this would be impassable in his ten-year-old Audi estate. The rain would form rivulets thrashing like eels desperate to reach the creek. And then the tractor would churn the track into black glue that could suck your boots off.

He was now driving along the edge of Lower Field and, if it weren't for the late-season sweetcorn, he would have been able to see the top of the farmhouse from here. A little further on, he pulled over and walked the short distance to a tiny creek. He followed the route the flood would take and stopped when he reached the path that cut through the grass close to the creek. Warm earthy air filled his lungs and he knew then that he was right to come back. This country—this Cornwall—was home. He didn't believe in a soul, and yet being here just felt right, inside.

Amid the background call of sea and river birds, kids' voices carried through the trees. They'd be in kayaks on the main river or crabbing off a jetty. They'd be further away than they sounded—the river could do that.

With the exception of the big houses on the Plynt promontory, most of the land, from Dan's boatyard to the tumbledown mine, was owned by the farm. Six hundred acres—although part of the Black Woods reduced that by almost a hundred. There were trees all along this stretch and on the other side of Plynt. The forest started a few yards from where Dan now stood and stretched dark and forbidding around the northernmost part of the small inlet known as Chycoose Creek.

To his right, the path followed and then cut down to a foreshore, exposed when the tide was out although the river continued just yards ahead. This was an idyllic spot but no good for a boatyard. The small inlet didn't have the depth or width of Trevelyon Creek, and his boatyard was the last place on the inlet where yachts could moor without beaching at low tide.

Dan walked along the bank and then sat. He dug his hands into the fluvial earth, feeling the grittiness biting into his fingers. His right hand closed around a stone and he flung it, trying to reach the water. The stone seemed to be sucked from the air and pulled into the silt, leaving a hole that would remain until the tide returned. He tried another and this time it disappeared into the fast flow. One more hour and there would just be nothing but a trickle running through the molasses.

He heard the kids again and recalled an incident a few years ago. He'd been here with Karen, though closer to the forest. She'd said the moaning in the woods was just the wind in the trees and nothing to be afraid of.

Two boys had been stuck in the creek with a rowing boat at low tide. One of them had been standing in the dark river mud, tugging at the boat. But it wouldn't move and the boy's legs were deep in the mud and probably sinking. In places the silt was so deep a person could sink in and never be found. Karen called the rescue service but they'd have taken too long.

Dan had found two wooden boards and used them to cross the mud. It had taken half an hour to rescue the kids. He'd been exhausted and covered in muck when the Fire and Rescue guys arrived.

He threw another stone and watched it get swallowed up. Would the boy have survived if Dan hadn't been there? Probably. Maybe he would have made it back into the boat and waited. One thing was certain: in future those boys would respect the river and its tides. Like Jade Bridger would have respected the river and its tides. Her disappearance just didn't make sense.

Dan sat for a while before he realized it was just an unconscious delaying tactic. He walked back to the car and stared in confusion. The door was open and his keys were on the floor.

Although he may have been mistaken about closing the door, there was no doubt he'd left the keys in the ignition. He picked them up. The keys had been on a medallion key ring. It had gone. Someone had taken the medallion. It didn't make sense. His phone was still plugged into the charger. They hadn't taken his phone. In fact, nothing else appeared to have been touched.

FIVE

Dan passed the Trevelyon village sign still pondering why someone would take the medallion. A bronze circle with a snake-like design, it was worthless, except for sentimental value. His mother used to wear it as a necklace or good luck charm.

In her will she'd left him the barns that he'd turned into a boatyard. The land was held in trust but it was effectively his. The only other thing of hers that he had was the medallion.

The gates of *Bluesky Boatyard* were open and gravel crunched under his tyres as he drove through. Long shadows from the two wooden sheds blanketed the yard. They looked no different from the day he'd left.

He'd forgotten how beautiful the lime-wood planks were. He remembered how forlorn they'd looked before he and Karen had painted them the colour of a cloudless sky.

He'd put windows in and Karen had designed and painted the signage. She had a flair for calligraphy, and he wondered whether she would have stayed with him if she'd pursued a different career than the high-powered job in London.

Parked on the right was one of those Far Eastern cars so popular with the elderly. It had once been bright red, although it had faded to dark pink in places. The sight of it dispelled his negative thoughts and brought a smile to his face. Auntie Margaret was here.

He parked as she appeared at the office door, her hands on her hips, her face as severe as her tied-back grey hair.

"And what time do you call this?"

Dan beamed and walked towards her.

His auntie opened her arms wide, pulled him into a bear hug and held him for a long time. She smelled of spring flowers and biscuits.

Still holding his shoulders, she pushed him away and started to speak. Then her mouth dropped open. "What the heavens? Just look at the state of your hands."

"Give me ten minutes and then we can take as long as you like to catch up."

He kissed her cheek and then took a suitcase from his car and climbed the flight of steps to his home.

Unlocking the door, he grinned. The house smelled fresh and clean. Yellow chrysanthemums adorned the coffee table in the lounge and surfaces gleamed with polish. A glass panel separated the lounge from his art studio. He walked through this and opened the glass doors onto his balcony. He placed his hands on the railing and breathed in long and deep before turning back to admire his home.

When he'd first moved in he'd constructed the floor and bathroom at the far end, but he recalled the hardwood sheets instead of the glazing. He remembered the nights in a sleeping bag on the floor. By the time Karen stayed, he'd built the bedroom partition and started to buy furniture. None of it had changed. Karen had bought the stone and glass coffee table and they'd chosen one of the sofas together. She'd also turned the loft into a home rather than a functional living space.

He took longer to shower than he'd predicted, letting the pounding hot water drive away the melancholy and the past. Skin still tingling from the heat, he went down the steps and into the office, where a pot of tea and two slices of cake were already on the table.

Auntie Margaret said, "I can't believe you're finally here. You know, there have been days when I thought you'd never come back, but here you are and it's good to have you back where you belong." She poured tea through a strainer, refusing to use tea bags because, she insisted, they contained *dust and scrapings off the floor.*

"How are you?" he asked, hugging her again. She seemed thinner and paler than he remembered. She'd been diagnosed with angina, which he was sure was caused by the stress of looking after the business for him. That was really why he'd come home.

"I'm fine." She smiled broadly and he guessed she was putting on a brave face. "Seriously, I am. And I'm very happy to have you home again. Now, tell me about what you've been up to."

Dan settled into an armchair and told her about his time working in Bristol as a barman.

Auntie Margaret was his father's cousin, so not really his aunt. He'd known her for most of his life and, over time, she'd acted like the mother he'd lost. She'd worked on the farm estate as office manager for many years and did the bookkeeping. With his mother gone, Auntie Margaret began part-time childcare. When he ran away from home, she took him in. And when Dan set up his own business, although officially retired, she joined him.

As he talked, she prompted with a few questions but never once mentioned the incident. Didn't mention Jade Bridger. Didn't mention prison. It was as if he'd just been away for a long holiday. And, when she finally spoke at length, it was about the business.

"Things aren't good," she began. "We're down to one mooring and a smattering of work. As you know, we stopped employing Nick, the young lad. Tom's been working on half pay, but even that's unjustifiable. Sales in the shop are right down, so I just cover if anyone comes in and rings for help. On the carpentry side, there've been a few small jobs."

She stopped as a stocky small man with a shock of grey hair peered into the office.

"Tom!" Dan said as he stood to vigorously shake the old man's callused hand.

"Good to have you back with us, lad," Tom said, and then waved an apology. "I have an errand to run and then a couple of doors to hang in the village. I'll be back later and we can talk."

After he left, Margaret said, "Bless him, for all his faults he's lovely."

Dan nodded with a smile. "I'm lucky to have him. I'm very grateful that you kept things going for me even though I was AWOL. I feel terribly guilty."

"Nonsense. You needed to get away. Anyway, there's some good news for you." Margaret took a sip of tea. "You've sold quite a few of your art pieces. If we have to close the yard, at least you'll have an income from your sculptures."

"How many?"

"Out of the eighteen left, fifteen went very quickly."

She didn't have to say it, but Dan knew what she meant by quickly. Notoriety could work wonders.

"Eighteen?" He knew Margaret would have thorough records, but he was certain there had been nineteen unsold works. He shrugged. "We can go through all the paperwork for the yard and sales tomorrow. Thanks for looking after everything for me." He stood and gave her a hug. As he pulled away he noticed tears in her eyes.

"You're a good boy," she said. "Everybody knows it. It just wasn't right."

As Margaret left for the day, he locked the double gates and proceeded to do the rounds. The routine immediately came back to him, checking everything was put away, secured and doors locked. Ominous clouds filled the horizon, replacing the last vestiges of daylight. A couple of seagulls looked black against the sky as they flew over the pontoon.

Eighteen months ago, nine boats had been moored to the pontoon and he'd felt the marina side of the operation could support the rest of the business. Now only one boat hung there, dejected, like the solitary mourner at a funeral.

He walked out onto the pontoon and checked the mooring. The boat was a Hardy Navigator; it was a few years old but in good condition. He walked to the end of the pontoon and watched the swell of the water. When was the last time he'd skinny-dipped at night? A long time ago, when Karen was still around. Her laughter had become a scream as he'd pushed her in. She'd thrashed as though unable to swim so that he'd dive in to save her. The water had been shocking compared to the warm night air but they soon became acclimatized, creating swirls of light in the dark mirrored water under an almost full moon. They'd made love afterwards, part hidden by the boats. Perhaps it was the thrill of being outside, but it had been one of those moments to capture for eternity.

He realized he was deliberately avoiding either footpath. He didn't want to be reminded of Jade's disappearance. He didn't want to think of the pink top that they'd said... No. He blanked the thoughts from his mind.

In the quiet of the early evening he heard a car on the lane. It came from the direction of Plynt, heading for Trevelyon. Nothing odd there. But then it stopped. Why would someone be outside the yard at this time? He looked towards the gates but there was just darkness beyond the buildings. He turned back to Trevelyon Creek and soaked in the moonlight shimmering across the water and the gentle calls of the birds. He looked up towards the main river and thought about the small creek. Who had been there and why had they taken the medallion?

He shook the thoughts from his head and ambled along the pontoon, heading towards the yard. As he climbed the steps to his loft, he realized there was a car on the far side of the gates.

The car that had stopped earlier. It was still there.

Its lights were off but the engine idled, and as he stared he could see someone inside, lit by the faint glow of a cigarette. Dan leaned in through the office door and flicked on the yard's rear spots. He ducked back out in time to see the car, a purple BMW, move away. He sprinted to the gates but it was out of sight by the time he reached them.

SIX

Dreams of dark forests disturbed Dan's sleep. Unknown creatures lurked there and, when something chased him, he couldn't run. River silt bogged him down, trying to claim him too. It was still dark when he finally got up. He sat in his studio with a cup of tea and stared into the cold night. At one point he thought he heard a boat put-putting quietly. He scanned the creek but saw no navigation lights or any other evidence of a boat. Apart from that noise there was nothing but the occasional bird call until the light changed from indigo to a smudge of pale grey.

A strong smell of earth and sea blew into the loft as he opened up the double doors. Autumn would be here soon and the harvesting season would be but a memory. As a young boy on the farm, he'd enjoyed the fruit picking—mostly. A permanent lump on his elbow was a reminder of when he'd fallen out of an apple tree and broken and dislocated the joint. A pretty young woman had helped carry him back to the farmhouse. She'd been a student working through the summer vacation. In those days most of the seasonal farmhands had been British students. He knew times had changed. The labourers were all Eastern European now.

The thoughts of the farm reminded him he was back and he planned to face the first of his demons today. But it was still too early so he decided to fill the time by catching up with Margaret's accounts. He'd also check on the sale of his artwork.

He unlocked the office and pulled out the books. It didn't take long to go through them. Income had died after a few small jobs in the spring. Each time a mooring was due for renewal, the entry was "nil". Dan presumed the problems would have started when he'd been arrested and charged, but he was wrong. The departures had mostly happened within the last six months. Some of the customers had been with him from the start. Later he would call a few to learn what was going on.

In the wages book he saw that the kid had been laid off in April. Margaret had put herself on half pay as well as Tom, but she had paid herself nothing for the past two months. Dan wrote a post-it note: "Pay yourself today!" and stuck it to her PC screen.

The sculpture sales were more encouraging, though most had been in the earlier months. As Margaret had said, he counted eighteen, but there was one missing: his final piece. The one he had finished on the night Jade had disappeared. It was two pieces of driftwood entwined with a strip of tin. He'd called it *Tin Heart* because, when rotated, the pieces could be seen to form a heart in one direction.

He went upstairs and checked his personal album. Here he photographed the work and commented on it. There was no record of *Tin Heart* being exhibited. He was certain the sculpture had still been in the studio when he'd left. He'd ask Margaret about it when she arrived. Maybe she'd given it to a gallery and forgotten to update the records. It was unlike her, but possible.

Still too early, he did the rounds, unlocking the workshops, and headed for the gates. One side of the gate hung ajar. The chain had been cut, the padlock hanging useless to one side. Removing the chain, he swung the gates apart and decided Tom's first job of the day would be to collect a new chain. There was no point in reporting it to the police—not with the relationship he had with them.

He turned back to the sheds and froze. Graffiti adorned both sheds, the beautiful lime planks covered with black spray paint. The messages included: "Scum", "Killer" and "Go to hell".

So much for thinking he'd had a bad night. He hadn't heard the gate open, footsteps on the gravel or the sound of people spraying paint. His immediate thought was to have Nick paint over the graffiti, but then Dan remembered he wasn't working for them anymore. He would have to do it himself.

After forty minutes of painting, he had covered most of the offending words before Auntie Margaret arrived. She opened the door and her little dog eased his old joints from her car.

Alfie was a cute brown poodle-cross mongrel. Only a few years ago he would have bounded from the car, eager to chase anything that moved. Now he shuffled beside his mistress whose face was blotched with anger. She shook her head, looked into Dan's eyes and gave him a big hug. "You don't deserve this," she said. "Some people are just ignorant. Ignorant hooligans."

Dan hadn't told the shrink about Jade Bridger. And maybe his inability to sleep was a result of his *demons*: his father and problems with a woman called Debbie. He would confront them now he was back, but there was nothing he could do about Jade's disappearance. Maybe

32

he could have handled her better, but he was innocent and there was nothing he could do to turn back the clock.

He sat in his studio and realized he was now looking at the path to the left. The tide was low, and because of The Ridge and stepping stones it swept around all the way to Plynt. If only it hadn't been a high tide that night then she could have just run away.

He knew the police had checked along the shoreline, and there was no evidence she'd swum to the edge and climbed out. No footprints. No disturbed undergrowth. She had just disappeared.

The papers had described her as a good student from a loving family. Dan knew that to be a gross exaggeration. She was a troubled child from a problem family. Maybe because other kids mocked her low intelligence, she regularly skipped school to play along the creek. Sometimes she'd hang around the boatyard. She occasionally helped, and once, under close supervision, Tom let her operate the crane. She frequently asked to borrow a canoe and, when Dan asked her to join his kids' dinghy club, she reluctantly agreed—reluctant only because she didn't want to sail with the others. She was a loner.

Dan let them sail Toppers, and when Jade showed more of an interest in the old Laser dinghy, he'd let her take it out. It wasn't long before he let her sail on her own. Of the five kids who sailed regularly, she had the most natural talent, and although she would have sailed every day, Dan made a deal with her: she could sail it any time at weekends—not just during the Saturday morning lesson—providing she attended school.

And then there was that evening and she disappeared.

He'd been open with the police. He'd shown them the video footage. Collick said he'd deleted something. He tried to get Dan to confess to going after Jade, but of course he hadn't. Nothing had been erased.

Dan had found her bra in his room and had luckily disposed of it before the police showed an interest in him.

They'd found her blood in his home and he'd told them about the cut on her head. Again Collick hadn't believed him.

Dan had kept telling them what happened. Told them he'd talked about sailing and discussed the upcoming competition. He'd told her he'd give her a prize if she won her class but she'd been distracted. He'd done most of the talking and she seemed to be deep in thought most of the time.

He couldn't tell the police what was distracting her or why she seemed confused, but he did tell them she'd asked if she could stay over.

Of course, Collick jumped on that, said it confirmed they were having a relationship.

And then, four days after she'd gone missing they'd found the pink top on the path, the one she'd worn around her waist after she'd put on his shirt. Two days after that they'd arrested him because his DNA was on it. Not because he'd hugged her. No, they made a ridiculous claim that it was his semen. And the press lapped it up.

He was a pariah. A child abuser. A murderer.

And that's where Debbie came in.

Debbie had been his stupid fling after Karen left him. Friends said Debbie knew exactly what she was doing when she got pregnant. She wanted a child and she got one. The mother wanted child maintenance but refused to let him see his four-year-old daughter, Bella. And when Dan tried to get a court order she responded by claiming he was violent. She'd applied for a restraining order against him. She even laughed. She knew he wasn't violent. She just wanted to prevent access and punish him.

The magistrate had seen through it and thrown out her case. But that hadn't stopped the press. When he was arrested by Collick, suspected of Jade's murder, the press brought up the old case as though he'd been guilty of that as well.

Confront your demons. It was time to see Debbie.

SEVEN

Dan drove to Penryn so deep in thought that he couldn't recall the last few miles. Debbie's old claim had blinkered the investigation, which led to him being charged with Jade's murder. He felt his chest tighten with an anger he'd tried to suppress. Six awful months awaiting the preliminary hearing, and all because of her.

But anger wouldn't help. The idea was to stay calm and move past this, to somehow find a solution.

After three long presses of her doorbell, he gave up and went in search of them. Bella loved play parks, and that's where he found them. He spotted her on a swing. She had curly blonde hair and a pretty face. Dan noted she appeared to be in her pyjamas even though it was after ten o'clock.

Bella looked straight at him as he approached. He saw recognition, but as she started to smile Debbie stepped into his line of sight. She, at least, was dressed, but she looked as though she'd done so in a hurry.

"So, you're back," she said with dead eyes.

"Debbie, I—"

"I prefer to be called Deborah now." She must have read something in his face, a reaction to the change of name. "What?" she snapped.

"Please be calm. I'd like us to have an adult conversation." He regretted the patronising words as soon as they left his mouth.

"How dare you!" She marched away from him and, when she reached Bella, snatched her arm and led her to the exit.

Bella gave Dan a surreptitious smile that warmed his heart.

He jogged ahead of Deborah and faced her. "Look, I'm sorry. I'm sorry. We need to talk…"

Still walking, she cut him off, raising a hand to his face. "Not here. I'll talk to you through my door."

He followed again but, once inside, she shut the door in his face.

"Hey!"

He rang the doorbell and tried to sound relaxed. "Deborah, please can we discuss this. She's my daughter and I have a right to see her."

To his surprise, Deborah called back that she needed a couple of minutes first. He waited, and eventually the door opened a crack.

"Right, you can talk now," she said, in a voice that suggested she was actually going to be reasonable.

"Can I come in, so that we can talk properly?"

She didn't budge, so he started as he'd practised: he was sorry that she'd had to bring up Bella on her own. He knew it must be tough to be a single parent. He was sorry that the money he sent wasn't much.

The gap closed to a sliver. "You're a bastard, you know that? You shouldn't have gotten me pregnant. You shouldn't have slept with me if you didn't love me." She continued a rant he'd heard many times, blaming him for everything.

He tuned out her moaning until he registered her saying something about his violence.

37

"You know that's nonsense, don't you. You hurt me with that accusation. How could you let Bella think I was like that?"

"Don't pretend you care about Bella! You should have been around for her birth. You should have helped me bring her up. And the money you give me isn't enough to bring up a little girl. Don't you want the best for your daughter?"

"Of course I do, Debbie... Deborah. Of course I do. Each time I've been paid, I've given you what I can. I wish it wasn't like that, but sometimes I've gone without so that you had the maintenance. I'd do more if I could."

"Are you hinting you'd like to come back? You want to move in and be a family?" She opened the door a little further and he saw expectation light her face. He hesitated, replayed what he'd said and wondered how she'd drawn that conclusion.

"Come back? We were never a family. I just want..."

"That's it, isn't it? Always about what Dan Searle wants. No consideration for me or Bella. No consideration for anyone else. You are a selfish bastard. You use people. Just like you probably used that girl— Jade Bridger. I bet you did it."

She was deliberately baiting him. He knew it, but the temperature still rose in his chest. He braced his hands on either side of the door, fighting back the urge to push it.

She continued: "They say you raped her. You killed her and hid her body."

"That's not—"

"You're a filthy man. For all I know, you raped and killed that girl. You're a filthy man. All men are filthy."

"Stop it!" He realized he'd shouted as she slammed and locked the door. He pulled his hands from the frame and looked at them, shaking. He stepped away and stared long and hard at the door. How could he ever get through to someone like that, someone so bitter and twisted? The shrink was wrong. You can't resolve something reasonably when the other person is crazy.

Dan headed for his car, disconsolate. Parked in front of his Audi was a metallic purple BMW. The same one he'd seen last night outside the boatyard.

He took two steps towards it and a man got out. DS Gary Collick wore a crooked smile beneath his short beard.

"Hello, Dan. I had a call that you were harassing this woman."

"Detective," Dan said with an incline of his head. "She called you, didn't she?"

"Walk away, Dan, or she'll get a restraining order and you'll find it even harder to get access to your daughter."

"Thanks for your concern," Dan said without feeling. He pointed to the BMW. "Seems I've seen this car before. What colour is that—the new pink?"

Collick's eyes narrowed before he controlled his expression. He winked. "Funny guy. I'm watching you and, eventually, I'll get the evidence to put you away."

EIGHT

Collick's car had been outside the boatyard last night. Had he come back later? Had he been responsible for the graffiti? It didn't seem likely. Collick may believe Dan to be guilty but at the end of the day he was a policeman.

There had to be loads of people who wanted Dan gone. Maybe a group of villagers were responsible for the graffiti. Perhaps they still thought he was guilty.

Dan drove along the lanes rather than the main roads into Trevelyon. As the village started, there were three tumbledown sheds on the river side and an area called Old Quay—the last remnant of when tin had been shipped from the area. The road split. The low road passing the village hall and doctor's before bisecting another boatyard. The upper road split again and looped around, with residences all along the roads that branched from it.

Dan drove up the hill and followed the road round. Before it descended again, it passed the *Cross Quays* pub.

Although it still wasn't lunchtime, people spilled out onto the road holding pints. There was one sure way to find out how the village felt about him.

Dan parked and walked back to the pub. No one outside paid him any attention as he squeezed past.

Inside, the barrage of noise reminded Dan of a typical night in a Bristol city centre pub. For a moment he stood in the doorway and looked around. Again there was little response and certainly no sense of animosity. He made his way to the bar and raised his hand to the barman, who nodded.

"Hi, Pete, how's things?"

"Good. Yourself? Are you back?"

"I am. Why so busy?"

The barman pointed to an oar on the wall. "We won the gig race this morning. Beat Mylor into second place. That's something to celebrate."

"Sure is." Dan grinned and ordered a pint from one of the real ale pumps.

Pete pulled the pint and set it carefully on the counter. "There won't be any trouble now, will there." He said it like a statement of fact.

Dan looked around and now saw that a few locals were watching him. Some nodded civilly, although most others just glanced away. He spotted Tom at the back with two other men sitting at a table for four.

"No trouble," Dan said to the barman. "It's good to be back."

Tom pointed to the spare chair. Dan sat and greeted the men nursing their beers. After a few nods they resumed a conversation about unemployment and immigration. Tom didn't join in. He leaned over and said, "Margaret told me about the graffiti."

"What do you think?"

"It's terrible. Some people…"

"Do you think it's someone from the village? Someone we know?"

Tom shrugged and took a long pull on his pint. "A year after you were released without a conviction? I can tell you I haven't heard anything. I haven't heard anyone talk as though you were guilty, except for maybe Bridger and his crowd."

Just as Tom said the name, a tall man entered the bar. Steve Bridger was skinny except for a beer belly and, although only a few years Dan's senior, he had the puffy eyes of someone much older and a heavy smoker. His skin betrayed years of alcohol and drug abuse. Dan stood, they locked eyes, and then Bridger pushed his way over.

"You've a bloody nerve," Bridger barked, pressing his face close to Dan's. "I want you out of this village, or you'll end up like Jade." He snatched at Dan's shirt with his left hand. "I'll ram my shotgun so far up your sissy arse that you'll beg me to pull the trigger."

Bridger pulled his right arm as if to throw a punch, but someone grabbed it. Other hands wrapped around the ranting man and pulled him back.

Pete, the barman, pushed between them, his back to Bridger.

"Sorry, Dan. Best you leave."

Dan nodded and squeezed past.

Bridger hawked and spat; a glob of spittle landed on Dan's face. He tried to turn but hands pushed him towards the door. He waited outside, heart racing, ready for Bridger, ready for a fight, but the man didn't appear. After a few minutes the red mist cleared and Dan drove back to the boatyard.

He didn't tell Auntie Margaret about the altercation with Bridger but got straight to work on the phone. He called all of the customers who had cancelled their moorings. He mostly left messages for a call back but two people answered. Neither said it directly, but Dan had the clear message that it was nothing to do with the murder enquiry. Both had moved to *Pentewen*, his competitor's boatyard, and claimed it was because Dan hadn't been around.

Afterwards, Dan worked through the list of previous customers and managed to secure the antifouling of two boats and some repairs to a wooden hull. A couple of others promised work on their boats over the next few weeks.

In the afternoon Dan went to the local yacht clubs and offered them a discount for work. He called in at the larger boatyards offering his services.

He was beginning to think he was wasting his time, when *Falmouth Boatyard* agreed to use him as a subcontractor.

Back at the office, he noted the details for Margaret to schedule and went to look at the part-built yacht in the workshop.

He ran his hand along the timbers from bow to stern, feeling out the areas for filling and sanding.

Tom stood at the shed entrance. "It'll be a beaut one day, that it will."

"One day, maybe a long way off. Maybe never."

"You're too generous. If the chap can't pay then he should take it away."

Dan had heard the argument before, but completing the job would be a pleasure and it wasn't as though they needed the space for anything else. "I'll call him tomorrow and discuss a storage charge. Maybe that'll prompt payment for the work instead."

Tom beckoned Dan to sit with him on a saw horse. "Come and talk to Tom. It's about time we properly caught up."

Dan complied and started by talking about the boatyard's lost business, but the old man cut him short, his thoughtful blue eyes seeing right through him.

Tom said, "When you get older, you look back at your life and you realize work just was…"

Dan couldn't help smiling. Tom was in his fifties but acted as though he were much older.

The older man continued: "Of course money is important, but people are what matter. That young girl mattered to you, didn't she?"

"You know she did."

Tom waited for Dan to maybe say more. When he didn't, the older man said, "All I'm saying is that Jade meant something to you. Not in the way people said, but you encouraged her. You gave her the opportunity to be herself. Maybe you should stop worrying about the unimportant things in life and focus on the people. What about Karen? What about your father? What about that little girl of yours in Penryn?"

Dan told him about the morning, talking through the door, trying to be reasonable but getting nowhere. He also mentioned Collick being there and watching outside the gates last night.

"Collick thinks you killed her." Tom paused. For a moment Dan saw sadness welling in his eyes.

"Tom?"

"You didn't kill her, so what did happen to Jade?"

"I don't know."

Tom gripped Dan's shoulder. "All I'm trying to say, lad, is this: focusing too much on yourself won't fix your troubles. You can't chop wood without creating chips."

He often used that phrase. Dan stared into the distance, wondering whether it made any sense. He wasn't so sure the older man was in touch with reality. Money would solve the problem with Deborah. Give her enough and she'd be happy, she'd let him see his daughter.

Tom continued: "It's not right... what happened. Not right that they would think you could do something like that. If only I could have been here and been a witness. I think now maybe I should have said I was."

"You were off sick—gastric flu."

"Yes, but if..."

Something by the river caught Dan's attention.

"Hey!" He jumped up and ran to the workshop entrance. A man climbed the perimeter fence and darted behind the wreck of a barge sunk in the mud.

"Hey!" Dan shouted again, sprinting to where he could get a better view. A man crouched beside the rotting hull. Dan could see him clearly now and knew exactly who it was: the scary guy who had lived in Black Woods forever, as far as Dan knew. When he was at school, the kids called the tramp Mad Mike, though no one could say where the name came from.

"Clear outta here!" Dan screamed at the man. He picked up and threw a stone that smacked into the barge with the sound of a gunshot.

The tramp jumped up, ran in a crouch back to the fence, scrambled over it, fell to his knees, and then scurried off along the path out of sight.

"Jeez!" Dan said, aware of his pounding heart. Tom came up beside him.

"You sounded like your dad." He paused and then said softly, "Maybe a bit of an overreaction?"

"That guy gives me the willies. Always has. Ever since..." Dan breathed out, the adrenaline subsiding. "Check he doesn't sneak back please, Tom."

Tom muttered something about the guy being harmless enough as he headed for the fence. Dan picked up a piece of driftwood, climbed the loft stairs and sat in the studio hoping for inspiration. He hadn't sculpted since he'd been away and wondered whether talent could

45

just disappear. He tossed the log to one side and tried sketching ideas, but nothing seemed creative or flowed from his fingertips.

After an hour he gave up and hit the phones again, calling prospects and people who had moved their moorings. By the evening he'd spoken to three more and all said they'd moved to *Pentewen*. Five out of five so far. Dan was starting to be suspicious that his clients were being poached. Tomorrow, he'd pay the owner a visit.

Before Dan began to close up, he heard a vehicle pull into the yard. A white van had reversed in and stopped just inside the gates.

He raised his hand to the driver. "Can I help you?"

A man in his early twenties got out of the passenger side. "It's OK, won't take long," he said, holding out a short length of timber. "Have you got any two by two?"

There was something about his demeanour Dan didn't like, but he dismissed it as paranoia. He started to explain that they weren't a timber merchant when the driver swung his door open and stepped out holding a baseball bat.

Dan raised both his hands, "Woah! Come on lads, there's no need for this." Never one to back away from a fight, he glanced left and right hoping he'd also find a weapon.

Nothing.

He could run and try and get to the shed, maybe find the crowbar, or... Hell! He picked the driver and charged.

With the element of surprise, he ploughed into the man's chest before the guy could react. As they crashed to the ground, Dan punched him and reached for the fallen bat. His fingers closed around it and, hearing the other man behind him, he swung wildly. He missed and

46

then saw the other man's wooden baton jab before his chest felt the impact. Then his ribs took a blow, causing him to spin and scrabble for balance.

He swung again, a wild blind swing that gave him time to stand.

The one with the baton bore down in front. Dan swivelled to see the driver behind him. He stepped sideways to have them both in front, but the man with the weapon immediately charged, using the stick like a scythe.

Dan blocked the blows and then realized too late that the driver was behind him again. A punch to the back of the head brought a shower of stars. He blinked in time to see and dodge the stick jammed towards his face, but then a sucker punch dropped him to his knees.

The baseball bat tumbled from his grip as a blow landed on his arm. Another in his side sent him sprawling on the ground.

One of the men said something, but Dan couldn't make sense of it and then pain exploded on the side of his head. Gravel pressed into his cheek. Grey tracksuit pants with a white line moved close followed by white Puma trainers. They were the last image he saw before blacking out.

NINE

Karen put down the phone and stared out across the Thames at the blinking lights on Canary Wharf. She could see the ferry and wondered whether her fiancé, Matt, was on it. Probably not. She didn't know how he did it—in the office before seven thirty every morning and increasingly home late. But he wasn't working, not really. He was out drinking and it was getting worse.

But that wasn't what the phone call was about. Margaret had been in touch. After a year and a half, Daniel had come home. How did she feel about it? She didn't know.

It was good to hear from Margaret and it was a relief that Matt hadn't been home to know. He wouldn't have approved of the contact. He would have been cross by the implication that she, Karen, wanted to know that Daniel was back home.

Sitting on the balcony with a glass of wine, she worked on finishing a press release ahead of the publication of the annual results in a couple of days. The main requirement was to not sound too upbeat, to get the balance right between investor and public perceptions. Really, it was the easiest one she'd done since joining investment bank BebelStreet Capital, and in a climate of industry disquiet and regulatory pressures, the bank's figures showed a healthy recovery. And she knew the internal results for the last quarter showed continued growth, particularly held up by Matt's FOREX department. So why was he out so much? She knew him. This wasn't the celebrating or client entertainment that he claimed. She could see it in his eyes: the tiredness, the stress. Was the pressure coming from above or was it self-inflicted?

Karen gave up with the communique and watched the ferry on its return trip to Docklands.

Daniel was back. How would he cope? What would he be doing about the allegations? As she thought about it, she realized that since the focus had been on him and then his aborted trial, there had been no developments in the search for the missing girl. Was that because of who she was—the troubled family background? What if it had been Nick who had gone missing? OK, as a boy there may have been less concern, but he lived in one of the big houses in Plynt. Karen bet Nick's parents wouldn't have let it go a year without a development. They had money—and money buys press coverage. And press coverage buys public pressure and public pressure can lead to results.

Karen pushed her press release away as though its blatant corporate attempt to manipulate public opinion was a sign of her complicity.

The City, with its bright lights, its glamour and yes its money, had been a big draw. It had taken her a few years to realize, but the ambition equation wasn't that simple.

The front door lock double-clicked and she heard light footsteps in the hall.

"You're still up." Matt hesitated in the doorway and then stepped over and kissed her head.

She looked at the kitchen clock, surprised it was after eleven. "Lost track of time," she said.

"You've been crying."

Had she? She dabbed absently at her cheeks. "What was it tonight, Matt?"

"Client meeting."

She really wanted to ask which client, to challenge him, but ended up just looking into his eyes. He looked wired. "Are you doing something?"

"Doing something?" He stopped himself, looked away and stripped his jacket off. "No, I'm not *doing something*. Maybe too much coffee, too late at night. I'll get a shower before bed, might help me sleep. Want to join me, baby?" He looked back and started to unbutton his shirt, trying to be sexy. But then he didn't wait for a response and started walking to the en suite.

"Matt, we need to talk."

Karen stood in the bedroom as the power shower kicked in and Matt was lost in a billow of steam.

She was still there when he emerged, naked, towel over his shoulder. "We need to talk."

"About what?"

"About what's going on."

"I don't know... What do you mean? About work? Everything's great. I've hit my targets for five straight months. I've been promoted. I'll get another million plus bonus..."

"I mean about us. About you. Why are you out so much? Are you doing heroin again? Something's troubling you. What is it?"

"Woah!" Matt flung his towel on the bed as though it were something that could smash. "I work damned hard for us. And it's mostly my money that pays for all this." He waved his arms around. "And it's me who pays for our expensive holidays, and who bought you your damned new car?"

Karen watched the anger flush on his face and then fade almost as quickly.

He blinked hard and sat on the bed, suddenly seeming exhausted.

TEN

Dan remembered a blue strobe and blurred faces. Later he heard disjointed voices and felt like he was on a rough sea, lurching backwards and forwards.

When he opened his eyes, the first face he saw was Margaret's. It was contorted with concern and an attempt to smile.

"Are you awake?" she said.

He grunted, "How long...?"

"Just overnight. You've slept most of the time. Do you remember anything, dear?"

Dan tried to prop himself up but felt a stabbing pain in his side. A nurse was on his left and helped adjust his pillows. She handed him a miniature paper cup containing two tablets and a cup of water.

"Cracked ribs," she said. "The doctors want to keep you under observation in case of internal bleeding, but they say you'll live. Fingers on your left hand were dislocated. Bruised but not broken."

He glanced at his hand, the fingers strapped together, now aware of the pain. He raised his good hand to his head and felt a lump the size of a squash ball at the back. Looking up and focusing, he noted the patterned curtain surrounded the bed, and through a crack he could see movement. The clatter of hospital noises became more than just a background hum.

"Truro hospital," Margaret said as the nurse left.

"How did I...?"

"Detective Sergeant Collick found you. He's here to talk to you if you're up to it."

After a moment, Dan accepted, and Margaret ducked through the curtain.

"So you're alive," Collick said, taking Margaret's chair.

Dan squinted at the detective, not liking the expression on the man's face. "You happy about this?"

"Let's be clear. I'm not happy about lynch mobs. Due process of the law is what I'm about. Now..." He took out a notepad and pen.

"Guilty until proven innocent, isn't that your approach?"

Collick didn't respond, just stared impassively.

Dan said, "Do you know what Exeter Prison is like? People say being on remand is worse than being a convicted felon. In a way it must be like being on death row: in limbo, innocent but impotent—locked away and unable to do anything but wait. You know, the only difference between prison and remand is I could wear my own clothes and make phone calls. Six shitty months and then the Crown Prosecution decides you don't have a case!"

Collick sighed. "Look, Searle, I won't pretend to like you, but I'm just doing my job, and if we went round thinking everyone was innocent until proven guilty, we'd never catch anyone, now would we? So let me do my job and tell me what you can about the attack. How many, and did you recognize any of them?"

Neither man blinked for a while, until Dan finally relented.

"Fine," he said, and began to recount the incident by starting with the van pulling into the yard.

"From the beginning," Collick interrupted. "I want to hear everything since you arrived back." He paused before adding: "Including your confrontation with Steve Bridger."

Dan rushed through a summary, including seeing Collick's BMW outside the yard on the first night and meeting him in Penryn. He mentioned the graffiti, and Collick wanted the detail of what was written before focusing on the incident itself.

When he got to the attack, Dan said, "The van was white—a Ford Transit, I'm pretty sure. There was no name on the side or markings except for scratches. It had a large blue padlock on the rear doors. And I'm pretty sure I remember the registration." He reeled off the number plate he recalled and then said, "The guys, I've never seen them before."

"There were two of them?"

"Right. They looked like squaddies or maybe stevedores—dock workers."

"I know what stevedores are."

"Early to mid-twenties. Short hair..." Dan stopped to think, to picture the men. "The driver had darker hair and had a blue beanie on. The other one was fair and unshaven. The stubble looked more ginger. They both looked pretty fit so I guess that's why I think dock workers or army. Both white. Both about my height—six to six-one. Maybe the passenger—the fairer one—was a bit shorter. They had tattoos. They both had grey hoodies or tracksuit tops."

"But you saw tattoos?"

"On their necks and when their arms were exposed. Intricate, I'd say, though I have no idea what. I didn't get the impression they were gang or prison tats. The driver wore jeans. I don't remember any brands or logos on the tracksuits. I had a close-up of a pair of Puma trainers. Show me a picture and I might pick them out, but apart from that I couldn't say."

"Distinguishing features, like Roman nose or scars?"

"Not that I can remember."

"Accents?"

"Nothing obvious."

"Excellent. You'd make a good detective."

"Really?"

"No. It was just my turn to be funny."

Dan studied the detective for a moment before speaking again. He said, "You haven't asked me how I am."

"The doctor told me what your injuries are."

"Not the same thing."

Collick let a tiny smile twitch the corner of his mouth. "You know, if those guys had wanted to, they could have caused serious damage. My view: this was just a warning. Someone wants you to pack up and leave—or they'll be back. And next time it'll be more serious."

"So are you going to investigate?"

Collick looked at his notepad, put it away and stood to leave.

"One question for you," Dan said when it was clear Collick wasn't going to answer. "Of all the people to find me, it had to be you. Were you watching my place again?"

"Good job I was, eh?" The smile flickered but stayed this time. "One question for you: are you going to leave now?"

"No." Dan hoped it sounded more confident than he felt.

Collick took a step towards the curtain and turned back. He shook his head. "Like I said, it could get worse. So if you're staying, I'd take more care if I were you."

Dan must have been asleep because he became aware of a cool, smooth hand holding his good one. He opened his eyes. A young woman rose and bent over the bed. Of a Hong Kong-Chinese mother and a white father, she had naturally tanned skin but eyes the colour of a clear Tuscan sky. She'd tied back her neat dark hair and used cover to hide the hairline childhood scar on her right cheek.

"Karen?"

She gripped his hand harder, her face warm with concern. "Yes, I'm here, Daniel. How are you feeling?"

Karen was the only one who called him Daniel. He loved the way she said his name. He smiled.

"To be honest, it hurts like hell—my head, my chest."

She touched his face and suddenly it was like a constricting belt being loosened. He breathed out and felt moisture on his cheeks.

"Everything will be all right."

He blinked at the tears. "Karen, I... I can't cope. I can't carry on." He didn't know where that came from. Up until that point his resolve had seemed strong.

She placed her head gently on his chest and held him. He breathed in the apple scent of her hair and closed his eyes. She lay like that for a long time, with only light pressure on his chest. He knew it couldn't be comfortable.

"Thank you," he said.

She lifted her head and perched on the side of the bed. "I know you, Daniel Searle. You're a fighter. You're not a quitter."

"Maybe I'm not the man you used to know." It had been more than five years since they'd been an item, before she'd decided to leave.

She watched him as though reading his thoughts. "That's different. You know I left you because I was ambitious. I needed to get out of this county. I needed to get my career going and only London was going to do that for me."

He'd tried to dissuade her from going to Exeter University and yet their relationship had survived those three years. He hadn't seen the split coming, but looking back, he should have. She'd encouraged him to study, to be ambitious the way she was. She needed a big career, felt the tug of the City. She had wanted him to be ambitious too but he'd apprenticed as a carpenter, then worked in a Falmouth boatyard.

He'd been content, setting up and running *Bluesky Boatyard*, with his hobby of creating sculptures out of driftwood. It hadn't been good enough for her.

"So what are you going to do?" she asked, breaking into his thoughts of the past.

He raised his shoulders in a slight shrug. "How long are you down for? How's what's-his-name—Matt? How's Matt's job?"

"You're avoiding the question." She gave him the stern look he'd seen many times. Her eyes burned into him. "You weren't guilty when that bitch from Penryn accused you of assaulting her and your daughter, and you aren't guilty of murdering Jade Bridger. Are you?"

"No, you should—"

"Of course I know you didn't do it! But this is a small place and not everyone knows and loves you like Auntie Margaret and me." She paused as if expecting him to come to the conclusion himself.

He shook his head.

She said, "When I said 'What are you going to do?' what I meant was what have you really come back for?"

"To resolve my issues with Deborah and my father."

"No."

"No?"

"You need to prove you didn't do it—prove you aren't guilty."

"Karen..." He shook his head. She had a purity he loved. To Karen, life always seemed straightforward. If it's not white then it must be black. Maybe she didn't understand the complexity—the problem of proving a negative. The problem of Collick being so blinkered he could see only one culprit.

She kissed his forehead. "Think about it. Tomorrow they'll let you out and I want us to start work. As soon as they say you can leave, I'll come and collect you. That's when we begin to prove your innocence."

ELEVEN

"Let's start at the beginning," Karen said.

She'd collected him from the hospital forty minutes earlier, arriving with bags of new clothes for Dan to leave in. She'd waved away his protests with a comment about a recent bonus. When they reached her car—a sporty silver SLK—he guessed she was doing all right for herself.

The SLK suited her high-flying image, and he enjoyed the roof down even though it looked like it could rain at any moment.

She'd driven to the King Harry Ferry and, after crossing the Truro River, she'd pulled off the steep incline. A concrete driveway took them back to the river and the Smugglers Inn. Dwight Eisenhower was said to have stayed here the night before the D-Day landings. Dan had come here to get away, to think, when he'd been a kid.

His father owned no land on the Roseland peninsula, and crossing the river was an escape from his father's world.

They sat on a bench outside and she pulled an expensive-looking notebook from a smart bag. Dan looked away and pretended to study a noticeboard which was covered with 1st Infantry photographs.

Karen said, "Daniel! Come on. I want to know your side of the story. Just talk and I'll prompt if I'm unclear."

"You sound like DS Collick."

She raised her eyebrows. "Is he on your side now?"

"Nope. I'm still suspect number one in his eyes. So what do you know? How much was in the papers?"

"Didn't you read them?"

He shrugged and watched the choppy water splash against a stake. "I avoided them. The lies bloody papers say…"

"Hey, watch it. If it weren't for the *bloody papers* I'd be out of a job."

For a minute he thought she was being serious, but then she grinned and said, "Anyway, there wasn't much about you, just your background and the suggestion of a relationship between you and Jade." She must have seen his reaction, because she quickly added, "You know, I didn't believe it. They mentioned you took her sailing but neglected to say anything about your little sailing club. Anyway, most of the copy was about the disappearance, about her, and there was an interview with her mother. Interestingly, no interview with the father."

That didn't surprise Dan. Steve Bridger was more likely to threaten a reporter than give them an interview.

She continued: "I know it never reached a preliminary hearing. The case collapsed and at the time there was a flurry of articles that regurgitated the same stuff, but nothing new. So, long story short, I have no idea what happened except she was last seen at your place and they found her top nearby and that somehow incriminated you."

"So no detail about the case against me?"

"Just that it was being treated as a potential sex crime and then they linked it to your acquittal for violence towards Debbie—it seems she's still bitter."

"And some!" he said, and tried to read Karen's face. Surely she must know about the trace of blood that prompted the police to conclude she'd been murdered. He swallowed. "What else do you know?"

"Enough about what I know. Let's just go over it from your perspective."

He nodded. Since she'd said it yesterday, he'd played things over in his head a thousand times, but there wasn't much to go over.

"Jade was sort of in my dinghy club and regularly came over to the yard and took the Laser out. On Saturday—the day before she disappeared—she missed the sailing club but turned up during the night. She was distracted and looked like she'd been crying. She never said what the trouble was." Dan saw the question in Karen's face and added, "Of course I asked her, but she was a teenager. I'm sure you know what teenagers are like. Wouldn't or couldn't talk about anything personal."

"So what did you do?"

"We talked about sailing, went over a route on the whiteboard. I wanted her to tell me what was troubling her so made her beans on toast and tried to get her to talk but she didn't."

"What did she say?"

"Not much. One odd thing was that she asked to take the dinghy out even though it was dark. She was cross that I wouldn't let her."

Dan hesitated a moment, wondering how much to say, how Karen would react. She was back, if only for a short time. She was here to help an old friend, but then she could get irrationally jealous. Would she still be like that even though they were just friends? Maybe. Maybe

61

he needed to be careful how he said things. He decided on an abbreviated version.

"She asked if she could stay and I said 'No'. She got cross with me when I said she should go home, said she was afraid. I offered to drive her, but she said some things. Trying to hurt me I guess."

"Like what?"

"Oh I don't know. Stupid stuff, like I didn't care about her. She said that you'd left me because I didn't care about you. That sort of thing. I didn't take it to heart. Then she ran off towards the creek. She fell over the fence and hurt herself. I saw and fetched her back, let her clean herself up."

"You took her up to the loft?"

Dan looked into her eyes so she could see the truth. "I let her have a shower and told her I'd drive her home afterwards."

"How did she react to that?"

"Not happy but accepted it. So I showed her upstairs, gave her a towel and left her to it."

"The police found blood."

Of course she knew about the blood. "A trace," he explained. "It was from when she banged her head. Anyway, when she came back down she ran off. That was the last time I saw her."

"A minute ago, you said *was a teenager*. You talk of her in the past tense. Do you think she's dead?"

"I don't know. I don't know what happened to her. She ran away many times, so there's a chance she just ran away and is OK—that she's out there somewhere, I guess."

Karen scribbled notes and circled some words. He watched a large seagull land on another bench, pick up something and launch its awkward body back into the air.

"Sorry," she said.

"Sorry?"

"For taking so long to write notes. You were saying?"

He shook his head. "That's it."

"Did you go after her?"

"No."

"She ran down the path towards Plynt. The tide was in. She couldn't have gotten very far."

"No, she wouldn't have even made it to The Ridge."

"Did she come back?"

"The police checked the security tapes. There was no sign of her after that. It showed her going but not coming back."

Karen thought for a moment. "Obviously no one else triggering the camera either?"

"No."

"So what happened? She go into the water?"

"Could have, but it'd be crazy. It was a dark night. You know what the mud can be like, and I don't think she was a great swimmer."

"Why did the police think she didn't wait for the tide to go out and then cross?"

That was the first thing they'd dismissed. Because the stepping stones on the far side would have been even more underwater, it would have been at least an hour after high tide before she could have crossed to The Ridge.

Dan said, "Two boats were out there before sunrise but it was light enough. They needed to avoid The Ridge, and neither crew saw anyone on it or the path."

Karen wrote a note and Dan had the sense she was delaying. Then she said, "What about the pink top?"

"I thought you said... The police found her top on the path. I'm not sure how..."

"And the DNA?" she prompted.

"Yes, they allegedly found my DNA on her top."

Karen held his gaze. "Dan, we both know it was more than just DNA."

And there it was: the big one. He took a deep breath. "Ordinary DNA I could accept. She was at my yard, touched things I touched. When she hurt herself I gave her a hug—she was that distressed. But that was it. God, I would never have done anything remotely sexual with her."

She waited and then said, "The papers said the top was pink with grey writing on the front: *Pineapple Dance*. She wore it a lot and they claimed it had semen on."

He felt his jaw tense with anger. "No way was my semen on her top!"

She wrote down and circled "Semen", "Other Evidence?" and "Witnesses?" and he suspected it was to give herself some time.

When she spoke, her voice was strained. "She was pretty, wasn't she?" Karen leaned away and looked out at the river.

His injured fingers pulsed and a lump locked into his throat.

"You don't believe me, do you?"

She looked back, her sharp eyes drilling him. "I do... I just..."

"I need a drink." He jumped up, alarming a seagull into flight, and strode towards the inn's front door.

He returned with what looked like two long glasses of juice. As he set them down, he said, "Still like vodka with your orange juice?"

She looked up. "You need to be honest with me." Her eyes pleaded with him. "We're closer than a brother and sister. You have to be totally honest."

Dan felt like biting back, by saying that they used to be close until she left him because he wasn't good enough, wasn't as exciting as her city slicker. He took a long pull on his drink.

"How long are you down here for, Karen?"

"Just a couple of days. Mum's a bit unwell so I thought I'd visit." She touched his arm. "Plus I knew you were back."

"Knew?"

"Margaret called Mum and... and then she called me."

He nodded. "Say hi to your mum, and I hope she feels better soon."

A long silence followed. Eventually she gave him a look he recalled. It meant something like *Come on, you know I can ask challenging questions and get you to think.*

"I'm not hiding anything, OK?" he said with a sigh. "Let's talk about the DNA. Allegedly there was a match... my semen... but something wasn't right. The prosecution were leading with it, but it clearly wasn't strong enough. Wilson, our family solicitor, was dealing with it. He's no expert—I couldn't afford anyone else—anyway, he went over the details, obviously asked the right questions because they dropped it. Never even got to the preliminary hearing."

"What questions exactly?"

Dan winced. "To be honest, I don't know. I knew I wasn't guilty, so when they realized they had no evidence I just accepted it."

"You should find out."

Karen scribbled some notes and waited for him to agree, then pointed to the other circled word. "Were there witnesses? The prosecution always come up with something, no matter how tenuous."

"I believe so."

"Believe so? So you don't know for sure or who they were?"

"Well I guess—Collick implied he had me *bang to rights*. Wasn't just the DNA. Who they were—I have no idea. They were never disclosed or called since the case against me was dropped."

"Other evidence?"

"Not that I know of."

"One thing I don't get: they arrested you for murder. Don't they need a body for that?"

"No, not these days. Not if there's enough evidence, although my semen allegedly on her top and a theory that I'd erased my security tapes was pretty thin."

Karen thought for a while and he guessed she was realising there wasn't much to go on. Then she wrote a word in capitals and underlined it. "Suspects?"

Dan shrugged. "Apart from me? I don't know."

"What about her dad, Steve Bridger? I did some digging about him." Surprise must have shown on Dan's face. "Yes, of course, I've been thinking about this too. He has a record of GBH, causing affray and possession of cannabis. I also think it's really odd that Jade wasn't reported missing until Sunday night. So the search for her didn't start until the following day and the stats…"

"Yeah, I know it's not good beyond twenty-four hours."

She wrote some notes against the father's name. "You know, the police hardly focused on the family, only questioned him once according to the papers. And yet ninety per cent of sex crimes are perpetrated by a family member."

"That's Collick for you. He was so convinced I'd done it, there were probably no other suspects."

"We should talk to him." She ignored the face Dan pulled. "Who else could be a suspect? What about the witnesses? If they claim they saw you do something then they must have a motive."

He shrugged, "I don't know who they are—their identities were protected. All I know is there was more than one, possibly two." He read her mind. "Who would know? Definitely Collick, the prosecution, but they're not going to say. Maybe my solicitor?"

"I doubt it, but worth a try. Of course, there's the obvious: the witnesses themselves. I think we focus first on finding who the witnesses were. We need to think who would have a motive."

He thought of Deborah, but he was sure she couldn't have kept that a secret. Apart from her, the only other person he didn't get along with, before Jade disappeared, was his father.

She said, "I know it seems crazy, but we have to start somewhere. Police call it shaking the tree to see what falls out."

The first spots of rain made them run for the car and put the roof up. Dan realized he was grinning as she drove him home. He studied her profile. She may have a flash car but she wasn't as hard and materialistic as he'd expected. If anything, she seemed just like the Karen he used to know. She may only be in Cornwall for a few days, but her enthusiasm lifted his spirits—higher than at any time for over a year—higher than since she had left him.

TWELVE

According to the Bristol shrink, he had two demons to face. One was Deborah and the other his father.

It had been many years since Dan had driven along the farmhouse driveway. He'd asked Karen to join him but knew she'd decline.

"This is about you and your dad. I'd just be awkward and in the way," she'd said.

She knew he had issues with his father and had told him to confront them many times before she ditched him for Matt, Mr City Slicker.

A tractor started up as he drove onto the gravel area between the house and old cow sheds. It was a sad sight: empty sheds and a hay barn beside a farmhouse that should have been demolished years ago. The main chimney still leaned dramatically and Dan marvelled that it hadn't fallen by now.

As the tractor stopped beside him, the driver swung the door open and leaned out. Geoff Jenkin, the farm manager. His large face barely lit with recognition, although he could clearly see it was Dan stepping out of the old estate car.

"Well, as I live and breathe, the prodigal son."

Dan nodded. "How're you doing, Geoff?"

"No complaints. Fine summer, drier than the last few." He looked Dan up and down, as though appraising him like a bull at the market. "Been in the wars?"

"Just a spot of trouble. Some people don't seem to be happy I'm back."

"You here looking for work? Guess you'll have to make amends first."

Dan shook his head and looked over at the farmhouse. "Not going to happen. Too much history between me and the old man. Is he in there?"

"Rarely comes out these days, ever since..." He looked askance for a moment. "You didn't know he'd had another stroke?"

"No." Dan knew his father had blood pressure problems and a temper like a spark to a bale of hay.

Geoff sat back and thundered the tractor through a three-point turn. "Take care of yourself," he shouted, and then drove towards the road.

Dan watched him go, uncertain how he felt about Geoff. The man had always seemed friendly, and yet he'd never been close in all the years Dan had known him, which was most of his life. When Dan had helped out on the farm in his early teens, Geoff treated him like all the other labourers: no special treatment, no compensation for his age.

Dan had worked hard only to be rewarded by the toughest work sometimes. And there was the time he'd been in the old barn stacking bales of straw conveyored up to him. He'd become stuck as he'd been too slow to deal with the bales near the top. He'd called to the farm manager to stop the conveyor, but he hadn't. The man had just enjoyed the spectacle of Dan struggling under the weight of them.

Exhausted and sweaty, Dan had managed to get out only to be berated by Geoff for wasting time and spoiling the stack. Now that he thought about it, he guessed the farm manager and his dad were cut from the same cloth: both hard men whose only life was the farm, a business that family got in the way of. The only difference between him and the old man was that Geoff had never been married and had no children. Not that you'd guess his father had either.

Where the tractor had turned, the gravel had been pushed aside leaving bare concrete. The grey concrete was easy to hose down to clear the muck of a working day. His father had laid the stones to make the yard more homely, he'd claimed. Instead of hosing, he'd rake the gravel smooth. From the look of it, the yard hadn't seen a rake for a few years.

There had been a farmhouse on the plot for over a thousand years, or so the story went. This one had been rebuilt by his great-grandfather and the grey stone front looked Georgian whereas the dog-legged sides were older brick. They were badly weathered on the south-west face beneath a tangle of ivy, dog roses and Virginia creeper.

Two old and twisted lemon trees stood either side of the front door. His mother had planted those.

Dan gritted his teeth and rang the bell. Instinctively he tried the door and, finding it unlocked, let himself into the house. It smelled worse than he remembered. There was always a lingering odour, like burnt toast, although in places it was less strong than the smell of earth and mould. He knew the earthy smell came from below the broad, oak floorboards, since large parts of the building had no foundations.

"Hello? Dad?" he called as he walked down the hall towards the large painting of his great-grandfather, a hard man with a face so stern, it was said, that one look could crack stone.

He found his father in the front room, the loud TV showing a black and white movie.

"The front door was open so I let myself in. How are you, Dad?"

John Searle jerked around, startled. There was no recognition in his craggy face, though Dan noted a grey pallor had replaced the ruddy complexion of a decade earlier. The old man pushed up, one hand on the arm of his chair, the other using a walking stick. He stood as tall as he could, trying to mask an unsteadiness in his legs.

"You're back," he said, one side of his face hardly moving.

His father turned the volume right down.

"It's good to see you too, Dad," Dan said, knowing his voice sounded strained and full of irony.

"Don't be cheeky with me, boy. I may not be the man I was, but I could whip your backside if I needed to." He tapped his stick to emphasize the point.

The room was stuffed with old furniture, some centuries old. Dan selected a green plaid sofa and sat. "I'm sure you could," he said, but then let silence fill the space between them.

Never taking his eyes off Dan, the old man dropped himself back into his armchair. "How've you been, boy?"

"I've been better. Prison was tough."

"But you got away with it."

Dan swallowed hard and took a long breath. "Pardon?"

"I said, 'You got away with it'."

"They released me because I didn't do it."

His father coughed what seemed like a comment. Then he said, "What's the reason for the visit?"

71

"Just to talk."

"Hmm... Have you found God yet? Prison can be good for reflecting on your life."

"How can you say that? You've not been inside. Prison's good for nothing—especially when you're innocent."

"And the great dragon was thrown down, that ancient serpent, who is called the Devil and Satan, the deceiver of the whole world—he was thrown down to the earth, and his angels were thrown down with him."

"What are you raving about?"

"You can take a stand against the Devil. Jesus rebuffed his three clever attacks. He defeated him and so can you. Read Matthew 4:11 and Luke 4:13. You can call on God's great protection."

"You're wasting your time. I don't believe."

His dad didn't respond. There was a long silence and Dan looked out of the window at the tyre swing and planks of wood in the walnut tree that had once been a tree house. His dad had put those up for him.

Movement beyond the tree caught his eye. He stood, peered out of the window and saw the tramp walk behind the hedge beyond the walnut tree. Dan turned back to his dad.

"Why don't you get rid of that creep?"

"Who?"

Dan almost said "Mad Mike" but knew his father didn't approve of the name. Instead he said, "The crazy guy you let live in the woods. You know, he's always lurking about and stealing stuff."

"He's no trouble, keeps himself to himself. Not as though I use the woods for anything, is it? And he keeps the vermin down. Never had any trouble with foxes, or badgers either, since he's been around. Don't bother yourself about him, boy. He's nobody. He's harmless."

72

There was a single photograph on a side table. It was sepia in a silver frame. Two people: his mum and dad on their wedding day. Both of them were smiling slightly, but there was a faraway look in his mother's eyes he could never read.

Dan took a breath. He was here to confront his demon, be rational, be calm, try and resolve years of hurt. He said, "It must have been tough for you, Dad. You lost your wife, and I know I wasn't an easy kid."

"No, you weren't. You could be a bugger. Didn't sleep, even as a baby. Always running off, getting into trouble. I wanted you to take over this farm. Three generations it's been in this family, and it looks like I'll be the last."

"I've always been such a big disappointment to you."

"My biggest disappointment is your lack of interest in the farm."

"At least you have Geoff Jenkin to run things."

The old man half nodded, but Dan had the sense that there was something else there, something about Geoff that his father didn't like. He looked down for a long time, so long that Dan wondered whether he'd dropped off. Eventually the old man looked at him with faraway eyes. "Promise me something. When I'm gone, I don't want Geoff to have the farm. He'll try and take it, thinks it's his right. He's just a bloody manager! Boy, I want you to promise me you'll run it."

"I can't. It's not what I want."

"I brought you up. Children have an obligation. You have an obligation, even if you don't love me."

Dan shook his head. How dare the selfish old bastard play the *you don't love me* card? Still, he forced himself to stay calm although he knew his tone was bitter.

"That's rich. Did you ever do anything for anyone else? In prison, when I needed you most, where were

73

you? You didn't help. You didn't visit. You didn't even write. They were the scariest and loneliest six months of my life."

The old man shook his head slowly, as though thinking. "I did my best for you."

"Like you did when I was at school? You never once came to any of my rugby matches. You were the only dad who didn't turn up. You only went to the school when I'd been in trouble, and your answer then was punishment. When I won the art award in Truro, you drove me there but didn't stay for the presentation. I had to get the bus home."

"I looked after you. I fed and clothed you. Hell, as a child, I even bathed you."

"You made me cry, you were so rough. You used to get soap in my eyes."

"You can be such a big baby."

Dan knew his face was flushed, felt adrenaline pumping through his veins. He bit his tongue and let a silence grow between them.

Eventually his father said, "There's still time to renounce the Devil."

Dan shook his head in disbelief.

His father continued: "If your mother was here now, she wouldn't be happy that you turned your back on God."

"Don't say that. You don't know... In fact, she's the reason I don't believe. If there's a God then He wouldn't have taken her from me."

"He acts in ways we can't comprehend. He must have taken her for a reason."

Dan tasted acid in his throat. He couldn't suppress the anger another second. "Unbelievable! You're just a miserable old bastard," he said.

"What?"

"And thanks for your help when I was arrested—falsely arrested!" Dan pointed to the well-thumbed Bible on a side table. "Is that what you did for me then? You prayed at St Just for me. Did you ask the Lord to forgive my wicked soul?"

A shadow of sadness crossed his father's face, and when he spoke his voice had none of the anticipated aggression. "That's not true. I did my best. I always did my best, and one day I truly hope you find God."

Dan left then, his father still talking about God. He marched out and decided he'd never return, and never wanted his father's inheritance.

His tyres scuffed up more of the shingle as he tore away from the decrepit house, his father's last softly spoken words—"You don't understand"—trailing in his wake.

THIRTEEN

Karen was waiting for him as he returned to the boatyard. "How did it go?" she asked. She looked expectant, perhaps believing he'd been able to mend the rift between himself and his father.

He shook his head. "He's changed, only he's become even more intolerable since I last saw him. And he's convinced I was guilty."

Karen shook her head.

He said, "You coming in?"

She put one hand on the roof of her SLK. "I'm just leaving." Her voice sounded slightly off, like she was holding back. "While you were with your dad, I thought I'd use the opportunity to talk to the guys here."

He raised an eyebrow, wondering if this had been the main purpose all along. Send him to his father's so she could talk to Auntie Margaret.

"Tell me upstairs then," he said, and walked towards the steps.

"I spoke to Tom and was pretty sure he knew who one of the witnesses was, but he wouldn't be pressed. I think he might have been hinting to you but is concerned he shouldn't get involved."

Dan was intrigued and thought back to his odd conversation with Tom in the shed. He'd said he wished he could have been a witness, not that he knew who was. Dan put it down to the old guy losing his marbles.

Dan shrugged. "I think he gets confused."

Karen said, "And then I spoke to Auntie Margaret." She stopped and he waited for her to continue.

"And?" he eventually prompted.

"You told me everything about the night Jade disappeared?"

Dan felt his throat tighten. It was better to stick to the simple version he'd told Karen. "Of course," he said.

"You need to talk to her. She's in the office waiting for you to come home. I'm going to leave the two of you to talk. Be gentle and try and understand, Dan. Just remember, no matter what, she loves you."

He saw now that the look on Karen's face wasn't expectancy, but something much colder. He moved towards her. "You said you're going. You *are* coming back, aren't you?"

She opened the car door and ducked in, not looking at him. "I'm not sure, Daniel. I've got things to deal with." She didn't explain, just closed the door and glanced up into his face.

"Call me," he mouthed, and held an imaginary phone to his ear.

He found it hard to breathe, and a couple of minutes passed after her car pulled through the gates before a constriction around his heart eased. Turning to the shed, he walked slowly to the office.

Inside, Margaret sat at her desk, staring out towards the river. She looked up as he came through the door. Her hands were placed either side of her face, her skin translucent, moisture on her cheeks and eyes rimmed with red.

"I'm a silly old woman," she said, her voice broken with emotion.

77

Dan leaned over and put his arms around her, squeezing tightly. She was his auntie, his stand-in mum.

In a quiet voice, he said, "Whatever it is you need to tell me, I have no doubt that you did it with my best interests in mind." He dabbed at her tears and kissed her, which caused more tears to flow.

He left her for a moment and made a pot of tea the way she liked it. He put two china cups on the table and beckoned her over. He waited and had poured the tea and taken a sip before she sat down and was ready to speak.

"I was to be a witness. DS Collick insisted that I mustn't tell you, said I'd be complacent..."

"Complicit?"

"Yes, complicit, and could go to prison. He said I would be seen as an accomplice to murder." She held his stare then. "But I know you couldn't have done it. Not you."

She reached across the table and he held her hand reassuringly.

He said, "Well, I'm no longer charged with her abduction or murder, so you can tell me what you saw."

"To be honest I said I didn't see anything, but he seemed to think what I told him was relevant. I said I didn't want to be a witness against you and he said I was just verifying a picture that would be confirmed by another witness."

"What did you say to him?"

"I can't remember the exact words, but I confirmed that Jade regularly came to the boatyard and that she had been all over, including your loft.

"I said I hadn't seen her on that Saturday before she disappeared, but that I knew she'd been because the sailing route on the board had changed, and only she had done that lately. I also mentioned that when I came in on Sunday there were dirty plates in the sink."

"Oh." Dan now realized why Collick was keen on her testimony. "So he was just building a picture of her being at the yard that night."

Margaret's eyes suddenly brimmed with tears. "There was something else. I didn't tell Collick but I thought it was all right to tell Karen. She said you'd told her everything, but she looked upset when I told her about Jade coming down the steps wearing your shirt."

Dan's mouth dropped open. "How did you...?"

"I came back. I'd left Alfie's toy in the office and he's... Well anyway, I couldn't sleep. I was at the gate about to unlock it when I saw her come down the stairs wearing hardly anything."

He said, "I was angry and that's when she ran away."

"I didn't see that. I just saw her coming down your steps and head for the office. If I'd stayed and watched or if I'd come through the gates then I could have told them what happened next. I'm sorry I didn't. I don't know why... I just felt I had to go."

Dan took a long breath. If only he'd told Karen the whole story. Now she might think he had something to hide rather than to save an awkward conversation. She'd always been so jealous—even of Deborah after she'd left him.

"Dan? Are you all right. I'm sorry..."

"It's fine, Auntie. It was totally innocent. The important thing is that Jade disappeared afterwards." He nodded slowly, trying to dispel the negative thoughts that were flooding in. Instead, he eventually said, "OK, I was told there were two witnesses. Do you know who the other one was?"

"Yes, but..."

79

"Auntie, it doesn't matter if you tell me now. There's no case against me, but, if I'm to clear my name, I need to find out what the supposed evidence was against me."

"He said he saw you on Mizzen Green with Jade."

"Who?"

"Jack Tanner, the owner of *Pentewen Boatyard*."

"You don't need to tell me who bloody Jack Tanner is." He shook his head, trying to get to grips with the nerve of the man. Was his motive to ruin Dan? Did he provide false witness to poach his business? Unbelievable.

Margaret placed a hand on his. "You're angry. I shouldn't have told you. I've known him for years. Jack's not a bad man. I don't know what he told DS Collick, but I'm sure he believes whatever he said."

"And you don't think he wants this boatyard or to put me out of business? You've seen we've lost most of the moorings, and I think they've all gone to his yard."

Margaret frowned. "You'll confront him, won't you?"

"Of course."

"Please don't mention that I told you."

After Dan assured her he wouldn't and thought they'd finished, she added: "There's also the chap from Redcastle Estates."

"What chap?"

"He came around a few times while you were in Bristol, wants the boatyard for development." She looked sheepish. "I didn't think I should trouble you with it, but Karen said I should tell you everything."

"Auntie, I don't understand. You're telling me that a developer is interested in buying the yard. That's no biggie." He looked at her quizzically. "You did say no, didn't you?"

"Of course I said no, but there's more to it. You know you lease the yard. You don't own it."

"Sure. Mum's trust owns it. That's who my lifetime lease is with."

Margaret swallowed hard and licked her lips as though her mouth were too dry. She rubbed Alfie's head as he brushed against her, not looking Dan in the eye. "Well, I don't really understand how it works. I thought Redcastle owns it or has rights."

Dan couldn't believe it. The trust was run by his father and Wilson, the family solicitor. How could his father agree to sell the land without letting him know? Margaret was still talking but her words were drowned out by his thoughts.

"Dan?"

He focused on her again.

"Your dad has been struggling financially," she explained. "In fact it's been ever since the BSE crisis in eighty-nine. You know he did well at first, because the farm was clear, but then in ninety-six the French and then everyone stopped buying British beef and the market collapsed. It almost wiped him out. You know the business isn't what it used to be. It's not just the boatyard, but other tracts of land that Redcastle were interested in. You must have seen the new housing development up at the Passingplace roundabout."

"How could he, Auntie? This is all I have."

She had tears in her eyes again, but this time, as they spilled over her cheeks, she didn't wipe them away. She got up and pulled him close. Her sobs wracked her body and he held her until they subsided. She shook her head, presumably realizing he was the one who should be crying.

Margaret tried a weak smile. "Well, I suppose Karen coming back is one small blessing."

He said "Yes" but, after what Margaret had told her, he doubted she would be coming back.

FOURTEEN

As the crow flies, Tanner's boatyard, *Pentewen*, was about two hundred yards down the creek, and Dan could see it when he walked a short distance onto his pontoon.

Old Quay was just beyond *Pentewen*. Until a hundred years ago, ships had docked there to load tin. When the trade stopped, dredging stopped and the creek had silted up so much that anything with a reasonable draught couldn't get much further than Tanner's even when the tide was right in.

Grey drizzle fell as Dan drove to Jack Tanner's yard. He passed the green without a glance, looped around into the main village and took the low road. This bisected *Pentewen* before passing the doctor's and the village hall. It became the main road out of the village and passed warehouses at Old Quay. Years ago someone had built the sheds to take trade from the creek but the silting had happened faster than expected and the business went bust.

On the land side of the road, Tanner had a giant green corrugated shed. On the other side was a wide concrete yard and slipway. Dan made a quick count of seventeen boats, propped up and under work. Beyond the slipway, Tanner had developed his mooring into a mini marina, with multiple pontoons reaching out into the creek like the top of a telegraph pole.

Bollards restricted the passing traffic as *Katie Bay*, one of the biggest local yachts at over forty feet, was being manoeuvred inside the shed. At the same time, an ugly grey boat called *Double Zero* was being taken out.

Dan spotted the apprentice that used to work at his boatyard. The young man acknowledged him with a nod.

"Good to see you've found work, Nick," Dan called out of his window. "Jack around?"

Nick pointed at the truck pulling *Katie Bay* and indicated where Dan could park.

Once out of the car, Dan walked alongside the tow truck and shouted above the echoing engine noise. "Jack, we need to talk."

Tanner's face showed surprise and then uncertainty and Dan reckoned he was wondering how to handle the situation. Finally, Tanner stopped and called another worker to take over from him. Climbing from the cab, he used an oil rag and then held out a hand to Dan.

Dan looked at it and then back at Tanner's face.

At the rear of the shed was an office. Dan nodded in that direction and then led the way. Once both men were beyond the door, he turned sharply.

"Give me one good reason why I shouldn't punch your lights out!"

Tanner raised his hands and backed into the door. Suddenly he looked all of his fifty-odd years, his eyes weary, his body no longer ramrod straight. "Whoa, Dan. I don't know what..."

"Cut the crap, Jack. You're trying to ruin me, trying to take my business away."

Tanner shook his head and sidestepped around a table, putting it between them. He sat down, the whole

83

time keeping his eyes on Dan. "You've not been around, my friend. People used your yard because of you. Since you've been gone—with no notice of returning—customers have been looking to go somewhere they know they'll get the service they need. I've not been pinching your business. You did it to yourself, my friend."

Dan felt flames in his chest rush up to flush his neck and face. He balled his fists and stepped towards Tanner just as the door opened.

"You OK, chief?" A young man with an Australian accent, built like a barge, biceps bulging from beneath a damp T-shirt, looked from Tanner to Dan and back again. "I heard raised voices. You want me to throw this guy out?"

Dan took a pace back and tried a smile. "We're cool here." His eyes met Tanner's and held them.

Tanner waited three beats then nodded. He waved the Aussie out and told Dan to sit. Dan pulled up a chair opposite and sensed the red mist evaporating.

Tanner said, "I don't want trouble. And Dan, there's no need for any. I have honestly done nothing to actively poach your business. We've been in competition for ten years, you and I, and there's been no trouble. I didn't complain when you first set up because there's enough business for both of us. And we've different areas of expertise. I can service bigger boats and you're more of a carpenter. I don't have anyone with your skills."

"So why the lies about me? Why tell Detective Collick that you saw me on Mizzen Green with Jade Bridger the night she disappeared?"

Tanner rubbed his hands slowly forward and then back across the top of the table. "What? You shouldn't know what I told the police! They promised you wouldn't know unless it went to trial."

"Well they were wrong."

Tanner looked at some paperwork on his desk as if distracted.

When nothing was forthcoming, Dan said, "I'm waiting for you to tell me what you told Collick. Tell me what you think you saw."

"I was out on a pontoon. One of the boats had slipped its mooring and I was retying it. I saw your lights go on. I heard you arguing. You know how sound carries across the water at night. I saw her run away from you."

Dan was about to interrupt but held back, deciding to let Tanner tell his whole story first.

"She climbed the fence and cried out. Then I saw you help her back over and walk back to your sheds. To be honest, I thought nothing of it really at the time, but then later saw the two of you on Mizzen Green."

"I wasn't there."

Tanner shrugged. "Just saying what I saw."

"You saw someone. It was dark and there was no moon."

Tanner looked uncertain. "Well, yes. I thought it was you."

"Because you expected it to be me and Jade."

"I suppose so."

Dan forced himself to unclench his teeth. "It wasn't me."

"But it looked like you."

"Describe him—tell me what you told Collick."

Tanner looked skyward, as if trying to visualize it. "He was your size—about a foot taller than the girl. He wore dark clothes—nothing distinctive. He had hair, your length, dark not blonde. From the way he stood and walked, I said he wasn't old. He had your build."

"So you told Collick it was me even though you couldn't be certain."

Tanner looked down, said nothing.

Dan said, "Did Collick lead you? Did he suggest it was me?"

"Maybe. I can't really remember."

"And you said you saw me on the Plynt path too. On The Ridge or before the stepping stones?"

Tanner looked up again. "No. No. I never said I saw you there. I just said I saw what looked like a confrontation or something and then later you were with her on Mizzen Green."

"With Collick's prompting."

"Yes."

Dan asked, "Was Jade wearing her top?"

"The pink thing that was found with... Yes, I think so."

"You could see it was pink?"

"No."

"Could it have been a white shirt?"

"It was darker. I'd have known if it was white."

"So you definitely saw her on Mizzen Green later?"

"That's what I'm saying."

"But you weren't sure it was me. How can you be sure it was her?"

Tanner shook his head. "You're right. I can't be sure."

"But you told Collick she was wearing her pink top?"

"I don't... Maybe... Again I can't remember if it was Collick's suggestion."

"Didn't that contradiction bother you? Didn't you question why it was found on the path, but you saw her wearing it on Mizzen Green? And presumably nothing happened between her and the man to make you suspicious at the time."

"I just..." Tanner rolled his shoulders and looked away.

86

Dan shook his head in disgust and pushed his chair back. "Who are you protecting, Jack? Why are you lying?" When Tanner started to protest his innocence, Dan raised a hand to stop him as if pushing away a bad smell. He opened the door and saw the Aussie waiting on the other side in case of trouble. Dan glanced back at Tanner. "When you decide to tell the truth, I'll be waiting."

He brushed against the big guy, who barely moved to let him pass, and marched outside into the drizzle. When he spun his car to face the right way, he spotted Nick looking around the side of the shed. Something like nervousness or even fear showed on his face, before the boy ducked out of view.

Dan thought about what Tanner had said. Collick had ignored the obvious lie and not worried that Jade may have had her top on when she left Mizzen Green with the man. How had she got from the Plynt path to Mizzen Green? The security tapes should have spotted her going back.

None of it made sense, and Collick seemed to just take the bits he wanted to prove his theory.

The windscreen wipers swished to and fro, making little impact on the fine rain. Karen had told Dan to shake the tree, but he wasn't sure what to do next. Was he like a wiper, part of something bigger, but ineffective?

In his frustration, he turned too fast and sharply into his yard. Braking hard, he skidded and then stomped up his steps and picked up the phone. He dialled Karen. Her voicemail answered and left a message to return his call.

Later that evening, he tried twice more. She didn't pick up.

FIFTEEN

Dan drove into Falmouth before Margaret or Tom arrived in the morning. Heavy overnight rain had left the roads black and slick. He found himself staring at the shiny surface, recalling the evening Jade disappeared.

He knew he couldn't have told Karen about Jade wanting to stay over or that she had worn his shirt without her being suspicious.

Maybe anyone hearing the full details of events would think the worst. He was glad he'd had the presence of mind to get rid of her bra. At least there was that.

As he navigated Falmouth's high street, he wondered what Margaret truly thought, whether she had deliberately told Karen about Jade in his shirt. He shook his head at the nonsense of it. Margaret would never think the worst and he should have trusted Karen to understand.

Outside the office of Hanworthy and Wilson Solicitors he parked on double yellows and strode through the front door. His legs felt heavy, his head light, but he was damned if anyone else was going to know that.

"Dan Searle to see Mr Wilson," he said to the receptionist, and he was shown to the small conference room on the ground floor. He was offered a drink and accepted a plastic beaker of cooled water.

After five minutes, Mr Wilson appeared at the conference room door and apologized for keeping him waiting. Wilson took a seat opposite, opened a box file and took out a notebook and pen, knowing Dan preferred a one to one, rather than have a secretary—or paralegal—taking notes.

"How can I help you today, Mr Searle?" Wilson asked, his tufty grey eyebrows sprouting above dusty glasses. His voice was soft but formal, even though he'd been the solicitor to the family for as long as Dan knew.

"I want to talk about my boatyard," Dan said. "But before I do, I've some questions about the case against me."

"Oh?" Wilson's eyes narrowed but, apart from that, his face remained impassive.

"They claim that it was my semen on her top. How did you undermine their evidence? I don't mean to be rude, but you aren't exactly an expert and I didn't pay for..."

"You're talking about Jade Bridger."

"Of course I am."

"Yes, of course. Well, I guess I just got lucky." Wilson's mouth drew into a smile, as though pulled by a suture. "Plus, as you know, the police can be misguided in their quest for the truth. I'm being polite, you understand?"

"That doesn't really explain."

Dan waited but Wilson didn't say more. "OK, let's talk about my boatyard... I understand that the trust has sold the land."

Wilson took his time to answer. "You appreciate that, however much I would like to, I can't discuss any of your father's transactions, Mr Searle. I can confirm that the rights to develop the land have been sold." From the box file he removed a document and explained that it was Dan's lease agreement. He read excerpts from it, that Dan only vaguely followed, and finally concluded: "In layman's terms, you have a lifetime lease, providing you pay the land rent. I can tell you that the ownership only transfers to the developer in the event that they trigger a purchase clause and commence development. However, they can't start developing with you there. The developer is hamstrung as long as you remain as tenant."

"Shouldn't I have been informed—as the leaseholder?"

"No, because they've effectively bought the right to buy."

"So the trust is still the owner."

"That's what I'm explaining."

Dan relaxed a little. He'd fretted all night worrying about losing the boatyard. "Just tell me one thing," he said, holding the solicitor's gaze. "Is the developer Redcastle Estates?"

"You should ask your father that question."

Dan wondered whether Wilson was unaware of the relationship he had with his father. Getting his father to open up about business transactions was like prising a barnacle from a ship's hull.

Dan said, "I noticed there's a Redcastle development of new houses by Passingplace roundabout. Looks about ten acres, so he's obviously sold that land to Redcastle. Just hypothetically, if I were open to negotiation, could I do a deal with the company—and let's, for argument's sake, say it's Redcastle—could I accept an incentive to end my lease so they could proceed with the development?"

Wilson looked a little confused. "Are you saying you'd give up the boatyard?"

"Maybe, for the right price," Dan lied. He hoped this would confirm who the buyer was.

Wilson's bushy eyebrows rose. "Well in that case, as your solicitor, I'd advise you to have a thorough agreement drawn up, otherwise as soon as you terminate your lease, Redcastle would have automatic rights."

So it was them. Dan smiled. "Of course, I wouldn't do anything less, and since you're my solicitor... I presume there's no conflict of interest."

"Not at all. We don't act for Redcastle Estates and, although we act for your father, he wouldn't be party to that contract."

Dan thanked him for his help and managed to persuade Wilson to part with contact details for Redcastle before he left.

Outside, he looked up and down the street hoping to see the purple BMW. He wanted to speak to Detective Collick, but it could wait. More important was a discussion with Jade's father. Overnight, Dan had decided it was the only other tree shaking he could do.

Bridger's house was on the outskirts of Trevelyon, a semi-detached with no drive or garage. The house was surrounded by a panelled fence that had been extended so that Dan couldn't see over, except for by the gate. It was bolted and clearly meant to deter visitors.

Beside the gate was a doorbell. Dan rang it and studied the property. Weeds dominated the flower beds and the grass had more patches than turf. Curtains masked the downstairs windows, although one was open and Dan could hear the TV. Possibly horse racing.

He thought he saw a curtain twitch and guessed someone was checking who'd rung the bell. Leaning over the gate, his fingers found the bolt and slid it back.

Five paces took him to the front door and he hammered with his fist.

"Steve Bridger, we need to talk."

Inside, it sounded like someone running up the stairs.

Dan waited.

He raised his hand to beat on the door again when it jolted open and a shotgun was thrust into his chest. The smell of stale beer, cigarettes and cannabis poured from the hallway. Dan took a step backwards and raised his hands. Bridger followed.

"Don't put your dirty Searle foot on my property," Bridger spat, the barrel of the gun pressing harder into Dan's chest.

Dan tried to sound calm. "Just wanted to talk to you. Since I didn't abduct Jade, I thought you'd want to find out who did."

"I ain't talking to you. You did it all right."

"Did you send those goons to beat me up?" Dan waved his taped fingers.

"I don't need no one else to fight my battles. When I come to beat you up, it'll be me, just me, understand? Only you won't know when it'll be. You'll just have to keep lookin' over your shoulder, won't you."

Bridger's eyes swam, black like crude oil on water.

Dan's hands started to drop slightly.

Bridger said, "You have a kid, don't you? A kid by a whore in Penryn."

Bridger's eyes flared and, as he jabbed the gun harder, Dan raised his hands high again. Bridger smiled. "When I've done you, I'm gonna…"

Dan dropped his bad hand, hitting the barrel down and to the left. It hurt like hell but, at the same time, his right lashed out at Bridger's face. The nose cracked.

Before Bridger could howl, Dan grabbed his throat and spun him to the floor. He stamped on the man's gun

92

hand and snatched the weapon for himself, jamming the butt end into Bridger's chest.

"You dumb..." Dan stopped. A boy and girl, under school age, looked out of the door.

"Steve?" the boy said.

"We're just messin'. It's OK." Bridger's voice distorted as he dabbed blood from his broken nose. "Go back inside. You can put the cartoons on."

Dan took hold of Bridger's shirt and pulled him up. His left hand hurt badly but he didn't want Bridger to see his pain.

Ejecting the two cartridges, he thrust the gun into Bridger's hands. "Let's go inside," he said.

His shoes stuck to the carpet in places and he tasted bile, although he was unsure whether it was caused by adrenaline or the terrible odour. "You should clean this hole," he said as he reached the kitchen and opened the back door to get air.

"You broke my nose," Bridger said, slamming the gun on the table and slumping into a chair.

"I've some questions that I want you to answer truthfully or, God help me, a broken nose will be the least of your worries." Dan took a breath. "Look, Bridger, we both need to know the truth about Jade. Now help me!"

Bridger looked up and Dan saw resignation, the bravado evaporated.

"Good. First off, did you send those guys to beat me up?"

"I said not."

Dan studied the other man's sweaty face. The adrenaline of fear seemed to be fighting either alcohol or drugs. He believed him and pressed on: "Did Jade arrange to meet anyone the night she disappeared?"

"Not as far as I know."

"Does she have a PC or access to one? Does she use Facebook or other social media?"

Bridger screwed up his face, thinking. "We don't have a computer. As far as I know she didn't use Facebook. Lizzy doesn't approve. That's why she couldn't have a smartphone—that and the cost."

"But she had a phone."

"Yes."

"Did they find it?"

"No, and the police said it wasn't used after the afternoon on the Saturday." Dan waited for more and Bridger offered: "No trace of the signal after, so looks like the battery was removed."

"Why didn't you report Jade missing straight away? Why did you wait until two days later when the school questioned her absence?"

"I don't know." Bridger didn't make eye contact and Dan scraped his chair closer.

"Not good enough."

"She was always running off—like her mother did when she was young. She was a wild one."

"Who? Are you talking about Jade or her mum?"

"Well, both, but Jade. She didn't do what she was told. We thought she was just messing. You know, teaching us a stupid lesson, like *look, I can scare you by staying out all night*. Only, she'd done it before."

Dan noted that Bridger talked about his daughter in the past tense, like he knew she was dead. He watched the man's bloodshot eyes until they met his. Then, taking a guess, he said, "Why did you hit Jade, the night she ran away?"

"Did she say I hit her?" Bridger's eyes flashed white.

"She didn't need to."

Bridger put his hands either side of his mouth as though the words weren't allowed to come out, but they

94

did. "We argued as usual, only it got a bit rough. She hit me."

"So you hit her back."

Bridger said nothing, looked guilty.

"Did you tell the police that?"

Bridger shook his head, so Dan continued: "Because they might suspect you? Because you beat her and didn't report her missing for two days—when you had no choice?"

Bridger looked down and away. Dan stood, thought about just walking out, but then said, "I want you to know I didn't do anything to Jade. I liked her. She was a good kid at heart and she had a talent on the water. Maybe I could also see she was a bit like me at that age. Angry with my family and labelled a rebel, a misfit. But I can tell you for sure, Steve, if she was abducted then it wasn't me. So start thinking about who it could have been and get off my back."

Dan walked out, leaving the front door and gate open. He thought he heard Bridger mumble something but it was lost in the noise of CBeebies blaring from the lounge.

When he got into his car, Dan realized his hands were shaking. Pain travelled the length of his left arm and into his neck. The fingers on his damaged hand were bent unnaturally. He coughed and pain stabbed his left-side ribcage. A&E, he decided, and called Karen as he left the village. Her voicemail kicked in. This time he decided to leave a message.

"Hi, Karen, only me. I've been shaking the tree. Nothing's come loose yet except for my fingers, but some updates for you if you'd like to hear them." He clicked off, uncertain how to end it. He then dialled the number Wilson had given him for Redcastle Estates. When it was answered, he said his name and the call was routed quickly. But then there was a long delay before someone called Alan Everitt spoke.

Dan said, "So you've purchased rights to the land."

"That's right, Mr Searle. We have development rights over your boatyard. It's ideal for exclusive, prestige waterfront properties with berths."

"But you need me to vacate as tenant before your rights kick in—is that correct, Mr Everitt?"

"That's it, and I'm sure we can come to an arrangement that would be financially attractive to you. And please call me Alan."

"How much of an incentive are we talking about…" Dan paused, trying hard to sound friendly, "…Alan?"

Everitt made noises like he was scribbling notes, maybe calculating. "Let's say ten grand."

"That's not nearly enough I'm afraid."

"I noticed the yard was closed today. Are you considering permanently closing up?"

Dan's hand throbbed. He turned at a double roundabout and could just make out the hospital sign ahead. "With the right money, maybe I am. How about fifty thousand, Alan?"

"That's beyond my remit, I'm afraid, Dan." Everitt cleared his throat trying to mask his obvious excitement. "I can stretch to thirty-five. Maybe."

Dan let silence tease Everitt as he found a parking bay, before saying, "I'll think about it." He ended the call and sat for a moment and wondered whether he disliked Alan Everitt for who he was or who he represented. Were Redcastle opportunistic vultures or was there something more to it?

SIXTEEN

The stillness of the evening and the mirrored river at high tide had a photographic quality. Dan sat in his art studio and watched the sun go down over the woods. He had the double glass doors open, although the temperature had a cold bite to it. He took a long pull on a beer and thought about Redcastle. He'd researched the type of arrangement they'd entered into with his mother's trust. There would have been an upfront payment securing them first refusal to purchase the land. This would have been substantial and non-refundable if Redcastle later backed out. There would be a maximum period to the offer, and ten years seemed fairly common. So if Redcastle didn't purchase, or couldn't because Dan remained as tenant, the agreement would expire. He wondered about the timing of boat owners cancelling their mooring contracts. They hadn't occurred straight after he'd been arrested. It was much more recent. He would have to find out when the Redcastle agreement was signed to establish whether a link was likely.

His phone rang. Karen.

"Hey you," she said.

"You sound like you're driving."

"Yeah. I want to hear what you have to say. What the truth is about that night."

He'd decided to tell her everything and had tried to plan what to say, but his mind wouldn't access his previous thoughts so he just spoke. "I'm sorry I didn't tell you the complete story. It was only slightly different. So she ran off after I refused to let her stay. I was worried so I went after her. I called to her as she jumped the fence and sprawled on the other side. She cried out. She had a gash on her forehead, which I gave her a plaster for. She agreed for me to take her home if she could clean up first. I let her into the loft... I stayed downstairs. After she'd showered, she came down in my... shirt..."

"Yes?"

He'd almost said "wet shirt" but had managed to stop himself. "I think she thought I'd let her stay if she was flirty. I was cross.

"The next I knew, she was running to the foreshore again. I saw her disappear but didn't go after her the second time."

"Because you didn't want her to get the wrong idea."

"I didn't think about it, but yes, that will have been the logic."

"And when she didn't come back...?"

"Like I said, I didn't really think about it. I just assumed she'd come back along the path and then back to Mizzen Green."

For a while, the only noise was of the wind and tyres, and then she said, "When I see you I want you to go over that again. With more detail next time." She paused. "In case there are any clues. But for now, tell me what you've found out."

Dan recounted the meeting with Jack Tanner, his nervousness, and the Aussie who seemed prepared to start something. Karen didn't know the guy, nor had she known that Nick was now working there.

She said, "So Tanner thought he saw Jade on Mizzen Green after. So she did go back."

"But my video..."

"Yeah, that doesn't make sense."

She asked if he had any idea how she could get round without triggering the lights and camera.

He couldn't think of anything unless she'd been in the water and that would be crazy because of the mud.

They chewed it over for a while and then Dan told her about Redcastle's deal with his father. "I told them I wanted fifty grand."

"You're not really considering giving up, are you?" She seemed genuinely concerned.

"No. Just wanted to know what I was up against. I also confronted Steve Bridger this morning, though I didn't get very far."

He told her about the shotgun and broken nose.

"Jeez, Bridger deserved it then, but my God how did you stay so calm?"

"I wasn't. The dumb idiot had left the safety on, but I was still shaking afterwards. I used the only useful karate move I remember from a course I did as a barman in Bristol."

She laughed, and he felt himself relax for the first time on the call.

"You've been driving for ages. Where are you going?" He almost added that it sounded like she was driving over the speed limit, but he held back.

"I've been in London. I've just left the M5, joined the A39. No traffic on the road, so I should be in Truro in under an hour and a half."

He heard road noise.

"Karen?"

"I know it's late, but can I call in and see you? I need a friendly face."

It was almost two hours later, past eleven, when he heard her Mercedes enter the yard. He was at the door and watched her climb out.

"What's up?" he said as she came up the steps.

Carefully avoiding the cracked ribs, she hugged him around the shoulders and the moment stretched out between them. "Let's go inside." She had a crooked smile that said she didn't want to talk about something. "Do you have anything to eat?"

While she freshened up and opened a bottle of Pinot Grigio, he threw together a meal of spicy chicken and rice. "I should have ordered takeaway," he said by way of apology.

She kissed his cheek. "It's lovely."

They sat in the studio looking out over the creek, lights dimmed so they could see the stars, blankets over their shoulders against the cold. The moon shimmered on the water like a silver coin on velvet. When she talked, she wanted to reminisce about becoming friends in secondary school.

"You were an enigma," she said. "Even though you were in the year above, I knew you had a reputation for being trouble and answering back to teachers and yet you were the best artist the school had ever known. I know helping out at the after-school art club was supposed to be punishment for you, but I could hardly concentrate when you were there. I tried over and over to be able to draw a perfect circle the way you could."

As a kid his father had told him Michelangelo had won the Sistine Chapel contract on the basis of being able to draw a perfect freehand circle. When Dan had asked how long it would take him to be able to do it, his father had laughed and said, "It would take you forever, boy."

Dan had practised every day, maybe a thousand times, before he could draw a four-inch-diameter circle freehand, perfect to the human eye.

Karen said, "Mr Jenks thought you were a star. Though I suspect he was also a little jealous of you. I, on the other hand, I thought you were a god."

"You didn't let on. It took until I had left and you were in the sixth form." He studied her, the line of her jaw, the freckles she hated. She still looked as good as when he fell for her at eighteen.

"I thought you'd guess I fancied you when I tried to talk on the charity hike to St Mawes. We both came from single-parent families, we both had an interest in art, and I worshipped you." She laughed and he shook his head and smiled.

"You needed to be more blatant."

"Like kissing you at the sixth form Christmas party?"

"I still don't remember what made me attend."

"I had a friend whose brother worked at the carpenters where you did your City and Guilds."

He nodded, recalling their early days and how the relationship had grown. "It was tough when you went to uni," he said, and he didn't just mean financially. He'd seen her as often as he could, mostly travelling at weekends to Exeter to stay with her. Three long years studying media and communications, but at least she'd come back to him, working for a mortgage broker in Truro.

At twenty-one, when he'd been bequeathed the old sheds with use of the land, he knew he would build a boatyard and carpentry business. When the loft was almost finished, Karen had moved in. Over four years and then she announced she was taking a big job in London. She hadn't even told him about the interviews. They'd argued and she'd moved in with her mother for a while. He thought she'd come back, but stubbornness wedged anger between them and then she'd left for her new job.

"I hurt you badly, didn't I?" she said in the grey light. The mood had changed and she'd heard the sadness in him.

He found it hard to answer, didn't want her pity. She was ambitious and he wasn't. He was just a happy, satisfied Cornish boy, always would be. She must have picked up on his hesitancy and surprised him with her next words.

"You took up with Debbie pretty quickly."

"Looking back I see she was a rebound. She was pretty and available. I don't know why I got involved—didn't have any feelings for her. She was a mistake."

"Did you tell her you loved her?"

"I've never told any other girl I loved them."

"What happened—how come she got pregnant?"

"She lied, told me it was all right. She didn't say she was on the pill, but she knew that's what I'd assume. She's crazy and... I know I shouldn't have taken the risk."

"How many others have there been?" Karen asked, although he suspected she didn't really want to know.

"What—that I took a risk with?"

"No. I'd hope you learned your lesson. I meant how many girlfriends?"

"A few. No one you know. Remember you used to say everyone has a soulmate and that we were born for each other? No girlfriend lasted more than a couple of months. It was always me who ended it, because it was going nowhere."

"So who was after Debbie?"

He reeled off a handful of names and she prompted for more details. He protested but succumbed to the pressure. It was as though she needed to put herself through some pain to atone for leaving him. There had been more in Bristol, more opportunity, shorter durations, and after the experience with Deborah, he was always careful.

Karen was silent a while, listening to the river birds.

He said, "See. This is why I found it awkward telling you about Jade. You get upset."

She seemed to shake thoughts from her head and swivelled back to look at him. "What happened to the girlfriend you had when... when you were arrested? What did you say her name was?"

"Amber."

"Are you still seeing her?"

"No. She never even wrote to me in jail. I haven't bothered to make contact."

"You weren't with her on the night Jade disappeared then?"

"I'd have had an alibi if I had been."

"Yes, sorry. Obvious. So when did you last see her?"

"The following night and then the night before I was arrested." Dan thought Karen was still being sensitive and was surprised by her next comment.

She said, "I would have visited you. If..."

"If you hadn't been engaged."

"We're not engaged. I had to stop writing. Matt found a letter I was writing and made me promise I'd stop. Said it was him or you and I couldn't..."

"It's OK."

"I let you down."

He reached out and touched her cheek, felt its familiarity.

In the small hours she stretched and said she should go. Two and a half bottles of wine said otherwise so he insisted she take the bed. He tried to curl up on the sofa,

103

but his ribs ached so he lay on the cushions on the floor and was soon asleep, his dreams full of the happy times before she'd left, before he'd screwed up by dating Deborah.

SEVENTEEN

Dan stretched to relieve the ache of an uncomfortable night and groggily checked the time: eight-fifteen. He scrubbed at his face with his hands. The bedroom door was ajar and it only took a moment to confirm Karen had already left. His phone pinged with a message, its second notification. He suspected the first ping had woken him.

Thanks for last night though I shouldn't have stayed. Going to Mum's—must look after her. Hope I didn't disturb you this morning. Speak to you soon. Love Karen.

In case she had just left, he opened the front door and peered into a grey morning, the first fog of the year. The air was damp and heavy in his lungs. There was no sign of Karen.

He was about to close the door when he noticed a brown envelope on the step second from the bottom. Back inside his loft, he opened the slightly soggy envelope and pulled out a Polaroid photograph.

The picture was of a young woman, possibly early twenties. Not posed; it was almost as though it had been taken by mistake. Colours were faded and the once-white border was grubby. He turned it over hoping for a clue. On the dirty back were marks in red pen: a circle with two lines. He turned his attention to the envelope, a standard small letter size. It too was grubby and it smelled of mould, but there was nothing else distinguishing it—no writing, no other marks.

Would Karen have left the envelope there? He thought it was unlikely. Just in case, he rang her mobile, but he got voicemail and left a brief message.

After making himself a pot of strong coffee, he decided to call previous customers once more. The first one he managed to speak to said he knew of Redcastle Estates but was reluctant to discuss switching to Tanner's yard.

"I have a theory," Dan said. "You don't need to tell me, just confirm or deny my theory."

The other man grunted what Dan took as a reluctant acceptance.

"My theory is that there was a financial incentive to move. Because without it, you would be out of pocket since you terminated before your annual renewal date. Right?"

"Ahmm." There was reluctance in his tone.

"And it was Redcastle who paid you—or Tanner."

"Look, I'm sorry, Dan, I'm not comfortable continuing this. I'm sorry."

Dan tried again, but the ex-customer ended the call. He tried others and left messages until another call was answered. He repeated the conversation only this time got the answer: "You're right about the incentive but not who paid it. I'm afraid I signed an agreement and can't discuss it."

Again Dan failed to get any more details. As he selected the next person, an incoming call interrupted him.

Collick.

The detective formally confirmed he was speaking to Dan and then said, "I'd like you to come to the station to answer some questions."

Dan knew Collick had nothing or the police would be at his door. No warrant for arrest, so no need to visit the police station voluntarily.

"Not going to happen," Dan said.

"Meet somewhere neutral, then?"

"Why?"

Collick ignored the question. "You know the pub on Custom House Quay in Falmouth?"

"I'll meet on the condition you answer my questions. And I mean really answer."

"All right, although don't expect me to divulge anything sensitive, anything that pertains to the case against you."

After agreeing, Dan went downstairs intending to ask Margaret about the photograph. The office was empty but he could see Tom setting up the shop.

"Hi, Tom, is Margaret about?"

Tom jumped at the sound of Dan's voice. "Goodness! I didn't hear you there, lad. No, Margaret's going to be a little late this morning."

"And yesterday? The yard didn't open."

"I was out and about working yesterday. Was Margaret not here? Anyway, I thought you were covering?"

Dan studied the older man, who looked away and busied himself. "Come on, Tom. I think you know Margaret wasn't here yesterday. And you know about today. Is there something people aren't telling me— something I should know about? Is Margaret planning to leave us?"

Tom pulled up a blind over the window and unlocked the shop door. Without turning, he said, "If she hasn't

107

mentioned it then I'm sure it's nothing to worry about." He came over to the counter and leaned against it as though thinking. "You did talk to her, didn't you?"

Dan nodded and gave Tom a look as if to say *I'm waiting for you to tell me what's going on.*

Tom said, "Good. You know it wasn't my place to say anything about her being a witness and all that, when we talked."

That made more sense of Tom's chat with him in the workshop but there was still nothing forthcoming about Margaret's absence. After waiting, he began to take the old photograph from his pocket.

Tom resumed his preparation of the shop. He brightened. "You know Ted Bryant?"

The name was familiar but Dan couldn't place it.

"He lives just down from Mizzen Green," Tom explained. "In the pub—before that idiot Steve Bridger turned up—he was sitting on the next table."

Tom continued when Dan nodded. "Of course, Ted was the one who saw that car on the night Jade disappeared."

"That's news to me. Why didn't you mention it before? What's it got to do with Margaret?"

Tom looked up sharply. "What? No. No! It's got nothing to do with Margaret."

"What else do you know about what Ted saw?"

Tom shrugged. "That's it, I'm afraid. The police looked into it but decided it wasn't relevant."

Dan checked his watch and guessed he'd be late for his meeting with Collick. He said, "Tom, before I go, did you see anyone this morning when you arrived?"

"No, but the gate was open."

Dan nodded, realising that Karen would have unlocked it. He pointed to the photograph he'd laid on the counter. "Recognize the girl in this photo?" As Tom

108

picked it up and studied it, Dan explained that it had been left on his steps.

"No, can't say I do. Looks old. Not very clear." Tom handed it back. "Think it has something to do with Jade's disappearance?"

"Maybe," he said, but he felt more excitement than he showed. Someone seemed to think there was a connection and it was the first real lead he'd had.

Love means selflessness. When you love someone with your whole being, normal life means nothing. You'd scale a mountain for that love. You'd drive through an inferno. But love wasn't about facing your greatest fear, it was about not wanting to grow old without the one you love. Karen had said that. She'd also said they were two halves of a whole. He thought they were just words—until she'd left him.

Dan thought about their evening together, their long comfortable silences, how he felt complete with her around. He thought about how her hair smelled of apples, like it used to, but then he stopped himself.

He forced the thoughts away. Emotion wouldn't help. Karen was with another man, a man who could give her much more than he could. She'd left him and was just a friend—his closest friend. The best he could hope for was that she could find a balance in her life where Matt accepted that friendship.

Trees crowded to the edge of the road that cut through the wood. They formed a tunnel with their boughs and trunks so dense that Dan couldn't see more than a few feet beyond. The darkness between the limbs seemed to beckon with the promise of oblivion. He knew Black Woods was his greatest fear.

What had he been, seven or eight, when he'd decided to find out more about the man who lived in the forest? He'd packed a canvas rucksack, moth-holed and stiff with age. He'd taken a penknife for protection and set off.

Almost a hundred acres and he decided to cut a zigzag path through the trees, starting at Chycoose Creek and covering the whole area in search of the crazy woodsman. At first, good light had made his passage to the river easy and then again for his return route to the ploughed field. By the third journey he'd had to focus hard on walking in straight lines; the trees started to look alike. Occasionally he would find the river and other times the fields but he had changed direction each time he thought he'd gone far enough. After what he'd estimated as a couple of hours, he'd been too disorientated to have any sense which way he'd been going.

When the trees formed a slight clearing, he'd stopped to rest, taken a drink and a bite of food. The first dead animal had caught him by surprise: a giant black rat had been hung at head height, nailed to a tree trunk. Dan had poked it with a stick until it flopped to the ground.

A few yards later he'd found a wire with six rotting starlings dangling by their necks. He'd held his nose as he edged around the grotesque sight. And then came more rodents. Again a string of them, rats and other poor creatures. This time they'd been hanging by their paws, their flesh dripping off white bone. One had been perfect except for having a skull for a head. Another wire had had a single giant crow hanging by its wings, spread out at arm's length. The feathers had moved, and when he'd poked it with a branch, yellow maggots crawled over the black body. He'd beaten at it until the bird's carcass had torn from its wings and thudded to the earth.

The smell of death had clawed at his nostrils and burned his throat. More and more animals, mostly crows, starlings and black rats, were hung from wires or were pinned to trees. Dan had half closed his eyes, held his breath, walked faster and faster.

Startled, he'd seen something big move between the trees ahead.

His heart had raced faster than he'd ever known. And then it almost froze as he realized the shape was a man. A man bending over a poor creature, a deer in the throes of death, sliced open, its guts oozing out.

Dan's heart had jolted back to life and he must have gasped because the man looked up, his hands red, blood dripping from his arms. Dan had run.

Later, he recalled the roots and vines grabbing at his ankles, the branches slashing his face. He heard the man crashing through the undergrowth, sometimes to the left, sometimes to the right, always too close. He felt a hand grab at his bag and the rucksack be dragged from his back. He stumbled but blindly ran on. Now only the sound of his blood rang in his ears. He fought and fought through tangled bracken and briar and then the ground gave way beneath him.

He sprawled into the crater-like dip as though the Devil himself was sucking him down into the depths. Earth filled his mouth, his fingers clawed air and white hot pain flashed in his skull and then there was nothing.

Auntie Margaret had found him on the edge of the woods near the farmhouse. They'd said he must have wandered for hours until he'd found the house, but Dan recalled nothing that happened after the blow to the head.

The gash had taken two weeks to heal, but the fear of the forest had never gone away.

EIGHTEEN

Mist rolled like waves over the walls of Custom House Quay. Dan sat on a wall and watched as Collick's BMW emerged between the buildings and parked.

When he got out and walked over, he hugged a North Face jacket around him like a polar explorer. Dan imagined the flecks of grey in Collick's unkempt beard to be ice.

"What's with this weather?" Dan asked, trying to sound lighter than he felt.

Collick shrugged, tossed a half-burnt cigarette to the ground, and sat on a table. He put his feet on the bench, waited a beat and then said, "You attacked Steve Bridger yesterday."

"He threatened me with a shotgun! He's got a bloody cheek to report me."

"He didn't."

"Who then?"

"A neighbour. And she mentioned the gun."

"Great! And the police are only just responding." Dan laughed mirthlessly. "I could have been shot."

"But you weren't, and I see that Mr Bridger came off worse—much worse." He dragged his fingers through his bearded chin. "So, what did you talk about?"

"Since I know it wasn't me, I wanted to know who else could be a suspect."

"You could have asked me."

"OK, that's one of my questions you promised to answer. Who else could it have been?"

"No one, because it was you," Collick snarled. "You had clever lawyers get you off on a technicality. We're all supposed to be equal in the eyes of the law, but truth is, those who have money can buy better justice than the rest of us. You're the OJ Simpson of Cornwall."

Collick had said something similar before and Dan wondered why. Wilson had handled his case, and as far as he knew, the old solicitor wasn't particularly clever and, since it never went to court, cost only a few thousand. Wilson had been lucky, that was all, but there was little point in arguing about it with the prejudiced copper.

Dan leaned forward and fixed Collick with his eyes. "The night Jade came round, her father had beaten her. He's an abuser. I think she was running away from him."

The stare became a game, neither wanting to blink. Dan thought the detective was trying to mask something. Finally Dan prompted, "What?"

Collick pulled a wry smile, seemed to relax. "I'm waiting to see if you have another question."

"It's the same question. You've not properly answered the first."

"Bridger didn't do it. His wife says he was on his lazy arse all evening. It took two days for her to get him to look for the girl."

"So Bridger's not a suspect because his wife says so! Maybe he beats her too. Maybe she's afraid of him. Have you thought of that?"

Collick said nothing.

113

"I asked him whether she had access to a PC, whether she used social media."

Collick shook his head, "What, you're playing detective now are you? I can't have you going around beating people up to get information."

"It was self-defence, and I promise it won't happen again. Look, I know the case has gone cold. I suspect Inspector Melville is no longer involved, is she?" Dan saw from the look in Collick's eyes that he was right.

Dan said, "So it's just you—and me. You may as well have my help—use anything I find."

Collick held up a hand as if partially signalling defeat. He said, "We checked for computers and phone records. No clues there. What are you thinking?"

"Just looking for other potential suspects. I guess I was thinking there may be mature friends on Facebook or something. Someone she knew, maybe a teacher."

"We checked all the usual: Internet, phone, friends, teachers..."

"What about registered sex offenders in the area? Did you check them?"

"I hope you're not going on some vigilante trip against paedos. All I can say is we checked—as we always do. It's a matter of routine in cases like this. Again, nothing to suggest any involvement."

"OK. Have you any leads on the guys who attacked me?"

"This is your last question."

"Did you trace the van?"

"The van reg number you gave me wasn't valid. You mustn't have remembered it right."

"It was right. If you couldn't trace it, then it was fake. Doesn't surprise me. It was either fake or the van was stolen. I asked Bridger about it and I'm pretty sure he didn't arrange it. I'm going to put up CCTV cameras at the front in case they come back."

Collick stood, attempted to shake some of the dampness from his coat. "That's it."

Dan said, "I'll buy you a coffee from the pub. Look, I have one more important question that isn't related to the case."

The detective squinted, considering, then nodded and requested white with two sugars. Dan fetched the drinks, struggling with his left hand to carry the second cup. Collick didn't offer to help, but when Dan handed over the steaming coffee, Collick seemed more friendly. He said, "What's old man Searle doing with the farm? Is he selling it off?"

"You know as much as me. He's obviously sold that tract up by the roundabout. I learned yesterday that he's also sold them rights to develop my yard as upmarket properties with berths." For a moment Dan thought he read genuine concern on Collick's face. "You worried about me?"

"No, just surprised he'd do that to you."

"Nothing surprises me about him. He's an old bastard who cares about nothing but his money." Dan thought a moment. "What about the odd guy who lives in Black Woods near the farm?"

"Mad Mike? What about him?"

"He's always lurking around, spying, pinching stuff. Did you question him?"

"No. We'd have needed good cause to question him. I don't know if you know this, but your dad refuses any authorities from setting foot on his land without a warrant." He shook his head. "You said the question didn't pertain to the case."

"I spoke to Jack Tanner."

"And?" Collick smiled with eyes cold.

"He said he didn't see anyone on the Plynt path that night. He also said he wasn't sure it was me on Mizzen Green."

"But it was."

Dan shook his head. Why couldn't Collick see anything other than his guilt? He said, "And it doesn't make sense. You found her top on the footpath and yet Tanner thinks she had her top on when he saw her later on the green."

"So? He was mistaken."

"But he wasn't mistaken about me… it was very dark that night."

Collick looked away and said nothing.

Dan said, "OK, let's assume she was on Mizzen Green later and met someone. How did she get there? You checked whether I erased the security tape."

The detective laughed. "You think I'm a fool, Searle? I realized you could have just switched it off. You turned off the recording so you could follow her towards Plynt and then were with her later on Mizzen Green."

Dan shook his head. Yes, he could have done that, but he didn't, and why would he then take her to Mizzen Green?

He said, "I think we do have another suspect. We need to find out who that other person was."

"What other person?"

"The one on Mizzen Green. The one that Jack saw later on."

Collick stood. "So are we done?"

"I haven't asked my important question yet."

Collick shook his head and started to walk away.

Dan held out the photograph that had been left on his steps.

Collick stopped.

"I just wondered if you knew who this is." Dan said without inviting Collick to take the Polaroid.

"Looks old. From the eighties, maybe earlier?"

"I don't think it's that old. Just faded. Do you recognize her?"

"No, should I?"

"I don't know."

Collick pulled a quizzical look. "OK, we're done," he said, leaving his half-drunk cup on the table. "No more private investigations, Dan. I need to warn you. If there are any more altercations, we'll be meeting at Her Majesty's pleasure. Understood?"

"I wouldn't expect anything less from you."

By the time Dan pulled into the supermarket on the outskirts of Falmouth, he could see a watercolour painted sun through the mist. He purchased provisions, and as he returned to his car, he noticed Jack Tanner with a trolley nearby. A woman instructed him as he loaded the boot.

"Jack Tanner." Dan strode over. He'd expected a rage to take over when he saw the man again but he felt only a chill in his blood.

Tanner started, his eyes darting left and right and then at his wife. "Not here," he said.

"Why, because your Aussie muscle isn't here? You've been lying, Jack."

Tanner shook his head but without conviction.

Dan said, "I know the truth."

Tanner's wife came around the car and snapped "We're going" to her husband. Tanner placed the last bag inside and closed the boot.

Dan followed him to the passenger door. The man's features distorted with suppressed angst. As he got in, Dan held the car door open and leaned in. "It's illegal to force a company out of business. You ever heard of anti-competition laws, Jack? It's a criminal offence—which means prison."

Tanner sunk into his seat, but a thin smile pulled a line across his mouth. When he spoke, the tension was gone. "I told you before, Dan, I've done nothing. I didn't tell your customers to switch to me. I'm not like that. I don't need to close your damn business." He tried to pull the door shut, but Dan gripped it harder.

"Whether your agreement was written or not, I'll find out and expose you, Tanner."

Mrs Tanner moved the car half a pace and Dan released the door. Tanner was no longer smiling and his voice fell to a whisper as he shut Dan out. He said, "You're wrong, Dan Searle. You're dead wrong."

NINETEEN

Dan barely noticed the Black Woods as he drove back to the boatyard. His head was in a million places. Jack Tanner had been afraid of the truth, but it didn't seem to be about Dan's business. The past customers said there had been an incentive to move so it must have been Redcastle Estates with Tanner just an unwitting beneficiary. Maybe.

Had Tanner been afraid because his wife was there? He'd glanced at her a number of times in a way that could have been nervousness. Dan knew nothing about her but their relationship seemed cold from the brief interaction he'd witnessed. Did the Aussie fit in somehow? Were they up to something illegal? Could they be involved in a series of boat engine thefts Dan had heard about? It didn't seem likely. But the Aussie wasn't your typical provincial boatyard hand.

He shook the crowded thoughts from his mind. He was mixing the need to clear his name and to find out what happened to Jade with conspiracy theories about his business.

Dan thought about his evening with Karen, and the thought of her leaving prompted the memory of the mysterious photograph. Who would have left it and how? Was the photo relevant to Jade's disappearance?

So far he had one suspect: Jade's father. He had to agree with Collick that the man was a waste of space, but complicit in something as sinister as abduction or murder? It seemed unlikely. If Collick was right then it wasn't a local paedophile, no one from school, not an arrangement with a friend. Of course, it all hinged on Tanner's witness statement. That brought him back full circle. Did Tanner really believe he'd seen Dan with Jade later? If he was lying, could Tanner have another motive? Could he be a suspect?

The timpani of wheels on cats-eyes jolted him back to the road. He'd overshot a roundabout, pulling across a Volvo. Dan raised an apologetic hand but the Volvo driver had already taken another exit.

Margaret stood outside the office as he crunched to a halt in the yard.

"Where've you been?" she asked, but before he could respond she added. "We've been waiting. There's someone needs to talk to you."

Dan's brow crinkled. He really wanted to ask where she'd been, and if something was wrong, but instead he responded with, "You're being a bit mysterious, Auntie."

"I just want to make sure…"

"Auntie!"

"It's Nick. He's on the slip by the fence." She paused a beat and Dan saw seriousness in her face. "He's something to tell you." As Dan moved towards the office door, she touched his arm. "Let him do the talking. Try not to judge, whatever it is."

Nick stood on the foreshore, staring out at the opposite bank and the last remnants of mist that greyed the distant oaks. He skimmed a stone but didn't seem to watch its bounces. When he turned to look at Dan, the

120

innocence in his face made him look like a concerned child.

Dan beckoned him over, into the office and then pointed to the couch. He dragged a chair opposite. "How you doing, Nick?"

The young man perched uneasily on the edge, hands clasped together so tight that his knuckles went white.

"Nick?"

"I... I want you to know..." Nick swallowed. "I need to tell you... I don't want you to think..."

Dan waited, tried to keep his face neutral. Tension built during a long silence that stretched like elastic between them.

Finally, Dan broke it. "I'm sorry we had to let you go, Nick. You know business has been bad. I'm glad you've got work, but I won't deny it, Jack Tanner..."

"Oh, that's a relief. I didn't want you to think me disloyal, working for a competitor and all."

"It's fine."

"Thanks. I also wanted to tell you he is all right. I don't think he's trying to ruin you, Dan."

"He said some things to the police that could have been a problem for me. He said he saw me with Jade on Mizzen Green that night and I was never there."

Nick said, "If he said it then I'm pretty sure he thought it. Anyway, couldn't Tom have been an alibi for you?"

"Why'd you say that?"

"Well he was there wasn't he?"

Dan said, "What makes you think that?"

Nick shrugged. "I saw him on the road, going home, I thought. I was on my way to Plynt—I'd been working for my uncle that day and he was driving me. Anyway, as we passed *Pentewen*, I saw Jack pottering around in the

121

yard. Then a bit further on, Tom drove past. I assumed he'd also been working through the night."

"He wasn't at work that day. So he definitely wasn't working late. You must be mistaken."

"Shame," Nick said. "You probably know Jade had a crush on you, but she was also fond of Tom. She didn't like many people but said she could talk to you."

After Nick had gone, Auntie Margaret said, "That seemed to go OK. I don't want to know what he had to say."

Dan hugged her. "Good. But I really would like Nick back here."

"When you can afford it."

Dan handed her the mysterious photograph. "This was left on the steps this morning. Any idea who it is?"

She studied the photo and shook her head. "Someone left it, you say? And you have no idea who?"

"Not a clue."

"Curious. How did you get on with Jack Tanner yesterday? Couldn't be linked to that in any way?"

"I got nowhere with him and I can't see how the photo could be linked. He claimed ignorance but I don't believe him."

After a moment's thought Margaret said, "Have you considered asking David Bishop?" She pointed to the solitary boat on Dan's pontoon.

For a second, Dan thought she was referring to the photo. She must have read confusion in his face.

"About why your other customers have left!"

The simplicity of it made Dan slap his forehead. "You're a genius, Auntie."

She dug out Bishop's contact details and handed them over. Dan immediately dialled and got a BT answering service.

"Does nobody answer their phones around here?" he groaned.

"How are you doing with suspects?" Margaret asked.

"I was starting to hope Jack Tanner was one, but Nick just gave him an alibi. He saw him in his yard. The only other person I have a lead on is Jade's dad, Steve Bridger. And he's as unlikely as a bowsprit on a barge."

"What about Lizzy—Jade's mother?"

"You think she's a possible suspect?"

Margaret chuckled. "Silly. I meant you should talk to her." She handed him a page from a notebook with times and place names. "I thought this might be useful. She has regular work, though I'm sure it's all cash in hand. She does part-time at Sally's Hairdressing and does a few cleaning jobs." She pointed to a line. "She's at the village hall right now if you're ready."

Dan hesitated. "Any suggestions on what I should say? Based on my chat with Steve Bridger, I doubt she'll just want to talk about my innocence."

Margaret gave him a hug and pushed him towards the door. "Don't assume anything. Just talk and see what she has to say."

TWENTY

Dan climbed the fence and stood on the path to Mizzen Green. He glanced down at the imprints his boots left in the damp, compressed earth. They'd found Jade's footprints on the path, but no one else's had been identified. He walked along the undulating track that ran beside the creek for a few hundred yards. Animals used it more than people, mainly because it terminated at his yard.

Unless the tide was high, the foreshore was more convenient to walk along. To the right the land was scrub and trees. On the left there was a short strip before the foreshore that mostly screened the track. It gradually rose so that there was a drop of twenty or so feet to the river before twisting and descending to Mizzen Green.

There were children crabbing off the quay, their parents helping transfer the crabs into buckets. There was an empty bench and three giant mooring posts, rusted with age.

On the far side of the green was a long building that had once been something to do with the tin smelting operation. Converted into a holiday let, it had been vacant on the night Jade had allegedly met someone here. Dan walked past wooden bollards onto the road where four cars were parked and then followed it towards the village. He now knew that Ted Bryant had reported seeing a suspicious car. Dan looked across the road and wondered which of the houses was Bryant's. While the properties were over a hundred years old, they had all been improved over time. None of them had a good view of the whole of the green but at least eight of them could have seen a car parked by the bollards.

Three houses short of the village hall, he shrank behind a wall.

Collick pushed open the double doors of the hall with a crash. He strode forward and turned just as a woman appeared.

Lizzy Bridger.

Dan could hear her angry tone but couldn't make out the words. Then Collick said something with a dismissive wave and walked away. Dan waited. He watched Collick get in his BMW and drive off. Lizzy Bridger sat on the wall outside the hall. She lit a cigarette and took a long draw.

Dan had seen her around, but not really looked before. From a distance he could some family resemblance to Jade: medium height, thin almost elfin face. Jade's hair was blonde and Dan wondered whether that was Lizzy's natural colour beneath the bubblegum-pink cropped style. He waited until she flicked the cigarette away before walking towards her.

She reached for another fag as she watched him approach. "I look like steaming cow guts to you?"

The surprise at the acid in her voice must have shown on his face, because she followed up with: "The way you're looking at me, as though I'm the one what's done something wrong. Me, the bloomin' mother!"

Dan sat on a post about three paces distant. There were hard lines on her face that must have once been attractive. The years had not been kind. Only a few years older than himself, Lizzy Bridger could have passed for twice his age. Compared to Jade's bright blue eyes, Lizzy's were cold and dull and supported by folds of tired skin.

He tried to imagine talking to a friend, soft and kind. He opened with: "How are you?"

Lizzy looked away.

"I just want to tell you face-to-face—it wasn't me. We all need to find out the truth about Jade."

She didn't respond for a long time, and when her eyes came back to his, there was less harshness in them. "You attacked my husband."

Dan held up his hands. "I'm sorry. I didn't mean to. I just wanted to talk and he came at me with a shotgun."

Lizzy smiled then, showing a black space where an upper canine tooth had once been. "Oh, don't apologize. That lazy git musta deserved it." She took a long drag on the remnant of her cigarette and flicked it away. "Did he tell you anything… you know, useful like?"

"Not really."

"He thinks you did it."

"He's not the only one. Collick does as well. What did he want just now?" Dan noticed her jaw tense and wondered if her bad mood was more to do with Collick.

"Nothing new. Nothing about finding my girl."

"Are you sure she didn't just run away?"

"I've asked myself that a hundred, a thousand, times. That, and who could have abducted her." Tears brimmed in her eyes, making them less cold for a moment. Suddenly she seemed a different person, as if her hard shell had cracked. She said, "I keep imagining her. If she's dead. Did she die in pain? Did he abuse her horribly? If she's still alive, what terrible things he's still doing to her body." She was unfocused, lost in her own thoughts and shaking.

Dan remained quiet, unsure whether to prompt her to keep talking, but Lizzy dragged a wrist across her eyes and the hardness reappeared. Her voice dropped to almost a whisper. "It was the Buccaboo."

"The what?"

She smiled then, but it was cold. "I don't want to talk to you."

Dan said, "As I said, I just wanted to tell you that it wasn't me and I want to find out what happened to Jade."

Her gaze drifted back to him. "To make you feel less guilty? Is that it?"

"That's not..."

"You're a Searle. Nothing good ever came outta that farm, no matter what the name. There's evil in that place. It's the Buccaboo, and you Searles are to blame." She stood and pulled open the village hall doors, then swivelled. Her voice came back, full of vitriol. "There's nothing but evil at that place, you hear me!"

And then she was inside with a slam.

TWENTY-ONE

Margaret was on the telephone when he returned to the boatyard. He hung back, trying to be discrete, but couldn't help overhearing part of the conversation. He guessed the person on the other end was from a hospital, after hearing the word *operation* and her make a date for an appointment.

"Auntie, are you all right? I couldn't help overhearing. Surely you don't have an operation for angina."

Surprise froze her features before she hid any emotion. "Yes, dear, I'm fine. As I said, it's just a routine check-up."

He had been so self-obsessed, so wrapped up in his problems, that he had been oblivious to everyone else's feelings and worries. He gave her a hug and suggested they have a cup of tea and cake.

The water was high, with gulls cruising on the channel, waiting for the tide to turn and bring the accompanying fish. They sat outside and, after he insisted, she told him the truth about a lump under her arm. A biopsy had shown there to be cancerous cells and she'd had it removed.

"What's the... what do doctor's call it? The prognosis. What's the prognosis?"

"The consultant is fairly confident this is isolated." Her eyes flickered away and he knew she was acting more bravely than she really felt. "I'm sorry, I've been a bit weak over this. I've been getting myself into a tizzy expecting the worst. But I'm OK. Just a scare, that's all." She began to cry and he pulled her in close so that the tears wet his neck. He held her for a long time, until she nodded and eased away, wiping first her face and then his neck.

"Sorry."

He squeezed her arm. "You should have told me."

"I didn't want to worry you."

She'd worried him about the angina but this was different. He said, "You know, I'll always be there if you need me. In fact, I'll be there even if you don't!"

She laughed and seemed almost back to her normal self, except he saw a shadow lurking behind her usually happy eyes.

After the tea and cake were gone, she asked about the meeting with Lizzy Bridger.

Dan hadn't expected much to come out of the conversation but it had been even more disjointed than he'd anticipated. "You know, Auntie, I'm not sure what to think. At first she seemed angry with me but then she became more reasonable. She didn't outright accuse me and didn't blame me for hitting her husband. But then she got all funny and made a comment about the farm."

"Searles Farm?"

"She said something like nothing good came from it. Presumably meaning I'm bad because I come from the farm. She said it was evil—said all Searles were evil—and mentioned someone called something like Bockaboo. I think that's who Lizzy Bridger thinks took Jade."

"Ah…"

"What?"

"Old Cornish fairy stories. Maybe Lizzy Bridger's a bit of a Pagan. She probably believes in the Knockers too. They're supposed to be people who live underground. Tin miners were afraid of them and had to leave food and gifts to appease them."

"And Bockaboo."

"Buccaboo. Actually it's a corruption of Bucka-Dhu. Dhu is the old word for black. Like the Black Woods used to be called Kosow-dhu. Literally *woods black*."

"And bucka is like Bucker Field on the farm?"

"That and Bucker Mine."

Dan said, "I'm still none the wiser."

"Buccaboo is a corruption of Bucka-Dhu. It's the black spirit. The Devil. This whole area is rich with stories of the battle between good and evil. Many places are named after saints for their protection."

"I know Helston is an abbreviation of Hell's stone."

Margaret nodded. "Your great-grandfather named the farm Searles. It used to be called Gwidden Farm. Obviously before my time, but in those days people were more superstitious and didn't like the change. You see, Gwidden means white, which would represent the good—you know, in an attempt to balance the spirits. The Bucka-Gwidden and Bucka-Dhu. Removing the Gwidden left nothing to fight the dark side."

"So you think Lizzy Bridger really thinks there's evil here?"

"I don't know, but it's a bit rich coming from her. She worked there for a while. Did you know that? End of the nineties."

"No. I wanted nothing to do with the farm after I moved out."

Margaret raised her eyebrows. "Well, what can I say? She was an absolute tramp. Very young, too young to be away from home in my view. She used to come from the area apparently, though I got the impression home was now one of the Scilly Isles. Anyway, she was good-looking and she knew it. There was some scandal involving Lizzy. Must have been pretty bad because he fired her."

"Did he ever say what it was?"

"He wouldn't talk about it. You know how puritanical he can be. Well, he just called *her* a Jezebel. So it's ironic if she's now saying he's the evil one."

Dan looked out towards the mouth of the creek. The gulls were dipping and diving for fish, a snowstorm of birds over the water. After a while he looked back at Margaret, a thought spiralling in his head. "Is Steve Bridger Jade's father, do you know?"

Margaret pursed her lips. "Who knows? She has three or four kids, I think. She's such a tramp I wouldn't be surprised if they're all by different men."

TWENTY-TWO

Squatting low, his wild eyes stared into the trees. Hardly a breath passed his lips as he strained to hear. They were coming and he was alone. His fingers shook on the soil and so he dug them deep to stop the trembling.

A bird fluttered in branches high overhead but during the next hour he saw and heard no other movement. Were they lying in wait or had they passed? He eased his hands from the dirt and slowly pushed himself onto all fours. He hesitated, watching for a response before crawling backwards, a small movement at a time.

He slipped over a mound and took longer breaths before raising his head to look for signs of anyone—anything—following.

In his head he recited passages from the Bible he kept in his vest. Remembering the words made him feel better, although he knew the words didn't stay long in his head.

His name was written inside the book: Michael. It seemed to have been a long time since he'd heard someone say his name. His only recollection of it being said seemed to be angry and harsh, like he'd done something wrong.

Perhaps that's why the men were after him. He called them men, and most of the time they looked human, but

Michael knew they were bad spirits that could take any black form, any black creature. He tried to keep them away with the words from the book and killing their own. He strung the dead ones up from trees to scare the evil away.

Michael looked over at his wheelbarrow. He kept his tools in there but there was no gun. Had he had a gun? He could imagine one in his hands, the weight of it. Had he lost it in the forest?

His home was in the forest but he daren't go there just yet. His treasure was there, in a safe place. He knew how to find it. Maybe the men—the things—wanted his treasure.

He pushed his hands through sticky hair and touched the scarred, bald patch. He recalled a blinding flash so brilliant it could have been beautiful if not for the pain. He couldn't recall how it had happened nor how long ago but knew it had something to do with the men who hunted him. They would do it again. They would take his treasure.

Beside his wheelbarrow was a dead deer. Wild deer were rare in Cornwall. It must have escaped from a game park. As he stared at it he remembered he'd snared and killed it shortly before thinking he'd seen the creatures in the woods. Picking it up and putting it on top of the wheelbarrow, he took up the weight and pushed it back to the faint track through the trees. Once there, he turned left instead of returning to the house. There were places in the woods where light fled, where he knew he should go.

Michael couldn't recall how often he'd had to hide, but as he passed a fallen tree he remembered that a green tarpaulin was hidden beneath. He would use that to build a bivouac. As he dug it up, he knew he'd done this many time before, hiding from the men, hoping they wouldn't find his house where his treasure was hidden.

Later, he found the perfect spot and built his temporary home with the tarpaulin and sticks. He skinned the small deer and decapitated it. After checking the area to make sure it wasn't obviously a camp, he went in search of dead animals. Black creatures were the best, the vermin of the Earth that he used to ward off evil. He found a dead rat and crow and strung them up. He stuck a branch in the ground and jammed the deer's head on top. He dangled the bloody skin from a tree and tied wires between trees at ankle height. If the creatures weren't scared by the carrion, at least a tripwire might get them.

Sunlight no longer filtered through the trees by the time he'd returned to the camp. Although desperately hungry, he hung the carcass from a tree nearby. If the creatures came that night, he hoped they'd take the carcass rather than him. If no traps had been triggered, and it looked safe enough by morning, he planned a fire and a feast.

Huddled in the bivouac, he risked lighting a candle so that he could read his Bible.

In the night he awoke to water dripping through the rips in the sheet. He closed his eyes and listened to the drum of the rain.

The farm, Michael knew, had a large tarpaulin. It covered a section of hay by the big house. Tomorrow he'd cut himself a big enough piece and then bury it by the fallen tree for next time the creatures came looking for him.

Before dawn, with the ground heavy with moisture, he uncovered logs he'd stored to keep dry and made a fire. The charred meat filled his gut and he drank rainwater that had pooled where the sheet had been tied.

Afterwards, he demolished his bivouac. He cut a section of tarpaulin and wrapped the remnants of the cooked meat. He dug a hole and buried the bones. With a makeshift broom, he swept the area and scattered twigs and other natural detritus to make it look like no one had been there.

He laboured for a long time and, when he was finished, he grinned and nodded to himself for a job well done. He looked around, breathed in the cool earthy air. The fears of the previous day were now just a taste in his mouth.

He began to walk, pushing his wheelbarrow of tools and wrapped meat. It was time to go back home. Home to where his treasure was waiting.

TWENTY-THREE

Tom was stacking timber outside the workshop after a delivery.

Dan approached. "Tom, the night Jade Bridger disappeared..."

"Yes?"

"Sorry, I have to ask, were you around?"

"No. What makes you think so? I was home with gastric flu. I didn't leave the house for a couple of days."

"It's just that Nick said he saw you driving your car that night."

Tom shook his head vigorously. "Must have been mistaken. Wasn't me. Can't have been my car."

"I thought not," Dan said uncertainly, but then another voice made him look up.

An elderly man stood in the entrance to the workshop. "Hello?"

Wiping his hands on his jeans, Dan approached and shook the man's proffered hand.

"I'm David Bishop," the man explained, and pointed to the solitary boat on the pontoon. "The blue Hardy."

"Of course!" Dan grinned. "Do you have time to talk?"

"That's why I'm here, young man. Do you have somewhere comfortable we can sit and chat?"

Dan led the way to the sofas outside the office. Alfie hobbled out, closely followed by Auntie Margaret, who offered them drinks.

Bishop declined with charm and then eased himself into the nearest seat as though bending his knees caused him discomfort. "I know how that little dog feels," he said. He had neat white hair, age spots on his hands and face, but bright eyes that hinted at humour. Something about his posture and smart, though inexpensive, clothes said ex-army.

"Sorry I didn't recognize you," Dan began. "You've been a customer from just after I started this place."

"Understandable. I hardly ever use the damn boat anymore. Janice—my dear wife—keeps telling me to get shot of it, but it's part sentiment and part aspiration."

Dan frowned sympathetically.

"These damn knees. When they're bad I can't get in and out of the boat, so I use it as an incentive to keep up the exercise in the hope that someday soon the pain will ease and I can get out on the water more. It's probably been five-odd years since we spoke, so don't feel too bad about not recognising me." He placed his hands on his knees and set his shoulders. "So, you wanted to talk to me about something."

Dan raised his chin in the direction of the pontoon. "You're the only customer who hasn't switched moorings. I wondered if anyone approached you."

"They did, about a year ago."

"Alan Everitt?"

"That was the man's name. I didn't like his tone, and then when he offered me an incentive to move my boat I liked him even less. I'm sorry it looks like your other customers didn't feel the same way."

Dan nodded, stood and picked up a notepad and pen before returning to the sofa.

"What deal did he offer?"

"Mr Everitt was very cagey so I played him," Bishop said with a twinkle in his eye. "He took a long time to get to any detail, really wanted to sound me out and see if I could be persuaded. Eventually he offered to pay my mooring fees for the rest of the year here and then a year at the yard down the road."

"*Pentewen*?"

"That's the one, though he later said he could get another deal if I wanted to move somewhere else."

"You don't happen to know the exact date he made this offer do you?"

Bishop smiled and told him. "Thought you'd want to know when you left the message, so I looked it up."

Dan wrote the date and some notes. He paused, his pen hovering over the pad. "And did he say why he was doing this to me?"

"Not straight away. I said we needed to meet. I said I never agreed to anything without seeing the whites of the eyes of the person I'm dealing with." The twinkle again. "But I wasn't really interested. As I said, I was playing him."

"So you met when and where?"

Bishop gave a date and an address in Truro. "That's his office I think."

"Not Redcastle Estates?"

"The people developing the field at Passingplace roundabout? No, I don't think so."

That surprised Dan, but he decided to come back to it after asking about the motive. "And at this meeting—Everitt told you why he was keen to do a deal?"

"He said it was because you were away and going to close the yard. I didn't buy that. It didn't make any sense. It could be a reason for me, but it didn't explain why he was willing to pay good money to help me out.

So I pressed him and he came up with a half-decent explanation. He said there was someone influential who thought you were guilty of abducting that girl who went missing. Probably murdered and you'd got away with it because you could afford the best lawyers, coming from a wealthy family as you do."

Dan shook his head. "Did you get a name?"

"I tried, but he wouldn't say. In fact, he made me sign a non-disclosure form before we started and insisted that our conversation was confidential and that he would take legal action if I were to disclose anything. In the agreement itself, there was also a gagging clause, I think it's called."

"And yet you're telling me now."

The corner of Bishop's mouth flicked up. "Non-disclosure my arse. I didn't sign his main agreement and I'm sure his claim of legal action was nonsense. It wouldn't have been very secret if he decided to publicly sue me."

"Did you get a copy of the actual agreement?" If Dan could get that, he was sure he could take action himself under the anti-competition regulations.

"Saw it, and said I needed to think about it. Everitt was prepared for that and took all the paperwork back."

Dan drummed his fingers in frustration. Then he remembered to come back to Redcastle. "So if you saw the agreement, you saw who the other party was. Was that Redcastle Estates?"

"No, Esparante—or something like that. Never heard of them." He spelt it out as Dan wrote it down.

They spoke some more, but Dan gained no new information.

After Bishop levered himself from the sofa to his feet, he said, "I believe in the old principal of innocent until proven guilty, and it's not right what that man has tried to do to you."

"Thanks for your loyalty. One thought," Dan added, "Hardy's have particularly high sides. If you'd like, I'll make you steps to make it easier to get in and out. No charge."

The old man chuckled. "I may just take you up on that offer, but for the time being I'll use the challenge as my motivation." He gave Dan a firm handshake and wished him success in rebuilding the boatyard business.

On the outskirts of Truro, Dan parked close to the address Bishop had given him. The properties were mostly Georgian, converted into salubrious offices with high-gloss black doors and gold fittings.

Before leaving home, Dan had searched the Internet for a company called Esparante but hadn't found anything that seemed relevant and there was no name plaque beside the entrance. Nor could he see through the opaque glass on either side of the door.

Dan rang the reception buzzer and found himself in a well-appointed foyer. A girl behind the desk finished sorting paperwork and looked up with a smile that didn't show in her eyes.

"Esparante Agency?"

She blanked him.

"I'm looking for a company called something like Esparante Agency. Alan Everitt?" he tried.

"Oh, you mean Esperar Land Agents Ltd." She pointed to a board on the right-hand wall. Dan didn't see the name, but there must have been over thirty companies listed.

She saw the confusion on his face. "We provide flexible office services. This is Esperar's registered address. We re-route calls and forward post."

"Ah," Dan said, looking disappointed. "And the forwarding address would be...?"

"Confidential." She gave him the smile that didn't show in her eyes.

"Are you expecting him today?"

The girl checked a page that Dan guessed was a schedule. "He occasionally comes in for meetings. We have rooms here but I can't see anything booked in for him for the next month." After a pause, she said, "You can leave a message that I can pass on."

Dan thought about it but decided he could get hold of Everitt via the Redcastle phone number if necessary. He thanked her and headed back to his car. He drummed his fingers on the steering wheel and an idea came to him. Using his smartphone, he searched a web phone directory for Alan Everitt in Truro. There was only one Everitt listed. The address was a village not far away.

It took Dan ten minutes to find the area and another ten to locate the house. It was set back from the road, partially hidden by trees and surrounded by a high fence. Security cameras covered the main gates. Dan walked up, ignored the intercom and looked through a crack in the wooden gates. Beyond, he could see part of a well-maintained garden and a large modern house.

Four ostentatious Romanesque columns ran along the front. Stone steps went up to the front door with an arched, modern window above. A mishmash of styles created by someone with more money than good taste, Dan decided.

No cars were parked on the herringbone paved drive and when he rang the buzzer no one answered. Dan returned to his car and realized the drive looked like it swept to the side of the house and another gate.

He followed the road round and turned down a track, following the high fence. He found the second entrance

141

and tried the gates. They were locked. Again he peered through to the house. An Aston Martin was tucked into one of three open garages but there was still no sign of life. As he stepped back he noticed another track to the rear of the property. Dan drove on round, turned down a further track and almost ran into a parked white van.

Dan walked around it. The registration was different but he had no doubt he'd seen the van before.

He got back into his car and dialled Detective Sergeant Collick.

"It's about the evening I was beaten up."

Collick made no attempt to sound interested. "What about it?"

"I know who was responsible. I've found the van the guys were in." He gave the location outside the village.

"And the registration matches?"

"No, but it is the van. It's a Ford Transit. I recognize the blue padlock on the back doors and a scratch over one wheel."

"Hmm. You said you think you know who was responsible?"

"A guy called Alan Everitt. It wasn't about Jade Bridger. That's what he wanted me to think. The guy wants me out of the boatyard. He's been trying to drive me out of business, and now he's resorting to intimidation."

Collick didn't say anything.

Dan added: "He was using the disappearance of Jade as a cover."

"And you know it's Everitt because…?"

"Because this guy has an expensive house just where the van was parked and it just suddenly all makes sense: the graffiti, the beating, the threats."

"Do you know how crazy you sound? The guy has a motive and an expensive house?" There was a tension in

Collick's voice, like he was holding something back. "So you're the victim, are you? It's all about Dan Searle, not about Jade Bridger at all?" Then the detective let the anger overflow, details of the case punctuated with invective.

Dan held the phone away from his ear and, after a few seconds, ended the call.

TWENTY-FOUR

Dan spent a long time staring out at the river, watching the darkness grow beneath the overhanging trees until he could no longer see the line where the water ended and the trees began.

He sipped bottled beer and listened to music. He had tried calling Karen but had only got voicemail. He wondered what she was doing and why she didn't answer. The urge to try again became an obsession until he couldn't resist any more.

She answered on the first ring.

"You been avoiding me?" He tried to sound casual.

"Sorry, Daniel. I've a lot going on and I can't talk long." Her voice was quiet, almost whispered.

"You back in London? Everything OK?"

There was a moment of silence on the line and then she said, "Best that I just deal with it. Tell me your news. What have you found out?"

Dan told her about meeting Bishop and the agreements Everitt had persuaded the boatyard customers to sign. He said he'd been to the office but hadn't got past the receptionist and the name of Everitt's company.

"Did you search Companies House?" When he said no, she explained: "It's a limited company, so you can find quite a bit from the legal documents."

He said he'd check, then told her about the van and the conversation with Collick.

She laughed. "What were you thinking, expecting Collick to be on your side?"

"I know. Pretty dumb, but I actually feel better that I know who's behind the attack. And that it wasn't about Jade Bridger."

"Don't do anything stupid about Everitt, though, will you? Promise me." She waited for him to promise before continuing. "Tell the police."

"Collick won't help."

"Just report it. Whether Collick helps or not, you'll have it on record. Anyway, I do think you could do worse than get him on your side. So he's an idiot. So he's convinced it's you. All the more reason to work with him." She shrugged. "I guess it's easier said than done. Anyway, how's your investigation going? Any progress on clearing your name?"

He told her about the conversation with Lizzy Bridger, how she didn't blame him for hitting her husband. "But she's an odd one—all over the place. Started going on about evil spirits and blaming the farm."

"Your dad's farm?"

"Yeah. Which is ironic, because, according to Margaret, Lizzy Bridger used to work at Searles Farm back in the nineties. And there was some kind of scandal involving her. Oh, I forgot to ask..."

"What?"

"No, there was this other thing. Did you notice an envelope on the steps when you left?" When Karen said she hadn't, Dan explained about the photograph. "Only, the photo looks old—thick paper, like it's from one of those old self-printing cameras."

"A Polaroid?"

"That's my guess. It's got to have something to do with the case though, hasn't it. Though I've no idea what, nor who left it."

He thought he could hear her thinking, the way she made a little noise with her tongue on the roof of her mouth. "Karen?"

"The photo. Could you scan it and send it over?"

"Sure."

"I may work for an investment bank but I know someone who may be able to help with this kind of thing. There's a research department at the press agency I work with. I'm pretty sure they have a machine that can scan photos and through some sort of recognition can find any images and associated press that have been published. Not sure how many years it goes back, but it's worth a try. What do you think?"

"I'm already scanning it," he said, standing over his computer. "There, scanned and emailed." He heard her phone ping and she said she'd got it.

"Back in a minute," she said, ending the call.

As he waited, Dan knew that with Karen around the weight of the world was halved. He answered as soon as his phone rang again.

"OK, I've forwarded the email. No idea how long it'll—"

He wasn't sure where it came from, but he suddenly said, "I love you, Karen."

Silence at the other end.

"Sorry," he said. "I know you're practically married and I don't want to come between you and—what's his face?—Matt, but I can't help how I feel about you."

"This isn't a good idea, Dan." He heard background sounds, wondered where she was. He'd been thinking about this, about what to say.

"You once told me that love was about facing your biggest fear."

"Daniel, I..."

"My biggest fear is never seeing you again. Knowing that I'll grow old without you."

He heard a man's raised voice then and guessed it was Matt.

She said, "OK, Mum, I'll get that first thing and email it over. Love you."

And then she was gone and he held the phone to his ear listening to dead air. Matt had stopped her from staying in touch while he was in custody. She'd pretended to be on the phone to her mother, which probably meant Matt didn't know she'd visited him either. Why have secrets unless she had feelings for him? She'd said she had things to deal with and he wished he'd found out what she was doing. His mind spun with possibilities and questions—and hope.

TWENTY-FIVE

Initially, the night was filled with thoughts and memories of Karen and, during the long hours, Dan thought he heard a boat out on the water. He wondered if it was the same one from the other night. The one without the lights.

As grey pre-dawn light played shadows on the ceiling he realized he was awake and thinking about Everitt. He took a sip of water, hoping to ease the tightness in his gut and tried to relax, go back to sleep. After a few deep breaths he found thoughts crowding back. There was no structure, just secret deals with individual boatyard customers. Jack Tanner must have known, maybe had a contract with a gagging clause himself. Everitt was a middleman. Did Redcastle know or was Everitt just a speculator? Would the anti-competition laws do anything? A legal fight could take years and what would be at the end of it—compensation? Dan was unsure he wanted compensation. Everitt was behind the graffiti and the beating. Compensation wasn't enough. Dan wanted revenge. Thoughts of returning the beating flooded his mind and it felt satisfying—until logic took over. The risk would be too great and Collick would be all over it.

The cycle of thoughts repeated and he came back to the relationship between Everitt and Redcastle, or

Esperar and Redcastle. Who were Esperar Land Agents? What had Karen said? Check with Companies House?

Dan got up and switched on his computer. He spent a few minutes trying to find information on Esperar before realising websites provided access to company information. Alan Everitt, someone called Impala and another man—Gavin Redman—were listed as shareholders of Esperar Land Agents. After an hour of abortive research he found Impala LLP. No shareholder's this time; LLP meant Limited Liability Partnership. His fingers shook as they hovered over the keyboard. Two partners: Redman, the man he didn't know, and one he did.

Geoff Jenkin, the farm manager.

Dawn was an angry streak of red as his tyres spun into Geoff Jenkin's drive. Things had changed since Dan had last been here. The old mobile homes, in which the temporary farm workers squatted, had gone, either towed or collapsed with rot. Old sheds had been replaced by modern ones. To one side, the metal dairy shed dominated and behind it barns with corrugated roofs formed a quadrangle. An open double garage with a room above housed a new Land Rover Sport.

The house had once been three cottages, but there was now just one main door and another to one side that looked disused. A big property for a single man.

Dan hammered on the main door and kept it up even when he heard Jenkin shouting he was coming as he thumped down the stairs. When the door opened, Dan felt the rage surge through his veins. He pushed, following through until his hand found Jenkin's chest and then he kept pushing so the bigger man staggered backwards.

"Whoa! Whoa!" Jenkin retreated, his voice desperate.

Dan kept pushing until the man's back hit the rear wall. He kept his left hand in the middle of the farm manager's large chest.

"You bastard!"

Perhaps the initial shock wore off, because the look on Jenkin's face quickly shifted, becoming stone-hard. Although more than two decades his senior, the man's move was faster than Dan anticipated. He grabbed Dan's forearms and squeezed with surprising strength.

"Enough!" Jenkin's shout hit Dan like a punch.

Dan squirmed free, pulled back. "You bastard, how could you?"

"What are you talking about? What the hell are you doing banging down my door first thing in the morning?"

"I know all about it."

Jenkin didn't respond. Their eyes were locked and Dan wished he could read the farm manager's thoughts.

A thin line of a smile formed on Jenkin's lips. "You look knackered. You been up all night?"

"I know what you're doing." Dan spat the words.

"What am I doing?"

"Driving me out of business, that's what."

Jenkin's tension eased. He shook his head and was about to say something when a vehicle drew up outside. Jenkin looked towards the door. "I haven't got time for this, Dan, I've got work to do. We've got the harvester up in Bucker Field this morning." He easily sidestepped Dan, reached the door, and called outside.

"I'll be right up." He stepped out and turned back to Dan. "Look, let's talk on the way. I'll explain and you'll see you've gotten something wrong." Jenkin strode to the garage, climbed in the Land Rover and swung open the passenger door.

Dan stared at the car door for a moment. "I'll follow you."

"Your heap of junk won't make it. You'll bust your suspension at best, but more likely an axle. Get in."

Dan stepped in and swung the door, hoping the slam would strengthen his position. But as he sat beside Jenkin, jolting with the ruts, he knew the older man had control. By the time the track hit the edge of the forest, Dan accepted his car wouldn't have made it.

Dan fixed his eyes on a tractor a hundred yards ahead. "You've some explaining to do."

"When we get there."

The tractor had stopped in Bucker Field but Jenkin drove on past it. He waved to the other man and continued to the boundary fence. He didn't turn off the engine. Without a word, he climbed out, unlocked the gate and heaved it open. Metal grated and groaned until it was wide enough to take the car. A sign beyond warned of danger and restricted access.

"Why are we going up here?" Dan asked as Jenkin drove through, the wheels scattering slate as the terrain changed from earth to stone. The barren outcrop caught the first rays of sun, showing an ochre crest over solid grey.

"Just up ahead," Jenkin said.

Under the Land Rover's wheels, the track smoothly wound up and round, down and then up until they reached the highest point. The broken chimney of the old mine jutted like a tombstone. Jenkin eased to a stop.

"Now, Dan, what's this nonsense about me driving you out of business?" His voice had the honey tone of a much-loved uncle.

"You're in business with Everitt."

"No."

"Oh come on! I've seen the evidence. You might not be a shareholder, but you are a partner in Impala. So indirectly you are involved."

Jenkin raised his hands, fingers outstretched like he was trying to push back the words. "That doesn't mean—"

Dan's blood surged. "You bastard, you're trying to drive me out of business so Redcastle can take my boatyard and develop it for upmarket waterfront properties. For God's sake, you were also behind those two guys who beat me up!"

"What?"

Dan swivelled and pinned the farm manager with a glare. "Don't pretend you don't know! Everitt works for Redcastle, who have development rights on my boatyard. They want me out—fair or foul."

Jenkin raised his hands like he was half surrendering. "Honest to God, I don't know anything about Everitt arranging to have you beaten up. If I'd known—"

"I don't believe you."

"That was nothing to do with me."

"Who's Gavin Redman?"

Jenkin shrugged. "A friend of Alan's. He's on the council." Again he raised his hands. "Look, he's the contact with Alan, not me. I'm like what they call a silent partner. Redman approached me, said it was a low-risk investment. Though he said I should just act like a middleman and ease any transactions between your dad and potential land buyers. Seriously, Dan, I had nothing to do with any attack on you."

Dan said nothing and glared, but Jenkin just looked back. He sounded genuine, and yet surely he knew what his partner was up to.

The silence stretched between them until Dan said, "So why the hell are you in business with the guy?"

A smile pulled a tight line across Jenkin's lips. "To make some money—real money. What other reason is there?"

A thought leapt unbidden into Dan's mind and was out of his mouth before he could stop it. "You want to take over the farm."

Jenkin shook his head, the thin smile still present. "Ah, there it is," he said and then opened his door. "Get out. I want to show you something."

They stood on a flat stone protruding over the wasteland that was the old Bucker Mine. Behind them a partial chimney jutted beside a building known as the engine room. After that was a crater, the ground sloping away into a gapping crack. This was where the mine had collapsed leaving a rough oval about twelve feet wide.

Dan surveyed the fields, the Black Woods and the river beyond. Rooftops in higher parts of Trevelyon could be seen from here.

Jenkin waved his hand over the panorama, places where darkness still pooled and others were streaked with morning light. "Beautiful, but I'm no damn poet, Dan. Most of what you can see has been in your family for generations."

Dan frowned. "I know this."

"Bear with me, kiddo. I just want to talk about the history. This is your family's land and it's been the source of great wealth. For a short time that came from this mine. Of course, it didn't used to be in the Searle family. And because Trevelyon was a centre for smelting and shipping, first of tin and then lead, it was a great business—until the disaster, that is."

Dan knew his history. The miners had rebelled at working the lead. People had died from poisoning, and after a dispute, an explosion crushed the seam, ripped the heart out of the mine. The owners had closed it and his great-grandfather had snapped it up for a bargain, managing to make a quick fortune until eventually the area had been condemned. A couple of years ago the council compulsorily purchased it on the grounds of it being a danger to human life—unsafe, although the only access could be across the field or through the forest. They claimed kids had been seen playing there and erected the protective fencing and warning signs.

Jenkin continued: "Bucker Mine made your family, but there was always money from the farm. Before you were born, this was the largest dairy farm in Cornwall. You must know your dad was once the farm manager here, for his old man.

"After your grandfather died, things got tough for your old man. The EU milk quotas of eighty-four made us rethink the business, diversify. Beef did well until BSE at the start of the nineties. You were—what—seven, when it broke out in Cornwall?"

Dan nodded. He recalled all the media coverage of the mad cow disease. He also remembered that was the time his dad and his previous farm manager had argued a lot. The guy had been sacked and Jenkin stepped up as replacement.

Dan said, "I remember you did all right out of it."

Jenkin reached forward, hooking his arm around Dan's shoulder. At first it could have been an affectionate gesture, but it held him there and Dan sensed it was more about control than a gesture of friendship. When Jenkin spoke, his voice was edged with emotion.

"Wouldn't have if our farm had been hit by it. We'd have gone bust overnight if we'd had to slaughter the cattle like other farms around. Compensation came too little too late for most. So we did OK for a while—until the Frogs banned all British beef."

154

Jenkin stared off into the distance and for a while there was just the drone of the harvester in Bucker Field. A cloud of birds swelled over the woods and then was gone.

Dan thought of pulling free but waited.

Jenkin said, "You know how much profit we can make on a head of beef today?"

Dan didn't. He had no interest in the profitability of the farm. Maybe that was Jenkin's point.

The big man breathed out, almost like he'd come to a decision, and his arm relaxed and dropped from Dan's neck. "Lucky if you make a tenner," he said. "The fruit did well for a few years, but even the Pick-Your-Own business isn't worth running these days. When I started, we would employ up to thirty labourers during the year. Now I just have a couple of part-timers. Oh, the arable, wheat and corn help us tick over, but we're struggling, Dan. Know what I'm saying to you? Farming has become a mug's game, and I'm not a mug."

"So, you're telling me you're not interested in taking over the farm because it doesn't make enough money?"

"That's exactly what I'm saying. But also that it's your family's farm."

"The new Land Rover—Dad didn't buy it, did he? That's from your business with Everitt."

"Partly, I have a few business interests. When your dad wanted to sell the land by the roundabout, Everitt acted as agent and Redcastle paid well. Your dad got what he wanted and we made a bit of money on the side." He raised a hand, like a Boy Scout making a pledge. "All straight up. Nothing dodgy."

"Why, Geoff? Why did Dad want to sell the land?"

"As I said, the farm business isn't good these days. He needed the money, I s'pose. You want details, you'd better ask him."

Dan squatted for a moment looking at the crack in the ground and realized that if Jenkin had jerked him backwards he could have slipped into the hole. Perhaps the grip around his shoulders was more than control. Perhaps it had been a threat. Or maybe Jenkin had considered throwing him in. Dan's pulse quickened and he picked up a stone. Jenkin stood over him as though willing him to act.

An ache grew in Dan's chest that was more than the bruised ribs. His breath shortened. The rough stone bit into his fingers as Dan squeezed it, making a decision, deciding this was not the moment. Trying to seem casual, he flicked it towards the hole. It skidded on the slope just short before disappearing over the edge.

Dan stood and faced the farm manager. "I'm waiting to hear the explanation you promised. You said I'd gotten it wrong."

Jenkin matched his glare. "I'm a partner in a business that invests in Esperar. That's what I've told you. I don't want to own the farm and I don't want to ruin your business. I'm not your enemy, Dan."

Dan narrowed his eyes, shook his head.

"Look," Jenkin said, "Leave it with me. If Everitt is trying to put you out of business I'll get him to stop. If he's done worse—if he was behind the attack on you— I'll find out. As I said, I'm not your enemy. If anything, I'm on your side."

TWENTY-SIX

It took Dan twenty minutes to walk back to his car. Jenkin apologized for not being able to spare the time to take him back, but Dan suspected the manager never had any intention of driving him back. He was about to get in when his phone rang, Karen's name on the display.

"Hey," Dan answered.

"Who is this?" A man's voice. He guessed it was Matt.

Dan said nothing, heard the tension in Matt's breathing.

After a few rapid heartbeats Matt said, "I know it's you, Searle. You're trouble. I want you to keep away from my wife."

"One, you aren't married."

Matt started to speak but Dan spoke over him.

"And two, I don't really care what you think. In my book, if she wants to be my friend, it's up to her."

"Just stick with your prostitutes and get your nose out of our life."

Dan didn't have time to respond because the call ended abruptly.

"Arsehole!" Dan muttered. He stood for a moment with his hands on the roof of his car wondering what was going on. He wanted to call Karen to check she was all right but guessed Matt would answer. As he stood there, he realized Jenkin had left his front door ajar. Curiosity carried him to the door, but then he backed off and got into his car.

He rolled it along the drive before changing his mind. He pulled through the trees and tucked it out of the way. A minute later he was standing in Jenkin's hall.

For a moment he hesitated, wondering what he was doing, but he shook away the guilt and headed for the kitchen. Dishes were piled high in the sink. Apart from that, the room was generally clean. Without leaving any sign of a disturbance, he checked the many drawers. Only a few had cutlery and utensils. The rest were untidily crammed with papers and detritus. He didn't know what he was looking for. Maybe something with Redcastle or Esperar's name on it. Maybe anything that contradicted what Jenkin had said at the mine.

Nothing grabbed his attention.

After the kitchen, he checked the lounge and found nothing of interest. The dining room had ageing mahogany furniture, probably inherited. A sideboard had tarnished silver cutlery and a photo album which again looked decades old. There was nothing else downstairs except for a toilet and a door that wasn't external. He wondered what was on the other side. A cellar or walk-in pantry perhaps. The door was locked. Not a pantry then.

Upstairs, he found three bedrooms and a bathroom. One was used as a junk room: boxes, an old TV set, clothes on racks. The smallest bedroom was used as an office, looking out over the garage. A grey safe, the size of bedside table, stood on the floor next to a metal filing cabinet. A desk, etched by years of use, had a computer and a set of drawers. The computer looked state of the art.

On the desk were unopened envelopes that looked like bills and a couple from the Inland Revenue. The loose papers showed nothing interesting but there were some geological maps of Cornwall that made him stop. They all had the farm marked out and one showed the boundary of Bucker Mine. He held it for a while wondering why Jenkin should have these, but eventually he shook his head before returning everything as he'd found it.

The drawers of the filing cabinet moved slightly but wouldn't open. He poked a letter knife along the top drawer and felt it catch. Try as he might, he couldn't work it loose and decided to stop before any obvious damage was done.

The main desk drawers opened easily, except a central one which was locked. Pulling out a sheaf of papers, he found bills and letters organized chronologically. Rifling through them, nothing jumped out as odd.

Dan tried the knife on the middle desk drawer. It caught and clicked open. He took hold of the handle but then froze as something creaked downstairs.

A door or floorboard?

He listened hard and was rewarded by the noise again. Breath tight and blood rushing in his ears, Dan looked out of the window. He hadn't heard Jenkin's car and there was no sign of it outside. Easing to the hall, he stood silently waiting for more sounds. Minutes passed and then he heard footsteps. It was as though someone had also been waiting and listening before continuing.

Could it be Jenkin?

New sounds came from the kitchen. Dan edged to the banister, considering whether he could get down the stairs and slip out. No way without being obvious, he decided.

A bang like a door slamming made his heart jump. He stepped backwards into the junk room and eased the door until it was almost shut. He stood by the wall, heart pounding in his chest, unsure what was going on or what to do.

Could he hear feet on the stairs? He looked through the crack of the junk room door but no one appeared on the landing. Instead, he heard a scuffling on the far side of the room. He stepped over to the far wall and placed his ear to it. Occasional scraping sounds seemed to be coming from the other side of the wall. Confused, because he'd assumed it was an outside wall, Dan hesitated before realising it could be his chance to get out. He moved back to the door and eased it open. He stepped out onto the landing and edged so that he could glance down the stairs. Seeing no one, he took two steps.

A noise below made him retreat sharply. He stood on the landing, his hands shaking, again filled with uncertainty. *Come on, move!* he told himself. Gritting his teeth and clenching his hands against the trembling, he crept to the office. Without hesitation now, he gently closed the door, stepped to the window and released the latch.

A small outhouse or coal bunker offered a short drop. Climbing through the window made him gasp from the pain in his ribs, but within a minute he was down on the bunker, the window left slightly ajar. He lowered himself to the ground and breathed for the first time in a while. In a squat, he ducked around the rear of the house, under the kitchen window and then along the far side towards the cover of the trees lining the drive.

The noise of the car engine seemed jarring in the quiet of the morning. Dan reversed to the driveway and threw it into first. As he drove away, he kept his eyes on the house, expecting someone to come out and watch him go. But no one appeared.

Instead of turning left for home, he went towards Passingplace roundabout, following the farm boundary until he reached the closest point to Bucker Field. The harvester spouted dust and debris and as it turned at the edge of the field and Dan saw the Land Rover.

It hadn't been Jenkin in the house.

Ninety minutes later, Jenkin called. He shouted incoherently down the phone.

"This is the day for angry callers," Dan said, trying to defuse the farm manager's anger.

"What the hell are you playing at?"

"You'll need to explain what's upsetting you, Geoff."

"You know bloody well. I've a good mind..."

Dan interrupted. "I blamed you for what Everitt was up to, for being attacked. But I've accepted your explanation."

"That's not what I'm talking about and you know it. You broke into my house."

"Of course I... What? Broken in?" What had Dan done to make Geoff think he'd broken in. Or maybe... Dan tried to act normal and sound concerned. "Are you saying someone's been in your house, Geoff?"

"Yes, that's exactly what I'm saying." The stress in Jenkin's voice dropped a notch, doubt creeping in. "So you're saying you know nothing about it?"

Technically, Dan was guilty of breaking and entering. He knew that, but he'd been careful. He was sure he'd left everything as he'd found it. Perhaps Jenkin was just fishing. Dan said, "Are you sure someone broke in? If it was just the front door... I don't remember you closing it when we left."

161

"It wasn't just the bloody door. There's..." He stopped himself from saying something.

"What?"

"Just... someone's been through my stuff."

"Anything stolen?"

"No, just a broken internal door."

Dan thought about the locked kitchen door and the first loud noise he'd heard. He said, "That's terrible. If you need me to give a statement to police, I'm happy to help, Geoff."

"Hmm."

Dan said nothing, certain that Jenkin wouldn't report it. The man had something to hide—and it wasn't just a broken door. Maybe the police would be more interested in why than whom.

Eventually Jenkin said, "OK." There was acid in his tone. "But believe you me, when I find out who's been in my house, been through my stuff, they'll wish they'd never been born."

Dan couldn't resist the urge. "Good job you're on my side. I could do with some of that attitude when you deal with Everitt."

Jenkin ended the call, barely able to hide his irritation.

Dan smiled. It was petty, but scoring a point felt good.

Perhaps it was a day for arguments, but he felt ready to confront Jack Tanner again. The man must have been in cahoots with Everitt. Dan wanted to make Tanner squirm. When he reached Quay, his phone rang with Karen's name again. Expecting Matt, Dan picked up but didn't speak.

He breathed and relaxed as he heard Karen's friendly voice.

"I'm so sorry," Karen said.

"You know Matt called me?"

"We had a row. He went through my phone history. Saw you'd called me last night. I thought he'd let it go, but he seems to have wound himself up this morning."

He heard something in her voice and was concerned. "Are you all right?"

There was a pause and then: "Yes. Don't worry about me. I'm fine. I just wanted to apologize for him, for what he said."

"Yeah, what was that about prostitutes?"

Again there was a hesitation. Her voice softened. "I've a confession, Daniel. The night I stayed for a while, I went through your things. I found the photograph of Amber in your bedside drawer."

"It's over with her. In fact it was never really on." He thought about Amber, how she'd come to the boatyard asking for advice about buying a boat for her parents. She looked like a model, great figure and flowing auburn hair. Out of his league, he'd thought, but she seemed interested, accepted his offer of a drink one evening. It developed into a meal and after that she stayed over a few nights. He'd always known it was temporary but it had been fun while it lasted.

Karen said, "I got a bit green-eyed, I'm afraid. She was very attractive and…"

"There's no need to explain."

"Oh there is, Daniel. I took your photo. I… I sent it to my friend at the agency—the one who can search based on images."

Dan was intrigued now. She hesitated and he waited, letting her find the right words.

"You said her name was Finn, right?"

"Yeah, Polish grandparents I think."

"Not true. Her name is Amber Finnigan. At least she told you her real first name. She was in the *Cornish*

163

Times. Headline: *Beauty queen turns to petty crime.* She'd won a pageant as a kid, hence the beauty queen label, but she was charged a couple of years ago for shoplifting."

"But what's that—?"

"That's not all. What I didn't tell you is Zach—my friend—dug a bit deeper. He has access to other sources of information and discovered that she's also been arrested on a few occasions for soliciting, but never been charged."

Dan's tongue stuck, his mouth suddenly dry.

"That's what Matt meant. He must have seen the email from Zach. Anyway, then he put two and two together and reckons your last girlfriend was a prostitute."

TWENTY-SEVEN

"You're going in!"

A couple of teenage boys in wetsuits pushed one another until one ended up in the water. His pal immediately dive-bombed after him. Other kids dropped lines, crabbing off Quay, and an old guy fished.

Dan smiled and, for a time, his desire to confront Tanner and other issues seemed insignificant. He sat on the bench on the green and squinted into the sunlight bouncing off the rippled creek.

As he watched the kids at play, he realized the importance of childhood, of having fun. His father may not have been the best but Dan recalled long summers when he'd played with friends and enjoyed himself on this quay.

Picking up his phone, he penned an email, remembering to use her preferred name:

Hi Deborah, it's beautiful on Quay. Kids are crabbing and I wondered if Bella would like to do it? He thought about the chance of her saying yes, and added: If you want to supervise, that'll be OK.

A few minutes later he was amazed to receive an affirmative response and replied that he'd pick them up. As he stood, he recognized the fisherman and walked over.

"Mr Bryant?"

The man propped his rod against a post and his face creased into a smile as he looked up.

"Morning, Dan, but please call me Ted."

"Do you have a moment?"

"All the time in the world—the one benefit of getting old." Ted's face creased into a forced smile. "What can I do for you?"

"Can I ask you something about the night Jade Bridger disappeared? Tom said you reported seeing a car parked at Mizzen Green."

"Told the police I did."

"But you must see cars parked here all the time. Why mention this one?"

"Well, it was just a bit odd really. It was in the bay for Mizzen Mast Cottage." He pointed to the holiday let at the end of the green. "I spotted it when I went to bed, parked there, but there was no one staying at the time and in the morning it had gone. Second night it was there again—the night the girl was... disappeared. I thought I could see someone sitting in it. Like I said, I told the police."

"Detective Collick?"

"No, not the first time. I don't remember his name, but then Detective Sergeant Collick came round and asked me for details. Then it was—what?—just after you were arrested, he came round again, said they'd looked into it and that it wasn't—what do they call it?"

"Pertinent to the case?" Dan suggested.

"Yup, that's it—pertinent."

"What can you tell me about it?"

"It was a while back now..." Ted scratched at his forehead. "Well, it was a blue car, funny-looking, but I don't drive and never paid any mind to types of car, so can't tell you what... Tab!"

166

"Tab?"

"I remember part of the number plate. The detective asked me about the number plate and I remembered the letters TAB. Funny what you remember without thinking. I remembered TAB because it looked like a cigarette glow in the car. We used to call them that, you know. Anyway, that's why I thought maybe someone was inside." His face creased again. "I'm sorry that I didn't knock on the window, but—you know how it is—when I saw the cigarette, I decided to back off and report it if it was there again another night."

Dan said nothing.

Ted shook his head. "I guess I chickened. I thought it seemed dodgy, but if it had been a tryst—a couple, you know—I'd have been embarrassed. On the other hand, if he was dodgy and casing a joint, I could have been risking my life."

Dan nodded and patted Ted on the shoulder. "Probably did the wise thing then." He glanced at his watch and realized he needed to get a move on. He thanked Ted and wished him luck with the fishing.

On the drive to Deborah's, Dan thought about what Karen had said about trying to work with Collick. Perhaps he should talk to him about the car. He took a breath, held it and then called Collick's mobile.

"The car Ted Bryant saw…"

"Searle, I thought we'd had a chat and you were to stop causing trouble."

"It's not trouble. I just have a question."

Collick grumbled.

"He said you investigated it…"

"What, exactly, did he say?"

"That he saw a car outside Mizzen Cottage the night before and on the night Jade disappeared. He said it was blue and had the letters T-A-B in the registration."

167

"Right, dark blue..." Collick paused as though deciding how much to say. "We traced the owner and he'd been walking his dog. He isn't from Trevelyon so thought parking in the bay was safer than an unlit street."

"I'd like to ask you..." Dan was unsure what to say but wanted to keep the conversation going and somehow find out what Collick had been arguing with Lizzy Bridger about.

Before he could finish the sentence Collick beat him to it. "I'm busy, Searle. You've got your answer, now let me get on with my job."

The phone went dead and, not for the first time, Dan cursed the ignorance of the man.

Bella and her mum were ready and waiting when Dan arrived at their house in Penryn. Bella's face lit with excitement and expectation and Dan put aside the irritation he'd felt talking to the detective.

They called into the convenience store in the village to get crabbing lines, a bucket, and some bacon to attract the crabs. When they arrived at Quay, Ted had shifted position and Dan took up the spot where he'd been fishing.

Deborah set rules on how close to the edge Bella was allowed, but then she backed off to let father and daughter play.

Bella insisted on pulling her line out almost as soon as she cast in but, after she had caught a couple, she learned to wait a little longer. When Dan pulled out a crab almost the size of his hand, he held it between finger and thumb and presented it to Bella. She squealed when he dropped it and then laughed as he scrambled to catch it without being pinched. They tangled lines and later Dan knocked his over the edge and couldn't reach to fish it out with the net. Besides the poor technique, and left with a single line, they filled their bucket with crabs.

Later, Dan looked back and realized he'd captured moments that would stay with him forever—he fun his daughter had and the squeals she made. He'd laughed as they tipped up the bucket and raced the crabs down the slipway. He was still smiling at the memory when Karen called. He put down his tools and stepped out of the workshop.

Karen started chatting as though neither of them had problems. He let her talk though he desperately wanted to ask about her relationship with Matt. Instead, she told him her mother's flu was almost gone and how good and understanding her boss was. In turn he told her about the crabbing.

"That's real progress," she said with genuine enthusiasm. "Have you arranged your next visit?"

"No."

She lectured him on taking advantage of the situation and building on it. Of course, she was right, and he kicked himself for not thinking about it.

"Next time," she said, "have something prepared—a plan to do something specific."

On their last call, he'd expected her to be upset about Amber but she hadn't judged him. She seemed to accept that he knew nothing of the ex-girlfriend's past. The photograph alone pointed to a proper relationship. However, when she said "Dan, the main reason I've called...", he held his breath.

"I've had a response to the old photograph you gave me."

"Yes?"

"Well, Zach at the agency has a match. The matches come back with a percentage likelihood, and this one's only seventy-eight, but he thinks it's someone called Nina Ivanova. There was a short piece in the *West Briton* on her—with a photograph, naturally—in the summer of ninety-seven. I'll send you the clipping and you'll see her face does look similar. Her hair is longer and looks darker—mousy I guess—in the paper, but of course she could have easily bleached it. There was an article because her father was in the country looking for her. She was Bulgarian and allegedly working illegally in the UK. He'd traced her to Cornwall, but nothing specific."

"And what happened?"

"Zach couldn't find any follow-up articles I'm afraid, so we don't know. Do you think she might have been at your dad's farm?"

"Could be." He tapped his lips, wondering what farm worker records were kept. Would they still be available? He realized who would know. "Can you ping the article over to me and I'll see if Margaret recognizes the name or photo?"

"Already sent."

He signed off saying he'd let her know if anything came up, opened the email and printed the attachment.

TWENTY-EIGHT

Conflicting thoughts worked their way across Steve Bridger's face.

Before he could decide on an unfavourable reaction, Dan walked straight up to him in the pub. Bridger's three drinking buddies looked from Dan to Bridger and back.

Dan said, "Let me buy you a drink by way of apology."

Four faces stared at him as though he'd said something in a foreign language. Dan added, "In fact, I'd like to buy for all four of you. What're you having?"

Each man placed an order—a beer and chaser. No point in missing an opportunity like this. Bridger was last and, with a shrug, succumbed to the desire of free booze.

As his drinks were delivered he continued to eye Dan with a mix of caution and suspicion.

"So you didn't do it?" one of the drinkers offered.

"I had nothing to do with Jade's disappearance."

The man nodded as though this was all he needed as approval and knocked back his whiskey.

Dan leaned towards Bridger. He said, "I'd like a word."

Bridger pushed his lank greying hair from his face and squinted. He said nothing and took a sip of his bitter.

"In private would be good," Dan said.

Bridger looked up. "You can say what you want here. I got nothing to hide."

When Dan had told Margaret about the Bulgarian girl, she hadn't recognized the name. She'd reminded him that in the nineties there'd been a lot of foreign temporary workers on the farm. Dan wanted to ask Lizzy Bridger, but seeing Jade's father here, Dan decided to ask him.

"Your wife worked on Searles Farm."

Again the suspicious look. "What of it?"

"Late nineties?"

"I guess. You should ask her."

"She ever talk about it?"

"Nope."

"Ever heard the name Nina Ivanova?"

One of the other guys made a coarse wisecrack and his friends laughed too loudly. Dan tuned them out. He repeated the name.

Bridger looked at his beer before savouring it. "Nope. Never heard of her."

"Ever heard of problems at the farm about the time your wife was there? The reason why she left?"

Bridger bristled but held himself in check. "I think you've asked enough questions. Thank you for the drinks, but we're done and you're spoiling my evening."

Dan nodded and backed away, sat at the other end of the bar and nursed his own beer. He waited an hour, hoping Bridger or one of his barfly friends would come over and say something. No one did.

At two in the morning his ringing phone jarred Dan awake.

Number unknown.

"What you doing?" Lizzy Bridger, her voice slow and thick with drink or drugs, maybe both.

"Mrs Bridger." Dan cleared his throat and blinked himself awake. "I'm trying to find out what happened to your daughter."

"You were asking about the farm."

"Yes, but—"

"What went on at that damn farm has nothing to do with her."

"Who was Nina Ivanova?"

Lizzy didn't respond.

"Who was Nina Ivanova?"

"Name sounds familiar."

"Did she work at the farm?"

"Maybe, but you're—"

Dan's pulse quickened. "What happened to her?"

Again a long silence. Dan broke it: "You called me, remember? You want to talk?"

"Just want you to stop stirring things up. You aren't helping none."

There was something Dan hadn't asked Steve Bridger because they weren't alone. It was just a wild guess, but it was worth a shot. He said, "Why was your husband searching in Geoff Jenkin's house?"

Lizzy scoffed. "You don't know shit."

"Then tell me what I should know."

"Steve wasn't in Jenkin's house yesterday, you idiot. You're just causing trouble between us, stirring up the past. It's got nothing to do with my poor missing girl. You know, there's not a day goes by…" Her voice trailed off as though she was muttering to herself. And then she became more lucid again, her pitch higher. "Leave me alone, Dan Searle. I've been fair. I've been fair, ain't I? This is my bloomin' life." The call degenerated into a stream of abusive nonsense about the farm and how the Searles were bad and should pay.

Dan had had enough and ended the call. He stared into the darkness, faint light playing on the ceiling. He had shaken the tree and it had finally yielded a result. He settled back down only to be disturbed by the phone ringing again a few minutes later. Number unknown again. He thought about turning the phone to silent but upon impulse answered.

"You know," he said immediately. "You know who was in Jenkin's house, don't you?"

The person didn't respond. He heard humming. A simple tune, but flat like nursery rhymes can be.

"Lizzy, I know it's you," he prompted.

Then she spoke, adding words to the tune:

"One, two, he's coming for you.
Three, four, he's under the floor.
Five, six, grab a crucifix.
Seven, eight, now it's too late.
Nine, ten, never sleep again.
In the woods, you better be good.
Under the stair, he wants you there.
In your head, he wants you dead."
Lizzy's voice dropped to a whisper.
"Listen to the wind, he's calling to you.
He's saying your name...
Bucca BOO!"

TWENTY-NINE

Michael felt in the roof space, his hands clawing through thick dust until they touched the suitcase. They traced the line of the box, finding the handle and pulling the brown leather bag to the edge. He lifted it down, carefully keeping it flat, and carried the suitcase into the dining room. Laying it on the table, he dusted the lid and released the catches, paused and then opened the case.

This was his treasure.

He ran his hand gently over the items lying on the top. He thought he'd find them neatly piled in the suitcase, but his things were in disarray.

He touched the metal design, the good luck charm he'd taken from the boy's key ring. He caressed it and then squeezed it tight between both hands until he felt the metal leave an imprint on his palms. He opened his hands and ran a finger around the circumference of the charm. Then another and another finger, each one giving a different sensation.

Closing his eyes, he tried to make the images come. Sometimes they did and he remembered things, flashing images like the old photographs, occasionally making sense. But often they did not.

He couldn't control the images and it made him angry when memories wouldn't come. In his darkest moments

Michael prayed to God, but sometimes God didn't listen. God didn't help.

He'd gone crazy once. He knew he had because two windows and a chair were broken. Looking at them, he recalled the red fog in his head and the weight of the chair. Now he remembered the weight of the suitcase and saw that a corner was dented and the side gouged where the glass had bitten deep. Now he remembered throwing his treasure. Angry with himself, he blinked tears from his eyes.

Replacing the charm he picked up the camera. He wondered when he'd broken it. No pictures came out anymore and he couldn't recall how long ago it had stopped. Perhaps the man at the farm would mend it for him. Then he could take more pictures of pretty girls.

He picked up a few Polaroids and studied their fading images. When had he taken them? Before the camera had broken, but they seemed much older than he expected. He held a picture up to the light and sadness rose in him like rain filled a hole. The girl wasn't looking at the camera; none of them were because he'd taken them in secret. Red pen on the back of one caught his attention: two lines and a circle. Who had put the mark on his treasure? He sifted through the other Polaroids and found four others with the marks, all photos of the same girl.

"No!" he shouted, but his voice was a grunt and in the corner of the room he saw the red mist seeping in. He blinked the fog away and wept then. He remembered there had been a time when he could use his voice, a time before the blinding pain and fear.

He carried the charm through to the lounge, sat in an armchair and looked at the picture over the mantelpiece—a bird, a colourful small bird, with a fine chain around its leg. *I am the bird*, he thought. *I am trapped, but this is my home, like the box is the bird's perch.*

Michael rubbed the metal charm as he studied the painting, and calmness descended. He may have slept, for when he awoke he saw the image of a beautiful young woman in the doorway. Tall with loose fair hair, she smiled at him and her eyes seemed to shine with a wondrous light.

"I know you," he tried to say, and he felt the cold of the metal charm in his palm.

He stood and stepped towards her and she reached out as though putting her arms around him.

"June," he uttered, and for a moment he recalled their life together, how happy he had been that she would have his child. "June, I'm sorry," he tried to say, but before she reached him she was gone.

He sank back in his seat, the smile still on his face, pleased he had remembered something of his past. He looked down and saw that he had dropped the photographs on the floor. No, they weren't of June, they were of another young woman. He didn't love her, didn't really know her, but he recalled the photos were important. He'd put the red marks on them to remind himself.

When the light faded, Michael made his way out of the forest. Every hundred yards or so, he shifted the heavy sack to his other hand and finally swung it onto a shoulder as he reached the track.

Checking that there was no one about, he cut across to the line of trees that led to the farmhouse garden and then shuffled along in a crouch until he reached the first barn. He looked in, and beside old farm machinery Michael espied a workbench with a box on top. He hadn't remembered the box until now. There would be food inside; tins of beans and fruit in sweet juice were his favourite. He grinned as he saw he was right. He'd come back for this afterwards.

The old man's car was parked next to the house and Michael ducked beside it to remove the dead animal—a badger—from the sack. The farmer hated badgers almost as much as Michael hated the black vermin—the black spirits. Perhaps that's why he left the food—to pay for the badgers Michael caught.

After he had prepared the dead animal as a gift, Michael followed the edge of the gravel area to the tarpaulin-covered hay. There he took out his knife and was about to puncture the material when he saw a slice already missing. He hesitated, ran his hand over the jagged cut, and the memory of removing it flashed back. Only days ago he'd hacked off a piece to replace his damaged sheet and had already buried it.

With the food in his bag, Michael ran home. For the first time for as long as he could remember, he felt good. The creatures weren't after him today, and he had remembered something.

Later, as he ate his tinned meal and stared at the bird, he realized it no longer reflected him. He saw the missing girl in its eyes. She too had been chained, and he needed to tell someone where she was.

THIRTY

Geoff Jenkin's Land Rover was parked outside the main farmhouse. Dan drove past and saw a Ford with disability stickers beside the rear kitchen door.

He climbed out and stopped.

"What the hell is this?"

Outside the back door a mass of fur and blood was spread across the flagstones: a badger, gutted and pulled apart to form a crude crucifix.

Stepping over it, Dan opened the door and entered the kitchen.

"Dad?" he called.

Footsteps echoed on the hallway boards and then Jenkin ducked into the room. Without preamble he said, "It's Sunday. Your dad's at church."

While he'd lived at home, Dan knew his dad had gone to church every Sunday, but he understood the old man's mobility problems prevented him now.

"I thought he didn't go anymore. And whose car is that outside?"

"It's your dad's, but he hardly uses it. I don't think he feels safe enough. Anyway, a friend picks him up for church these days."

"He's still going then?"

Jenkin ignored the question. "So what're you doing here? Looking for me?"

"Know the name Nina Ivanova?"

Jenkin let puzzlement pull at his features. "No, should I?"

"I think she worked on the farm in ninety-seven."

"Long time ago, and you'll remember we used to have a lot of temporary workers in those days. What's this about, Dan? Our issue, or do you mean the missing girl?"

"Day before yesterday, you were denying *we* had an issue."

Jenkin's hand rasped across the stubble on his chin and he leaned back against a kitchen worktop. "Come on, let's not beat about the bush. You know I didn't deny investing in Alan Everitt's business, I just don't have anything to do with his underhand tactics."

Dan shrugged and looked out of the window, past his car at the old cowsheds, corrugated asbestos on the roof. Judging from the state of the building it would become a problem soon. He looked back at Jenkin, who seemed a little too comfortable in his dad's house.

"I think she has something to do with Jade Bridger's disappearance."

"Who you talking about now?"

"Nina Ivanova."

Jenkin raised an eyebrow.

Dan showed him the photograph Karen had emailed and summarized the newspaper article from ninety-seven. He decided against mentioning the Polaroid or how he'd received it.

Jenkin said, "Tenuous. What makes you think there's a connection to the missing girl?"

Dan didn't say anything and Jenkin looked out of the window as if considering or recalling something. The silence stretched between them like a taut bailing cord.

Finally, Dan said, "Did she work at the farm?"

"Who? This Nina Ivanova?"

"Yes." Irritation edged his voice.

"She may have. Name sounds vaguely familiar, and I remember questions."

"Questions?"

"By the police. Your dad wouldn't let them on the farm without a warrant and they had nothing but hearsay to suggest the girl had been here. You know that's always been his way, always your grandfather's way, with authorities—would never let them on the farm, whether it was the police or council or even DEFRA. Whoever. No legal right, no entry is his motto." Jenkin grunted and looked Dan in the eye. "If this Nina girl worked here then she moved on after the summer. So even if the police did search the farm, they wouldn't have learned anything. And she could have gone anywhere afterwards. Kids did that. We didn't ask where they came from or where they went afterwards. We put a roof over their heads, we paid them and no questions were asked. Have you asked Margaret? She kept the books and did the payroll."

Dan said that Margaret couldn't remember her. "Presumably the books are still here?"

"I guess. You'll have to see your dad about it."

"Will you tell him I'll be back later?"

"When I see him, sure."

Dan retreated to the back door, turned the handle.

Jenkin followed. "About the other thing—Everitt. We're cool, right?"

"Yes. Sure," Dan said, distracted by the disembowelled badger on the threshold. "What's this outside?"

"Just a present from that nutter in the woods, is my guess." He nodded. "I'll get it cleaned up before your dad gets home."

Dan had never met Karen's partner, but he immediately reckoned the man leaning against a silver Mercedes—like the grown-up version of Karen's car—was Matt. Tall, dark hair, glasses, designer clothes and sports jacket; a city slicker out of place in the boatyard, out of place in the countryside.

Dan drew up beside him, stepped out of the car and saw a weary face, like the man had been driving all night.

"Matt, I presume?" Dan held out his hand in greeting.

The other man took it reluctantly, his hand soft and weak.

"I'm looking for Karen," he said.

Dan shrugged and pointedly looked around. "She's not here."

"I'd like to see for myself."

Dan hesitated, thought and decided it was better to get rid of the guy than have another confrontation. After all, she wasn't there and he had nothing to hide. "Not a problem," he said and led the way up the steps to the loft. He flung open the door and Matt was immediately inside. The man strode quickly through the sitting room, glancing through to the studio and then on into the bedroom. Dan waited by the door, his hand still on the knob.

"As I said, she's not here."

Matt marched back, reached Dan, but kept going towards the steps.

As he passed, Dan said, "What's happened?"

Matt didn't stop, but Dan grabbed the man's arm, held him there, and said, "Tell me what's happened. Why are you looking for her? Is she all right?"

"I'm sure she's fine and no concern of yours." Matt snatched his arm back. "Just butt out of our business and there won't be any trouble."

Dan stood on the top step and watched the man stride back to his car. He felt a sense of victory, although he wasn't quite sure what for.

The Mercedes kicked stones up as it swung through the gates.

Dan unlocked his phone. He dialled Karen, got her voicemail and left her a message about Matt's little visit. He asked that she call him back to confirm everything was all right.

He sat in the studio with an artist's pad and a chunk of driftwood and sketched sculpture ideas. Nothing felt right so he thumbed through his catalogue of previous work for inspiration. The last piece was the missing *Tin Heart* sculpture, two sea-bleached branches intertwined and shaped into giraffes' necks with their heads facing one another. It was probably the most corny, commercial item in his collection and it was gone. The only conclusion he could reach was that someone had stolen it, but they would have needed access to the loft. Only Margaret had a spare key and he trusted her implicitly. He was still puzzling over the issue when Karen rang.

"Where are you?" he said, picking up.

"You're not looking for me too are you?" She sounded different, muffled.

"You OK, baby?"

He heard her breathe. Then she said, "Yes, I'm all right."

"Matt paid me a visit this morning. I was on my best behaviour. You'd be proud. I didn't react badly at all." He told her about Matt wanting to come up into the loft, even searching the bedroom. "He probably even checked under the bed."

She said, "Have you had lunch? Would you come over?"

"You'll have to tell me where you are, though."

She laughed before giving him an address on the Falmouth seafront.

THIRTY-ONE

"What?" Karen sat in the lounge of the Saint Michaels Hotel in Falmouth, overlooking the gardens. In her lacy cream top and jacket, Dan thought she looked stunning. He glanced down at his own windcheater, polo shirt and jeans, and grimaced.

"You look great. I, on the other hand…"

She shushed him and waved him into a seat, smiled and said, "I took the liberty of ordering for you. I hope you still like shrimp and linguini."

He laughed. She still liked to take charge.

"So, you're staying here then?" he said.

"No. Just wanted to have lunch by the sea. I'm booked into a boutique place just outside Truro. So where are we? What have you learned?"

"That you haven't changed."

"I'm serious, Dan." She took a sip of sparkling water and fixed him with her penetrating blue eyes. "I've been a bit distracted these past few days. Bring me up to date. Tell me what you've learned about what might have happened to Jade."

"I'm not sure I've learned anything."

"That's not true. You suspect her dad was abusing her in some way."

185

"But I did before. I guess I could see it in his eyes when I confronted him about it. He said something like: 'Who told you?' and he sounded guilty. So I've sort of confirmed it, but I'm sure he's not Jade's actual father."

"Do you know who is?"

"I suspect Lizzy Bridger is the only one who knows and I don't exactly have the kind of relationship with her for her to tell me. Did I tell you? I had an odd call from her—pretty nasty actually—she sounded drunk. Anyway, I'd bumped into Steve Bridger at the pub and accused him of being in Jenkin's house."

"Woah! That's news. What was Steve Bridger doing at Jenkin's place?"

Dan told her about the incident with Jenkin, being taken to the mine for a history lecture and then, after walking back, deciding to search his house. "Someone else was there, searching too, so I took a wild shot and accused Bridger."

Karen waited for the waitress to put their meals on the table and check they didn't need anything else before saying, "I don't get it. Why would Steve Bridger—?"

"No, Lizzy said it wasn't him, which sounded very much like she knew who it was. Oh, and the other thing that surprised me was how angry she seemed with Collick. I don't know if I told you, but I saw them arguing."

Karen had a faraway look in her eyes and he knew she was trying to make sense of things before speaking.

The smell of the pasta made him suddenly famished. He took a forkful.

"We should eat this before it gets cold."

"OK, but tell me what you've found out about the girl in the photo while we eat."

He shook his head. "No, let's talk about other stuff for a while. Nothing serious. Tell me how your mum is and what crazy things she's been up to lately. And tell me how your job's going."

She reluctantly accepted and they made small talk and enjoyed their meal. He probed about her work and Dan suspected things weren't as fine as she alleged, but he didn't challenge her on it. When they finished, the waitress delivered poached pears that Karen had pre-ordered for their dessert.

Sated and relaxed, they walked along the coast road towards Pendennis Castle. A chill breeze swept in from the sea and clouds gathered threateningly. On the rocks below the road a few hardy tourists looked like they were trying to pretend the weather was better.

"So what do you think?" Karen asked.

Dan said, "It's going to rain."

"What do you think about the photo of Nina Ivanova? What have you learned?"

"Not a lot really. People seem to recognize her name. Jenkin said she may have worked at the farm."

"May have? Surely he'd know. Even if he can't remember everyone who ever worked there, surely he'd remember someone who'd gone missing."

Dan nodded. "My dad has the accounts. I know it's fifteen years ago, but I'm hoping he'll have the payroll records. If she's in there, then the connection is the farm."

"The connection with Jade Bridger's disappearance?"

"That's my assumption."

"Because?"

"Because she was reported missing and someone left that Polaroid. Someone was trying to tell me something."

Karen didn't say anything for a while. The wind picked up so they turned back and Dan put his arm around her shoulders for warmth.

Before they got back to the hotel, she said, "Do you think Jenkin's involved?"

"It could implicate anyone involved with the farm, including my dad, but Jenkin is my number one suspect right now."

"Of course we don't know yet who left the photo of Nina, do we? The whole thing could be a deliberate misdirection."

"Maybe," Dan said, guiding her along the path as the first raindrops fell. They ran and made the decision to duck under a shelter rather than make it all the way back to the hotel.

Sitting on a bench out of the rain, she said, "I've been thinking about what you said earlier. If it wasn't Steve Bridger, could it have been Lizzy who was in Jenkin's house?"

"It could have been Lizzy." He let the thought sink in and watched the grey clouds streaking down into the sea, the rain sweeping across the bay. Then he recalled her words: *Steve wasn't in Jenkin's house yesterday.* Yesterday. Had Dan said when? He didn't think so.

He nodded to himself. "You know, I think it *was* Lizzy."

Karen said, "You told me she's the one who has an issue with the farm. Maybe her issue is with Geoff Jenkin. Although if it's an old issue, then why would she be there now?"

"Unless it's actually linked to Jade's disappearance."

"But she seems to have relied on her waster of a husband to look for Jade. If she suspected Jenkin, wouldn't she have done something eighteen months ago?" She thought for a moment. "Did Jade know Geoff Jenkin?"

Tanner had said he'd seen Jade meet someone on Mizzen Green. He'd assumed it was Dan because she

188

seemed to know him. Did she know Jenkin? He shrugged. "It's possible, but as far as I remember, she never mentioned the farm."

"I'm cold," she said, and he put his arm around her.

A man with a Scottish terrier scurried out of the rain and both animal and master shook water from their coats. He nodded to them. "Nice to see such a happy couple. Shame about the weather. Autumn's come early this year."

Karen responded, but Dan wasn't listening. He was still thinking about who Jade might have known, who she might have mentioned, but the only name he kept coming back to was Steve Bridger. If he'd been at Quay that night and had been the other person in Jenkin's house, then maybe he could be the connection. But Lizzy said it wasn't him. Then again she could be lying.

Karen pulled in tighter, watching the rain blowing from the west, and he wondered what she was thinking, wanted to ask whether she was happy with Matt, but the other man sat nearby.

Eventually the rain eased, the sky lightening. Karen asked, "Do you have plans for this afternoon? I wondered if you fancied going somewhere like the Lost Gardens of Heligan?"

"Heligan—is that a reference to Hell?"

Karen gave him a quizzical look. "I've no idea. What made you ask that?"

"Just another odd thing Lizzy Bridger said. I'd never thought about it—obviously many towns have Cornish saint's names, but so many places also refer to the Devil and Hell."

"So what did she say?"

"She said maybe the Buccaboo took Jade."

Karen shook her head. "Cornish folklore. It's voodoo nonsense."

189

"And then last night she started chanting a nursery rhyme or something. I'd not heard it before but it was about the Buccaboo."

"It's nonsense, Daniel. She was drunk, wasn't she?" Karen waited for Dan to nod. "There you go. She's a crazy drunk. Don't get distracted by her nonsense. OK?"

"OK."

"So are we going to the Gardens or what?"

He held his hand out, felt the last fine drops of rain. "What about the weather?"

"Makes it more fun."

She laughed, and he realized he hadn't heard that laugh for more than five years, when she used to be his Karen.

She said, "But there are three conditions: No more talk of devils and such. And no talking about the past, because I'd just like an afternoon away from our problems."

"Agreed," he said with a smile. "And the last condition?"

"You buy me an umbrella."

THIRTY-TWO

The afternoon with Karen had been refreshing, almost like old times, and for a few hours he'd felt a contentment that had been a faded memory.

He saw a glint in his eyes as he drove back home.

Just before Mizzen Green, Dan saw Ted Bryant walking along the street. They exchanged waves and Dan drove on. But then he looked in his rear-view mirror and stopped.

Ted walked up the path to a house well beyond Mizzen Green and the long, thin holiday let next to it.

Dan reversed back to where Ted had gone in. The old man was at the door now.

"Do you live here?" Dan asked.

"I do."

Dan got out and walked towards him.

Ted said, "Do you want to come in?"

Dan stopped at the door and turned around. He looked up and down the road and shook his head.

"Tell me again what you saw that night Jade Bridger disappeared."

"I saw a car parked outside Mizzen Mast—"

"The holiday let that should have been empty."

"That's right." Ted seemed a touch hesitant but added: "I think I saw someone inside."

"One or two people?"

"Erm... One I think."

"But you're not sure?"

"No."

"Tell me about the car."

"Blue and funny-looking. I don't drive and never paid any mind to types of car, so I can't tell you what make. I remembered the number plate TAB because it looked like a cigarette glow in the car. That's why I thought maybe someone was inside."

"It's funny, but they are almost exactly the same words you used last time."

"I'm remembering our conversation now."

"OK. How many nights did you see it—the car?"

Ted shook his head. "Why so many questions, Dan?"

"You said you saw it from your bedroom."

"Did I...? Yes I did. That's right... from my bedroom window."

Dan looked up and pointed. "That window?"

"Uh-huh."

"Shall we go up and look?"

Ted tried to smile. "Dan..."

"Is there something you want to tell me?"

Ted put his hand on the door as if to close it.

Dan put his foot on threshold. "You didn't see the car, did you, Ted?"

"I might have done."

"What the hell is that supposed to mean?"

"I think I saw something there the night before."

"But not from the bedroom window. Because it looks to me like you can't see the parking bay of the cottage from here—or from your window for that matter."

Ted looked confused and said nothing.

192

Dan said, "What's going on? Why would you make up something like that? Why say there was a car there and give a partial number plate."

The old man had tears in his eyes. "I... I..."

Dan softened his tone. "Please, Ted. Help me. Please."

Ted nodded as though his head weighed a tonne. He said, "Ask Tom."

"My Tom?"

Ted nodded again. "I can't say more... I promised him."

THIRTY-THREE

Dan clenched his teeth as he marched up to Tom in the yard.

"What are you doing here today?"

Tom looked taken aback by Dan's abruptness but smiled. "Oh hi, Dan. Nothing better to do so just thought I'd catch up."

"Why?" Dan asked, but then shook his head. "I've been too distracted," Dan said. "Distracted by who's trying to ruin my business. I kind of lost track of what happened that night. The night Jade disappeared."

Tom nodded and looked at the fibreglass dinghy he was repairing.

"Tom, look me in the eye and tell me what you were doing that night."

"Why? You can't think I had anything to do—"

"I can't rule it out. Let's go over what happened. You were where?"

"At home with gastric flu."

Dan said, "Jade ran from the office a second time, unhappy that I wouldn't let her stay. She ran down the Plynt path. But the tide was high and there was nowhere to go.

"Later Jack Tanner says he saw her talking to someone on Mizzen Green and her top was found on that path. She'd been wearing the pink top when she ran to the left and yet it appeared later on the path to the right.

"That wouldn't be so surprising if it weren't for the fact that my security cameras didn't record her coming back. The police checked to see if I'd erased them but I hadn't. However there is another way. Know what it is?"

Tom shook his head, his eyes still on the dinghy.

"If the lights or the cameras were switched off."

Tom said nothing.

Dan said, "I would know how to do it. Aunty Margaret would know how to do it. And guess what? You would know how to do it. Right?"

Now Tom looked up. "Yes. But I didn't. I promise you I didn't have anything to do with Jade's disappearance."

"I'm going to ring that inspector—Melville. I'm going to tell her what I know."

"What do you know?"

"I know that you told me to find out what Ted Bryant knew. Maybe that was a distraction from your guilt."

Tom shook his head.

Dan continued: "I know that Ted is lying. It was almost like he was remembering a script. Both times I asked him it was almost word for word the same. And the chance he saw someone smoking in a car at Mizzen Mast Cottage from his bedroom window is highly unlikely. The angle is too shallow."

"What are you saying?"

"He's lying and practically confessed. He told me to talk to you. He was covering for you, wasn't he?"

Tom reached out to put a hand on his shoulder but Dan stepped back.

"Let's go up to the office and sit and have a cup of tea. I can see you're angry. Let's just talk this through."

195

"Jesus, Tom! Just tell me. Are you guilty?"

"Let's get a cup of tea." He stepped past and took a couple of paces towards the office.

Dan grabbed him and spun him around.

Tom raised his hands, afraid he was about to be punched. He blinked tears from his eyes. "Please, Dan..."

"Did you do it?"

"No!"

"For God's sake, Tom. Just tell me."

Tom took a long breath and sighed.

"Did you ask Ted to lie for you?"

"Yes."

"Why?"

"I saw the car that second night. It was nine-fifteen or so. I was driving past."

Dan sat on the edge of the dinghy. "So Nick did see your car go past *Pentewen* that night."

"Probably."

"So tell me. Why did Ted lie for you? Why did you say you weren't there?"

"I couldn't be the witness so I asked Ted to say he saw the car. I told him what to say. Everything he reported was what I saw, although he does think he saw the car there the night before. He'd seen it from the road and didn't pay it any attention until I told him what I'd seen. Of course, Jade hadn't disappeared then so it wasn't important. I just wanted to help."

Dan's fury started to ease. He could see Tom's distress. This man had been his friend and support for almost ten years. He'd always been loyal. He also realized the older man couldn't have been the one on Mizzen Green that night. He was the wrong build. Tanner had thought it was him, but Tom was shorter and stockier. Even from a distance in the dark they couldn't be mistaken.

Tom said, "So Ted covered for me."

"All right, but—"

"I was having an affair with a married woman." Tom shook his head. "It was stupid I know. I'd rather you didn't ask her—"

"Who?"

"She lives in the terrace opposite the green. I'd worked on her kitchen a couple of months before."

Dan knew who she was.

Tom continued: "It started just as a bit of flirtation, I guess. I didn't think anything of it because she's much younger than me. Then her husband went away and she invited me over. I was at her house the day I was supposed to be sick. I saw the car by Mizzen Mast on my way home. It only lasted a couple of months." He was shaking his head again. "Her husband doesn't know. I'd appreciate it if you didn't say anything."

"I won't promise not to. But for the moment I believe you."

"I just wanted to help. I thought the car and the note might be evidence that you were innocent. Of course I know you're innocent."

Dan stared at the older man. "What did you just say?"

"About you being innocent?"

"No. Something about a note."

Tom looked confused. "I found a piece of paper a week or so after you'd been arrested. It had numbers on it and looked like Jade's writing. You know she had terrible handwriting. I'm sure it was hers. Anyway, I gave it to the police."

This was the first Dan had heard about any note.

"OK, you can make amends by calling the police and asking for it back. Since you gave it to them they should return it. Will you do that for me?"

"Of course."

This made Dan think of something else. He pulled out the photograph of Nina Ivanova.

"Do you recognize this girl?"

Tom shook his head and asked how it was relevant.

Dan said, "I want to hear from you that you didn't leave it for me to find."

"I've never seen it before in my life. Honestly, I don't recognize her or know how you got it." He studied Dan's face for a moment then added: "So what are you going to do now?"

He may still have been referring to Ted's lies and the affair but Dan assumed otherwise. He said, "I'm going to ask my dad. Apparently the girl worked at the farm in the nineties. If anyone knows anything it should be him."

THIRTY-FOUR

Searles Farm loomed darkly from the trees, only a slight interior glow hinted of someone's presence.

He was determined to stay calm but Dan could already feel a tightening in his chest as he rang the farm doorbell and let himself in.

He switched on the kitchen light and saw signs of a Sunday lunch. Despite his disability, his father continued to insist on cooking a proper meal on *The Lord's Day*.

Dan called out a greeting and heard his father call back from the lounge. He walked through and the smell of food and soot suffused the usual mustiness.

His father sat hunched in his armchair, beside him a small table with a reading lamp, a book and a bottle of something amber. The room danced with light from the blaze in the inglenook.

Dan reached for the main light switch.

"Leave them off." His father's voice was thick with alcohol and something else that was probably self-pity. Dan noticed the framed photograph on the floor.

His father said, "Good, you've come to talk?"

Dan stepped closer, breathed in and out, felt the tightness ease. His father was just an old, infirm man, full of sadness and regret. In his mind he imagined

Karen telling him this and he tried to focus on it rather than the anger from the years of hurt.

His father swivelled, his face contorted by the flickering shadows. "Pull up a chair and a glass."

Dan picked up a tumbler from the sideboard and held it out as his father poured a good measure of whiskey into it. He sat at an angle across from his father and saw that the photograph was of his mother.

Dan felt his father's eyes on him as he glanced down and back. He placed his glass on a mat, studied it for a while until the old man spoke.

"It would have been very different if she hadn't left me."

"Dying isn't leaving. And don't go saying it was my fault."

"I was too old and too busy to be a proper father."

"The farm always came first," Dan said, and thought he saw a flicker of temper in the old man's eyes, although it could just have been the light from the fire.

His father took a swig of whiskey. "It had to come first, and your mother—God rest her soul—couldn't cope. It was too much, what with a difficult child too. The doctors said there was a chemical imbalance, something in her head, something hereditary." His voice trailed off, melancholy choking his words. "I never really understood."

Dan knew that was as much as his father would ever say about her. He could never say suicide or talk about what she did.

John Searle placed a log on the fire and watched the bark catch and crackle until he seemed to return to the present.

"So you've come to your senses? About the farm?"

"That's not why I'm here. I want to ask about someone who may have worked here. Does the name Nina Ivanova mean anything?"

"No."

"I think she worked here in the late nineties. Jenkin seemed to think so too."

"Jenkin doesn't know anything. That damn fool thinks we should change everything, go to the American method of cattle rearing—the feedlot system. You heard of it? It's all about quick turnaround and high intensity. No more dairy and raising calves. It's about feeding and fattening and turning as much profit as possible. He says it's the future— that we can't go on with such low margins. The land as well—he'd sell off as much as he could, you don't need it with cattle that can't roam."

Dan waited a beat before saying, "You have employee and payroll records. I'd like to find out if she worked here."

"Who?"

"Nina Ivanova."

"That's not what we're talking about, boy. This is important. I need you to take over the farm and do things the way they always have. We could be successful again, focus on quality, you know, organic. There's money in quality food. That's the future for Searles Farm. Let the rest chase cheap meat."

"Dad"—Dan leaned closer and held the old man's stare—"I'd like to see the records."

John Searle's focus went far away. With meticulous care, he refilled his glass and took a deliberately slow drink. "I know the truth, son," he said into his glass.

"What do you mean?"

"I know the truth about you and that young girl, Jade Bridger."

Dan felt his chest tighten and blood suffuse his neck. "What are you talking about?"

The old man looked up, his eyes like they'd seen a thousand years of pain. "I've got the evidence. I bought it..."

"You've got what evidence?" Dan couldn't believe what he was hearing. Had the old man finally gone senile?

"In my safe, I have the evidence of your relationship with the girl."

Dan pushed up from the chair. "You're drunk and talking rubbish."

"I didn't want to have to do this, but you leave me no choice. Take over the farm so I can get rid of Jenkin once and for all."

"What? Are you trying to blackmail me?"

The old man's eyes glistened, wet with emotion. "Look, son, just accept that I know the truth..."

Dan was already striding to the door. He spun at the last moment, acid in his mouth. "You wouldn't know the truth if it slapped you in the face."

He walked down the hall, past the painting of the great-grandfather with his austere, disapproving look. The study was the door on the right before the front entrance. It was a mess of magazines, envelopes and receipts, mostly on a large oak desk. Above it, the shelves were a muddle of knickknacks and books. The combination safe to the right of the door was the size of a washing machine.

Behind him, his father's stick thudded on the wooden boards. John Searle stood in the doorway.

Dan stared at the safe and then his father, challenging him.

"Open it. I want to see this fake proof you've got."

The old man snorted, defiant. He glanced down the hall and back. "It stays there. You manage the farm and it doesn't exist."

"You're an idiot."

"How dare you talk—"

"Where's all the old paperwork—the employee records?" Dan shouted, cutting him off.

When the old man didn't respond, Dan pushed into the hall and jabbed open the opposite door. This used to be the office where Margaret had worked. Now it was a bare room except for a single bed, a side table and a temporary rack of clothes.

Behind him, his father said, "The stuff's in the dining room. I'm sorting things."

Dan strode back down the hall, through the dingy lounge into the dining room that had never been used while Dan lived at the farm. He stopped at the door, the memory of his mother suddenly overwhelming, her body slumped at the dining room table, her hands cold, her eyes unseeing.

Dan had been three when she took the overdose. Although so young, he remembered the image.

His father shuffled behind him.

"You weren't there for her," Dan said. "She was sick and she needed you."

"I had a farm to run." Emotion made his voice quaver, but Dan didn't think it was for the same reason. "And you're not the only one to suffer. Yes you lost your mother, but I lost my wife. I had to deal with everything alone. I had to bring up a kid and run the business. And you were a difficult kid. She couldn't handle you. That's why—"

"Don't you dare!" Dan couldn't look at him, knew his father's eyes would be black and unyielding. He pushed the ghost of his mother back into the dark recess of his mind where she always lurked and scoured the piles of box files that ran round the room.

Everything was labelled, many in Margaret's handwriting, most in chronological order. The 1997–1998 payroll was a grey speckled file. He picked it up, checked inside and then collected the prior year's just in case.

His father stepped back as Dan moved to the doorway.

Dan said, "I'm taking these."

His dad shuffled after him as he strode back towards the kitchen. When John Searle spoke the aggression was gone, replaced again by the pitiful voice. "Don't go. Run the farm for me. I need you."

Dan didn't respond, just stormed through the kitchen and left the door gaping open. From the corner of his eye he saw the old man looking out of the kitchen window, watching as Dan over-revved his car and tore down the drive.

THIRTY-FIVE

Rain fell again, thudding onto his windscreen. The wipers smeared it away like bad memories.

He couldn't recall the drive to the hotel in Truro, just dark trees flashing past and then a blur of lights through the town. As he stopped outside the hotel he felt the tension in his chest evaporate and then he was outside her room, knocking softly.

She opened it in a bathrobe, the light behind her pale. He stood silent, wondering what he would say, how he would say it. For a moment he read nothing in her face and then she smiled and nodded him in.

"Would you put your arms round me?" he said in a quiet voice.

She pulled him in close, his head in the crook of her neck, her arms around his shoulders and head. He smelled jasmine on her skin and five years melted away.

"Karen?"

"Shush," she said.

She moved them to the bed and they sat, his head still bound in tight. She kissed him lightly on his wet cheek, made calming sounds and he let himself become weightless, lost in her comfort. He wasn't aware of when things changed, when his hands started to feel the curve of her. He felt her hand on his back easing the tension and then lower. His hands were under her robe, her body responding to his touch. Her robe fell open and she pulled his head up and kissed him hard, tongue probing. Then the comfort stopped and the passion became everything, all senses burned away but that of each other's body. And then suddenly she pushed away.

"Sorry, we have to stop."

He cupped her face in his hand. "What's up?"

"Daniel, I'm with another man remember. I shouldn't have done that."

He almost commented but saw real distress in her eyes. "I'm sorry."

She turned away for a moment and then back, their faces almost touching. "It's not your fault." Her words were slow and small. "I made a promise—to myself. Because of my dad, what he did. I promised myself I would never sleep... would never be unfaithful."

Dan pulled her in close, his breath mingling with hers.

"Can I just hold you?"

"Yes," she whispered. "Just hold me."

At first her body felt awkward, unyielding but gradually she relaxed and he eased her down under the duvet, holding tight, his body fitting hers. With her head on his chest she eventually fell asleep and stayed there for two hours. Dan watched the digital clock tick to 3am. He'd been staring, he realized, a myriad of thoughts spiralling until they settled on what his father had said. *I've got the evidence. I bought it. I have the evidence of your relationship with the girl. In my safe.*

Whatever his father had in that safe, Dan needed to see it. A fist in his gut said he needed to refute the supposed evidence. Not merely to convince his father, but to show him he was wrong, expose him as a fool.

Dan slid from the bed and dressed. He leaned over Karen and kissed her lightly on the forehead.

206

She stirred. "Honey?"

"Something I need to do," he whispered.

"OK, baby." She was barely awake but turned her face, offered her lips.

He kissed her again.

"I'll see you in the morning," he said.

She mumbled something and he reckoned she was asleep again by the time the bedroom door clicked shut.

The road glistened, slick black with bright orange patches beneath sentinel street lights. Beyond Truro, his full beam fought against the torrent, the only let-up being when he travelled under tunnels formed by overhanging trees.

He was beyond the Passingplace roundabout before he saw something different through the dazzling rain: an eerie glow like the street lights, only pointed up and fading from orange into a crimson bruise.

Flames lit windows and were sucked upwards into the grey above the main section of the farmhouse like a pointed hat. Dan slewed the car at the rear of the building and jumped out, the engine still running. His father's car was still there.

He barely registered that the kitchen door was open. The room was pitch black, the wiring burnt, fuses blown presumably. But the fire hadn't reached this far—the end of the dog-legged building. Smoke caught in his nostrils and, as he approached the next door, he saw it pouring through the cracks.

"Dad! Dad!"

Dan tested the handle for heat and then opened the door. The grey air was so thick that he ducked back gasping. He located the Aga's rail and found a tea towel hanging there. He ran it under a tap, covered his mouth then pushed back into the hallway. At first the sound was a distant growl, but as he edged his way along the corridor the dense air was ochre and the sound became a roar.

"Dad, are you in here?" His voice burned raw and he realized he'd been repeatedly shouting.

Outside the dining room, he stopped. Something flashed yellow up ahead and a crash heralded a wave of black dust that stung his eyes.

He felt the heat now. He crouched low, his breathing laboured, and considered whether he could make it to the lounge. Another boom and a wall of flames told him it was hopeless.

He crawled back to the kitchen and shut the door to buy time. Opening the garden door on the other side, Dan staggered through it spluttering and clearing his throat of dust-choked mucus.

Long shadows stretched over the lawn, and the trees, edged with gold, seemed to dance to the beat of the inferno. Recovering his breath, Dan ran around the side of the house to the first lounge window. It was already blown out, fire licking up the wall above it.

The next window was the same.

As he ran, he moved further away from the house, the heat forcing him back. After the lounge, the dining room was ablaze but the windows were still intact. Beyond, he looked into his father's downstairs bedroom. The bed was engulfed in flame, bedding balled and burning like a bonfire.

"Dad!"

Dan grabbed a branch and smashed the window. Immediately, air sucked in and the room bloomed into a molten ball. Dan staggered on, past the front porch that now burned, the timbers bent with heat. Even one of the lemon trees had smouldering branches. On the drive side, the rooms all burned like the bedroom. Dan peered inside, through smoke and flames, but saw no sign of his father. He looked up, wondering if his father could make it upstairs anymore, but the flames came out through windows that could show no life. And then above the whoosh and roar of the fire he heard the first siren.

Someone must have called the fire service.

The headlights swept along the road he'd just driven. For seconds he stood frozen—until headlights bobbed down the drive. Then instinct took over. Dan edged away, headed to the old cowshed and watched as first one then two more engines positioned themselves. One ploughed onto the lawn at the front. The other two stopped at the side. For a few minutes he watched the men move in unison as though they were dancing with the fire. Then the hoses began to pound the roof with their jets, the building seemingly impervious to the new force.

A police car arrived and, by the time a second one joined it, the flames from the upstairs were clearly losing the battle of the elements.

Had it been sensible to hide from view? Should he have immediately let the authorities know he was here? It had been instinctive, perhaps because of Jade's case and Collick's attitude.

There were four policemen on the scene, all in uniform, so DS Collick was an unlikely witness. But then wasn't it natural to fear the police? If a police car was behind him, he'd immediately wonder if he'd done something wrong, if a light was out or he'd been speeding. Human nature. And now the longer he stood and watched, the bigger the problem became. If he showed himself now, would he look even more suspicious?

Dan followed the line of the sheds until he reached his car. In a moment he was in and driving away from the house, taking the track towards the woods that would eventually lead him around to Lower Field. He could have kept going but there were unanswered questions.

He stopped close to where he'd parked on his first day back and realized that his hands were shaking. Switching on the interior light, he studied his soot-smeared face and red-rimmed eyes. They stared back with incomprehension. Rain had plastered his hair to his head. It had created lines like black warpaint on his skin. Clenching and unclenching his hands, he breathed in and out to calm his thundering heart.

When he felt able, he climbed out of the car and stood in the rain. From this vantage point he could see the top of the house above the ears of corn, but little more. Climbing on the bonnet and then the roof, he sat with legs dangling and watched the firefight as water pounded his body and sloughed off the car.

How much time passed, he was unsure, but the fire seemed out and vehicles were leaving. The rain had abated and he thought a drop in temperature was the cause of his shivers.

In the boot he had an old towel he kept for cleaning the car. Using this, he scrubbed the sooty water from his skin and threw it on the seat inside.

The box files he'd picked up earlier were still on the passenger seat. He wanted to search the farmhouse, but it was too soon. He reached over and picked up the first file—1996. He opened it and flicked through the records and found no mention of Nina Ivanova. The second file had the same documents: end of year PAYE returns and monthly payroll records from the accounting system Margaret used. No one named Ivanova appeared on the computer printouts.

A book showing the manual calculation of weekly pay per person yielded nothing. The other paperwork was a bundle of sheets showing hours worked. Presumably Margaret used this to calculate the figures entered in the book. Dan scanned through the 1997 details and then went back, taking his time. No mention of an Ivanova. He was about to give up when he realized the handwritten records were in pencil, sometimes in different handwriting and occasionally with corrections and rubbing out.

Nina's father had been looking for her in September, although, according to the article, her last known whereabouts had been in May. Dan started with the last week of September and studied the hours-worked sheet, checking the names again and each correction made. He worked his way back, week by week. When he got to the second week of June he stopped. A line had been rubbed out and overwritten. The name on the line was Pete Ashworth. Underneath was not a misspelling, but a different name. Dan checked the other sheets and saw that Pete Ashworth appeared for the first two weeks of April and both times his name covered an erased record. Dan could see a capital *A* and the letters *va* at the end. He held up a sheet to the light, flipped it over so he could see the reverse and there it was: the indentations as clear as they'd first been written.

Nina Ivanova.

The person who had signed off both sheets was Geoff Jenkin.

THIRTY-SIX

Dan stepped out of his car. The track squelched under his shoes and rivulets raced down towards the creek.

Dawn was about an hour away but would be suppressed by lowering clouds and a pall of smoke that hung like a blanket over the field and beyond.

He climbed onto the door sill to see over the sweetcorn. The farm was a black outline against the pewter sky with no lights and no sign of the fire service or police.

Satisfied that they had left, he dropped down and back into the driver's seat. Driving cautiously over the slick mud, he reversed the route he'd taken earlier and stopped at the cowshed, out of sight of the driveway.

Close up he could see definition: the blown-out windows, black holes against the stone. The main roof looked distorted whereas the rear section seemed virtually unscathed.

Entering the kitchen, his feet sloshed through thick water. He switched his mobile to torch mode and saw the liquid was black and dusty like a kid's flour paste mixed with liquorish. Apart from ash and soot, the kitchen itself appeared intact. The door through to the hall was baked with bubbled paint on the far side. He shone the light on floorboards, burnt and buckled, and made his way into the heart of the house. As he walked, the damage intensified as though in waves, like he imagined the rings of Dante's inferno. It culminated in a ruined lounge.

His torch light flickered over degrees of blackness. Beams hung down, partially destroyed. The ceiling was mostly gone and, above where his father used to sit, he could see distorted roof timbers and the sky. A jagged chimney wall explained the pile of rubble where the fireplace had once been.

Most of the floorboards were gone, presumably in the goo around the remnants of the joists. Here and there, bits of furniture remained. He reckoned a grotesque lump had once been the TV. There was also part of a sofa, jutting from the ground, its metal frame a skeleton in the lifeless room.

Walking on the best joists, he moved on and looked into the side rooms, each of them baked black but slick and with holes where window frames had once been. The ceilings hadn't collapsed here, and in the hallway the painting of his great-grandfather, although charred and peeling, was otherwise intact. His glowering visage looked like he'd challenged the fire and remained defiant.

In Dan's father's bedroom, the bedframe remained but nothing else—except a mass of something distorted out of all recognition. Dan swallowed, wondering whether this could be the remains of his father. With a knot in his stomach he approached, flicking the light over and round. He breathed again when he was satisfied that it was something embedded in plastic. Maybe once material on a dresser.

Ash and broken plaster filled the study. The desk had been partially burnt but remained in place. The safe, however, looked unscathed.

Crouching, he tested the combination dial and it moved easily. He rotated it clockwise to his mother's birthday and imagined the discs click into place. Then to the left he dialled her month. To the right he dialled the first part of the year and finally the second, anticlockwise. Now he did hear a click. He held the handle for two heartbeats before swinging the door open. The safe was empty.

Dan rocked back. His father kept all the important documents here. He always did. No reason to change. And he'd said the *evidence* was in the safe. What did he have and where the hell was it?

A creak of wood in the hall made him swivel. "Dad, is that you?" His voice boomed loud in the stillness.

He stepped into the hall and glanced towards the front door in case someone was coming in. He heard a noise again, this time from the direction of the lounge.

"Who's there?"

Dan ran through to the destroyed room, his feet slipping on wet boards. And then, stepping onto the joists of the lounge he heard someone moving quickly in the hall beyond. He followed as swiftly as he dared, shining the torch down and then ahead with each step. The kitchen door that led to the garden had been closed.

Now it was open.

Blood coursing through his veins, his breathing shallow, Dan stepped through into the porch between the kitchen and garden. The coal bunker for the Aga was here. He flicked the torch around and stepped onto the outer flagstones.

The torch light was lost against the dark garden. He scanned the side of the house and waited but saw no movement. An owl hooted as if defying that anything had changed tonight. Turning back, he stepped through the porch and stood in the kitchen doorway. The noise of a door creaking made him spin, light sweeping.

The old coal cupboard door was ajar.

Movement in the kitchen made him spin again, just in time to see someone looming over him—someone, something, swinging towards him.

And then a flash of pain tore across his temple before all fell dark.

THIRTY-SEVEN

Dan was aware of children's voices chanting.

"One, two,
He's coming for you.
Three, four,
He's under the floor.
Five, six,
Grab a crucifix.
Seven, eight,
Now it's too late.
Nine, ten,
Never sleep again."

Although soft and far off, he knew they were taunting him. There were two of them standing a few yards away but he couldn't make out their faces. The more he tried to focus, the more blurred their faces became.

Dan said, "Who are you?"

The children just continued their eerie chanting:

"In the woods,
You better be good.
Under the stair,
He wants you there.
In your head,
He wants you dead."

"What do you know?" Dan shouted. "Who started the fire?"

He tried to look around but realized everything was blurred shades of grey. He blinked rapidly, hoping to clear his vision and remember.

He'd been struck. Someone had been waiting for him, probably hiding in the coal cupboard.

Was he now lying outside the farmhouse? Was the attacker still there? Again Dan tried to look around but even the children had faded into the dark mist. They continued to chant but it was getting further away.

Maybe he shouldn't make a noise in case the attacker was nearby. Maybe the children thought it was the Buccaboo.

There was something so familiar about them. Who were they? He seemed to know and yet couldn't find their names or faces.

The safe had been empty. In Dan's experience the safe was never empty. Which raised two possibilities: either his father had emptied it and escaped the fire, or someone had stolen the contents. If it was someone else then it was surely the attacker. Had that person also started the fire? And if that was the scenario then didn't it imply that his father was dead?

Blinded though he was, Dan knew he wasn't going to find any answers lying on the floor. He tried to move. At first his body wouldn't respond and then it was like he was under water, his limbs only half connected to his brain.

He became aware of something cushioning his head. He twisted and the sharp smell of rotted wood, mildew and dirty clothes snapped him to his senses.

His head was on an old army blanket. Another covered his body. He shook it off and sat up. Fingers of pale light filtered through a single boarded window. The floorboards were warped and rotted with age and he could see woodlice in the dirt between them. The room, the size of a small bedroom, was bare except for the blankets. He listened and heard nothing but his own ragged breathing. He guessed then that the children's voices had been imagined. Dreamt or perhaps remembered. Then he thought of his phone, checked his pockets and guessed he'd dropped it when he'd been hit.

If he was being held captive, why wasn't he tied up? Presumably the room had been secured, although the panelling on the window looked flimsy.

Before checking the wood on the window, he clasped the tarnished brass doorknob. He turned the cold metal and the door moved. Easing it a fraction, he looked through the crack. Beyond he saw a hallway, floral paper peeling from the walls. He slowly opened the door wider, stepped out, and lightly moved along the hall.

The next room was larger than the first. He guessed it had once been a dining room but now the only furniture was a simple trellis table against one wall. On it lay a battered brown suitcase. Bits of a wooden chair littered the floor by a boarded-up window. Papers, photographs and other objects were scattered about on the table and floor. There were odd items such as a recorder, a broken action man, a woolly hat, a beret, a single framed photograph.

Dan's hands shook as he picked it up. The picture was of a boy in a green school uniform. It was Dan. He'd been six when that photo had been taken. He wasn't looking into the camera, but past it, an inquisitive expression on his innocent face. He recalled sitting on the stool with a metal screw stem and the bright sunlight coming through the school doors behind the photographer. He'd seen a face at the window and pointed, but the man was gone when the photographer turned to look. Had the man taken this before Dan had spotted him?

He put the picture down. There were many other photographs, maybe a hundred. All of the others were similar to the Polaroid of Nina Ivanova, yellowed with age. He picked up a handful and flicked through them; he recognized a lot of people, mostly from the farm and many from the village.

He turned each one over to check for writing or marks of any kind, but there were none. And then he found one of Jade. On the back was a mark: two circles. He found a second one of Jade, again on a different day, but this too had the two circles.

There were newspaper clippings about the farm. The oldest dated back thirty years, crinkled and stiff with dirt and age. Amid the papers he found a metal ring: his mother's broach. The one taken from his key ring on his first day back. Pocketing it, his attention was then drawn to newspaper clippings cleaner than the rest. He sorted them and noted the recency of their dates—all within the past year. And the stories were either about himself or Jade Bridger. Again, all the pictures of Jade had the two circles. There was no mark against pictures of Dan.

What was it that made Jade different? Was she connected to Nina in some way?

Dan put his hands on his head but immediately stopped himself touching a painful lump on his temple. He squatted and pinched the bridge of his nose. He felt so close and yet the pieces wouldn't fit together.

A human groan disturbed his thoughts and he scrambled to the window. Nailed-on plywood covered broken glass and he peered through the gaps. Outside he could see nothing but trees and undergrowth and the darkness between them.

The groan again. This time sounding frustrated and perhaps desperate.

Dan picked up a loose chair leg as a weapon and, moving as quickly as he dared, stepped back into the hall. A few paces later he stood in a lounge. Here the windows were mostly undamaged and one by a front door wasn't even boarded up. The room had a single armchair and three packing cases. Keeping to the best floorboards and hugging the wall, Dan crept to the window. He could see now that he was in the heart of a forest, green and dark with shafts of light. In a clearing he saw the back of a man crouched on the ground.

The figure rocked back and forwards and then groaned. He dug his hands into the earth, raised them above his head and let it fall. Then the rocking stopped and, in a smooth inhuman movement, the man was on his feet. He picked up a spade and swivelled. Dan ducked to the side of the window, his childhood fears crushing his chest. Mad Mike was going to kill him.

Through a gap between the frame and wall Dan saw now that the crazy man was not merely in the dark, but blackened with charcoal and earth. His face seemed distorted, more terrible than Dan's worst nightmares of the man.

Dan's grip on the chair leg tightened. Could he fend off a man armed with a shovel? But instead of advancing on the house, the man drove the spade into the ground and at the same instant let out a banshee howl. He did this twice more and then dropped to his knees and dug with his hands.

In that moment Dan knew that Mad Mike was digging him a grave.

Dan tore his eyes away and forced himself to retreat to the room with the suitcase. Using the chair leg, he prised pieces of the window frame away and then pushed against the loosest-looking plank. The end came free and it pivoted on the other. Now that he could get his hands out, he gripped the next and tugged it free. Within minutes the gap was big enough to climb through.

He glanced both ways to check for the man before pulling up and cocking a leg through the hole. Ignoring the pain from glass that bit into his hands, he dropped over and squatted on damp grass. He held his ragged breath and listened.

Hearing nothing, he hugged the brick building and followed a line away from the front. He didn't know which way was out but knew he had to run in the opposite direction to where he'd seen Mad Mike. He passed the bedroom and turned the corner to the rear and stopped, frozen with fear.

Mad Mike glared, his face half-melted like a Halloween mask.

Survival instinct moved Dan's legs. He was running. He couldn't remember starting or in which direction. He just ran.

Branches whipped his face and arms. Undergrowth snatched at his feet. He stumbled and slid but kept going. And then he saw the crows, their black wings stretched out, and childhood terror made him veer away.

He switched back, left right and left again, avoiding more and more dead crows.

And when a wire finally caught him across the chest, he already knew it was over. He wouldn't get away.

THIRTY-EIGHT

Dan was pulled to his feet. The man held his shoulders and looked at him with wide, red-rimmed eyes, like a bullock's in a slaughterhouse. His hair was singed to the scalp in places, part raw, part black. The man's hands were bound in cloth and Dan realized the grip caused him pain.

As Dan thought about twisting and running, the hands dropped. Mad Mike nudged his elbow and took two awkward steps towards the house. He then stopped and looked back. With a nod in the direction of the house, he took another step and beckoned.

"I must be crazy," Dan said under his breath as he started towards the house.

The tramp led the way, his left leg dragging, taking half a pace each time.

Dan said, "My name is Dan."

The grubby old man froze a second, seemed to nod and turned. He indicated his chest and grunted something.

"Michael? Did you say Michael?"

The distorted face showed a flicker of acknowledgement. So, Dan realized, the name Mad Mike was right.

Rather than go into the house, Michael rounded the side and led him to where he'd been digging. Beside the shallow hole was a wheelbarrow piled high with tools.

Dan recognized them.

"Hey, these are from my boatyard!"

Michael ignored him, sank to his knees and wailed.

Dan squatted in front of the distraught man and watched him for a while. "What is it? Can I get you help?"

Michael looked up and, after a moment, raised his hands as if beseeching. He then showed the palms covered in the dirty cloth.

"Your hands hurt too much?"

Michael barely nodded.

Dan went on hesitantly: "You're trying to dig this hole, but your hands hurt too much." He pointed at the ground. "Is it a grave? What are you burying?"

Michael grunted something that Dan couldn't understand.

Frustrated, Michael finally pointed into the woods and Dan saw a bundle of something that at first he thought to be the man's dead dog, and then the realization gripped his chest.

"Is that… Is that my dad?"

Michael mumbled something that became a keening, and scared birds took flight above their heads.

Dan sat with his face in his hands, eyes closed, breathing earthy air through his tight palms. He was unsure how long he stayed like that but, when he took his hands away, he saw that Michael had pulled the body to the edge of the grave.

Dan held the tramp's slaughterhouse eyes and then finally nodded. It seemed bizarre but, however crazy Michael was, he was doing this because he cared and

223

was distraught. Dan swallowed. He could do this for now—for Michael.

He stood and, taking the spade in both hands, drove it into the ground with all his might. Again and again, he pounded the earth, his own tears blurring his vision and stinging his cheeks.

In places the ground was soft, and he soon had to step into the trench to keep digging. He paused for breath and realized his hands had blistered with the effort. And then he began again, using the exertion to dull his mind.

He stopped again, exhausted, and saw the old tramp looking at him with what he guessed to be gratitude, a half-smile formed on damaged features.

Dan took a rest and said, "You tried to save him, didn't you?"

Michael grunted, *yes*.

Dan studied the old man. "Can't you talk?"

Michael's lips moved and Dan squinted, trying to read them, but the noises and movement made no sense.

He smiled and nodded as though he'd understood.

When he'd dug about three feet down, Michael got up with exaggerated slowness. Dan stopped and watched the other's eyes and read that it was time to put the body in the ground.

In the last few minutes Dan had been thinking clearly again. He knew that his father couldn't stay buried here, maybe even that a coroner would need the body for evidence of foul play, and yet logic didn't matter. He was in a microcosm; a world that existed only in this wood; a thousand trees, a house and a man who couldn't speak; a man who had risked his own life to pull his father's body from a fire.

Dan couldn't look as he picked up one end of the tarp that covered his dad. Michael gripped the other as best he could. They dragged the body to the edge of the hole and then let it tumble in.

Using his forearms to scoop the earth, Michael began to fill the grave in. Dan drew a long deep breath and took up the shovel.

A shower beat a rhythm across the canopy above them and the smell of the earth rose up. As Dan had piled the last of the soil in a mound over the grave, he realized Michael was reading from the Bible. The words didn't make sense but Dan felt the sentiment. He studied the crazy old man as he mumbled, head bowed, reminding Dan of someone at the Cenotaph on Remembrance Day.

When Michael finished, both men stood, the silence a palpable bond between them. And in that moment, Dan saw the truth of it. This tramp loved his father and cared about the farm, probably out of some time-hewn gratitude for being allowed to live in the woods. But it went much deeper than that; he was a watcher, a witness. He took the photographs. He had left the photograph of Nina Ivanova on Dan's steps.

He knew something and had been trying to tell Dan.

"Nina Ivanova," Dan said.

Michael looked at him with blank uncomprehending eyes.

"The photograph. You left me the photograph…" He squared his forefingers and thumbs to show the size. "There was a mark—two lines and a circle—on the back."

Michael's brow creased, eyes rolled up. And then he nodded as though the memory came, pieces slotting together to make sense. His eyes went bright and he grunted, *yes.*

Animated now, he pointed to the house and beckoned.

Michael staggered to the building, drunk with exhaustion. Inside, he scrabbled on the floor, picking up Polaroids and studying each one before tossing it down. Then he found one of Nina and handed it to Dan.

"She's called Nina Ivanova. She worked at the farm about fifteen years ago."

Michael didn't respond or acknowledge the information. Instead he looked over the array of photographs.

"Are you looking for a picture of Jade?" Dan found a newspaper cutting with Jade's photo. He showed Michael and asked, "Is there a connection between Nina and Jade Bridger?"

Michael cocked his head like a spaniel waiting for instructions.

Dan tried Jade's name again, but there was no recognition in the old man's eyes. What was he missing? Maybe Michael didn't know Jade's name.

"This girl—what happened to her? Where did she go? Was she murdered?"

Michael's eyes flared wide, his breathing exaggerated.

Oh my God, Dan thought, she was murdered. He said, "Where? Where is she?"

A low animal sound came from Michael's throat, like a suppressed wail. He looked beseechingly at Dan and then turned his head as if shaking his brain to dislodge the memory, despair written large across his face.

"It's OK. It's OK, Michael. Can you tell me who did it? Who murdered the girl?"

Michael stopped thrashing and, with desperate hands, filtered through the papers until he had what he was looking for: a newspaper cutting with the photograph of a man.

He held it up like a trophy for Dan to accept. The paper was old and tatty, but the photograph was clear enough: a photograph of a man with his cows. And that man was Geoff Jenkin.

THIRTY-NINE

Dan ran. He had grabbed a log-splitter from Michael's wheelbarrow and used it to clear a way through the undergrowth.

He had no doubt that the crazy old vagrant was dying of his burns. Michael had found strength in his need to try and save and then bury Dan's father but now he was spent. When Dan left, Michael had pointed out the direction of the farm before collapsing into the armchair, his glazed eyes fixed on the small painting of the bird.

Dan had promised to go after Jenkin and this seemed to satisfy Michael, but Dan had every intention of getting him help too. As soon as he could, he would call for an ambulance. The cuts on the trees would mark the way for them to find the house.

When he emerged from the woods, he'd expected to come out near Jenkin's property. Instead he was nearer the main farmhouse. The police were there, a couple of cars in the drive. He scraped a crude arrow on the track and then ran hard.

When he saw the first uniformed cop in the yard, he started to shout and wave.

"Here! I need help! Call an ambulance. He's in the woods." His voice was ragged even to his own ears so he wasn't surprised that the policeman didn't immediately react.

A second cop joined the first. This man started to shout, his tone angry.

"Listen!" Dan called. "He's in the woods. We need to get an ambulance."

He was close now, the gravel of the drive scuffing under his shoes.

They weren't listening. The second policeman raised something in his hand, like a gun.

"Would you just call a bloody ambulance?" Dan screamed at them. And then the policeman's words came through the red mist in his mind.

"Sir, drop the weapon."

It didn't make sense. Dan stepped closer, trying to explain. He realized too late that he had the log-splitter in his hand and he'd been gesturing with it.

"Taser, taser," the second policeman shouted.

Before Dan fully grasped what was happening, fine wires spun from the gun and something instantly grabbed Dan's chest. Then searing pain shot through his bones. His body felt like it was trying to tear itself apart and turn inside out.

Gravel bit into his face as he sprawled on the ground. Rough hands pulled at his arms, a knee in his back. He felt his wrists bound and then he was pulled to his feet. He tried to speak but his breath was gone.

Offering no resistance, he was escorted to the nearest car and forced into the rear. Dan closed his eyes and felt exhaustion hit him like a tsunami.

As the car drove along the lanes and then the main road to Truro, he saw it in his mind. He had a sour taste in his mouth and kept his eyes closed, afraid of the nausea that could consume him.

He must have spoken his thoughts because a window was cracked and he felt cool air on his face and began to breathe again.

The room in Truro police station smelled of disinfectant with a faint suggestion of vomit and sweat. The cuffs were tight on Dan's wrists. He wanted to stand under a scalding shower and scrub the grime from his face and hands and wake himself up.

Opposite, DS Collick sat with another detective. He had been introduced as Detective Constable Bateman. Dan took an immediate dislike to the constable, who had small, bulbous dark eyes that stared with the intensity of a praying mantis. Dan renamed him Bug-eyes.

Dan said, "Stop wasting time and get an ambulance to the farm to help the old guy there. He's—"

"In good time," Collick said.

Dan clenched and unclenched his hands. "For God's sake, Collick."

"Answer our questions first."

Dan leaned forward. "Are you arresting me?"

"What for?"

"I don't know. I'm sure you can trump something up."

Collick shook his head, real disappointment written in his eyes. "Look, we could charge you with threatening an officer with a dangerous weapon—"

"It was a log-splitter, for Christ's sake. I used it to—"

Collick raised his hand and spoke over him. "It had a ten-inch blade... Jesus!" He took a deep breath as though composing himself and placed his hands together on the table, prayer-like. "Listen, Dan. It doesn't need to be like this. We just want to talk. We want to understand what happened last night."

"What happened? You bloody well know what happened! My father's house burned down and he's dead."

Bug-eyes stiffened. "Mr Searle is dead?"

Dan saw some unfathomable thought distort Collick's face until it ended in a half-suppressed smile.

Dan sat back again and closed his eyes.

Bug-eyes said, "It doesn't look good for you, Dan. We found your phone at the crime scene."

"OK, I'll do you a deal," Dan said. "You get an ambulance out to the farm. There's a house in the woods. You'll find it if you follow the marks I left with the splitter. That's why I had it. I wasn't threatening... Anyway, you'll find a severely injured old man in the house. He's badly burnt. You'll also find my father's body there..."

Bug-eyes started to speak but Collick stopped him. "Go on."

"I know it sounds crazy, but get a crew out there and I'll explain everything. Firstly though, I need painkillers—my ribs are killing me. And secondly, I want my phone back."

Bug-eyes whispered in Collick's ear and the two exchanged a glance before Collick said "OK", stood and left the room.

While he was gone, Bug-eyes watched Dan intently. "This story had better be good," he said. "And if you've got an alibi, it's gonna have to be tighter than a gnat's arse. Why are you smirking?"

Dan said, "Was I? Maybe it's because gnats are bugs."

Bug-eyes narrowed his small black eyes, but somehow they still bulged.

Collick came back into the room, disapproval on his face that Dan guessed was aimed at his colleague. Of course, there would be a microphone in the room. Collick placed two tablets and a plastic cup of water on the table.

Dan knocked back the painkillers and said, "I should have a lawyer present."

Collick shrugged and raised an eyebrow. "I could cancel the ambulance."

"You're not going to do that, because I've said my father's body is out there."

Collick ran his fingers slowly over the hair on his lip, waited a beat, then said, "You got me, but let's just talk. Remember, I could charge you with attempted assault on a police officer."

"Since we're just talking then uncuff me... and I'll have a cup of coffee. White, no sugar."

Collick inclined his head in response, and Bug-eyes got up, went behind Dan and removed the cuffs.

Dan flexed his hands and rubbed his wrists. His fingers were thick and ingrained with dirt and his nails were black and split. The door opened and a young uniformed policewoman came in carrying a plastic cup of coffee and Dan's phone.

Collick said, "You can have the phone on the condition you don't use it until you're outside the station. Agreed?"

Dan agreed. The phone was scuffed and dirty but still working. The coffee was weak and generic with powdered milk substitute, but he showed gratitude with a nod and the flicker of a smile.

After two sips he told his story, both Collick and Bug-eyes scribbling longhand notes. He finished his coffee as he spoke and started with his arrival at the farm and finished with being tasered.

For a while only the sound of pencil on paper filled the room. Then Collick put down his pencil with deliberation, took a long breath and looked like he was making a decision.

"So, the fire was already underway when you arrived?" He waited for Dan's agreement before continuing: "What about the argument you had with your father earlier that day?"

"Who said we argued?"

Collick didn't answer.

"Yes, I went to see him earlier and it didn't end well. That's why I went back."

"At three in the morning?"

"I couldn't sleep."

"You were seen at the house before this—and arguing with your father..."

"It's Jenkin, isn't it? He's stitching me up, don't you see?" It struck Dan then that Jenkin was probably one of the people who might either know the safe's combination or be able to guess it. "Jesus, I bet he started the bloody fire!"

"Mr Jenkin saw the fire and called it in."

Dan felt his throat flush, his pulse quicken. "You need to arrest that guy. He had motive. There was something between him and my dad. My dad was unhappy. I think Jenkin was threating to take over the farm. And Jenkin is linked to Jade's—"

"Dan!" Collick barked his name, shocking him into silence. "Let's deal with one thing at a time. Do you have an alibi for the night—as you say—for you leaving home to go to the farm at 3am?"

"I wasn't at home." Dan halted himself. He'd already thought about it and decided he couldn't drag Karen into it. She was racked with guilt for almost sleeping with him. It would be unfair to her to make it public, to cause her problems with her boyfriend Matt. His mouth pulled a line like it was stopping him from speaking.

"You need to explain."

Dan said, "I can't say who I was with."

Bug-eyes tutted.

"It's complicated."

Collick said, "It always is with you."

"I can't."

"OK, Dan, so let's move on. Why did you really go back to the farm?"

"I'd rather not say."

Bug-eyes said, "You're not helping yourself here."

"It's not relevant and, since we're just talking, I'm the one who decides what I say and what is private."

Collick said nothing for a while, tapping his pencil on the pad. "So the fire was too intense for you to get past the kitchen?"

"I got into the hall beyond but could see I was too late—if my dad was still inside. The kitchen door was open so I guess I half hoped he'd got out."

"And now you think it was open because this Mad Mike went in and got him?"

"Yes. He's badly burnt."

Bug-eyes asked, "Do you think he started the fire?"

"No. I've already said. I think Jenkin started the fire. Why aren't you listening to me?"

"So why not Mad Mike?"

"I honestly believe the guy tried to rescue my dad." Dan switched from Bug-eyes to Collick. "Look, He was distraught and needed my help to bury him."

Collick said, "But you've got to admit, this whole burial thing sounds bizarre. Why would you go along with it? After all it was your dad he was burying and he may have been trying to hide the evidence—if he'd killed him. And from what you've told us, you can't possibly know what he was guilty of."

Dan shrugged. "I'm not a hundred per cent sure. Call it instinct. He was genuinely distraught at my dad's death. I guess the guy's emotion got to me. At least we know where the body is."

"His emotion, not your own?"

"Yes, mine too."

"And yet it's well known that there was no love lost between you and your father."

"All kids argue with their parents, it doesn't mean they want them dead. Yes, the old man could be a cold, selfish bastard, but he's all I have."

"He didn't visit you in prison. He didn't support you. He didn't believe you were innocent."

Collick stopped and watched Dan's eyes closely. It was like he expected Dan to expound more on his feelings, but nothing came.

"OK then," Collick said, "tell me why you didn't let the first responders know you were there and why did you go and hide in—what did you call it—the Lower Field?"

Dan ran his hands through his hair and combed out some debris. "I need a shower," he said. "I'd like to freshen up and then talk about Geoff Jenkin."

"One more question first. When you went back to the house, what did you do?"

"I told you. I looked around, I guess to see if Dad's body was there. And then I heard a noise—the crazy tramp."

"But you missed out the detail, Dan. The bit about you going into the study…"

They looked at each other, two poker players about to raise the stakes. And then Dan saw the trap in Collick's eyes. The detective knew.

"I opened the safe, but it was empty."

Bug-eyes wrote this down, but neither detective spoke.

Dan said, "Either it was already empty or someone got to it before me."

Bug-eyes scoffed, "Not very safe then if other people knew the combination."

Dan shrugged. They must have searched his car, knew he had nothing but the employee records. "If I took the contents of my father's safe, then where are they?"

"You tell us." Bug-eyes voice took on the tone of a taunting schoolchild and was becoming annoying. The man said something else but Dan tuned him out, kept holding Collick's gaze.

"The boxes in my car—the employee records. I took those from the house earlier." Dan forced his voice to express gravitas and realized he sounded like his father. "They're relevant. I'll tell you about the employee records but first I need a comfort break and I'd like to clean up now."

Bug-eyes took him to a toilet and waited outside. There was no shower but Dan ran the water hot and scrubbed at his skin with a tablet of white soap that had the softness of a house brick. Using paper towels he blotted the water off and stood at the mirror. A stranger with an ashen face looked back at him with yellowed eyes.

A knock on the door snapped him away from the apparition in the mirror. "Just one more minute," he called back to the impatient detective. Taking out his phone he dialled Lizzy Bridger.

Eight rings and then her voice: "What do you want?"

Dan whispered, "I can't talk long, but I've found something." Bug-eyes banged on the door and shouted.

Dan pressed himself against the door, felt the detective try the handle and push.

"Lizzy, listen. Geoff Jenkin's involved. I've got the evidence. I'm at the police station…"

"What the…?"

Dan didn't catch the rest. The door was punched open and he dropped the phone. A uniformed cop grabbed him, pulled both arms behind his back, lifted him onto his toes and then propelled him into the corridor where Bug-eyes glowered.

"Into holding three," the detective said.

The policemen started walking him down the corridor. Bug-eyes didn't move.

"You charging me? Look, we need to get Geoff Jenkin," Dan called back over his shoulder. "Not only did he start the fire and murder my dad but I think it's all about Jade Bridger. I think Jenkin killed Jade."

"Shut it, Searle," the detective said.

"For God's sake! Tell Collick. Jenkin killed Jade Bridger!"

Bug-eyes shook his head. "You've lost the plot, Searle. Enjoy our famous hospitality for a while and use the time to think about whether there's anything else you want to tell us. And in the meantime"—he paused like he thought he had comedic timing—"we'll see what we unearth in the woods."

FORTY

The room smelled stale. There was a blanket on a metal bench bolted to the concrete.

They'd taken Dan's belt and shoelaces as if he were a suicide risk. The bulb in the ceiling had a wire cage around it and even standing on the bench it'd be out of reach.

The metal was icy so he spread the blanket and lay on the bench, staring at the ceiling.

Jenkin called the fire service. Because of the timing, he must have called before Dan arrived, maybe earlier than three o'clock.

Karen had been his character witness and had personally vouched for him before. She'd defended him against Deborah's stupid violence claim—said he'd never been violent in the ten years she'd known him. But she hadn't been with Matt then.

Dan tried to dispel negative thoughts and focus on the possibility of Karen coming back. Would she? Would she leave her city slicker and come back to him? If she did have to split with Matt, he knew it had to be on her terms and not the result of an affair gone public. If she acted as his witness again, the press would be all over it. But then the press would be all over it anyway. Would she lose her job? He had no idea how these things worked. Could a company—would a company like BebelStreet Capital, where she worked—dismiss people for such things, for being involved with him, for bringing the firm into disrepute, however false the accusations?

Dan forced himself to think about happy times with Karen, and there had been many, but gradually the other thoughts came back and he realized it was no use avoiding them.

If he understood what Michael was trying to say, then Jenkin had been involved in Nina Ivanova's disappearance. Maybe her murder. Had Dan's father known? And if Jenkin had started the fire, was it to silence the old man over that? Did he think Dan was close to discovering the truth? Did the truth involve Jade Bridger?

He tried to make sense of it in the fine cracks that ran across the ceiling. *Let's go back.* Jenkin had taken over as manager a few years before Nina's disappearance. He didn't know why the old manager was replaced, but Jenkin seemed in charge, seemed comfortable with his father. Until recently. What had changed his father's mind about the man?

Dan closed his eyes and fought tiredness that made him sick and lightheaded. He'd had maybe two hours sleep and he guessed it was now early afternoon. Think, he repeatedly told himself. Lizzy must have worked for Jenkin. Did that mean Jenkin knew Jade? Did he kill Jade too? Dan had wanted to ask Lizzy about Jenkin and now regretted the call, wished he'd planned it.

Did it make sense that Jenkin would try and kill his father? If the two men had fallen out, then surely Jenkin wouldn't expect the old man to leave him the farm. What would be his motive then? Dan opened his eyes, felt excitement tear into his chest.

Jenkin's motive was to implicate him. Jenkin would have called the fire service. He would have told Collick about the argument, whether he heard it or guessed. And in that moment, Dan knew that Jenkin had been the one to get to the safe before him. Could Jenkin have guessed the combination? Probably. Maybe taking the contents of the safe wasn't about the evidence against Dan. Could it be about evidence against Jenkin?

Dan couldn't hang around here. He jumped to his feet, called and banged on the door. The peephole was slid open and a face he hadn't seen before peered through.

"What's the problem?" The tone wasn't aggressive, just matter of fact.

Dan said, "It's important I speak to Detective Sergeant Collick. I need to get out."

The peephole slid closed and Dan wondered whether he was being ignored, but moments later it opened again. Same guy.

"DS Collick is unavailable. He's at your father's farm following up on the information about the house in the woods. I'm afraid you'll have to wait."

"But I'm not being..."

The peephole closed and Dan lashed out at the door in frustration. After five minutes of no response he settled back on the bench and closed his eyes.

He must have fallen asleep because the sound of the door opening made him jump. He swung his legs round and rubbed grogginess from his eyes.

The cop who had opened the door stepped back.

Dan stood. "What's going on?"

Bug-eyes stepped into the doorway, hands on hips. "Seems like you're free to go."

"What do you mean, *seems like*?"

"Don't be a smartarse, Mr Searle. Just sign for your things at the desk and you may leave. If there's any following up to do, you can be sure we'll be in touch."

And it was over as quickly as that. Shoelaces in, belt on, he looked at his phone and saw he'd missed six calls: two from Margaret, one from Wilson—the solicitor— and three from Karen.

In the morning, Karen had tried to call Daniel to explain that it had been a mistake and that she needed to speak to Matt. She was already on London's South Circular when Margaret called her in tears.

"There's been a fire and John Searle is dead."

"Oh my God, Margaret, that's terrible."

"And they've arrested our Dan."

"Why?"

Margaret seemed to have difficulty answering. Then she swallowed and said, "They think Dan might have had something to do with it. Of course he wouldn't... there's no way he would try and kill John. No matter how angry he was. I can't believe they can possibly think that."

"When did it happen... the fire... when do they think it started?"

"About three this morning."

"Then he can't have done it. Margaret, call his solicitor and let him know that Daniel was with me until the early hours. If the fire was called in around three o'clock, then I'm Daniel's alibi. There's no way he could have gotten to the farm in time to start the fire."

Margaret choked on her relief.

Karen said, "I'll come back."

Margaret wanted to understand the situation and when Karen explained, she said, "It's all right, let us deal with things here and I'll keep you updated."

"OK. If there's anything I can do…" Karen wasn't sure what else to say and after a pause ended the call with: "I'll be back as soon as I can."

Karen stared at the long line of traffic. Events were taking over their lives, like the cars being drawn inexorably towards London. Only, her head and her heart were still in Cornwall.

FORTY-ONE

The station was quiet as he heard his name called.

"Dan."

He looked up from the phone and saw Tom sitting in the waiting room. The older man rubbed his knees and stood, tears in his eyes. "I'm so sorry about your loss, Dan."

"How did you...?"

"We heard about the fire, of course, but Karen's been trying to find you. And then Margaret—anyway, she sent me to get you. I've been here almost two hours. Apparently Karen would've been here but she's had to go back to London. We wanted to check you're all right, guessed you didn't have your car."

Dan patted his friend on the back and said, "Would you drop me at the farm, please?"

They walked to Tom's van and, once in, the old guy talked the whole way, but his words barely registered. The police wouldn't take action against Jenkin—not without evidence—but Dan knew he was involved. Dan had to confront him. As they approached the farm entrance, that would take him to Jenkin's house, he asked to be let out.

Tom said, "So you aren't interested in the note?"

"What note?"

"I thought you weren't listening." Tom shook his head. "I said that the police had given me back the note I'd found." He pulled out a piece of paper and handed it to Dan.

It had been torn from a spiral notebook. It was tatty and grubby and covered in numbers that could have been Jade's scruffy handwriting.

Dan shrugged. "It could be anything. Maybe some note of time trials. Anyway, whatever it was, I don't think it's important." He tucked it into his pocket. "I'm pretty sure someone's going to tell me what happened."

"Dan, don't—"

Dan got out of the car. "I'll be fine. Tell Auntie Margaret I'll be home soon."

He watched Tom drive away before walking down the drive.

He heard Jenkin's Land Rover before he saw it as the car reversed onto the track. Dan ducked behind a tree and was surprised by two things: firstly, he expected it to come towards him but it didn't. The second surprise was he saw Lizzy Bridger hunched in the passenger seat. He felt an idiot. He'd called Lizzy and warned her about Jenkin, she'd confronted him and now... what? Uncertain, he stood for a moment and watched as it bounced away. And then it came to him. Jenkin was driving her to Bucker Mine to intimidate her, maybe to threaten her, maybe worse.

Dan started to run down the track and realized it'd take him half an hour to catch up to them. At the side of the house a bicycle leaned against a wall. Though rusty and with a slightly buckled rear wheel, the tyres were inflated. He tested it and was happy it would suffice. Then, instead of chasing the Land Rover, he took off towards the main road, heading for the side gate into

Bucker Field, the entrance used by the harvester three days ago.

Ten minutes earlier, Lizzy had arrived at Jenkin's house. She'd walked all the way from Trevelyon and carried a holdall, her hands raw from the straps.

At the door, she dropped the bag, pulled out her husband's shotgun and clicked off the safety. She knocked.

Jenkin's face flashed mild surprise and then shock as he noticed the gun levelled at his midriff. "Lizzy…" His voice was controlled and smooth. "Now let's take it easy. I don't know what you're thinking or what you've been told, but whatever it is you're mistaken. Believe me."

"I've had enough." Her voice quavered with the emotion she'd been suppressing.

"Look, let's talk. What—"

"Talk?" She snapped, cutting him off. "It's almost twenty years too late. All those bloody years of worrying."

"You've been drinking. I don't think—"

"Enough of the thinking. It's time for you to confess, because if you don't then I will." She advanced a pace into the house and he took a step back.

"And what will it achieve, apart from easing your troubled mind?"

"Don't patronize me, Geoff. It's time to confess, because that Searle boy has probably worked it out and, if he hasn't, then you burning his father's house down will certainly give him the message."

"Woah! I didn't start that fire."

"Tell that to someone who'll believe you. I know you're a liar, so don't go coming the Mr Innocent with me."

Jenkin held up his hands in his half-surrendering gesture. "Let's not forget you're as much to blame as me. It's been in your interests to keep quiet. I've not forced you."

Lizzy shook her head in disbelief. "In that case, hand over the photographs."

"I'm not going to do that, Lizzy. They implicate me as much as you. You want to do something stupid, then fine, be my guest, but I'm not giving you the ammo to take me down with you.

"OK, enough bullshit. Let's go."

"Go where?"

She walked around him, barrels unwaveringly aimed at his middle, then walked him out towards his car. "Get in and drive."

"Where we going?"

"You know where. We're going to the mine."

FORTY-TWO

Michael sensed them early. After the boy had run off, he made it to the grave and just sat. When he breathed in, it was like sucking air through a straw and his lungs rasped like sandpaper and burned like hell.

Two people, he thought, coming from the direction of the farm. They were either clumsy or making no effort to be quiet. He levered up to his feet, his left leg awkward and restrictive. Half pushing, half leaning on his wheelbarrow, he shuffled from the open to the cover of dense trees. Here he had a screen, made many years ago and freshly restored. After he removed the suitcase and covered the wheelbarrow, he squatted and waited and listened. He heard other men in the woods, further back than the first two.

Fifteen minutes later, two uniformed policemen stopped forty yards out. They were still in the trees but clearly visible. One started talking on a radio. After a brief exchange, the two men advanced, heading straight for the house. They took a quick look inside and then scouted around outside.

It took them only a few minutes to locate the grave. An hour later there were men in white jumpsuits and a couple in plain clothes who seemed to be coordinating things. When the police started to search the woods,

Michael decided it was time to move. He had to stay alive. Something was nagging him—there was something vital he needed to do. With tremendous effort, crippled by the pain in his leg, he eased away silently. They never heard a thing and, as soon as he was out of their earshot, he forced himself up, used a branch as a crutch, and made his way to a bivouac.

Once there, he rested. He tried to think about what the boy had said, about what he'd asked. *What happened to her? Where did she go? Where's her body?* Opening the suitcase, he handled the newspapers, sifted through them to find the photograph of Geoff Jenkin. Michael had seen him with the girl, seen him with the body. Rocking backwards and forwards he tried to think, squeezed his eyes tight to let in the memories. And then it came to him; he had something in his suitcase, something deliberately taken to remind himself. Rummaging through, he found it: a lump of grey rock, a smear of white paint on one side and the lines and circle he'd painted.

As he held it, the images came back and he knew where he had to go. The trauma of recent events had at last unlocked the painful truth.

Dan cycled hard, his legs going too fast because the gears were stuck. Black skies threatened rain and, when a passing car sounded its horn, he wished the bike had lights. At the gate to Bucker Field, he dumped the bike and ran along the scrub on the edge of the freshly cleared maize field.

At the end of the field, where the farm track ended and the secured land of the old tin mine began, he saw Jenkin's Land Rover. Dan placed a hand on the car's bonnet and felt the heat as he wondered why Jenkin would stop here if he were going up to the mine. Where else would he go?

Dan glanced up the track Jenkin had taken last time they were here—when he thought the farm manager was threatening him. Rather than take the same path, Dan decided to take a circuitous route, a track worn smooth by dirt track riders.

Breathing hard, he rounded the first mound and stopped to catch his breath. Now he could hear voices, raised and angry. Lizzy and then Jenkin arguing.

He walked fast, still listening, trying to understand what they were saying. It didn't make sense. Lizzy appeared to be in control, threatening the farm manager.

A moment of silence was punctured by a scream— Lizzy's. Then Jenkin laughed and Dan knew the dynamic must have changed. The farm manager had control. Lizzy screamed again and then Dan saw her. She crouched on the barren rock close to the chimney. Her hair was dishevelled and she held her arm like it was broken. He couldn't see Jenkin so tried to get her attention. When her eyes found him, he saw desperation and fear in them.

Dan bent and his fingers closed around a fist-sized stone. He still couldn't see Jenkin. Where was he?

Glancing left and right, Dan slunk across the space towards Lizzy. Her mouth was bloody and one eye looked painful. A wrist dangled at an unnatural angle. "Where is he?" Dan mouthed. She flicked her eyes towards the slope and then Dan heard Jenkin climbing back up, slate sliding and rattling like dry bones.

"Got it," Jenkin said as his head emerged above the ridge. He stopped and then smiled, his eyes bulging like a crazed dog's. His hands held a shotgun and he levelled it at Dan.

Jenkin strode towards them. "Well, well, well, what a cosy meeting we have going on here." To Lizzy he asked, "Have you told him?"

Lizzy looked down, said nothing. Four more strides and Jenkin was right there. He slapped her across the head so that she sprawled on her side. For a second the gun was down and he swung it back towards Dan. But Dan had already moved back and sideways and then he threw a roundhouse, stone first. He aimed for Jenkin's face but missed. The first deflected off the big man's shoulder.

Jenkin spat, "You little runt." Hatred burned in wild eyes.

Dan caught him again, this time on the meat of his arm as Jenkin blocked the punch. Dan didn't see Jenkin's other hand and was knocked back on his heels. He blinked stars, realized he'd dropped his weapon and then doubled up from a kick to the groin.

A blow to the back of his head made his face rasp against hard slate. He saw Jenkin's scuffed black boots and then darkness rushed in.

Dan felt the stabbing in his chest, the cracked ribs holding him like a vice. He jolted into consciousness. Arms pinned to his sides, he was held in a bear hug by Jenkin behind, pushing him down the slope, towards the maw of the mine hole.

Dan's eyes flicked left and right, desperate for some sign of hope. Rocks, slate, lose stones. He skidded closer to the pit.

Lizzy scrabbled to the engine house but showed no sign of coming to his aid. Above her, the broken chimney looked like a mournful, silent witness.

Three steps away, Jenkin hissed, "You ruined everything, you little runt."

"I don't know…"

At the base of the chimney, Dan saw a painted mark: a circle and two lines. He double blinked. The symbol on the old Polaroid!

Jenkin was still talking.

"This farm should be mine. And now it's too late... there's no way the old man has left it to me."

Dan spoke, but Jenkin was ranting, unable to listen. He said, "This land is worth a fortune. And I deserve it. All the shit I've taken over the years. All for nothing? Well it's not going to be like that. It's not..."

He'd forced Dan to within a step of the edge.

Cool dry air came up out of the blackness and Dan dug his heels in, felt himself pitching forward, drawn into the hole. Jenkin squeezed a final time and Dan screamed.

And then there was another scream, a feral yell. Jenkin's grip was released. Dan sunk to his knees and rolled away. When he looked up, Jenkin was staring up the slope at something dark and monstrous, an apparition, black with soot and dirt, charging wildly down the scree.

With a guttural yell, Michael barrelled into Jenkin, lifting him from his feet, tumbling through the air like pirouetting wrestlers locked in a deadly embrace. And then they were falling, dropping over the edge, falling into the hole that was once a mine.

The whole incident ran in slow motion in Dan's mind, ending in a distant thud before another. And then all was still, except for a small green bird that fluttered up from the shaft and flew low over the grey rocks.

Lizzy stood on the ridge and, for an odd moment, Dan thought she intended to charge down and throw herself into the mine. Or maybe she planned to take Dan with her. Her face was contorted with emotion he couldn't read but, after a second, she howled like an injured animal, sank to her knees and began to sob.

As he climbed the slope, his ribs burned like hell and breathing came in shallow gasps. He dialled 999 and gave the briefest of detail. When the operator tried to keep him talking he ended the call. He crouched next to Lizzy, wincing with the sharp pain. Between sobs, Lizzy mumbled incoherently.

"Lizzy." He held her shoulders and tried to get her to look at him. "Is this where... Is Jade here?"

"Jade?" she said in a faraway voice. Now she looked at Dan, her eyes shot through with red, her grubby face wet with tears. "Jade." She shook her head as though it were weighed down by the sadness. "This isn't about my girl. Wish it was as simple as that."

She talked then and, although he suspected she had taken drugs, her words started to make sense. Lizzy needed to confess, but it was not what he'd expected.

FORTY-THREE

Collick arrived with other policemen after only five minutes, explaining that he'd still been on the farm because of the body in the woods. He wanted Dan and Lizzy to explain what had happened but they both sat in silence. Collick paced about and, between phone calls, glared at Lizzy.

When paramedics arrived, they said both were suffering from shock. Lizzy had a broken wrist and collarbone. Dan had a suspected punctured lung and was given oxygen as he was stretchered down to the field where the police and ambulances had parked.

On the way, they were passed by a fire crew in a Land Rover going up to the mine.

Forensic photographer Callum O'Donnell descended the nine-metre ladder into the darkness. He wore a blue protective suit provided by the fire service and a borrowed yellow hardhat. The head torch flickered to and fro as he glanced at the rappel ropes, the nails hammered into the grey rock face and the rungs of the ladder. He knew it was pinned at the top and bottom and it hardly moved under his weight, but he kept a firm grip of the rope in one hand just in case. The chief had said that they originally planned to fix ladders the whole way, but it was too deep and irregular and had taken too long, so after this it was just ropes all the way down. Callum looked up at the grey sky beyond the mouth of the hole and hesitated.

"Five more steps," a voice crackled in his earpiece.

Callum glanced to the side and down and saw the Fire and Rescue officer below, his head torch bright in the gloom.

"Taking the weight," Callum said as instructed and hoped his voice didn't betray his nervousness. He breathed in, felt his heart beating in his chest, released his hold on the ladder and leaned back. The rock jutted slightly and he knew this was why the fire service hadn't used their longest ladder. Keeping his focus on the wall of rock and imaging this was just a simple abseil, he planted foot after foot and descended to a level almost one hundred feet below the surface. The grey rock gradually became black and looked slick in the torchlight.

Plant, step, plant.

"Almost with me," the voice said, and began to count him down.

At the count of "two" Callum felt a tap on his leg and then his lead foot felt the bottom of the shaft.

As he swung his light onto the helmet of the other man, he felt hands pulling the ropes through his clip and then the carabiner attached to a new rope. "You're secure," the fireman said, and patted his shoulder. "Done this before?"

"Down a mineshaft? Never." Callum returned the officer's encouraging smile.

"The body's right here."

Callum stepped carefully across rocks that appeared wet in the torchlight, feeling the new rope pull through his clip and he saw it was being fed through by the other man.

The body was almost horizontal and in an ungainly pose. Exposed skin showed signs of very recent first degree burns. "You've not touched it?" Callum asked.

"Not me. My colleague only touched the neck to check for a pulse. Nothing else disturbed, don't worry."

Callum pulled open the bag he carried on his back and handed a torch to the fireman. "If you wouldn't mind..." he said, and, once it was fired up, directed the other man where to hold it as he took photographs of every angle. When he was satisfied, he nodded and said, "OK, he's good to go."

As Callum packed his equipment, the fireman called up with a brief report and asked for something called a linebag. Moments later Callum heard feet on the rocks above and then the light of a second fireman. He dropped quickly and smoothly to the ledge, reconnected ropes and, after a bob of the head, walked backwards a few paces and then disappeared.

Callum switched his attention to the first fireman, who was pulling on a rope. A yellow bag flickered in the torchlight and scuffed its way down until the fireman disconnected it. He turned to Callum. "Ready for the second one?"

Callum gave a nod and watched hands at his belt, attaching a new rope and unclipping the one connected to the fireman. The man patted his shoulder and said, "OK, watch out for the drop. You'll take five paces and feel it start to slope. Turn and I'll lead you to the edge. You've got another drop of about thirty feet."

Callum followed instructions and, after the slope, was told to lean back and start to abseil again. He could no longer see the opening to the sky and the black rock sucked light from the torch. The air was dry in his mouth and tasted of death. He shook the thought from his head, like he had the one time he had gone potholing.

Two friends in Yorkshire had taken him down a hole only big enough to squeeze through and then crawled for almost six hours in the dark and occasional wet. Even though his friends were there, they had hardly spoken and at times he had lost sight of them. But there was always the confidence that these guys had done it before and they knew exactly what they were doing.

At times his drysuit had snagged and the walls pinned him until he had found a way to wriggle through. The fear wasn't like claustrophobia, because he didn't suffer from that. No, the feeling was the polar opposite, like he was in a void, still air that he couldn't breathe. Time had lost all meaning, it had become about surviving, about not giving up. He had never told anyone, but at his darkest moment he had thought he'd heard a voice, the slightest whisper, and wondered if it were God. The words were indistinguishable, but they seemed to tell him to relax, to let the walls close in, to succumb. When they had finally surfaced again, he had seen the relief in the other men's eyes and knew then that they had been lucky to survive an uncharted route.

Something touched his leg and he snapped back to the present.

"You're down," the voice said in his ear, and he shone his light into the face of a second fireman. The man forced a smile. "Let's get this over with. I've only been here a minute and it's already a minute too damn long."

Callum turned, his light illuminating the opposite wall almost touching distance away. He looked down and saw he was on a ledge about three feet wide. "Where…?" His light picked up the crumpled body of the second victim, beyond the fireman. They hugged the wall and shuffled over. The fireman stepped to the other side and blood reflected black against their lights. A large man, the victim was at all angles and half of his skull was missing.

They went through the same routine as before with Callum being attached to a second rope that the fireman had connected to himself and then handed the man the torch so that the photographs could be taken. The cruel light lit the body and Callum manoeuvred along the ledge and captured the corpse from all angles.

"Done?"

"Yeah."

"Seen this?" The fireman aimed the light above their heads on the opposite wall, first highlighting a streak of blood."

"Main impact," Callum suggested.

The light swept left and right, picking out unusual marks like giant claws had randomly scraped a broad area. "What do you think?"

"Odd." Callum fired off a few shots of the blood and then the scratches. "Can't see how they are..." He stepped back for a shot and his foot slid on something wet. He reached out to steady himself and slipped again. And then he was falling feet first into the void. The scream choked in this throat just as the rope snapped tight and he felt the air squeezed out of his lungs. His shoulder struck stone and he spun, dangling only feet beyond the ledge.

"I've got you," the fireman's voice both crackled in his earpiece and echoed off the rock. "You OK?"

Callum closed his eyes, breathed the dry dead air, and opened his eyes. "I'm fine, just a few bruises. Oh God! Oh my God!"

"What?"

"Oh God!" Callum swallowed and blinked, trying to process what his torch light had picked up. Twenty or so feet below, a mess of white patches blinked back in the light. Bones. Hundreds of bones at the bottom of the shaft. In that moment he knew that it had not been God's voice he'd heard in the Yorkshire pothole.

FORTY-FOUR

Karen sat at the kitchen table nursing a cup of coffee. It had gone cold. She'd waited a long time. Now she wished she'd just waited at the hospital until the police had let her see Daniel.

"Oh, you're back," Matt said as he dropped his keys in the bowl by the front door but remained there.

She looked up and knew he could see her eyes were rimmed with red. She glanced into the lounge, at the bags she'd piled there, and back.

Matt followed her look, breathed in and sighed. "Oh, Karen."

"I'm leaving, Matt."

He walked forward to the table and placed both hands on it. "Honey, I thought we talked about things. I thought we were OK."

"We're not OK, Matt. We've probably never been OK."

He shook his head and smiled, but she saw the strain in it. "Everything will be fine, I promise, sweetie. We've both just been a bit stressed, what with work and this thing with Dan Searle."

"It's not about Daniel."

Matt rounded the table and walked behind her slowly. She didn't turn, but heard him get a glass. "I'm going to have some Châteauneuf. Want some more?"

"No."

He sat at ninety degrees to her, a large glass of red wine in front of him, his big hand reaching out. After a moment like that, he said, "Honey, hold my hand."

She looked into his eyes and moved a hand towards him. "I'm sorry, Matt." Her voice trembled slightly and she fought back tears. He placed his hand over hers and held it there.

"Look, why don't you take some more time. Go back to Cornwall and switch off for more than a weekend. You obviously need the break." He studied her face. "And I'm sorry I went chasing around looking for you. I should have accepted that you needed the space to deal with stuff. I'm sorry. OK?"

"I'm sorry too." She nodded and the tears brimmed. "I've realized this past week that my heart isn't here. Work seems so fake, not real life. In fact my whole life seems so fake."

"I'll start coming home at a reasonable time. I'll stop doing the entertaining and other stuff. I'll give you... I'll give us more time." He smiled again as if willing her to smile back and accept his offer.

"Matt, this isn't about you. This is about me. I can't go on."

He removed his hand, took a slug of his wine and sat back. "So, what, it's over? Is that what you're telling me?"

"Yes."

"This is him versus me, isn't it?" His voice was cold now. "I won't give you a penny. Don't expect half, because you won't get anything. I know the best solicitor."

Karen pushed to her feet, scraping the chair back. "This is not about Daniel. You should have trusted me. You should have let us remain friends. The fact that you didn't shows that we had a problem. Maybe we could have gone on longer if you hadn't reacted the way you did. But, you know what? I think I was always running away, thinking I was better, thinking that work could give me something better, that would make me a better person, but we can't change who we really are. And just because you have a big job and earn a ridiculous amount of money, it doesn't make you any better than the next man." He looked like he was about to argue, but she continued. "I'm not saying you're bad. I'm accusing the system, the culture, the whole damn industry. It's about making money, by fair means or foul. I don't want to be involved any longer."

"That's ridiculous!"

She waved away his protests and walked into the lounge. "Matt, I'm leaving you. Everything I'm taking is in these bags, so don't worry, I'm not going to fight you for half the apartment or half your money. This is all I need." She picked up a clothes carrier and suitcase, saw that Matt wasn't going to help and left the flat. She returned four times to load her car, and never once did Matt look up or say anything.

As she shut the door for the final time, Karen's last image was of Matt sitting at the table, drinking his wine as though nothing were happening.

FORTY-FIVE

In the hospital, Dan's punctured lung was confirmed and an x-ray showed one of the cracked ribs had broken. A nurse talked to him and then a doctor described what was going to happen. It barely registered through the fog of painkillers and tiredness, but as he was anaesthetized, he knew he was going into surgery.

When he came round, a doctor told him the operation was a success. He would now always set off metal detectors and have a six-inch scar. Providing there were no complications he would be discharged within five days.

He had a lot of time to think about Lizzy's confession because he had no visitors until the following morning. She said she had worked on the farm after leaving home. Dan knew that, but what he hadn't known was that she'd moved in with Jenkin.

"She's down there," Lizzy had said, her voice hoarse with pain or sadness, Dan was unsure which. "The missing girl from the nineties," she explained. "She died... an accident. Jenkin threw her down the shaft."

"And you knew?"

"He made me help." She had looked at him then, pleading. "Don't tell the police."

He had spotted Collick's and a marked police car driving along the edge of the woods, "Give me a good reason not to," he'd said.

"We both hate Gary... DS Collick."

Dan had said nothing. He'd just raised his eyebrows and glanced at the approaching cars.

Lizzy then added: "I'll tell you more. I promise I will."

So Dan lay in bed wondering what more there was to tell. Did Lizzy really know what had happened to her daughter? If she did then he had to get her to confess. It was the only way he'd clear his name. Lizzy had been the one in Jenkin's house. What had she been looking for? Was it linked to Jade's disappearance? And why was Lizzy so afraid of talking to Collick?

He also thought about Michael. The crazy tramp must have known the girl was in the mine shaft—the marking on the back of the Polaroid was a reminder of where she was. Michael had been dying and yet he'd managed to get to the mine and find some kind of energy to attack Jenkin—or maybe it was more about protecting Dan than punishing the farm manager.

Michael had been the one who had taken his mother's good luck charm on Dan's first day back. The stuff in the suitcase suggested he was a kleptomaniac. Had he also taken the missing sculpture—*Tin Heart*? Dan hadn't seen it in the house in the woods, but Michael could be the explanation. Did he just steal things or did the items have some meaning—like the photographs? Did his mother's good luck charm mean something to him? And why did he have pictures of Dan as a child?

Another burning question: if Lizzy was connected to Nina, did that mean there was a connection between Michael and Lizzy? Dan had confused the two girls when trying to understand Michael. Had Michael been confused too?

Thoughts of the case were still cycling through his mind when Collick and the bug-eyed detective came into his room.

They sat beside his bed and without preamble Collick said, "Tell us your side of the story."

In a monotone, Dan recounted being at the police station, having a sudden flash of inspiration and believing that Geoff Jenkin was involved in Jade Bridger's disappearance.

Collick's eyes narrowed as he interrupted. "Why? What made you think it was him?"

"Just everything seemed to come together. He wanted the farm. He wanted my boatyard for development—although he denied it—and he set me up. He told you I'd started the fire at the farm, when it was probably him."

Bug-eyes looked up from taking notes. "So you called Lizzy Bridger and told her your suspicions."

"Something like that. I didn't get the chance to say much. She was the only one I knew who would be driven enough to do something."

"So you're saying that Mrs Bridger went to the farm to confront Jenkin about her missing daughter?"

That's what he'd expected but it wasn't the truth. Dan forced his voice to stay deadpan and said, "I can't answer for Lizzy Bridger. I don't know what she was thinking."

Collick grunted. "OK then. So what were you thinking when you went to the mine?"

"I was thinking Jenkin was guilty of all of it. Yes, I went there to confront Jenkin about Jade Bridger."

"Tell me again why you suspected him. And why the mine?"

"Jenkin had taken me up to the mine, but after Michael showed me the picture of Jenkin and linked him to another missing girl then it seemed to add up. I think part of taking me to the mine was to intimidate me, suggest it was where he disposed of the body. But it wasn't about Jade, was it? It was about a young woman who went missing fifteen years ago."

Collick ignored the question. "OK, so you arrive at the mine. What then?"

Dan told the story of seeing Jenkin threatening Lizzy with a shotgun and how he'd become involved. "I thought he was going to kill us both," he said.

Bug-eyes looked up from his notes. "Why? You've been saying a lot but none of it explains his motive."

Dan shook his head and waited.

Collick prompted, "Go on. What happened next?"

"I thought he was going to push me down the slope into the mine shaft, but that's when Michael appeared."

"Mad Mike from the woods? The same man who may have killed your father?"

"As I explained before, I think he tried to rescue my dad from the fire. I got the sense he cared about him. I think he cared about me too."

"So he dived into the mine with Jenkin." Collick couldn't hide the disbelief from his voice.

"That's what happened."

"He deliberately killed himself to save you."

Dan sighed. "Look, you seem to want me to justify other people's actions. I can't. Maybe he meant to die. Maybe he just didn't think about it. I don't know."

Collick said nothing. The silence swelled and he seemed to be trying to read something in Dan's face.

Dan held Collick's cold-eye stare. "Tell me what you found in the mine."

265

Collick pursed his lips and then relented. "Obviously we found two bodies: Geoff Jenkin and the man you call Michael. Both dead. But we also found bones that'd been there a long time. SOCO are still there processing the site."

"Nina Ivanova?"

"There are bones of a woman. It's too early to know whose they are, but they're over ten years old. Bulgarian authorities will be contacted to check DNA."

Bug-eyes said, "There were other bones too. Lots."

Dan waited.

"Cows' bones." The detective shook his head, but his eyes didn't move. "Over a hundred cows down there. Know anything about that?"

"That doesn't make sense," Dan pinched the top of his nose. Why would cows be up there by the mine? They never had any cows in Bucker Field so they couldn't have just wandered up there. He said, "I can't explain it. What about Jade? Did you find her as well?"

Bug-eyes leaned forward, ignoring Dan's questions. "Lots of cows' bones. Maybe some kind of ritual? Some weird Devil worship maybe? Ever heard of anything like that?"

"No."

"But you know it's associated with evil spirits—the mine?"

Dan studied the detective's face and wondered whether he believed what he was saying or was just trying to get a response. He then looked back at Collick. "So, what about Jade?"

Collick said, "No other human remains. No Jade Bridger." He waited a beat, then: "Tell me what you know about Lizzy Bridger's involvement. What was she doing at the mine?"

The way he asked made it sound like he was fishing. Dan arched his eyebrows. "Same as me, I guess. As I said, I rang her from the police station, said I was suspicious of Geoff Jenkin."

"The shotgun at the scene was Steve Bridger's. So it looks like Lizzy took the gun."

Again Dan raised his eyebrows.

"You know how this looks?" Collick said, leaning forward, putting weight on the edge of the bed. "You and Lizzy Bridger were working together and you got rid of the man who you thought killed your father and the one you thought had taken Jade. And you know why it doesn't make sense that Jenkin took Jade? Because Lizzy Bridger knew that Jenkin had changed. After a prostate op he lost the desire."

"I don't know what you mean."

Bug-eyes interjected, "Jenkin liked his women— mostly young women. But years ago he was diagnosed with prostate cancer and had an op. Sometimes it affects the ability or the libido. And that's what happened to Jenkin."

"And you say Lizzy Bridger knew this—knew Jenkin wouldn't have been interested in Jade."

Collick inclined his head.

"So why was Lizzy Bridger there?" Dan asked. "What did she say?"

Collick studied him, dark eyes trying to bore through skin and bone. "Tell me again why you think Jenkin started the fire at the farm?"

Either Collick didn't want him to know, or Lizzy really hadn't told him. What was it between Lizzy Bridger and Collick? Why didn't she trust him?

Dan shook his head. "I thought you had me down as responsible."

267

Collick sat back. Bug-eyes said, "Timeline. It was called in before you got there."

Dan opened his mouth to ask how they knew what time he'd arrived, but then realized there was only one person who could have vouched for him, for the time he'd left Truro. Karen.

"Sounds like avoidance," Collick said, impatience edging his voice. "Guilty people try and divert questions. Why Jenkin? Tell me why you thought it was him?"

Collick was an idiot. Dan repeated his logic slowly, pausing after each word.

When he finished, Collick said, "You know what it looks like?" He smiled like someone holding something back. "It looks like you were deliberately setting the two of them up—Lizzy Bridger and Jenkin—making Lizzy think that Jenkin had something to do with Jade's disappearance." He nodded as though thinking. "Like you were trying to divert attention from yourself."

He paused again and Dan had the distinct impression Collick had planned this speech, maybe even practised it.

The detective continued: "So no, I don't have you down for starting the fire, but I still have you down for Jade's abduction. Did you do it alone or was Mad Mike involved? You know I have another theory forming: that Jenkin was on to you so you planned to get rid of him. You planned to get him up to the mine. Maybe you hoped that Lizzy Bridger would kill him and in the end Mad Mike had to save you... or maybe you planned for your accomplice to die as well as Jenkin. Nice and clean that way,"

"Rubbish."

Bug-eyes said, "It's a theory."

"It's a stupid theory."

"We'll see." Collick smiled. "DC Bateman will write up your statement. We'll leave you to have a think. If you'd like to modify your statement it will be better to do it before I get the evidence."

After they left, Margaret and Tom came in. They told him that Karen had waited for many hours but the police refused anyone access until he'd given his statement.

"She's gone to check on her mother but promised to return soon," Auntie Margaret said. She confirmed that Karen had been his alibi and Tom said he'd been interviewed by the police about when and where he'd dropped Dan, whether Dan had said what he was doing and whether he had a weapon.

Dan was surprised that his next visitor was Lizzy Bridger, her wrist in plaster and arm in a blue sling. She sat by his bed and said nothing for a long time. Eventually she asked if she could have some of his water.

"I didn't tell them," Dan said, and her eyes narrowed.

"Are you going to?"

"I haven't decided yet. At the mine you just said you were involved in Nina's death. You didn't murder her, did you? Tell me the whole story—then I'll decide."

When she spoke, Lizzy whispered so that she wasn't overheard. "Geoff Jenkin used to like girls. He'd often pick one from the farm girls and make her feel special. He made me feel special once. I was eighteen, had run away from home at sixteen and... well, as I said, he made me feel special. But it never lasted with him. There was always someone else. And his tastes weren't the usual."

"What do you mean?"

"He was rough, liked it when... you know, liked to force them to do things they didn't want to. He used the house joined to his as their accommodation. It started as a reward, better than the communal caravans, but then it

269

would become their prison. Anyway, Nina was different. She was an illegal and Geoff threatened to report her when she refused to play his games. She couldn't get away, so I guess that's how she had an accident."

"That doesn't make sense."

She looked uncertain.

Dan said, "What sort of accident was it?"

She took a long breath, "I don't know. Honestly. She looked strangled. Sometimes I think she killed herself. I don't know… maybe I told myself it was an accident because it's less distressing.."

"Did you have anything to do with her death?"

Lizzy shook her head vigorously.

"That doesn't explain your guilt."

"I worked for him. I was a fool. It was money and favours and I just turned a blind eye to what he was doing." She sighed.

"And Nina?"

"He said I was complicit, made me help him take the body up to the mine and dump it in. He caught me on video in the house with the body."

"Was it you in Jenkin's house the other day?"

"I was looking for the video." She widened her eyes and Dan thought he saw the real Lizzy Bridger for the first time. "So, what do you think?"

"You have to live with it. Can you do that?"

Her mouth smiled but her eyes stayed the same. "I don't know. I honestly don't know. Sometimes I think the guilt will eat me up." There was a long silence as she seemed to just stare right through him.

When she finally got up to go, she said, "I'm sorry you had to be involved in this."

"What do you mean?"

She shrugged. "Just sorry, is all."

"I thought he must be the Buccaboo you mentioned—the one who had taken Jade."

A dark shadow seemed to cross Lizzy's eyes. She was far away for a while then shook her head. "No. Geoff Jenkin was an evil devil but I don't think he took her."

"Because of what you know about his operation?"

She smiled. "Yeah, ironic ain't it. A snip in the wrong place and the whole thing changes."

"But then who do you think did take Jade then?"

The smile disappeared as quickly as it had come. After studying Dan for a while she started to cry and buried her head in the crook of her good arm. When she finished she just wiped her face, nodded and walked away.

After she left, Dan stared at the ceiling and thought about everything he knew. He seemed no nearer to finding out what had happened to Jade. Michael seemed to be the only one who knew anything. But he had been obsessed with Jenkin, his girls and the disposal of Nina in the mine. Maybe even he didn't know what had happened to Jade.

FORTY-SIX

The following morning, Dan asked a nurse to check his pockets for a scrap of paper. She found Jade's note and handed it to him. There were sixteen numbers on it, or maybe eight pairs:

20-1 4-16 18-2 4-21 19-3 4-00 18-4 4-30

Although the writing wasn't neat, the numbers were clearly in some kind of order. Dan was certainly not a mathematician, and no matter how hard he studied the numbers he couldn't see an obvious progression. Of course, Jade wasn't good at maths so it couldn't be a clever code. Could it?

He used the browser on his phone to search for combinations of the sequence. He found nothing of interest.

When Auntie Margaret visited, he asked her if the numbers meant anything, but she too drew a blank. "Nothing to do with her sailing—her competition?"

"I can't see how," Dan said. I can't see any pattern or relationship at all."

Their conversation turned to the mystery of Jade's disappearance, and they were still talking about her when a man arrived. He introduced himself as Femi Sisoko from the National Crime Agency. He was built like a rugby player and his black face held sharp intelligent eyes. His card had a phone number but no job title.

He asked if they could speak alone, and when Margaret left, he said, "How are you feeling?"

"It hurts when I laugh," Dan said, nodding, although he couldn't help suspicion edge his voice. "How can I help you...? Do I call you Officer or Agent or something like that?"

"Call me Femi, please." Sisoko flashed his teeth in a grin. "I'm running a small operation down here and wondered whether your incident fits in somehow."

"Incident? The word somehow makes it sound insignificant."

"Sorry, wasn't my intention."

"What are you investigating?"

"The connection between people. For instance, start off by telling me about Geoff Jenkin. How well did you know him?"

"Hardly at all really. He worked for my father, though lately there was a tension between them."

"What was the tension about?"

"I can't be totally sure, because my father and I rarely spoke, but when I last spoke to him, he seemed to think Jenkin was trying to change the way the farm worked. My father was a traditionalist and proud of the heritage of the farm. I suspect he also thought Jenkin was trying to take over. You know, ownership as well as being the manager—my dad was pretty unwell towards the end so Jenkin pretty much ran everything, so I thought the same."

"But you aren't so sure?"

"Jenkin made me go up to the mine with him. He is—was—a big guy. Almost as tall as you, but more solid. I'm not sure if he intended to scare me or what, but he

273

lectured me about caring for the farm, its history and my family. He seemed to make a big effort to convince me of his good intentions." Dan hesitated. "Maybe it was for show. Maybe he wanted me to believe that."

"Hmm." The NCA officer looked like he was thinking, then surprised Dan with: "What did you know about Jenkin's pornography business?"

Dan recalled Lizzy telling him about Jenkin had caught her on video. He must have had cameras set up. For the moment, he decided to say nothing about it. He shrugged. "Jenkin had a pornography business?"

"He had a collection of sex videos—amateurs—home-produced stuff. But we think maybe it was more than just for personal consumption."

"But porn isn't illegal."

"It is when the girls don't consent."

Then the connection made sense. "Like Nina Ivanova?" Dan asked.

"Yes, she was filmed—so a victim in more senses than one."

"And Lizzy Bridger?" Dan asked, probing.

"Mrs Bridger has been very helpful. While she consented, she has confirmed that many girls had no idea they were being filmed." He read something in Dan's face and added: "No I don't think there will be charges against Mrs Bridger. She's been very helpful. From the way she tells it, I think any court would say she was as much a victim as some of the other girls."

"What about Nina Ivanova then?" Dan asked, wondering about what Lizzy had told him. "Can you tell me how she died?"

Sisoko didn't hesitate. "No, that's not my area."

"I thought you were investigating connections. Surely…"

"Tell me about Alan Everitt."

"He owns an agency—Esperar Land. Jenkin was a partner in a company listed as a shareholder of Esperar."

Sisoko flashed his teeth. "There you go, a connection. What can you tell me about them?"

"Esperar? They were the agents who arranged the sale of the land by Passingplace roundabout. My dad sold it to Redcastle, the developers."

"So your dad was linked to Everitt and Jenkin."

"I guess—if you look at it like that. But then so would I be."

"Was your dad involved with porn?"

For the first time, Dan felt annoyance prickle his neck. "No way!"

"Why do you say that?"

"Because he was a God-fearing Christian, who would do nothing..."

"But he must have known." The NCA officer tapped his front teeth, his eyes studying Dan's. "As I said, we've spoken to Lizzy Bridger. We know she was an employee at Searles Farm. She also said she'd been dismissed by your father because of her sexual activity. So he knew all right."

"But he fired her. Surely you can see that he wouldn't have done that if he'd been"—he used his fingers as quotation marks—"*involved*, as you put it."

"Let's go back to Alan Everitt. Are you aware of anyone else connected to him?"

Dan recounted his search for the company and then the one that invested in Esperar. "The name Redman was listed as the partner."

"Know who he is?" Sisoko asked, in a way that made Dan suspect the officer had an idea.

"No. It's the only time I've come across the name."

"And no one else?"

"No one else?"

"Connected to Jenkin?"

"No."

"OK," Sisoko said, switching track, "tell me about the beating you received."

Dan described how two men had arrived in a white van and beaten him up. He'd assumed it was about Jade Bridger. "But they were Everitt's men. I saw the same van with different plates parked off-road at the back of Everitt's house."

"They didn't beat you too severely by all accounts. So how do you explain the attack?"

Dan's pulse raced. His face flushed. The way the officer looked at him. Was he under suspicion of being involved with Everitt? "Look, I just have a boatyard that Everitt wanted for development. I can get you evidence that he'd arranged the right to purchase the land and was also trying to put me out of business."

"Because your land is so valuable? Really?"

"That's what I've been told."

Sisoko thought, his fingernails tapping his teeth, before his piercing eyes locked back onto Dan's. "That takes us back to your father, doesn't it? He sold the rights to your boatyard. I'll ask you again and I want you to think hard. Could he have been involved with Everitt?"

Dan shook his head. "No way."

Sisoko smiled. "OK, look, I'm sorry to raise these things and distress you while you're recovering, but I needed to know. Let's go back to the guys who attacked you." He pulled a pack of photographs from an inside pocket. "Take a look at these. See if you recognize one or both of those guys. If they work for Everitt, then they're probably involved on the drugs side of the operation."

"Drugs?"

Sisoko said nothing, just handed him the first photo. Then the next and the next, until Dan had looked at twenty mugshots.

He handed one back to Sisoko. "That's the driver of the van, the one with the baseball bat. No doubt about it."

Sisoko was pleased, but then he surprised Dan by pulling out a book of photographs. There were six to a page and over one hundred in total.

"Take your time. I just want to see if you recognize any of these people. And to be clear, if you do, it doesn't mean anything. I'd just like to know."

Dan studied each face, turning each page slowly, hoping for some glimmer of recognition. About three-quarters of the way through, he stopped. The guy looked different, shaved head instead of long hair, but it was him. It was definitely him. The picture he was looking at was of Gerry, the big Aussie working at Tanner's yard.

FORTY-SEVEN

Dan was left wondering about Senior Investigating Officer Sisoko. On the surface he seemed likeable, but he was all over the place. When asked about Gerry, all he would say is that it was one of the mugshots they held. It didn't mean anything.

It left Dan wondering whether Sisoko was as ineffective as the Truro detectives he'd dealt with. Would he discuss Jade Bridger's case? Dan asked.

"I've spoken to DS Collick," the big guy said with a shrug, "so I pretty much know all there is to know about it."

"Since you're looking for connections, is there any way there's a link to her?"

"It's an ongoing investigation. And not mine." He raised an eyebrow. "Look, I understand there's issues between you and the detective sergeant, but you should leave the investigation to the authorities."

"But Lizzy is connected, and so, by extension, is her daughter. You know, you said I was connected so by implication so is she."

Dan got nothing else out of Sisoko except for being asked to call should he think of anyone else who might be connected to Jenkin or Everitt. As the big agent left, he adjusted the curtain beside the bed, which was odd.

Dan was the only occupant of the room and there was no need for a privacy curtain. Perhaps he just had some kind of OCD, Dan explained to himself.

Karen checked on him via text every day. On Friday she surprised him by being his first visitor. When she came into the room, her face was creased with mock seriousness.

"Daniel Searle, what are you like?" She grinned and kissed him on the cheek. "It's good to see you looking all right, but what were you thinking going to your dad's in the middle of the night, risking your life by going into a burning house, hiding from the police, and going to confront Geoff Jenkin who had a gun?"

"I didn't hide from—"

"How are the ribs?"

"Like I've a knife in my side and a corset around my chest. Apart from that, I'm as good as new."

She laughed and he felt his spirits rise. Four days in bed with very little to do except read the papers and check the Internet for news. Karen dropped a paperback onto his blanket: a crime thriller called *I Dare You*.

"I thought about getting today's paper, but guessed you'd be sick of reading the news. However"—she winked mischievously—"there's bound to be stuff that they don't know, but you do."

"Probably. I'm refusing to give any interviews. You'd be amazed at the lengths they go through to try and get access to me. Second thoughts, you probably know all about how the press behave. Tell me what you've learned."

Karen went over what she knew. The fire at Searles farmhouse had received nothing but local coverage and was believed to have been an accident as a result of the open fire and a chimney that hadn't been swept for a decade. Jenkin's involvement in a porn video business was more widely covered by the tabloids.

Dan said, "I thought Jenkin's videos were just for personal use."

"That's not how it's been reported. The papers are saying there were about sixty girls abused on those films," she said. "Though only a handful have come forward so far. And then Nina Ivanova—the girl in the photograph—they say she killed herself and Jenkin disposed of the body in the mine. But what I don't get is where Lizzy Bridger fits in."

Dan waited until a nurse had been in the room, checked on him and left again. Almost as though she were still there, he felt the need to whisper. "Lizzy Bridger was one of Jenkin's girls. She's on some of the videos and apparently she was forced to help dispose of Nina's body."

"Wow! Do you think she's telling the whole truth?"

"About Nina killing herself? As I understand it, there's no evidence to the contrary. The bone damage is consistent with a post-mortem fall. And there was her confession to me. She was distraught and it sounded genuine. She asked me to keep it a secret, so when I gave my statement, I didn't mention it."

"Why? I'd have told them."

"I'm not a hundred per cent sure why I didn't—apart from hating Collick. And maybe feeling sorry for her because of Jade. Anyway, I'm sure she's said something to the NCA officer. And if she hasn't... well, I don't feel bad because it looks like she was really a victim even though she kept quiet about it for fifteen years."

"You've probably seen, but this morning the Bulgarians have confirmed they're Nina's remains. Weird about the cows' bones. Any idea what that's about?"

"None."

"Well at least it's over and you're all right." She said it convincingly, but they both knew it wasn't really over.

FORTY-EIGHT

Sisoko looked into a room that was little more than a cupboard. It smelled of stale coffee and armpits. "Anything?" he said to the man squashed up next to a folding desk. A laptop was open in front of him and he wore headphones, one covering an ear, the other resting on his head.

"The latest visitor was a woman—looked a bit Chinese, if that's OK to say, sir?" The man swivelled the screen so that Sisoko could see an image of Karen. "My guess is she's a girlfriend. She knows a lot about the case—said she'd been following it."

"Let me hear," Sisoko said, and the other man hit rewind, made a few adjustments and unplugged the headphones.

Karen was talking about the cause of the fire and Jenkin's amateur porn business.

The surveillance man commented: "She hasn't mentioned our man."

Sisoko signalled for the recording to continue. When they started talking about Lizzy Bridger he got excited. Dan had looked furtive and lowered his voice.

"Play that bit again," Sisoko instructed.

After checking the nurse had left the room, on the screen Dan said, "Lizzy Bridger was one of Jenkin's girls. She's on some of the videos and apparently she was forced to help dispose of Nina's body."

Sisoko shook his head. "So that was it."

The camera and microphone had been in the room from the start. The only visitors had been the local police, Dan's aunt and employee, Lizzy Bridger and the girlfriend. Sisoko had noted the strange interview by DS Collick and put it down to personality. The detective constable had returned later with the statement written up and Dan had signed it without complaint. The elderly couple—Dan Searle's aunt and the boatyard employee— didn't say anything of interest. It was Lizzy Bridger who had piqued his interest. She'd whispered something that the mic hadn't picked up. That was the main reason for his visit to Dan—to adjust the microphone that'd been knocked by an orderly.

Lizzy Bridger had whispered a confession and it was nothing to do with his case. Damn! He'd really hoped she'd mention McNally. Now that would have been a breakthrough.

Sisoko listened to the end of the visit with the girlfriend.

"He never says her name. Who is she?"

The surveillance guy let his pride show. "I think she's the Karen referred to by the old couple. Remember, they said she'd come and gone—her mother is unwell. I've had the office check her out. She's Karen Chamberlain. Lives in a swanky apartment opposite Canary Wharf."

"Money then."

"Must have. And she works for BebelStreet— BebelStreet Capital. Apparently used to be called BebelPlatz," the guy added. "Changed their name shortly after the war."

"BebelPlatz sounds familiar."

"Famous for the Nazi book burning."

"Ah. Job?"

The other man looked uncertain.

Sisoko clarified: "What's her job at BebelStreet?"

"Communications and public relations manager. The interesting thing about BebelStreet is that they're under investigation—something to do with fixing foreign exchange rates. And here's the most interesting part— Ms Chamberlain lives with a guy called Matthew Pedersen..." The surveillance guy paused. "He also works for BebelStreet and is one of the people being investigated for their involvement."

Sisoko nodded, thinking. Could this be a money laundering connection?

The surveillance guy prompted, "Could it be linked?"

"Could be. Who did you use in the office?"

"Wills."

"OK, have Wills dig a bit deeper. Has our man Searle made any phone calls?"

"No." They'd cloned Dan's phone so they could monitor everything. "Not sent any emails either. He's exchanged a few texts, mostly with Karen. I don't think there's anything suspicious. I'll print everything that's come in and out on his phone for you."

Sisoko was about to escape the smelly room when the other guy said, "Sir... he seemed a bit bemused by your visit—he doesn't seem to be inclined to act on it."

The agent patted the surveillance man on the shoulder. "Keep at it, you never know." It was possible that Dan was suspicious and was being particularly careful. It was also possible that his seemingly innocent messages were code. "The book that Ms Chamberlain gave him. Before he's discharged, have someone pick it up and check it while he's asleep—just in case. Also, let's get a copy of that piece of paper they discussed."

Sisoko took a walk. He was grasping at straws. If the connections couldn't be found and operations closed ranks or ceased before he knew what was going on, he may never get his man. He'd give it a few more days and then try something else. If monitoring Daniel Searle didn't lead them anywhere, then a further prompt would be necessary.

And Sisoko had an idea about what might work.

FORTY-NINE

The conservatory at the rear of Margaret's cottage overlooked a garden that would be resplendent with colour in the spring. Now there was a damp look to the overlong grass, and half-barren bushes clawed the air. A small heater belted out warmth so Dan and Karen sat in comfort reading the Sunday papers. He had been discharged on Saturday evening and Margaret insisted he come home with her so she could look after him until he had fully recovered. Chicken broth appeared to be her main remedy, but it was good to be out of the hospital and cared for. He hadn't been here since he'd lived with her as a teenager and the cottage hadn't changed in more than a decade.

"Any more thoughts about that piece of paper with numbers on it?"

"Maybe times. The highest number after a dash is thirty so maybe that's seconds. So 4-30 could be four minutes thirty seconds."

"Or a time: half past four."

Dan stared at her. "Have you just thought of that?"

"Of course. It was because—"

"It was about four o'clock that night she disappeared along the Plynt path and Tanner claimed he saw her

286

later on Mizzen Green. Maybe that was four thirty. Maybe they're all times."

He wrote the numbers out and stared at them.

20-1 4-16 18-2 4-21 19-3 4-00 18-4 4-30

If they were in pairs then every other number was a four. Then he spotted something odd. If they were times then why had Jade written 20-1. Surely it should have been 20-01 like 4-30?

"Oh," Karen said. She had her head down reading the Review section of the paper. After a moment she slid it over for Dan to see.

There was an article entitled: *What Really Happened to Jade Bridger?*

He read it slowly, all the details of the case regurgitated: her disappearance from Mizzen Green; Dan being the last person witnesses saw her with; the security footage; Jade's top; the arrest and the collapse of the case.

Dan expected the article to cover the legal case in more detail and perhaps challenge his release, but it didn't. That would probably come later in the red-top papers. Instead, *The Sunday Times* moved on to the death of Geoff Jenkin at the farm—the farm being the link to Dan and his involvement in Jenkin's death. Nothing new so far, but the main focus of the story switched to Geoff Jenkin and his penchant for making sex videos. The journalist had got a statement from someone who confirmed that Jenkin had prostate cancer and that explained why his activity seemed to have gone into decline at the same time. And then came the denouement: the relationship between Jenkin and Dan. Because Dan used to live at the farm and was still in contact with the farm manager, maybe he was also involved in the porn video business. Perhaps it hadn't ended the demise of Jenkin's desire. It seemed tenuous but the reporter suggested that Jade might have been lured into the sex industry.

The reporter had got a quote from Detective Sergeant Collick. He had said, "We can't rule it out. Geoff Jenkin is dead and we have a suspect who was involved in his death. You have to question what their relationship really was."

Dan felt blood drain from his face.

Karen put her arms around him for a while before speaking.

"It's scary isn't it? That they can report such things even though the courts rejected them."

He said, "I can't believe Collick has done that... stirred it all up again. And based on nothing but speculation."

"Hey, the main thing is that I know you're innocent."

Dan rubbed his face and looked across at the garden and Margaret's rose bed. In the spring there would be a stunning array of perfect yellow blooms. For now it was just stunted sticks in the earth. He thought of how both wonderful and terrible the world was. "Do you think evil makes us appreciate the good things in life?"

"Not for one minute!"

They sat in silence for a long time, watching the birds and insects, and the wind feathering distant trees, until she said something he'd been dying to ask.

A little awkwardly she said, "How did you get on with the book I gave you?"

"Sorry, I must have left it at the hospital." He studied her face. "That was just something to break the silence, wasn't it?"

She laughed. "Boy, you know me so well." She took a breath. "Dan... you probably guessed that I've left Matt. For good I mean."

He said nothing.

"I've also given in my notice. I'm coming back to Cornwall. I'll live at Mum's for a while until I find my own place, I guess."

"What? The great, ambitious Karen Chamberlain coming back to the sticks?" He grinned. "Are you sure?"

"As sure as I've been about anything for quite a few years," she said. "Now then," she picked up the *West Briton* and turned to the Appointments section, "time for you to help the great, ambitious Karen Chamberlain find a job that's going to be challenging enough."

FIFTY

Two weeks had passed since Jenkin and Michael had died at the mine. Dan and Margaret sat in Wilson's office, the warm smell of leather and polish strong. Wilson had read John Searle's will with impassionate formality, the light behind him making his dusty glasses virtually opaque, and Dan couldn't see if there was any empathy in them either.

The will passed almost everything to Dan with the exception of some personal items listed for Margaret. Specifically listed for Dan was the damaged painting of his great-grandfather. It was almost like his father was poking fun at him from beyond the grave, knowing the painting represented the farm, the way of life and knowing Dan had always hated it.

Wilson explained there would be a stipend of twenty thousand a year for Margaret, although it depended on the remaining assets. Regarding the land, there was a covenant on the woods so that they couldn't be sold with the farm.

When he finished, Wilson took off his glasses, rubbed them semi-clean and replaced them before asking if anything in the will needed clarification.

Dan said, "The provision for the woods was for Michael, wasn't it?"

"Well there are inheritance tax benefits but I believe so, although he wasn't mentioned, and even if he was—"

"Why?" Dan interrupted. "What did Michael mean to my dad? Did they have history?"

He saw Wilson and Margaret exchange looks. Then Wilson said, "It's not my place to say anything."

Margaret nodded almost sadly and said, "I have a story to tell you, Dan, but can we finish off here and then I promise I'll explain everything?"

"Turning to the financial situation," Wilson said, "I have liquidated the assets, although I'm sorry to report there was barely enough to cover the inheritance tax. Although a working farm qualifies for agricultural relief, all machinery and livestock are non-exempt. Margaret"—he waited for her to focus—"the stipend will have to come out of the net profits of the farm, so, based on recent years, I wouldn't recommend you anticipate much, if anything at all. However, if the farm is sold within five years, you will be entitled to fifty per cent of the net proceeds." He looked back at Dan. "You understand this was designed as an incentive for you to maintain the farm rather than dispose of it."

Wilson answered some more questions and again covered the funeral details requested by his late father. "You can organize them if you like, but I'm happy to handle the arrangements if you prefer."

He read something in Dan's face and shook his head, eyes washed-out behind his dusty glasses. "I know you clashed with John, but I think you judge him harshly."

Dan bridled. "He never did anything—"

"Stop it!" Wilson's voice cut through his complaint, surprising him with its fervour. It looked like the solicitor cared about his father after all.

Wilson stood and nodded to Margaret. "Would you excuse us, please Margaret?"

"Of course. Dan, I'll see you for tea at Cavendish's. I'll tell you the story then."

Dan agreed, watched Margaret close the door behind her and turned to Wilson, wondering what the solicitor had to tell him.

"Firstly, I want you to know that I was ready to represent you after the fire at the farm. Karen told me you'd been arrested. I called but—"

"I saw. Thanks."

"But that's not what I want to talk about. You think John, your father, didn't try and help you, but he did. He sold the land by the roundabout so that he could afford the best lawyers and barristers—if needed—to defend you against the abduction charge."

"But you were my lawyer."

"That's what he wanted it to look like but I didn't have the experience. I wouldn't have known how to challenge the DNA evidence. And later, he came to me about other evidence. Before you ask, I don't know any details because he wouldn't say, but the sale of the development rights to your boatyard was to fight those charges."

Dan pursed his lips. From what his dad had said, he hadn't fought anything. Instead he had paid for the evidence. When he spoke he said, "But he was willing to sell something—the boatyard—that was precious to me. Strange idea of help, that is."

Wilson stood and offered his hand. "Think about it, Dan. He knew you wouldn't just give up the boatyard, so the small amount he raised cost nothing except your anger towards him. If John Searle had a fault it was that he saw the best in people and expected the same in return. He loved you…"

"And had a funny way of showing it."

Wilson walked Dan to the door and wished him well. "I hope I'll see you at the funeral, Dan. Perhaps after you've spoken to Margaret, maybe then you'll have a better understanding."

"This is a story about two brothers," Margaret began as she poured a cup of tea, held the china cup to her lips and blew on the surface to cool it and maybe to take her time. She didn't make eye contact, preferring to focus on the tea and tell her story like she'd practised it over and over. "The brothers were quite different, but they had a bond as strong as any brothers could. The younger, by three years, was taller and handsome and looked up to his older brother for his strength of personality and, I think, protection. The older brother was more serious, but nonetheless caring, with all the pressures of being the eldest and expected to run the family business, which he did. Both men fell for a pretty girl and at first she walked out with the older of the two. Then, at some point, one brother realized she was in love with his brother and gallantly stepped aside and watched as romance blossomed between the other two."

"This is all very cryptic, Auntie. Couldn't you just—"

"Bear with me, I'm almost finished." She composed herself and began again, almost like she was reading from a long-prepared script. "Their father died and the older brother took over the business and the house. The younger brother had joined the army, and when he came home on leave, he stayed in the big house with his brother. When he married the girl, she moved in as well and then she fell pregnant. She had a boy, and although her husband was away a lot, I think for a while they were very happy."

"Even the older brother?"

"I think so. He was still in love with the girl, but he loved his brother too. And he had company in a house too big for one man to live in alone."

"And there were never any other women?"

"The older brother was mostly too busy, but also, I think, a little awkward with people. Anyway, what happened next is important. The boy was only months old when his father had to go away again. A war was coming..."

"The Falklands." Dan felt his neck tingling as if touched lightly by a hand, but one that was prepared to grip hard.

"Yes, the Falklands War. The brother was part of an advance party. Anyway, I don't know the detail, but he was badly injured and in a coma for months. They thought he was going to die, but he didn't and he was eventually released into the care of his wife and brother. But he was a shadow of the man he had been, haunted by what had happened, and worse, physically unable to talk. He would have wild fits and screaming nightmares and would run out of the house and take days to be found and returned. The therapists said he had claustrophobia, but it was more than that. He needed to feel safe, and it seemed the only way he could do that was to keep moving and hiding. They tried therapy and of course drugs, but one day he ran away and never came back into the house."

Dan swallowed hard to clear the blockage in his throat. "He stayed in the woods."

"Yes." Margaret's eyes blinked tears, and for a long moment Dan thought she would break down, but she managed to compose herself to continue with a weak, comforting smile. "The mother and her son stayed in the house. I don't know what happened—maybe the pressure with the farm, maybe the stress of Michael's injury—but the older brother John and your mother became closer. But it wasn't straightforward. Your mother struggled with it. She was on medication too and, to be honest, she found it difficult to be a mother. You weren't an easy child, Dan, but that's not your fault. It must have been a difficult time, a complicated situation. I think perhaps she was conflicted with her love for John and a husband who no longer seemed to recognize her. Why she finally took her life, we don't know. Michael would have days when he seemed to remember and often came back to the farm. Maybe he came back that day. Maybe it was guilt, maybe it was the drugs, or maybe she just couldn't cope anymore. They say that most people who try to commit suicide do it as a cry for help."

Warm tears ran over Dan's cheeks. "And I was too young to help her."

"Of course you were. It wasn't your fault. And your dad—I mean John—didn't come home until the evening. It wasn't his fault either. He had a struggling farm to run and mouths to feed. You know he wouldn't openly admit it, even to me, but he blamed himself, and he was a man who found forgiveness hard."

FIFTY-ONE

Sunlight filtered through the stained glass, splashing colour on the heads of the congregation, and dust motes spiralled in the void above. Karen smiled encouragement as Dan climbed into the pulpit. He inclined his head almost imperceptibly in response and began to read Corinthians 1:13. Her heart swelled. He'd come so far in such a few days and she was certain there'd been a tear in his eye as someone read an excerpt from *Merchant of Venice*, the first part of the Portia speech that began "The quality of mercy is not strained". John Searle had planned his funeral to perfection, and no better subtle words, begging forgiveness, could have been directed at the man he called his son.

"For now we see in a mirror dimly," Dan read, but then stopped as though the words blurred on the page. The silence crept and Karen willed him to continue. Eventually he said, "I'm sorry, I only really got to understand the real John Searle these past few days. I'm not a well-read man, but at school we read Thomas Hardy's *Far From The Madding Crowd*. I can't pretend to have enjoyed it, but when I think of John I think of Gabriel Oak: a man of honour and integrity; a man with a strong sense of duty; a trustworthy, straightforward man; a stoic. John Searle was that man."

No sound followed but the tap-tap of Dan's shoes on the stone floor as he returned to the pew and sat beside Karen. She held his hand tightly and they both stood as the vicar asked the congregation to say the words Jesus Christ had taught them. She had never before heard Dan pray, but he bowed his head and recited the Lord's Prayer as though it were familiar.

Afterwards, once everyone had filed out and said their condolences, Karen hugged him.

"I'm so proud of you."

He nodded slowly. "What a perfect setting." He looked out over St Just Creek just a stone's throw away. "You know, I don't think I've ever been to St Just's before. Can you believe that? This is possibly the loveliest setting for a church."

"I was moved," she said as she led him up the path through the gardens. "You may mock me, but I felt something in there. Whether it was John's spirit, or that of the living or... or the Holy Spirit, I don't know, but I felt it and I'm so glad we came."

"Just for once—for today," he said, "I'm not going to mock you." He put his arm around her until they came to the gate to the car park where Margaret stood beside Karen's Mercedes.

Margaret's cheeks were moist and she seemed unable to speak as she hugged Dan.

He smeared her cheek with his thumb. "I'm amazed at how many people came. It looks like he was more popular than I thought. I guess I just saw the bad side of him."

Karen drove and Dan wedged himself on the small back seat. She kept glancing at him through the mirror to check he was all right, and he seemed fine. Just like the day before when it had been just the three of them at the crematorium service for Michael. It seemed unfair that the man who had given his life to save Dan—and probably Lizzy Bridger—had such an insignificant send-off.

"Do you think it matters? Does God count who comes to the service as a measure of the man?" she asked, almost to herself. The others didn't respond and she found herself thinking about Michael and the struggle Dan's mother must have faced.

FIFTY-TWO

Over the next few days people made enquiries about wintering their boats at his yard and paying for next year's berths. The order book was so busy that Dan wondered whether he should extend his pontoons to cope with the demand. It seemed *The Sunday Times* article had worked in his favour as publicity for a great location close to Falmouth.

Karen helped in the office so that Margaret could take time off. Her consultant said she shouldn't work at all, but she still turned up every day.

Karen saw how Dan relished the increased work and distraction from the case that had been like shackles around him. They stopped discussing Jade Bridger's disappearance, although she suspected it would always be there, like a dark stain. It never crossed her mind that Dan wasn't innocent, and yet something didn't add up. His lawyers had beaten the charges because the DNA was tainted. But his semen *had been* on Jade's top.

That made no sense for two reasons: Tanner had seen Jade on Mizzen Green wearing the top, and she had left with a man, walking in the opposite direction to the path where the top was later found. Not only was she wearing the top after the green, but it wasn't found for two days. The path wasn't particularly overgrown and, in Karen's mind, there was only one conclusion: the top hadn't been there until two days later. And since she believed Dan, then someone else had put it there. Someone had put his semen on it—someone had planted it.

Tanner had described the man on Mizzen Green as of Dan's size and build. This ruled out Everitt and Jenkin. Both men were taller, Everitt slim and Jenkin heavyset. She'd done some research into Councilman Gavin Rudman but found nothing suspicious and he could also be ruled out since he was shorter and rotund.

Karen had a strong suspicion of what had happened, if not who had met Jade, but seeing Dan's contentment, she didn't want to upset him. She was determined to wait until she had proof.

When Dan wasn't around, she went up to the loft and found the photograph of Amber, Dan's girlfriend at the time Jade disappeared.

Dan had a secret of his own. He had kept some of Michael's photographs and used them to make a scrapbook. He hadn't intended it, but as the book grew he realized he was constructing the evidence as well as information about his true father.

He had a section dedicated to Nina. He took a photograph of the marks at the mine and compared them with Michael's red marks on his Polaroids, the circle and two lines.

On a page with clippings about Jade and Michael's Polaroids of her, he noted the two circles. Was that a clue to where she was? Had Michael known?

He devoted a page to Jade's numbers but still didn't know whether they were relevant.

He added newspaper clippings about Everitt and Jenkin with details of their past.

Dan learned that Michael had been a sergeant in the Royal Marines: Four-Two Commando based near Plymouth. The beret in the suitcase had been his. Dan had posted on forums and made contact with former colleagues who had nothing but praise for the young man who had been shot in the head approaching Fort Stanley from Mount Kent. He'd been airlifted out and his friends had expected the worst. They said his survival was testament to his strength and courage. Dan included their emails in his scrapbook.

"I wish I'd known the man," Dan said to Auntie Margaret on the day he'd decided to move back into the loft at the boatyard.

"You did, dear," was all she'd say, and he knew she referred to their similarity. The deep love they had for someone special and an undeniable drive to do the right thing.

FIFTY-THREE

Dan took a walk along the path to Mizzen Green.

A cold wind funnelled down the creek. Up ahead he could see someone on the green, face to the wind, staring out towards the Fal and wrapped in a black cloak. Intrigued, Dan continued towards Quay. From the shape and sad posture, Dan soon suspected who it was.

"Everything all right?"

Lizzy Bridger looked up, scowled, and then forced a smile. "Just remembering."

Dan stood beside her for a while. Eventually he said, "In the hospital... you didn't finish telling me everything."

She lit a cigarette and stared at the distant river. The smoke trailed from her mouth.

Dan said, "You worked at the farm until my dad made you leave."

She nodded almost imperceptibly.

"Why?"

"He saw what I was doing... Jenkin was filming me..."

"Doing what?"

She took some long breaths, maybe wondering how or what to say. "Something I shouldn't have. Let's leave it at that. I'm not proud of what he made me do."

Dan thought for a moment. "Why just you? Why didn't he get rid of Jenkin as well?"

"I don't know. At the time I thought he was just anti me. But later I wondered whether Geoff had something on your dad."

"Like what?"

"I've no idea, it was just a feeling... because of the way they were. Because of Geoff's cocky attitude. He just seemed to know he could get away with anything."

"OK, I get it that Jenkin also had something on you because of Nina, but you could still have gone to the police. They would have understood."

She laughed. "Really? From your own experience, I can't believe you think that. Especially because of DS Collick."

"At the mine, you said you hated him."

"I do. You know how obsessive he can be."

"I don't get it."

Lizzy pulled he cloak tighter. "It's getting colder. Do you think there'll be an early snow?"

"Lizzy! Why do you hate Collick?"

"He doesn't think my husband should be allowed to look after children. He was the one who charged Steve with GBH. Said he was an unfit parent."

"And you disagree? You think he's good with children?" Dan realized he sounded a little too scornful and quickly added: "I got the impression you weren't that happy with your husband."

"I might not be happy but he's still Jade's dad and..."

When she wasn't forthcoming, Dan prompted: "And what?"

"You know. It's life, ain't it. Sometimes you just have to put up with the hand you're dealt. He's not perfect. No one is."

"So you hate Collick."

"For a while he threatened to have Jade taken off us."

That made Dan look up. "How long ago? And what about your other kids?"

"Oh ages ago, when Jade was small. And the other two aren't mine. They're Steve's sister's. He looks after them most days while she works."

"So you think your husband is OK with kids?"

"Not really. He's a waste of space, but someone for Jenny—Steve's sister—to leave them with."

"I know I asked you before, but you're certain Steve didn't have anything to do with Jade's disappearance?"

"Yes."

"And you know that because he was home with you the night she disappeared?"

"No, he was working that night. He does odd jobs when someone needs him. It's extra cash so—"

Dan couldn't believe what he was hearing. "He was out when she disappeared!"

She looked at him with eyes that were deep pools of sadness. "It wasn't him."

"Where was he then?"

"Look, Dan, he may be a useless shit at times but not that. He wouldn't... he didn't hurt his own daughter."

Dan could see there was no point in pressing her further. "What about this whole Buccaboo thing?" he asked. "It's been haunting me... The rhyme... I thought it was Jenkin. I thought you were telling me Jenkin was the Buccaboo."

"At the hospital you said you wouldn't..." She shook her head. "Look, the whole farm, you know the history... As a kid I was brought up to be afraid of the Buccaboo. My ma used to threaten us with him if we were bad. He was under the stairs—at least that's what we believed. Punishment was to be locked in a cellar where he might come and take us."

"Sounds awful."

She shrugged. "It was just her way of controlling us kids. She had a hard life and we were poor. Worked damned hard and had nothing to show for it." She turned to look at him. "You don't really remember, do you?"

"What?"

"*One, two, he's coming for you. Three, four, he's under the floor.*"

Dan studied her and thought about the rhyme.

She continued: "*Under the stair, he wants you there. In your head, he wants you dead.*"

"It's very familiar."

"It should be. We used to chant it at you. We didn't like you. The Buccaboo was evil and everyone knew there was some connection to the farm and your family. We liked to taunt you. In a way, I guess you were the Buccaboo. Mainly because you came from money and we didn't have any."

"I don't remember. So you did live around here as a kid?"

"We moved, and when I ran away, I came back. Though I don't know why. Only place I knew I guess."

"And you still think I'm the Buccaboo?"

"Not really."

"So when you said the Buccaboo had taken Jade, it was just a saying? You didn't mean you knew who had taken her?"

"No, and it's like saying I'll never know. Just like Ma wouldn't have known what had happened to me if I'd gone someplace else. Maybe Jade is just out there, getting on with her life."

"Do you believe that?"

"I can hope." She started to walk towards the road.

Dan said, "I thought you would wait at least until it gets dark."

She shrugged. "Sometimes. A bit cold today." She took another couple of steps and stopped. "I guess I should say sorry."

"What for?"

"Well, I mean thank you, really. Thank you for not telling anyone about... you know... my involvement. But it's probably just a matter of time. That NSA agent said they were going to go through everything. If there was something to hide then they'd find it." Her eyes were heavy with weariness. "And sorry for what you've been through." She shook her head and then walked away.

FIFTY-FOUR

Karen told Dan she was going for interviews, and it had taken three visits to Amber's home town before before someone recognized the photograph of her. They suggested she look for her in Bodmin.

There, Karen went into a hairdressing salon where the photo was passed around and one of the ladies said Amber had once been a customer. She thought the girl had moved to Saltash, although that was the extent of the hairdresser's knowledge and no one else in the salon made a contribution. Charged with renewed enthusiasm, Karen immediately drove to the small town on the opposite side of the river from Plymouth.

Going from shop to shop, she saw the same reactions when people didn't recognize the photograph. However the manageress of a travel agency reacted differently.

Her response was casual, too casual, and there was a hesitation before she said, "No, but why are you looking for her?"

Karen played it cool. "She used to be a beauty queen." She pulled out the poor-quality photograph from the article her media friend Zach had found but had folded back the headline. "My boss is putting together a story. You know, a *where-are-they-now?* kind of thing. A *West Briton* follow-up." She couldn't bring herself to pretend to be a reporter from the paper, but the manageress clearly interpreted it as such and read the opportunity.

"Will there be a mention of Plym Travel?"

"Tell you what, give me some details and I'll see what I can do. I'm sure he'll want some depth and colour for the story." Karen hoped that sounded like something a reporter would say and the girl seemed to buy it. She took out a pad and pencil. "Let's start with your name."

The manageress was called Tracie Wicker, and she made sure Karen spelt Tracie correctly. After she'd provided enough history of the business and detail about the most popular destinations and deals to fill half a broadsheet, she said that Amber was an assistant and worked on Thursdays and Fridays, ten till three, and Saturdays, nine till six.

"She joined us—let's see—about eight months ago?" Another girl at a PC nodded confirmation. The manageress continued: "She's only a junior, but she's very good with people and I think she has a future in the travel business. The customers like her. She has... a way about her."

Tracie smiled in a knowing way and Karen suspected Amber's popularity was mostly among the male customers. To appear genuine, she asked what Tracie knew of her employment prior to Plym Travel, but the girl knew little and Karen realized that the title *manageress* didn't mean *owner* or *hirer* either. She wanted to ask for contact details, but, rather than be faced with a standard *Data Protection Act* response, decided to leave on a positive note. She asked for the other girl's name and promised them both they'd get a mention.

On Thursday afternoon, Karen returned to the town and positioned herself in the Starbucks opposite the travel shop. She watched Amber at her desk, dealing with the only customers inside. For thirty minutes she tapped on her computer or fetched brochures for the couple to consult. Finally she shook their hands and showed them out. After they'd gone, she and Tracie performed a discreet high-five before they both returned to their desks and pretended to look busy but available. In the next hour, one man briefly went inside and picked up a brochure, but the rest of the passing trade either looked in at the window or just walked on past without a glance.

At three o'clock Amber came out and Karen left Starbucks. Once they'd rounded a corner, on a quiet lane up to a car park, Karen jogged up, panting. "Excuse me, it's Amber, isn't it? I called round earlier this week. Maybe Tracie mentioned me?" Close up she could see Amber wore thick foundation and was inwardly relieved that the girl wasn't as good-looking as she appeared in the photo from Dan's loft.

Amber smiled. "Oh, hi. You must be the lady from the *West Briton*. Yes, Tracie said you'd be doing an article that'd plug Plym Travel."

"I'm Kate," Karen said by way of introduction and shook hands. "Can we go somewhere I can do an interview?"

Amber made a step back towards the high street. "There's Starbucks."

"Somewhere more private... more conducive to a personal story..."

"Do you have a car?"

"Yes—parked in the main car park. Shall I drive us someplace?"

"No, I've a car—at the back of the shop. I thought maybe we could do it at my house."

Karen hoped she hid her excitement. "Sounds perfect."

Amber smiled, provided her home address and added: "See you in about ten minutes then."

It took Karen a little longer to locate the one-bedroom flat on the outskirts of the town and Amber welcomed her in with a smile.

"Nice pad," Karen said, noting how tidy it was in a minimalist way. Most of the furniture looked like it had come straight out of an Ikea catalogue. The lounge had a sofa, chair and coffee table, and a giant famous black and white print of New York on the wall. "Been here long?"

"Just over six months. Would you like a drink—tea, coffee, squash, water?"

When Karen declined, Amber pointed to the sofa and took the chair, sitting at a right-angle to Karen.

Amber said, "So, where do you want me to start?"

"Let's start with why you sometimes use the surname Finn."

"Sorry?" The girl's face was a study in confusion. "I don't see how—"

"I'm not here to write an article, Amber. I'm here to find out why you stitched up Dan Searle."

Now she got it. Amber's neck went red, and a moment later her face flushed, anger replacing embarrassment. She pushed out of her chair, glowered. "How dare you! Get out! Get out of my house right now!"

Karen didn't move, forced her voice to stay relaxed. "I don't think so, Miss Finnigan."

Amber inched closer, looking down on Karen, muscles in her cheeks working as teeth clenched.

Karen said, "I suggest you sit down and listen to what I have to say." She was calm and in control and the other girl wavered.

Amber stepped back but remained standing.

"You committed a crime," Karen said calmly. "I know you did. You know you did. So why don't you sit down and talk to me." Karen waved towards the chair. "Sit. Otherwise I'll be forced to go to the police."

Amber dropped back into her chair. There was a look in her eyes that Karen couldn't fathom, but she saw the teeth hadn't unclenched and the mouth didn't look like opening.

Karen decided to do the talking. "OK, let me tell you what I know. You were put up to it. Someone asked you to date Dan Searle for a reason." She was bluffing, but she could see she was right so far. "Then you were asked to get a sample of semen."

Amber gave a slight nod.

"You were worried about it."

Now Amber spoke. "Bloody right I was. Dating the guy for a joke was one thing. Getting his spunk, well..."

"And you had no idea what he'd do with it?"

"No!"

Karen smiled inwardly. She'd confirmed it was a man and somehow he had power over the girl. And then it clicked.

"He paid you, but you were forced to do it, weren't you?"

Amber didn't respond, but her discomfort was enough confirmation.

"Tell me who he is."

"I can't."

Karen waited for more, but Amber said nothing, just fidgeted and shook her head.

"I want to help you, Amber."

311

Amber looked up and harshness returned to her voice. "You can't help me. No one can."

"He has something on you, doesn't he?"

Amber stood. "I think you'd better leave. This can't end well. If he finds out…"

Karen stood and reached out but stopped just short of touching Amber. "Look, Amber, I can't believe… Whatever it is, it seems to me like all the more reason to go to the authorities. The guy's done wrong. Your friend's the criminal. He forced you to help."

Amber started to dispute something then stopped herself.

Karen said, "This man—he's not a friend is he?"

"No, but… I can't. I can't talk to you. I can't do it." Amber shook her head, her eyes becoming glassy and unfocused. "Please leave me alone. I can't help you."

"Why can't you talk to me?"

Amber said nothing.

Karen waited, hoping to get a response but none came. She scribbled her phone number onto a scrap of paper and left it on the coffee table. "In case you change your mind," she said.

At the door, Amber said, "I won't call you." Her eyes had a blankness to them, like she was no longer there. Her voice fell, dull and far away. "And if you do report this to the police, I'll have to deny it."

Karen sat in her car and wondered what she could do if Amber wouldn't give up the name of the man she'd worked for. He'd paid her well, but it was fear that was keeping her silence now.

FIFTY-FIVE

Dan was about to open his book on the Falklands War when a phone call disturbed him. Femi Sisoko from the NCA wanted to drop off some things and asked if he could come round. Forty minutes later the officer accepted a cup of coffee and stood at the studio window overlooking the creek.

"You've got a great view here."

"I find it inspires my sculpture, though I confess I haven't done any since I've been back. Somehow the inspiration isn't there." Dan stood next to the big NCA officer and took a sip of his drink. "So, you said you had some documents for me?"

The agent handed Dan a paperback. "You left this at the hospital."

Dan took it—the thriller that Karen had given him.

Sisoko said, "Do you like stories with codes?"

Dan frowned. "I'm sorry?"

"The book—it's all about the protagonist locating her ex-boyfriend by cracking a code." The agent seemed to be studying him.

"I didn't get a chance to read it all."

Sisoko flashed his teeth. "Oh, sorry, hope I haven't spoiled it." He continued to study Dan's face for a moment before smiling again. He opened a briefcase and

313

handed Dan a thick manila folder. "They belong to John Searle. Found in Geoff Jenkin's house."

Dan frowned. "What are...?"

"We reckon they were stolen from your father's safe." He glanced out across the river, watching the seagulls dip and dive. "I needed to check them out, you know, in case your father was involved with Geoff Jenkin's illegal activities."

"And?"

"I'm handing them to you. So make your own judgement."

Dan opened the file and flicked through receipts and statements.

After a few minutes, Sisoko said, "There are some investments in there that the executor of his estate probably doesn't know about, but don't get too excited, it isn't a fortune."

As Dan looked at the folder, Sisoko said, "I'm sorry about before—about suggesting your father might be linked to what was going on at the farm."

"John Searle? He can't have known."

"Or it really had stopped. We searched Jenkin's house but found nothing."

"What about the adjoining house?"

"The boarded-up one with access from Jenkin's kitchen? Yes, we checked and found nothing of interest there either. Lizzy Bridger seems to think Jenkin's activity stopped following his prostate cancer. Of course, he doesn't need to have a libido to maintain a business exploiting women. We were hoping he was still active... in the porn business, I mean."

Dan waited. Would Sisoko mention Lizzy Bridger's involvement in Nina's death or the disposal of her body? They'd found Jenkin's video library so... Then Dan realized: Sisoko hadn't found them because they were never there. Lizzy had been living in fear for over a decade and Jenkin hadn't got the evidence.

"Anything else?" Dan prompted.

Sisoko did that thing with his fingers tapping his teeth. "Does the name McNally mean anything to you?"

"No, should it?"

"I guess not. He owns a farm of sorts near Penzance. Well, he has horses." Sisoko tapped his teeth. "I thought you might remember the name from a few years back. He owns a meat supplier business in Ireland. It was one of the operations accused of switching horse meat for beef. You must remember the case. All the supermarkets were involved."

"Sure." Dan shrugged. "I remember the news, but not the name. McNally, you say?"

"McNally. He's at the centre of my investigation. At least that's what I think. He's into drugs, sex, and of course money laundering."

"But...?"

"Well he's clever. We can't pin anything on him. We think he operates in a kind of web, with people involved in parts but no one with a complete picture. Some of the businesses are legit and some operate behind legitimate businesses."

"With this McNally guy at the top?"

"That's what I think. That's what I'm trying to prove."

"I found the link between Jenkin and Everitt by searching company records at Companies House. Could you do the same to see the bigger web? Maybe see where this McNally guy fits in."

"If only—the registered directors and shareholders might not be genuine people."

Dan was shocked.

Sisoko said, "I know. It's unbelievable in this day and age that there's no validation of identity regarding something so important."

"Didn't you get him on the horse meat scandal then?"

"No. They managed to prove they were just part of a chain and that they weren't doing the substitution. The business was fined, but McNally's direct involvement wasn't proved. Even though he ships horses to Ireland all the time. Looks obvious, but circumstantial evidence doesn't stand up too well in court—especially when he can pay for the best lawyers."

Dan said nothing. He wondered whether this was an oblique reference to his own case. Sisoko was relaxed and friendly. He didn't seem the sort to play subtle games. After a long silence, with Sisoko appraising the loft, Dan offered him another drink.

"I'm fine thanks," the agent said, but showed no sign of leaving.

Dan said, "Perhaps you should try and get this McNally guy for something different—like the FBI caught Al Capone on tax evasion rather than for his actual crimes?"

Sisoko raised an eyebrow then nodded. "Not bad. An alternative crime might get us what we're looking for."

"What about the other name I found—the other investor in Everitt's agency—Redman? Is he a real person?"

"Councillor Redman, responsible for planning application approval. A bit of corruption going on there, it seems. But again no evidence of a link to McNally. We're digging deeper, but he may just be Everitt and Jenkin's genuine business partner." Sisoko tapped his teeth, thinking. Then he said. "A huge amount of illegal drugs come into the country via Cornwall."

"You think they might be coming in via the creeks?"

"Just a possibility," the agent said. His dark brown eyes seemed to deepen before he continued: "Look, I shouldn't say this, but I'm going to. We are making progress on a few cells in various operations. We're gathering evidence so that when we move we take all of it down. I can't say more, because it could jeopardize things, but we're closing in on Mr McNally and his gang. We'll get him soon."

When Sisoko left he shook Dan's hand warmly and said he was glad the boatyard seemed to be thriving. He beamed and hopped down the steps.

Dan waved him goodbye and returned to the studio and manila folder. He spread out the papers and began sorting them, identifying what Wilson would need to investigate and the receipts that Margaret might need for the farm accounts. As he looked, he wondered what Jenkin had been so desperate to find that he'd risk going in after the fire.

At the time he'd thought Michael had been there and hit him. Now he realized it was more likely to have been Jenkin. Michael must have found him outside the kitchen and taken him back to protect him from Jenkin.

The documents yielded nothing special and Dan wondered whether Jenkin had found and already destroyed whatever he was looking for. Perhaps it was even the evidence that his father had spoken of, which would suggest Jenkin may have been involved in the abduction.

Before he thought it through, Dan rang Sisoko's mobile.

"I'm surprised to hear from you already," the man said, road noise behind his voice.

"I need to tell you something in case it prompts anything."

"I'm listening."

"My father—John Searle—well, he said he had evidence that I was guilty. I think he paid someone for it to keep it quiet. But here's the thing: I know I'm innocent of Jade Bridger's abduction, so the evidence is faked."

"And you think maybe the blackmailer is really the guilty person?"

Was Sisoko disappointed? Dan said, "That's exactly what I think."

"Or an opportunist. What sort of evidence are we talking about?"

"I've no idea, but the implication was that it was in the safe. So, did you find anything else or something that could suggest blackmail?"

"No." For a moment there was just the sound of wind and tyres, then: "Obvious thing you should check—go through his bank statements. Though, I have to say, any smart blackmailer wouldn't leave a simple bank trail."

Dan thanked him and laid out the bank statements. It didn't take him long to find something odd he couldn't explain. A payment of £1,000 was made every month with the reference *H Croggan*. The name was familiar but he couldn't immediately place it. He called Margaret.

"Auntie, sorry to disturb you, but does the name Croggan mean anything to you?"

"Of course, it's a fairly common Cornish name. In fact, the farm manager before Geoff Jenkin was a Croggan. Patrick—Pat Croggan." There was silence and Margaret said, "Are you still there, dear?"

"What about an H Croggan?"

"His wife was called Harriet. You must remember them. They had four kids. Two older boys. And two younger children. The young boy was your age I think."

318

"Alan and Elizabeth." Dan remembered them now. He recalled Alan Croggan from primary school, a year below. The girl was a couple of years ahead. They had jug ears like their father and he occasionally saw them around the farm. "I always thought they were grubby and a bit rough. I never had anything to do with them. So why would Dad have been sending money to Harriet Croggan every month?"

"Really? I think I would have known."

"What if it's only been in the last few years—after your time—after you stopped doing the farm accounts?"

"Well yes, but why?"

Dan thought for a while. "What do you know about Pat and Harriet? What happened after they left Searles Farm?"

"Well, let me see… Firstly, I know Pat was unhappy about leaving. I never did understand what your father— I mean John—what John saw in Geoff Jenkin. As I recall… yes, I think Pat was paid off pretty well, but he wasn't happy."

"And where are they now."

"Well there's the thing I heard that Pat died about six years ago. I'm not sure, I lose track of the years. Maybe it was longer ago. I remember Harriet coming to see John afterwards. I heard they'd moved to the Scilly Isles, where she was originally from, virtually retired with a smallholding." She paused. "Maybe John felt sorry for her after Pat died. Maybe that's why he sent her money."

"Auntie?" He waited for her to acknowledge. "I need to talk to her. Do you know anyone who knows how I can get in touch? An address in the Scilly Isles would be good."

Margaret ended the call saying she'd try, and the following day she handed Dan a piece of paper with an

319

address on it. Before she released her grip, she said, "What's this really about, Dan? I hope it's not about that missing girl."

He sat her down on the office sofa, but before he could speak Margaret said, "You and Karen are getting on so well, it'd break my heart if you fell out again, and bringing up that old case will just cause more pain."

"I have to do this. Please understand."

She said nothing and he saw concern on her face.

When she spoke she changed the subject. "By the way, did you find your missing sculpture?"

"*Tin Heart*, you mean?"

"I don't think you ever told me what it was called. Anyway, if you haven't found it, I had a thought. Maybe it went with the others to the gallery at Trelissick. You know what my mind is like! I might have sent it unwittingly. Might be worth asking them if they have it. Could be they don't even know who it belongs to."

"Good idea," he said, "but I don't feel like we quite finished our other conversation. Promise me you won't tell Karen. I don't want her to think I'm still worrying about this thing. Anyway, it's probably nothing. I suspect the old man just felt sorry for Mrs Croggan. He gave money to charity and the church even when he couldn't afford to, so why not give money to an ex-employee who's fallen on hard times."

Margaret was silent for a while then said, "I'll cover for you. Just make it quick and let's hope it's as simple as you say."

FIFTY-SIX

Karen stopped at lights and realized she didn't know where she was or anything about the road or villages she'd been through. Her mind was spinning with what Amber had said about her history, her record. Suddenly it became clear.

A car behind her honked that the lights were green and she waved an apology, drove on and found somewhere to pull over.

She called Truro police and was put through to DS Collick.

"I think it's a policeman," she said after introducing herself.

"Woah, back up. What are you telling me, Ms Chamberlain?"

She took a breath. "After the disappearance of Jade Bridger, I know you think Daniel Searle did it, but it must have been a set-up."

"So, if it wasn't your boyfriend, you're telling me you know who abducted and probably murdered her?"

"He's not my boyfriend, DS Collick. Don't try and undermine me before you've heard what I have to say."

"I'm sorry, I didn't mean it like that. So you have a theory then. Who do you think abducted Jade?"

"I don't have a name, but I think you'll be able to find it out."

"Go on."

"I've just spoken to someone who confirmed the conspiracy to frame Daniel. She was part of it. And I'm pretty sure from what she said that the man must be a policeman. He has some power over her which I think relates to either a previous conviction or a crime she hasn't been convicted for."

"Excuse me if I say it sounds like a stretch, Ms Chamberlain. A little desperate to make Dan seem innocent. You might not be his girlfriend as such, but you're hardly unbiased."

Karen looked at her reflection in the rear-view mirror and wondered how impartial she could be, whether she was connecting imaginary dots.

"Ms Chamberlain, are you still there?"

Karen said, "Are you still looking at Daniel Searle as a suspect or have the police moved on? You know, are the police looking at the theory that her abduction was linked to Everitt and Jenkin?"

"I can't discuss that sort of detail about an ongoing investigation, but I'll tell you what. You tell me who you've been talking to and I'll look into it."

"She needs protection."

"Who, the witness? That can be arranged once I think it's necessary. So who is it?"

"Amber Finnigan."

A pause from Collick. "The name rings a bell."

"She was supposedly Daniel's girlfriend at the time Jade went missing. Only, she used the name Finn then. It was part of the set-up."

Again a pause. "I think it best that you come down and give us a formal statement. Actually, if this is true, we better just keep it between us before I can investigate and determine whether it's genuine and she does need protection. Where are you?"

Karen looked around. "About half a mile east of Lostwithiel."

"Look, I tell you what, I'm about to go up to Searles Farm to pick up some papers from Geoff Jenkin's office. I'll meet you there in say thirty minutes?"

FIFTY-SEVEN

The Skybus flight from Newquay to St Mary's in the
Scilly's felt longer than the thirty minutes his watch said
it took. An uncomfortable seat and constant droning
from the twin propellers and buffeting wind made Dan
wonder if a phone call would have been better.

The handful of passengers either walked into the
capital or were collected, so Dan walked straight to the
front of the taxi rank and a row of expectant drivers.

"Anywhere on the island for five pounds," the driver
said as Dan got in.

He gave the address and earned a "Ah, Harriet
Croggan's place" in response. Then he saw the driver
studying him in the mirror as he pulled away.

"You know her then?"

"The Croggans? Sure. Everyone knows pretty much
everyone on the island. You a relative?"

"Nope, just a quick visit."

"Is it Harriet or one of her boys you're after?" He
continued to glance back and Dan wondered just how
much attention was being paid to the road.

"Harriet."

"You know them?"

"Not at all."

The taxi driver pulled a face in the mirror that Dan couldn't interpret. "She's a tough one, is all. Just a word to the wise." The taxi stopped.

"Here already?" They'd travelled less than a couple of miles and were outside a stone-built house fronted by high stone walls and hedges.

Dan handed the taxi driver a five pound note and, when the man made no move to offer change, got out and stood at the gate. Either side was a stone bench, the kind used by smallholdings to display their wares, although there was no sign of use.

The driver hadn't moved. He wound down the window. "Want me to wait?"

Dan was about to say "no" when he had an idea. Leaning in, he said, "How much?"

"Depends how long, but let's say five pounds for every fifteen minutes. And then four back to the airport."

Dan took out his iPhone. "Can you use this as a video recorder?"

"You show me what to do and I'll try and do it." He shrugged. "For a price."

"OK, here's the deal for you: you video my meeting and I'll pay you twenty quid. Twenty quid whether it's thirty minutes or two minutes."

"Plus the waiting time?" the driver asked, his eyes already glistening.

"Plus the waiting time."

"Thirty."

Dan accepted and the man got out of the car. After a couple of practices with the phone, Dan was happy the taxi driver could do it. He positioned him by the wall where there was enough gap in the hedge to film the door clearly.

"Don't start until someone answers the door."

325

Dan opened the gate and walked up the path to a heavy wooden door. After glancing in a window to check no one was looking, he ducked around the left-hand side where he found a shed and backyard. Beyond that he could see a field of over three acres broken up into regular patches, growing vegetables mostly. On the other side of the house he found a once-white caravan that looked like it hadn't moved for decades. On the far right he could see a couple of people working the field—a woman and a young boy, he judged.

Returning to the door, he glanced at the taxi driver, checked the man was watching, gave a thumbs-up, and knocked.

A woman, Dan guessed her to be late sixties, answered. She had a weathered face and the hint of a smile.

"Mrs Croggan? Harriett Croggan?"

"Yes." She rubbed soiled hands on an apron, still smiling. "Can I help you?"

"I'm Dan Searle."

The woman's face froze with hard edges. "What are you doing here?"

"My dad—John Searle—well, he died a few weeks ago and I wondered…"

"I heard." She swivelled and called into the gloom behind her, "Trevor!"

Dan said, "I know your husband used to be the farm manager."

A man appeared beside Mrs Croggan, his face ruddy and enquiring, something familiar about it, though he didn't look like the woman. Dan guessed this was Trevor.

Trevor said, "Ma?"

"John Searle's son."

The man stepped around her, close enough to punch Dan, his large hands clenched. "What do you want?"

"I want to know why my dad was paying a grand a month to your mum."

The old woman disappeared from the doorway. Dan couldn't see where she'd gone.

"You know what your old man did to us?" Trevor's voice bristled with pent-up anger. "He was paying for ruining us. Now, before you cause Ma any more upset, you'd better get off her doorstep."

"I just…"

Trevor stepped forward, forcing Dan back.

"Just bugger off!" Trevor stiff-armed Dan on the shoulder causing him to spin.

"OK. OK, I'm going." He walked to the gate, sensing Trevor right behind him. And then a hand jabbed him between the shoulder blades so that he stumbled out into the street.

"What the…?" Trevor glared at the taxi driver recording with the iPhone. "What do you think you're doing?"

The driver didn't hesitate. He shimmied around the bonnet of his taxi and scrambled in. Dan jumped in beside him just as Trevor slammed his hand on the roof.

"Go! Go!" Dan shouted above the noise, but the driver didn't need instructions. The car, which had probably never been over thirty in its life, did a wheelspin and jammed Dan into his seat.

"Jesus!" the driver said. "My bloody hands are shaking. What the hell did you say to them?"

Dan shook his head. He'd expected a difficult conversation, possibly with Mrs Croggan asking for more money, but he hadn't anticipated aggression. "I have no idea."

Later, waiting for the flight back to Newquay, he took out the phone and watched the video over and over. The reaction really didn't make sense, and the more he thought about it, the more familiar Trevor looked.

He called Margaret. "Auntie, what do you know about Harriet Croggan's boys?"

"Well, when she was at the farm there were four kids, three boys and a girl. We talked about this before, didn't we? The older boys were quite a bit older than you. Maybe the younger one could have been your friend—but you didn't want anything to do with him. And the older ones were too old, I guess."

"Were they into anything dodgy?"

"What do you mean?"

"Did you think they were bad, I guess?"

"I don't know, dear. I just remember you avoided them. I think they taunted you a bit maybe."

Dan felt there was a connection he wasn't making. Then he had an idea. "What was Harriet Groggan's maiden name?"

"I've no idea. I didn't really know them. Why do you ask?"

"Just wondered whether I know the son, Trevor, by a different name." He noticed his gate was announced, boarding soon.

Margaret said, "Maybe Trevor was one of her sons from the first marriage. I've a vague recollection that the two eldest weren't Pat Croggan's."

"How about her previous married name?"

"Would you like me to find out, dear? Will probably only take a few minutes."

"Please. Then call me back."

Dan had a coil in his stomach as he waited. A sense of unease pulled at his gut. He sent a text message to

328

Karen, hoping she was having a good day and that the interview had gone well.

The announcer called passengers forward for the flight to Newquay. He stepped forward, six people in the queue. His phone rang.

"Margaret?"

"You won't believe the coincidence," she said.

The crew member checked Dan's boarding pass and asked him to end the call. "One second," he said to her frown.

Margaret said, "I asked Phyllis Cook. She knows everything. She even knew of the Upshalls, Harriet Croggan's parents."

"Sir!" the crew member said. "If you don't end the call this minute, you will not be able to board the flight."

Dan held up one finger. He couldn't breathe, the coil in his stomach too large, too tight.

Margaret was speaking. "Well, here's the thing. Before Pat Croggan, Harriet was married to a man called Arthur Collick."

FIFTY-EIGHT

The front door of Jenkin's house was ajar, although Karen couldn't see Detective Sergeant Collick's BMW. She pushed the door and called out, "Hello?"

After no response, she swung the door fully open.

She leaned in. Beyond the hall, she could see a kitchen with a coat over a chair.

"Hello? Is there anybody here?"

Something like the sound of footsteps came from inside, but far off.

"Detective Sergeant?" She stepped into the hall and walked to the stairs. She looked up and listened. Then she heard the sound again and followed it around the foot of the stairs into a room with a door at the far side. This door was partially open, and within four paces she was holding the door knob and leaning in.

Carpet became black and white linoleum floor tiles. It appeared to be another entrance hall with its own staircase. There was an odd, almost warm smell, like a second-hand bookshop.

Floorboards creaked overhead.

"Detective?"

"Come up," a voice called back, and Karen mounted the stairs, holding onto the wooden banister as the treads squeaked beneath her feet. Near the top, she realized that all the light was from a bulb rather than the window ahead. Although curtains hung either side, white boarding was tacked to the frame.

"I'm in the second bedroom," the voice said, and she followed it along a carpeted landing.

Collick was sitting on a single bed with a bare mattress, flicking through a pile of papers, an open tin box beside him. The carpet had been peeled back and a section of floorboards taken up. He looked up as she approached.

"Amazing what you find," he said.

She glanced around and noted the boarded window here too. "What is this place?"

"A house within a house. The door you came in through downstairs is the only way in or out. The windows are all boarded up and an old front door is permanently sealed."

"But why?"

A smile flickered on the detective's face. "I'll show you afterwards. You *will* be amazed, but it all makes sense... kind of." He pointed to an under-stuffed armchair in the corner for Karen to sit on and he swivelled on the bed so that he was facing her.

He steepled his fingers in front of his lips. "I apologize for making you go through this again, but I'm more focused now, so tell me what you've found out."

"I managed to track down Daniel's ex-girlfriend—the one from the time Jade Bridger disappeared."

Collick nodded slowly. "You make it sound like she was difficult to find?"

Karen explained that the girl had given Daniel a false name to hide her past and that she'd discovered it with help from an ex-colleague.

"Impressive." Collick's prayer-like hands stroked his beard as he spoke. "And that was how you discovered the girl had a—what shall we call it—a less than reputable past?"

Amber had said, *You can't help me. No one can.* She'd been afraid of either what she'd done or a person. Karen said, "She's being controlled."

"And you think it's a policeman who's controlling her in some way, right?" He waited for Karen to nod. "Did she give you a name? Did she even actually say it was a policeman?"

"Well not exactly, but because of her past—"

"No name."

Karen leaned forward. "You can check the records, though. You can see if someone was dealing with her, maybe a reported crime that an officer seems to have ignored?"

"Yes I can do that, but tell me again, you think he's involved because…?"

Karen told him about the girl's confession, that she'd been asked to be Daniel's girlfriend and then have sex. "She gave him the semen that was used as the DNA evidence on Jade's top."

"We can't say that for sure. You're drawing conclusions without direct evidence. However weird, it's one thing to take a sample of a man's semen, but it's quite another to use it in relation to a crime."

Karen shook her head. Surely he could see the obvious link? If DS Collick couldn't see it then surely a jury would.

"Why else would someone want Daniel's semen?" she asked, and then regretted the sharpness of her tone.

Collick shrugged. "There are some weird people out there. You wouldn't believe…"

"I don't."

"You know about Deborah?" Collick asked. "Of course you do. Well I wouldn't be surprised if she wanted to get pregnant."

"I agree, she wanted a baby so tricked Daniel and then retaliated when he didn't want to go along with it. But that's totally different."

"How so?"

"Whoever arranged for Amber to be Daniel's girlfriend and then take the semen planned this. And if you follow the logical conclusion then he had something to do with Jade's disappearance too. He was just waiting for the right time."

Collick sighed and was about to respond when his phone rang.

"Excuse me, I have to take this." He stood and walked out onto the landing.

Karen could no longer see him but, although hushed, his voice was clear enough. When he answered he said, "What's up?"

The other person must have spoken, then Collick said, "I understand. That changes things." Then: "Yes." He was quiet again, presumably listening, until he said, "Don't worry, I have insurance." He listened again, agreed and then ended the call.

For the first time, Karen noticed that some of the papers on the bed looked like agreements, legal documents perhaps. She turned, and Collick stood in the doorway, looking from the bed to her.

He said, "What do you hope to achieve?" His voice was flat with no hint of what he expected her to say.

"I know without a doubt that Daniel is innocent." She stood up. "Something's been going on. Someone set him up and I just want you to see that it's a real possibility and investigate it."

"OK, Karen"—his poker face creased into a smile—"for you, I'll do just that." He collected the sheaf of papers, put them into the tin and said, "Right, let me show you what's so interesting about this house." He raised his eyebrows. "You really will be amazed."

Karen followed the detective down the stairs. He pointed out the windows and explained that from the outside they just looked dark, so no one would guess they were boarded. He mentioned the front door being sealed as well and said, "This is where Jenkin used to keep his girls—the favoured ones. I'm sure you read about what he was up to." Collick was standing by the understairs cupboard and opened the door. The space was shallow and empty.

Karen waited.

Collick reached forward and pushed the wall. It opened stiffly. The dim light showed steps.

"A basement?"

Collick flicked on a dim yellow light and descended. "From the papers you'd think modern slavery was a recent development, but Jenkin had it sussed years ago. OK, he was small time, one girl at a time, starting out by treating them well, getting them out of the farm workers' communal Portakabin and into their own house. Grooming them probably. No doubt they felt like girlfriends at first."

At the foot of the stairs he turned the handle of another door and stepped into the basement. "And then he introduced them to his special room."

Karen couldn't see anything at first, and Collick's proximity compelled her to step forward into the gloom. The room was small, maybe ten by fifteen feet. She could make out a single bed and something dangling from the wall. A click of a switch and then pale light brought detail. The hanging thing was just a black cloak.

The bed was just a metal frame, old, the type with a wire base and no mattress. It swivelled and...

"Oh my God!" she gasped. There were belts tied on to the bedframe, like restraints.

The door behind her shut and then she heard a key turn.

Collick's breath was hot on her neck. He said, "I knew you'd be impressed."

FIFTY-NINE

Light bowed through the plastic window, making the expanse of water appear even bigger. In the distance, Land's End, the westernmost point of the English mainland, was an illusory hint of dark grey. Dan found himself staring at the distorted shifting sea like this was the whole microcosmic world.

The reason he'd thought Trevor was familiar was the similarity between him and Detective Sergeant Collick. Gary Collick. They were the older boys from the farm.

Back then they were Gary and Trevor Croggan. Of course, they left when Pat Croggan had lost his job. Dan must have been eleven or twelve at the time. He recalled seeing the removal van outside the house Jenkin had moved into. Later, his father had explained that Geoff Jenkin was the new farm manager.

What had happened? Why had John Searle replaced Pat Croggan with the awful Jenkin?

Looking back, maybe it was obvious something was going on, but as a child he hadn't questioned it or, if he had the answers, they hadn't been significant enough to remember. Was it something the old farm manager had done? Margaret said Pat Croggan had died. Did Gary and Trevor blame Dan for what had happened in some way? Could it be something like that? In the bubble of glass, his eyes reflected deep thought but no insight.

Karen was smart. If only he'd involved her. Perhaps if they'd travelled together she'd have been able to talk to Harriet Croggan, to get her to open up, to get her to explain why his father had been paying her a thousand pounds a month.

Mrs Croggan must have known it had stopped. Perhaps that was why Detective Sergeant Collick hated Dan so much. Perhaps that was why he was so determined Dan was guilty of abducting Jade Bridger. Was the detective's anger and prejudice getting in the way of common sense?

A large passenger returned to the seat in front, his weight pushing the chair against Dan's knees.

Dan looked out of the window again. Did it make sense that the detective would hate him because of the past? Again he wished he was looking at, and talking to, Karen.

He tried to imagine her talking through the problem, discussing it, dissecting it in her analytical way. The timeline was wrong. His dad was still paying the money when Collick came after him for Jade's disappearance. Surely he knew about the money going to his mother and could guess his father would be upset. That thought made Dan realize that his father would have known that Collick was the boy they'd known as Gary Croggan. Was that why his father had stopped paying the money? He focused on the propeller and thought his mind was a similar blur.

They were over land now with less than ten minutes to go. He'd call Karen when he landed to talk it through. She'd get it. She'd work out why Harriet Croggan had been unhappy to see him on her doorstep. Surely Harriet Croggan should have welcomed meeting Dan. She could have tried to persuade him to resume the payments. It would have been an opportunity to pressure him. Trevor was a labourer, a strong-looking guy, surely he would have been better off threatening Dan, pressing him for money, rather than throwing him off the property?

Dan sat back, closed his eyes and felt the plane begin its descent. He found himself visualising Harriet Croggan's grey stone house and its plot of agricultural land. Was it a comedown from the position at the farm or was it better to have your own land however small? He saw the walls and bushes and outbuilding with its yard and the old caravan. It reminded him of the days when there'd been the Portakabins on Searles Farm for the itinerant workers. It was tough work for labourers on the farm, but nothing like it must be on Croggan's plot without farm machinery. He'd seen nothing mechanical. The only vehicles had been a blue Fiesta, spotted with rust and patched up, and one of those little three-wheeler trucks, presumably for transporting the farm produce. He thought about the people he'd seen in the field, probably working by hand, backbreaking stuff, maybe harder than any of the workers on Searles had for a hundred years. Was that the attraction of living on a remote, windswept island? Escape, maybe.

He thought back to the day Karen had left him over five years ago. They hadn't rowed and he'd guessed it was coming. They sat across the coffee table from one another and she had used the word *escape,* but in the opposite sense. She had felt trapped in provincial Cornwall, unable to breathe, unable to feel challenged, wanting the maximum out of life. And yet she was back. Was it the failure of her relationship with Matt or a desire to return? He was afraid to ask. And in that moment he realized that he had to ask, had to talk about everything with Karen. Perhaps if he'd been able to talk about feelings, to understand hers, she'd never have left. He knew he'd been afraid to talk, afraid that by asking he'd make the worst happen, make her leave, but now he realized how deluded that was.

SIXTY

"This was a punishment room," Collick said. "Ma used to put us down here if we weren't good. It didn't happen very often because we were so afraid. You see, it wasn't just about being tied to the bed. It was about the Buccaboo. She said he lived down here—under the stairs—under the house. The black cloak was his. I used to lie here watching that cloak, terrified it would move, terrified it would suddenly fill out and become the Buccaboo."

"Why?" Karen croaked, her throat raw from the belt across her neck.

"I said. It was to keep us in check. Be good or the Buccaboo will eat your soul."

"No—" Karen closed her eyes, tried to relax. "Why are you doing this to me?"

Collick laughed. "Well it isn't so the Buccaboo can eat your soul, I'll tell you that for free." He walked around the bed and made sure the bindings were as tight as they'd go.

Horses tense when they're being saddled, they expand their chests so that the straps won't be too tight. She'd learned that from riding lessons as a kid. When Collick had first bound her, she'd tried to make her muscles big, to tense and hold her breath. The trick with a horse was to tighten, wait and tighten again as they relaxed. Now her body weakened and Collick was quick to tighten the straps a notch.

The Skybus hit the runway with such a jolt that Dan's head and neck felt like luggage had fallen on him from the overhead.

Checking that no one could see, he surreptitiously took out his phone, switched off flight mode and texted Karen. Landed. I'll call you when I leave the car park. Hope the interview went well x

As he climbed into his car and connected an earpiece to his phone, Dan wondered why Karen hadn't left him a message about how the interview had gone. Hadn't the interview started almost three hours ago? Either things were going so well she hadn't finished, or it had gone too badly to talk about on the phone.

He dialled her number and was relieved she answered after a few rings.

"Did it go badly?" he began.

"It's DS Collick, Dan. I'm here with Karen and she's too upset to speak to you right now."

Dan negotiated the car park exit barrier, sucked in two breaths and then said, "What's going on?"

"Calm down. There have been developments."

"Too right," Dan snapped back. "I've been to your mother's property on the Isle."

Collick's voice remained flat. "I know, but it's not about that."

Dan waited a beat. "So, what's it about then?"

"Evidence. I found the evidence at Jenkin's place. I reckon he stole it from your father. It was with the things from the safe."

341

A car coming the other way swerved and Dan realized he'd crossed the central line, not paying attention to the road. He pulled over, heart thudding.

"What are you talking about, Collick? There's no evidence because I didn't do it! You're trying to stitch me up, aren't you?"

When Collick didn't respond straight away, Dan added: "You there, Collick?"

"I was just going to say you should protest your innocence to your girlfriend. She's as convinced by the evidence as I think your old man was. Oh dear, she's shaking her head, too upset to even talk to you right now."

"What bloody evidence do you think you have?"

"In my hand I have a letter from the girl—from Jade Bridger to you, Dan."

"I never received a letter from her."

"Lizzy Bridger has confirmed it's legit, that it's Jade's handwriting. And *she* wouldn't want to stitch you up, not after you sort of saved her from Jenkin, now would she?"

Dan said nothing.

"It's a love letter, Dan. In it Jade refers to something you gave her as a token of your love—"

"This is rubbish!"

"You gave her a sculpture—something she refers to as *Tin Heart*—like it was an engagement gift or something."

The missing sculpture. Dan's mind was a whir. He hadn't given the sculpture to anyone and he certainly hadn't received a letter from Jade. Then, like a cycle gear engaging, it started to make sense. He said, "*You* know the letter's a fake."

"I don't—"

"Let me talk to Karen."

"I've got it on speaker, Dan, and she's shaking her head. You'll have to be more convincing than that. In fact you'd better convince me before you're picked up. There's a warrant for your arrest, but I'll let you explain to me first. Tell me why it's not evidence of grooming."

"Where?"

"At your old man's place. The farm."

The phone went dead and Dan stared at it for a moment before shunting the car into first and burning rubber.

SIXTY-ONE

Dan's car slewed to a halt outside the kitchen. He jumped out and looked desperately for any sign of Collick. Slamming his hand on the roof he pulled out his phone, ready to dial, fingers shaking. An incoming call from a withheld number interrupted him.

"Dan."

"Collick," Dan said, looking about. Somehow Collick must have known he'd arrived. The timing was too perfect. "Where are you, Collick?"

"Let's stop the pretence. You know, don't you?"

"Know that you set me up? Know that it was you from the start?"

"It wasn't personal."

Dan laughed, his voice sounding robotic. "Wasn't personal? How can it have been anything other than personal, you arsehole?"

"It was always about your old man, not you, not really. But I guess it's beyond that now. So yes, it has become personal. What made you realize?"

"Because the sculpture you claim I gave to Jade was in my studio on the night she disappeared. In fact, it was still there when I was arrested. I hadn't catalogued it and even Margaret didn't know what it was called and never saw it. It didn't go to the gallery at Trelissick. It was never sold. I know I didn't give it to Jade. So someone is using it to frame me again. They took it. No one other than Margaret had access to my home afterwards, no one that is except for the police—you and your team—who crawled all over it after I'd been arrested. That's why it mysteriously disappeared, isn't it? *You* took it and…" Suddenly another piece dropped into place.

Collick said nothing.

"Oh my God! You abducted Jade!"

"OK, here's the thing," Collick said, his voice changing like he had switched to an impersonal monologue, like a local radio station newsreader. "I need you to do something for me. Your dad owes me. He paid the first instalment for the evidence, but I know he's got more. He thought he was going to have to pay for your legal defence. A criminal defence costs big money."

"How much are we talking about?"

"A hundred grand at least. I know what you're thinking. You've been through his affairs and didn't find that sort of money. Well it didn't go through his bank or show up as an investment, because he kept it off the books. That's what I insisted for the initial instalment. He has it as gold bars and they're somewhere in the house."

"I don't think so." But as he said it, Dan was already pulling the police tape from the kitchen door.

"Just go in and look. And, in case you need some extra incentive, I've got someone who'd like to say a word."

Karen's scream froze Dan's blood. There were words but too distorted, too desperate to make any sense.

"Karen!" His voice filled the kitchen and echoed somewhere in the main house. He steadied himself on the soot-coated worktop and tried to sound composed when he next spoke. "What have you done to her?"

"Just bought myself a little insurance, that's all." He paused and Dan knew he was enjoying the moment, Dan's distress at not knowing what he'd done—what he could do—to Karen. "Would you like to talk to her...? Oh, sorry, you can't. She's a little tied up at the moment." His laugh was like a cheese grater on Dan's heart.

"You sick—"

"Seriously though. It's quite a clever contraption because the more she struggles, the tighter it gets. I would guess she could last about an hour before she either suffocates or dies by cutting off the blood to the brain. You know I'm not a doctor, so it's only a guess, mind. But I reckon you have an hour to find the safe and bring me the contents." He laughed again. "Oh, sorry, I almost forgot. You had an hour starting about twenty minutes ago. I'd hurry if I were you."

Dan said nothing, his mind trying to process options.

Collick interrupted his thoughts. "I know what you're thinking, Dan. You're considering calling the police. Well, be my guest. Remember, they're looking for you. DC Bateman knows about the evidence and believes you're guilty. You start involving them and you'll have questions to answer. By the time you convince them to look for Karen, it'll be far too late." He seemed to want Dan to think about that for a second before adding: "And I should say that when they find her there will be enough evidence to make them believe you did that too. They'd see that trying to divert the attention to me was a clever ploy. You'll say I fabricated evidence that you were guilty of abducting Jade Bridger and had abducted and killed your girlfriend. It'll be a couple of minutes before I convince them otherwise. Oh, and Dan?"

"Yes," he said, his voice lost in his throat.

"You've now got about thirty-five minutes. Good luck." Collick ended the call.

Dan tested a tap for water. It worked. He splashed his face, and gulped air to calm himself and think.

Would the NCA see Collick was framing him? It could be his only chance. He dialled Sisoko's number but got voicemail. He left a hurried message and hoped it made sense. He checked the time on the phone before sticking it into his pocket.

He walked through to the hall, his feet slack-slacking on the drying grey residue on the floor. Where would his father keep something precious other than in the safe? He made his way to the study.

It had been ripped apart and floorboards torn up. Someone had been here since the fire. He could think of only one explanation: Collick had been here looking for the gold. He stood in the doorway. It would make sense, using the safe as a distraction for the treasures buried beneath it. He looked around the room and tried to think like the man he'd grown up believing to be his father. The gold would be downstairs, since John couldn't get up to the first floor without assistance. His downstairs bedroom, then.

Dan opened the door to the room where John had slept. The part-burnt bed and the black molten mess were still there. He found an exposed, split floorboard, got his fingernails underneath and tugged.

Cursing his failure, he glanced around, spotted a clothes rail and dug that into the boards. On the second wrench, it came free. He pulled up another and another, exposing earth and debris but nothing else. He sat back and blinked sweat from his eyes.

He was wasting time. If there was something under the boards, a random search could take hours. John

Searle was a rational man above all things. There had to be a more logical place.

Dan returned to the study and stood at the door looking at the open safe, now lopsided on broken floorboards and joists. He tried to take himself back to the confrontation with his father. They had argued about the fake evidence that his father had bought to protect him. John had been agitated, glancing in the direction of the safe when Dan said he wanted to see the evidence. Or had he?

Dan positioned himself where his father had been and imagined he was looking at himself in the study. Yes the old man had looked in the direction of the safe, but he'd glanced away first. Dan glanced to his right. The painting of his great-grandfather looked back, impassionate.

The damn painting, specifically mentioned in the will.

All these years—could it be? Dan felt the edge of the painting and brittle, damaged wood came away. Then his fingers touched cold metal. He worked his fingers around the circumference, pulling, but the painting was fixed firmly to the wall. And then something clicked. A push had released a catch and the painting swung on the left to reveal a safe set into the wall.

Holding his breath, he turned the dial to his mother's birthdate. It opened. Inside was a pile of documents and gold bars.

Dan snatched up his phone and went to dial Collick, but the previous number had been withheld. Instead he dialled Karen.

Collick answered.

"I've found it. I've found it." Dan swallowed adrenaline. "Release her and I'll—"

Collick cut him off. "You have about five minutes to get it to me." He was quiet for a moment and then added: "She's looking rather pale. I'd hurry if I were you."

"Where the hell are you? You need—"

"Tut tut, Dan. I expected you to work it out. Stop talking and bring me everything you've found. I'm at Jenkin's old place... My folk's old place."

"I want to know she's still breathing. Let me—"

"Seven minutes." Collick ended the call.

Dan ran, slipped on the remains of the lounge boards, banged his shin but kept going.

In the kitchen he pulled a couple of reinforced shopping bags from a cupboard. He thought he heard a gunshot and glanced out of the window, but seeing nothing, he rushed back to the safe behind the picture.

There were about twenty small gold bars in the confined space behind the picture. He unceremoniously scooped them out and dropped them into the bags. A bundle of documents was tied with a green ribbons. He chucked it on top and set off again, this time taking a little more care to cross the lounge. Reaching his car, he just threw the heavy bags onto the passenger seat and jammed the gears in reverse. Then forward, he accelerated hard to the main road, slamming on his breaks just in time to stop, check the road was clear, turn and press his foot hard to the floor again.

With half an eye on driving, he held up his phone and tried Sisoko again. No answer.

Ahead, he saw a blue car on his side of the road, but it was beyond the second turning to the farm which came up fast and Dan skidded into the entrance, the rear slewing and crunching into the gate post. The Audi bounced off it and he kept going until Jenkin's house loomed beyond the trees.

Collick's purple BMW was there and he skidded to a halt next to it. He grabbed the bags and scrambled out.

There was probably a smart play, something like leaving the bags or maybe one bag in the car and confronting Collick first. But he couldn't think of what to do. Karen was dying in there and if he played games with Collick, it might then be too late to save her. If Collick had killed Jade Bridger to get what he wanted, then Dan had no doubt he'd allow Karen to die.

Collick was sitting in the kitchen, facing the door, hands below the kitchen table. As Dan stepped forward he realized the door between them had a hole punched through it the size of a dinner plate, surrounded by a peppering of holes from shot. There was a shotgun on the table as well as an open grey tin and a legal-looking document.

Dan dropped the bags. "Where is she?"

"Not here. Put the bags up here, I want to be sure you've got it all."

"Where the hell is she?" Dan banged his hands on the table. "If she dies—"

"If she dies, it'll be your fault. Now calm down and empty those bags on the table." Collick brought his hands above the table and pointed a gun at Dan. "Do it, now."

Without taking his eyes off the detective, Dan turned the first bag upside down and the documents and gold bars spewed out. He picked up the second and wondered whether he could swing it at Collick before he pulled the trigger.

"Don't even think about it," Collick said. "I can shoot faster than you can either throw a bag or reach the shotgun. But be my guest. However, it'll be pointless because, for the moment, Karen is fine. Providing you do as I ask, nothing will happen to her."

Dan emptied the contents and let the bags fall to the floor. "What now?"

"This house wasn't Jenkin's, it was ours. My brother and I used to have the section Jenkin defiled with his sordid little games. This was Pat Croggan's house and your father took it away from us, took away my father's dignity. Do you know how hard it is for a farm manager to find another position? Do you?" Collick shook his head, his brow creased. "It killed him, you know. We had to go back to where Ma came from and eke out a living from land that her folks left her."

Collick pointed to the papers in front of him and said, "Sit down, I need you to sign something and then we're done."

"What is it?"

"A transfer document for the deeds to this house." He pointed to a signature on the last page. "It's already been witnessed by a solicitor, so all you need to do is sign it."

As Dan sat and picked up a pen, Collick continued: "The deeds for this house were always separate, from when Searles was Gwidden Farm—in fact it was two farms. Funny that they were in this house all along, hidden under the floorboards in my old bedroom. You see, Pat Croggan wasn't as dumb as your old man thought. He found those deeds and kept them just in case."

Dan signed the legal papers and slid them back to Collick. "So what? You intend your family to come back and work this half of the farm again?"

Collick scoffed. "It's the best half. The animals are all here, the new milking shed's here—again a smart move by Pat Croggan to bring it from Searles onto this half of the farm. But no, I don't intend to farm it. Not now. It's got to be worth at least a million, so I'll just sell."

Dan nodded. He'd planned the same thing; he had no love for the farm, and sharing half with Auntie Margaret

351

felt like the right thing to do. He watched Collick's eyes and tried to stay calm while all the time his mind was screaming *Find her!*

He shouted, "Karen?"

Collick laughed.

Dan ran out of the kitchen shouting her name and listening. He heard nothing.

He ran from room to room in the main house and then back into the kitchen, realising the locked door was now open. He tore into the adjoining house still shouting. He quickly confirmed she wasn't upstairs and then found the basement room.

Shaking and sick to the stomach, he returned to the kitchen.

"She's not here," Collick said. "Look, I lied about the deadline. Karen's fine for the moment."

"Where is she?"

"Let's talk first. Let's talk about Jade."

Collick was crazy. He was sweating and there was a strange pallor to his skin. Dan tried to calm his racing heart. "Fine, tell me about your clever plan to have me put away for Jade's abduction—"

"That was never really my plan, you idiot. It was all about getting you off and your father paying for it. He'd have eventually given me all his money and signed over the deeds himself if he hadn't gone and burned himself to death."

"But the lawyers got me off."

"Yes they did. I didn't reckon on your old man paying for the best, who'd realize the DNA was tainted. Stupid girl was supposed to have a condom, not have her own DNA mixed in it. But then I was going to have the evidence tainted anyway, once your old man had paid the first instalment."

"And that's why there was the two-day gap?"

"That and the need to get the evidence planted without suspicion. The love letter from Jade was just a backup plan."

"OK, all very clever and you've done it, so now tell me where Karen is."

Collick pulled a disappointed face. "Don't you want to know the truth?" His eyes lost focus as he explained more. "Lizzy was never right and that Steve Bridger is a waste of skin. We knew Jade wanted to escape, and Ma wanted her with family. After all, she isn't Bridger's anyway. So the plan was to set you up—get our revenge—and rescue Jade at the same time."

"You abducted her. She wouldn't have trusted any random person. She trusted you, a policeman. You groomed her for it, didn't you? Just like you set me up with a girlfriend. What I don't know is what you did with her." And then something clicked. "Wait! She was family. Lizzy is your sister. She's Elizabeth."

Collick laughed mirthlessly. "Just worked that out, have we?"

And then Dan put it together. Tom had seen the car and asked Ted Bryant to be the witness. The blue car with the partial registration TAB. He said, "I should have realized. You said you'd found the car that was parked at Mizzen Mast Cottage, but you only knew part of the number plate and there was no description other than blue."

Collick smiled.

Dan remembered the Fiesta outside the Croggan's house on the island. He said, "It was your mother's car, wasn't it? You both met her on Mizzen Green and took her to the Scilly Isles."

"Close, but no cigar. Right about the car, wrong about me. It was Trevor, but he didn't take her. She never turned up. Jack Tanner must have seen my mum with him and assumed it was you and Jade."

"So Jade didn't go back down the path to the green."

"No, because you met her. You switched off the security system and helped her run away. Where is she?"

"For Christ's sake, Collick, I did not do it!"

"Is that your final word?"

Collick stood up, the gun pointed at Dan's head. The man's left arm dripped blood, his sleeve in tatters.

Dan took a deep breath. "Tell me. Tell me what you've done with Karen?"

Collick smiled again and Dan read something in the man's eyes. He was crazy and was going to shoot him. Collick had shot himself as though he'd been shot at. And in that instant Dan realized it was never Collick's intention to let him go. He would say that Dan fired first and Collick retaliated, aiming to wound, but the injury affected him. Dan was killed. And then, somehow, the detective was going to make it look like Dan was the bad guy.

Collick smiled and pointed at the detritus on the table. "I caught you stealing this gold and other stuff you found under the floorboards in my old bedroom. You came at me with your shotgun—yes it's from your farm—and I defended myself."

He said something else, but Dan wasn't listening. He'd dropped one hand low to hold a table leg. Throwing himself sideways he pushed off from the table, but too late he realized the table was far too heavy to throw over. The chair toppled and Dan found himself going with it.

Collick was smiling. "Self-defence," he said, aiming the gun.

Dan squeezed his eyes shut and his body hit the floor before his head. Pain from his damaged ribs burned white hot and the gun went off just as the back of his head hit the stone floor.

SIXTY-TWO

Dan's ears rang with the explosion, but he couldn't feel anything except the pain in his chest. Was it shock? Was this what the moment of death felt like?

And then his hearing rushed back. Noise. Shouting. Through it he heard "DOWN! STAY DOWN!"

Dan opened his eyes, saw blurred black shoes and trousers. Then another pair of feet and legs. He turned his head, saw a swarm of people in the room, guns out, pointing with them though not at him. Hands went under his arms and he was helped to his feet. A big guy, his dark face set both serious and concerned.

"Sisoko," Dan choked.

Sisoko gave a curt nod but looked at the prone body on the other side of the table. Another man bent over Collick applying pressure to a wound in his chest.

Dan took a step towards the door and staggered. Sisoko reached out and held him up.

"Don't try to go anywhere," the officer said.

"Karen's been kidnapped." Dan tried to sound calmer than he felt. He needed to persuade Sisoko, to get away, to find Karen.

Sisoko held up a finger. "I need an explanation. You can't—"

"OK, look." Dan gulped air. "Collick wasn't working alone. He had Karen here... captive, but he must have had help." He wondered if he was gabbling and not making sense. "He... look at the set-up. Somehow he shot himself in the arm with the shotgun. And the shot went through the door. Look where it is. It's a set-up. Collick couldn't have shot through the door *and* his arm without help. It's his brother." And as he said it he remembered the blue car in the road. He pulled out his phone. It was still connected to Sisoko's. When he'd rung the officer on the way to meet Collick he'd left it connected to voicemail so the confrontation would be heard or recorded.

Dan ended the call and brought up the video the taxi driver had taken. He froze the image as the camera followed Dan from the house and captured the back of the car. The one with the rust patches.

"There," he said, "It's a dark blue Fiesta." He'd hoped to be able to see part of the registration number but couldn't. If only he'd thought to check, thought to look for the letters Tom had seen. Dan gave Sisoko an imploring look. "I need to go."

"You're in no state—"

"I need to go!"

The senior investigating officer nodded to another man. "Davis, go with him."

Dan was already heading for the door—as fast as his painful ribs would let him. Outside, he cursed as he saw that his car was blocked in.

Davis came up behind and pointed to the furthest vehicle. "That one. Get in the passenger seat, I'm driving."

The doors of the grey Ford Taurus were already open. Dan scooted in and slammed the door shut.

357

"Where are we going?" Davis asked, gunning the engine and accelerating down the track.

"Penzance. The ferry to the Isles of Scilly. That's where he's taking her."

Davis drove maybe faster than Dan would have. Flashing lights on the dash showed he had the blue strobes on.

"How much of a head start has he got?"

Dan checked the time. "Almost twenty-five minutes. He could be over halfway."

Davis called someone, got put through to the Penzance police and provided details. He instructed them to provide an armed response. After the call he said, "We have a choice: cross-country shortcut or main road."

There was no hesitation. "Shortcut."

Davis turned off the main road. "We'll cut across and join the A30 further along. Hold on then," he said, and hit the siren.

Dan's fingers dug into the leather of the seat as he focused on the road ahead. Villages rushed by. Other road users pulled over and were lost in the Ford's wake. The minutes ticked slowly. Dan tried to work out timings. At normal speeds it would take three-quarters of an hour to reach Penzance, but these were far from normal speeds. Could Davis do it in under thirty? That'd put Collick's brother, Trevor, there ten minutes ahead. He wouldn't be rushing. He'd expect Collick to have done his job, killed Dan and now be processing the crime scene.

They reached the A30 without incident and Dan's mental calculation knocked the excess ten minutes off.

"So what's going on?" Davis asked now they could cruise on the dual carriageway.

"A girl was abducted a year and a half ago. I was blamed and arrested. It was a set-up. Ironically by the detective who was shot at the farm. And now his brother has got my friend."

"Why?"

"Revenge… Money. Seems they blame my father for ruining them. It's a grudge that goes back nearly twenty years."

On the outskirts of Penzance, Dan said, "The brown signs. Follow the brown signs to Scillonian. It'll take us to Penzance Harbour where the ferry docks."

"I know," Davis said, his eyes intent on the road.

The Ford weaved in and out of the increasingly dense traffic, and as they reached Wharf Road leading to the quay, Dan spotted a blue car three vehicles ahead.

"There!"

"That the one?"

"I think so."

Davis flicked the siren and lights off and slowed to thirty. He was on the radio to police already waiting at the terminal and provided a description.

"It's approaching the terminal. Slowing…"

For a second Dan wondered if Trevor had seen something suspicious and changed his mind, but then he turned into the terminal.

Davis said, "OK, he's just entered."

When they reached the same spot, Dan saw that the delay was caused by a queue where tickets were being checked. The blue vehicle was through and joined the queue. As Davis waved his ID at the gatekeeper, the police were already confronting the driver of the blue car. A man stood either side of the car, weapons raised.

"Armed police!" Dan heard the one on the driver's side shout. "Step out of the car, keeping your hands where I can see them."

With the lights flashing, Davis pulled up behind the blue car, said, "Stay here!" and climbed out.

Both car doors opened and two people got out.

"Down. On the ground!" the armed police shouted.

As the two people dropped and spread-eagled themselves, Dan was out and walking their way. He shook his head. This wasn't right. It wasn't the car he'd seen outside the Croggans' house.

"These are just kids," he shouted to Davis. "We've got the wrong car!"

Dan put his head in trembling hands. He'd blundered. It was under three hours since he'd left the Isles. If Trevor had gone by boat, he'd be arriving now. The ferry took two and a half hours. The blue car on the road outside the farm—maybe that was just an ordinary car, nothing to do with Collick. He hadn't seen it come out of the farm. He'd just jumped to that conclusion. He hadn't even registered the make, so it might not have been a Fiesta.

The police were opening the boot as he neared and saw there was nothing inside other than luggage. He'd screwed up. Davis seemed to be scrutinising him. Was he now doubting Dan's story?

Dan turned and walked along the wharf to the water's edge. The ferry was docking and, when he reached the railing on the quay, he stood and gulped in the sea air. Maybe Collick hadn't had an accomplice after all. He watched the cars coming off and tried to think. Collick couldn't have shot himself like that. It was a physical impossibility with a shotgun. There must be someone else involved.

He turned back to the queue. The first car was waved forward onto the ramp. What if it wasn't a blue car? It could be any car. At least one with a big enough boot space for a person—which would be most. Tom had told

Ted Bryant it was a blue car. It had been night and there were no streetlights. It had been Collick who'd said dark blue. Dan knew Collick had lied about finding the car, so why not lie about the colour. *Close but no cigar*, he had said.

Dan glanced at all the vehicles in the queue for the ferry. Could another colour look blue in moonlight? He pictured Karen's car in the dark at the boatyard. Silver could look green or light blue at night. Could other colours be confused with blue?

The third vehicle along from him was grey. Hard to tell what colour a grey car really is in the dark. It was a kind of pickup. From the front it looked like a small Fiat, but it had a covered load bay at the rear. Bryant's view would have been from the front, he wouldn't have seen the rear, plus he didn't know much about cars.

The Fiat started moving. The number plate had the letters TA and then an 8. Could Tom have misread TA8 and TAB? Maybe.

Dan peered in at the driver who glanced away; a man in his thirties with nervous eyes under a baseball cap. Dan stared as the Fiat moved past. The man had jug ears like Pat Croggan and there was facial similarity. *Jesus!* It was Collick's younger half-brother: Alan Croggan, the youngest boy from the farm.

Ignoring the pain, Dan ran up to the Fiat, grabbed at the passenger door handle and banged on a side panel when the car accelerated. But there were vehicles in front and the driver had nowhere to go. Dan ran screaming, "He's here!" He came up to the driver's side and yanked open the door. A yellow-vested ferry worker was beside him, another in front of the car and then Davis and the other policemen were in control. Dan was pulled away from the door and heard them yelling at Croggan to get out and down.

The rear of the vehicle had a black clipped-down cover. Dan pulled one eyelet free and then another, working his way around to get inside.

He saw feet.

"Karen!" Dan frantically jerked more of the cover free and saw her curled on the floor, leather bindings around ankles and wrists, pulled tight behind her back. Desperate eyes implored him to help. He clambered in and pulled a gag from her mouth, heard her gasp for air and began to fumble with the harness that bound her.

SIXTY-THREE

The following day, Dan left Karen's room at Truro hospital. She was dehydrated and traumatized by the ordeal and they were keeping her in for a second night. She was a fighter and he knew he'd have his old Karen back soon.

He spotted Agent Sisoko in the corridor and nodded to him. "Thank you."

"Just doing my job," the agent replied mysteriously.

"What do you mean? I rang you but couldn't get through. Did you get the voice message I left?" And then a thought struck him. How did you get there so quickly?

Sisoko cracked his broad white smile. "Good job we were."

As he spoke, a cupboard door opened and a man in a suit stepped out. Rotund and with a jolly face, he glanced at Dan and then Sisoko.

Dan looked hard. "Have we met?" He seemed familiar and yet he couldn't place him.

"Agent Simmons," the man said with a nod.

"I'm sorry, have we met before?"

Simmons let embarrassment pull at the corner of his mouth. "Busted," he said.

"What?"

"You probably saw me on that rough Scillonian flight. I was in the seat in front. Not ideal, but it was the last available."

Sisoko said, "I should apologize, Dan. I led you to believe we weren't interested in the farm and didn't think there was a link to our case, but we did. You seemed genuine but I couldn't be sure, couldn't know that you weren't somehow in the network. I wanted to make you think I might be closing in on McNally, thought you might warn him."

"You were shaking the tree."

Sisoko nodded.

Dan said, "So you were tailing me."

"Good job we were." Simmons grinned.

Dan nodded, thinking. "So when I rang you—"

"I didn't answer because I didn't want to give anything away. Thought it was best to just follow."

"So when you burst into Jenkin's and shot Collick, you weren't responding to my message."

Simmon's said, "No, but smart thinking. We did get DS Collick's full confession on voicemail."

"And now?"

"Now we think your connection to our case is just coincidental. Collick was setting you up for the girl's disappearance."

"So where is she?"

Sisoko raised his large hands as if in submission. "Sorry, I have no idea what happened to her."

"But we don't think you were involved... to blame, I mean," Simmons added.

Dan took a deep breath. "That's good to hear." He switched his attention back to Sisoko and asked. "What about the Aussie, Gerry, from Jack Tanner's yard?"

"What about him?"

"You had his photo."

"As I said, it was just in the pack. I shouldn't tell you this, but forget him. We have nothing on him."

"What about Jack Tanner?"

"Nothing."

"Everitt?"

Sisoko shook his head, his eyes set with a serious look. "Our investigations are ongoing. Do not get involved. Understand?"

Dan nodded.

Simmons said, "The book with the codes."

"What book?"

"The one Ms Chamberlain gave you in hospital. It caused us some consternation."

Dan was surprised. "Why? It's just a novel."

"But you wrote a code in it. We spent ages trying to link it to McNally."

And then Dan wondered whether Karen had written down Jade's numbers while trying to work them out. He said, "I have no idea myself."

Simmons said, "They seem to be in four pairs."

"Four? Not eight pairs or sixteen numbers? How do you get four?"

"I don't remember them all now," Simmons continued, "but I started to think maybe every other number was a date. They seemed to progress, add a month and then a day or so either side."

"Why—"

"The first was twenty dash one, wasn't it? So twentieth of January, I thought. Then the next one ended in a two. So that would be February. And then March and April." He narrowed his eyes. "Mean anything to you?"

"Are you still testing me?"

"No. Anyway, the pattern isn't great because, like I said, the other number varies between eighteen and twenty. So maybe they aren't dates."

Dan drove home thinking about the numbers. It felt like he almost had it but the meaning was just out of reach.

SIXTY-FOUR

Two days later, Dan travelled back from visiting Karen at her mum's house. November's biting cold winds were over and mild air blew down the creek. It was the middle of the afternoon and already getting dark.

Someone was on Mizzen Green, sitting on the ground with a row of candles in front of them. Lizzy Bridger.

He parked and walked up to her.

"Here again?"

She didn't respond immediately and seemed to be in a trance. Eventually she looked up at him.

"Here again?" he repeated.

"This is the day. I come here every month on this day and light candles for her. You know, it's kind of symbolic—a light to guide her home."

Dan was confused. "This isn't the day, Lizzy." He felt awkward saying it but pressed on. "It was the nineteenth of April... the night Jade disappeared."

Again she took a while to respond, and he suspected she had taken something, only this time she was placid and far away rather than incoherent and aggressive like the night she'd called him and recited the Buccaboo rhyme.

"Jade liked the new moon," she said. "Funny how people call it that when there's no moon at all. Jade liked it when there was no moon. You know, the stars seem so much brighter."

"So you do this every month on a new moon?"

She gazed far away.

Dan asked, "And you stay... what, all night?"

"Until the time she went. Until the stones are covered and the tide is high."

"High tide," Dan said.

She focused on him then. "What?"

"High tide tonight is at four fifty-seven," he said automatically, but his mind was whirring. Was that what Jade's numbers had been about? He had to check.

Dan picked up the tide tables for the previous year and checked the dates of the new moon. Agent Simmons had been right. Every other number was a date. The penultimate number was eighteen-four: the eighteenth of April, the day before she disappeared. She had written down the dates of each new moon between January and April. Jade had disappeared in the early hours of the nineteenth.

He checked the tides and confirmed his suspicion. The second number was the time of the high tide during the hours of darkness.

It was the twenty-ninth today. If Jade had written last night's high tide the numbers would have been 29-11 4-57. She had disappeared a day after and Lizzy Bridger was on Mizzen Green—again a day after. Maybe Jade counted the night as the same day. It wouldn't have surprised Dan if she had.

He spent thirty minutes deciding on a plan and finally rang Agent Sisoko. He told him what the numbers meant.

* * *

Shortly after three o'clock that night, Dan eased the Laser away from the pontoon and into the creek.

The darkness was almost absolute, with heavy cloud blocking the starlight, just like the night Jade had disappeared. But Dan didn't need any lights. He had a sixth sense of where he was on the water. Without seeing it, he knew where the channel was and the position of the yachts strung along the creek. It struck him then that maybe Jade had the same sense. What had she said? *I've been out in the dark before—many times.*

She'd tried to persuade him to let her use the Laser in the dark. Maybe it was true. Maybe she regularly sailed at night when he didn't know about it.

There was a light wind and he reckoned to be able to do at least five knots, which he hoped would be enough.

Crossing the creek, he came alongside a large yacht and tied up. He was on the channel side and opposite were the stepping stones and then The Ridge. The stones would be underwater soon like they were that night.

Eyes straining, he waited.

And then he heard it. A low burble. An exceptionally quiet engine on very low revs. Seconds later it was close: a grey mass looming out of the darkness, a boat without navigation lights.

Dan waited, straining his eyes, and then he saw it. The name of the vessel.

Double Zero.

And piloting the boat was none other than Gerry, the Australian.

SIXTY-FIVE

Dan's instinct was to confront the man, but he didn't. Mainly because the boat was going downriver. Based on Jade's numbers, the time of the high tide was important. Whatever the Aussie was up to, Dan suspected it would happen later.

Dan passed The Ridge and then rounded the Plynt promontory.

The water of the Carrick Roads was choppy and he cursed himself for not following closer. For a minute, he scanned left and right trying to locate *Double Zero*. And then he heard it. Gerry must have opened the throttle slightly.

He had turned left, upriver, in the direction of the ferry and ultimately Truro.

Dan turned the Laser and got on a reach. He was moving more quickly now but guessed *Double Zero* was going faster.

He passed Chycoose Creek and the shore on the left became a black maw as the thick forest began. There were spots of light on the far bank and one suddenly blinked. The other boat briefly blocked its light and so Dan knew where it was. Gerry was sixty, maybe seventy yards ahead and mid-stream.

Dan used all his skill to get as much speed out of the little dinghy as he could but sensed he was losing the other boat.

He passed oyster beds and then saw a giant chain angle out of the water. Dan moved over to avoid the ship moored there. In fact, there were four of them all laid up in pairs. Now Russian-owned, they were old passenger ferries. Cheaper to pay mooring fees here than scrap them.

Dan was past the first two when something made him slow.

A sound. There it was again. A clunk of metal on metal coming from the shore. Or was it one of the boats?

He tacked left behind the first ship, moving slowly, listening.

He heard what he guessed were boots on metal. And then he saw someone climbing a ladder from *Double Zero* into the ship.

When the man disappeared over the top, Dan eased alongside the other boat and checked there was no one aboard. When he was certain it must have been the Aussie who was now on the ship, Dan tied up and climbed over the other vessel to the ladder.

The metal groaned as it took his weight and Dan held his breath.

He hung there for a moment, his heart loud in his ears. Then he started to climb. The rungs bit his palms with rust and the few yards seemed to take an eternity. At the top, he poked his head up and checked no one was around. The deck was dark and silent.

Dan stepped cautiously over the side. After ten paces there was a door. He slowly turned the handle and was relieved it didn't creak.

He was inside.

The air was stale and tasted of iron. He was standing in a corridor that was dark but a dim light was coming from somewhere ahead. After treading carefully forward he came to some stairs and saw it was brighter on the deck below.

He crept down the stairs and stood at the bottom. He could hear voices. The Aussie wasn't alone.

The floor was carpeted, so he walked swiftly and silently to the next door. It had a rectangular window above it, too high to see through.

He placed his ear to the door and could hear the Aussie talking as if trying to explain something. Then he heard another voice. A woman. A foreigner.

Dan's heart stopped.

A gloved hand was over his mouth, and an arm locked around his chest.

SIXTY-SIX

Dan was pulled backwards, away from the door, by someone very strong.

His mind screamed *fight* but he felt helplessly pinned.

And then a voice said "Shush" calmly in his ear.

A torch was turned on and shone in his eyes before being turned on the man holding him. A policeman in a Kevlar vest. It flicked to another policeman and Dan saw an assault rifle in his hands. Then the man with the torch briefly pointed it at his own face.

Agent Sisoko.

Leaving the other two policemen at the door, Sisoko led Dan up the stairs, along the corridor and outside.

"Jesus!" Dan said quietly. "I almost had a heart attack."

Sisoko patted him on the shoulder.

"We'll take it from here," he said. "I want you off this ship and away."

Dan hesitated.

"Now!" the agent hissed, telling him there was no argument. "I'll come and see you tomorrow."

Dan descended the ladder and saw that there were now two ribs with large engines tied up next to *Double Zero*. There were two policemen with assault rifles on the Aussie's boat and another one in each of the ribs.

One of them waved for Dan to hurry up and get in his Laser.

As he was about to push off, one of the men leaned close.

The policeman said, "Don't just hang around. Understood?"

Dan sailed back to Plynt and the entrance to Trevelyon Creek. He couldn't help but glance back each time he tacked. Finally he saw two sets of blue flashing lights appear and head in the opposite direction.

It was almost midday by the time Sisoko arrived at the yard. He grinned as he appeared at the workshop entrance.

"Thank God," Dan said, flicking off the radio and stepping around a saw horse, "I've been bursting to know what was going on last night."

"You should have just left it to us," Sisoko said.

He reached out and shook Dan's hand.

"So?" Dan prompted impatiently. "I know Gerry—the Aussie—met someone on board. A foreign woman. Maybe more than one…"

Sisoko said, "Let's talk outside."

The agent placed a hand on Dan's shoulder and walked with him into the sunshine. "Beautiful spot," he said, "when the sun's shining."

"Stop teasing me and tell me what was going on."

"I thought you knew."

"To be honest, I don't have a clue." Dan glanced towards the Plynt path where Jade had disappeared. "Apart from knowing I'm not guilty of course."

"Guilty of what?"

"Jade Bridger's murder."

"Maybe you should sit down," Sisoko said. He was smiling again.

"Just bloody tell me!"

"People trafficking," Sisoko said seriously. "Well, worse than that, frankly. You've been a great help, Dan."

Dan shook his head.

"Shall we have a cup of tea?" Sisoko suggested. "I've quite a story to tell you."

In the office, Auntie Margaret made them a drink while Alfie paid too much attention to the agent's shoes.

Dan pulled him away with a ruffle of the old dog's collar. Then Margaret took Alfie and left them to talk.

Sisoko told Dan that they'd found thirteen young women on board the old cruise ship. Twelve of them were Asian and they were between sixteen and twenty years old. They were being smuggled into the country.

"We haven't got all the information yet, but it looks like they believe they're being smuggled into the country to meet wealthy husbands met through the Internet. But Gerry Hunt has confessed. They're being smuggled for the sex industry."

Sisoko took a long slug of tea before continuing. "Unfortunately, he's bound to be a small cog in a much bigger machine. The girls are dropped at the ship the night before. He says he doesn't know who by. He takes them to a shed just down from the boatyard where he works."

"Old Quay," Dan said. "That explains the timing. I guess Gerry could only get to it at high tide a few times in the month."

"He's said as much. Also that the girls get dropped off the night before because there's guaranteed no moon."

Dan waited for more.

"The girls were kept in the shed until the following night when they were collected. All very slick," Sisoko said. "We can't get much else out of Hunt. He calls the man who arranges the drop off the *courier* and can only tell us the first name of the guy who picks them up—which is undoubtedly fake. However, you'll be amazed to hear who Hunt's accomplice is. The man who handled the girls at Old Quay."

The agent paused for dramatic effect and then said, "None other than Steve Bridger."

Dan sat back, stunned.

"We turned up and he was just waiting there to unload the *cargo*. He's given a full statement and, according to Bridger, he just did what he was told by Hunt. He claims to know nothing about the cruise ship."

"Incredible," Dan said.

"We've got a team on board taking DNA samples and it looks like quite a few girls have been through their system. If you hadn't called me with your suspicion…"

"But I didn't know what was going on. If anything I would have guessed drugs."

"Doesn't matter. You put two and two together. You were right about the code."

"Do you think the trafficking has been stopped?"

Sisoko shook his head. "As I said, Mr Hunt was probably just a cog, just one route in. Stop that and another one starts up. That's what we usually find."

Dan remembered seeing his mugshot when Sisoko had asked him to review the photographs in hospital. He asked, "You said he was just in the pack. Had you been monitoring him?"

"Gerry Hunt had served time in his homeland but we didn't find anything there, and his job with Jack Tanner seems to have been legit. As I said, we've not managed to connect Hunt with anyone else except Steve Bridger. And we suspect Bridger's telling the truth and is just dumb labour. The obvious connection would have been between Hunt and Everitt. Everitt has some rights over your boatyard. I've a theory Hunt would want it because of the location. Old Quay limited what and when they could bring things ashore. With your yard they needn't have worried about the tides. And you have two big sheds in good condition. Clearly, Hunt and Bridger weren't working alone. The operation had to be set up in the first place. Someone knows the *courier* and who's picking them up after Hunt."

"Everitt then," Dan said.

"It could be but he's not talking. We'll keep working on him. Maybe he'll crack."

The agent stood as if to leave but Dan detected a twinkle in his eye.

"What aren't you telling me?"

Femi Sisoko gave his big grin. "Weren't you paying attention?"

"I thought so."

"I said we found thirteen girls on the ship."

"Yes...?"

"Twelve of them were Asian."

Dan now realized Sisoko had something big to tell him.

He said, "There was another girl. Jade Bridger. Jade Bridger is alive."

"What?"

"She was in a cabin on the ship, held on a deck below the water level. She's in hospital but doing fine bearing in mind she'd been held there for a year and a half."

Dan shook his head, trying to process the information. "Alive?" he said. "Thank God. I can hardly believe it."

Sisoko patted him on the shoulder and stood.

"I'd better be going."

As they walked out of the office, Dan prompted, "But her dad was involved!"

The agent walked all the way to his car before he said anything more.

"We've not got her side of the story yet," he said, "but according to Hunt she knew what they were doing and tried to blackmail them. So he locked her up."

"But Steve Bridger genuinely seemed to blame me."

"He claims he didn't know."

Dan shook his head. It seemed the only reasonable answer, he guessed.

Sisoko got into his car. Before he closed the door he said, "If I have anything more to tell you, I'll let you know. And Dan…"

"Yes?"

"If you find out anything else. Please, please, please don't get involved. You were lucky this time. Next time just tell me and leave it to us. Agreed?"

Dan nodded and waved the agent off. He had no intention of getting involved with anything else. Jade was alive and his innocence was finally proven.

Auntie Margaret joined him and linked her arm through his.

"Everything all right, dear?"

"He seems to think I was smart but I wasn't. And I missed an obvious clue. Michael Searle drew something on the photos of Nina Ivanova that pointed to her location. On Jade's photo he drew two circles. I should have realized he was telling me it was Gerry Hunt's boat, *Double Zero*."

She gave him a hug. "Come into the office. Have another cup of tea and some cake and tell your Auntie all about it."

* * *

The papers at the weekend were full of the story of how the NCA had foiled a sex trade business. As always there were little new facts but considerable general material about the sex industry and the abuse of women. Dan learned that thousands of girls were trafficked into the sex trade each year throughout the world and many of them disappeared from the system. The majority of women in the trade hadn't started by choice. They were conned or forced into it. They were vulnerable and many turned to drugs in their despair. The Association of Chief Police Officers estimated that over twelve thousand women working in off-street prostitution in Britain had possibly been trafficked.

It was an astonishing statistic and the trade Dan had interrupted seemed to have dealt with over a hundred girls, based on the DNA results. But none of them had been traced. Maybe the articles would prompt something or someone to confess.

Jade's story was bought by one of the red tops, and if it was true then she had worked out that her dad and Hunt were smuggling. She claimed she didn't know what, but it was hard to believe since she had followed Steve Bridger to Old Quay and seen the sheds. She also said she'd followed Hunt to the cruise ship and knew he travelled on the night after the new moon.

She admitted to asking for money and wanted to run away. On the night she'd disappeared she expected to meet her father but Hunt had been there. He'd hit her and she'd woken up on the ship.

Had he meant to kill her? Maybe. Maybe he couldn't go through with it and just locked her up instead. He hadn't abused her, and each month he gave her a supply of food and water.

Perhaps the most surprising revelation from Jade was the involvement of her uncle, DS Collick. She claimed

...at he'd intended to take her to the Scilly Isles and she'd agreed only because she wanted him there in case anything went wrong with the blackmail.

Another paper picked up on the link between Hunt's business and Geoff Jenkin's. There was no evidence, but it enabled the paper to pull out the sordid details of the farm manager's past.

Dan's exoneration got little mention.

The following week, Dan was surprised to see Sisoko again. The big man knocked on the office door just before closing.

"I thought I'd give you an update," the agent said with his usual broad smile.

Dan shook the man's hand warmly.

"I've read the papers," he said.

"More than that," Sisoko said. "And to say you may be right."

"Right? About what?"

Margret offered them tea.

The agent seemed to use the interruption to change the subject. He said, "I hear you're selling the farm."

Dan had divided the farm into two, along the old boundary lines, recreating the farm that had once been Croggan Farm. It was being heavily advertised in what the estate agent called the "alternative market". This meant for non-farming purposes, but that was as far as Dan understood it.

"Just half of it—where Jenkin lived," he said. "Too many bad memories I'm afraid." Even though he knew the agent had gained a lot of information from Lizzy in the days after Karen had been rescued, he explained, "Way back, that farm didn't used to be part of Searles. It had been in the Croggan family for generations before my great-grandfather acquired it. I thought the grievance was about Pat Croggan being kicked out in favour of Geoff Jenkin, but the feelings ran much deeper than that. I never understand how hatred passes down generations, but I guess they hated anyone controlling Searles Farm."

Sisoko waited for Margaret to give them a cup each and then leave them to talk in private. Then he said, "We have Jade and Lizzy Bridger in protective custody."

"Are you concerned about the Croggans or is this about the sex trade business?"

Sisoko didn't answer directly. He said, "In her statement, Lizzy told us she ran away at sixteen—the same age as Jade was. She said she was sick of the life on the island, sick of the way her mother treated her, and maybe wanted more opportunity, I guess. She blamed her mother for not liking her. For the fear she instilled in them, especially her. I guess you know her reputation, but it must have been hard for a sixteen-year-old... When she returned to this area she changed her surname. Working for Geoff Jenkin at the farm she got mixed up in his porn video business and was too afraid to tell anyone—even her half-brother."

Dan nodded. "If I'd known Lizzy Bridger was Elizabeth Croggan and Collick's half-sister, I might have guessed he was trying to set me up. I even saw them arguing and just assumed it was about his failure to find her daughter."

The agent said, "That makes sense. Alan Croggan has finally given a full confession and said that the Bridgers didn't know about the plan to take Jade away from them."

Dan knew Alan had pleaded guilty to Karen's abduction and found it ironic that he would be on remand at the same prison where Dan had been held.

"Has Alan said anything else?"

"He's confirmed the plan was to implicate you. DS Collick seems to have been trying to kill two birds with one stone. Ruin you and your father at the same time as save the girl from what he saw as an abusive household."

They finished their tea and Dan studied the other man's face.

He said, "You didn't come all this way just to talk to me about Jade and Lizzy Bridger." Dan studied the other man's face. "So, what did you really mean when you said I was right?"

Sisoko beamed and said, "McNally."

"McNally? The Mr Big you knew was involved but couldn't prove it?"

"You see, we think Jade knows more than she's admitting. The dates on her note were when the girls were dropped off at the cruise ship. It's possible she saw something. Maybe she knows who they are. And she was following her dad, so maybe she knows more about the other end of the connection. She's not saying much, but maybe she will... when she feels safe."

"How does that lead to McNally? Have you now found a connection to Gerry Hunt?"

"No. I wish. Hunt is sticking to his story that he didn't know who he was dealing with and so is Steve Bridger."

"So what?"

Sisoko raised an eyebrow. "Who owns the tin mine?"

Dan knew he couldn't see it from the boatyard, but the agent looked in the direction of Bucker Mine.

"Well, since it was condemned, I guess the council own it."

"And who, in all these related dealings, do we know on the council?"

"Redman. Are you saying he owns it?"

"No, the council should own it, but Redman arranged the sale to Alfa Explore. And Alfa have applied for a licence to investigate fracking on the site of the old mine. In fact, it's a dead cert that it's a prime location."

"I don't get it."

"Fracking exploration is a legitimate McNally business. He owns Alfa Explore and by implication is connected to Redman, who transferred the land to his company. Redman is connected to Everitt through the legitimate land agency business."

Dan still didn't get it, but he said, "That's great."

Sisoko smiled, "But it wasn't that. Just like you said about Al Capone—we might not get McNally for the sex trade business but maybe we'll get him on tax evasion. By having the mine transferred to him for next to nothing, he avoided stamp duty. Geological surveys show a high potential for shale gas, so the value of the mine was significant."

Dan said, "But there's no fracking in Cornwall."

"Yet. It will come and when it does we'll get him. Plus Councillor Redman will be keen to cooperate. He'll face corruption charges, so, of course, he's likely to claim coercion."

"I'm pleased for you."

"There's a long way to go, but the tax evasion issue will let us seize McNally's computers and documents, so we hope to make all the connections."

As usual, Auntie Margaret wanted a full update once Sisoko had left. Dan updated her on Alan Coggan and McNally. Then he said, "One thing we haven't talked about is what you'll do with your half of the money?"

"From the sale of the farm—assuming you do sell?"

"The estate agent is confident."

"Aren't they always?" she said, laughing. "Well then, let's assume I've half a million to play with. First I'm going to climb Machu Picchu, and then perhaps Kilimanjaro, and then visit Tibet and then the pyramids of Egypt…"

Dan must have looked agog, because Margaret began to chuckle.

"No. I'm possibly going to take a cruise somewhere for a couple of weeks. You know I've never been abroad before, so that'll be an adventure enough. But my priority is health. I'll make sure both Alfie and I get the best medical help we can. And after that, if there's much left, I want to give most to charity. Save the Children and Refuge, I think."

Dan turned his attention back to his auntie and said, "It must be hard for Bella too."

Margaret showed concern. "I wasn't implying…"

"I know, but it's tough only having one parent." Especially one so crazy, he thought. Then, out loud he said, "At least when I was growing up I had you. I always knew that I had someone who would listen, someone to turn to, someone to run to." He hugged her then. "Auntie, you've always been there for me. Thank you for everything."

If Dan hadn't returned from Bristol and if Margaret and Tom hadn't kept things going, maybe none of this would have ever been stopped. Maybe the yard would have been developed by Everitt, not for waterside houses, but for Hunt and his sex trade.

"Thank you," he said again.

"Good," she said with a grin. "Since you're in such a grateful mood, I need you to fix the ceiling in my lounge."

SIXTY-SEVEN

Bella gave Dan a hug. She said, "Bye, Daddy," and skipped to her mother at the door.

Karen sat in Dan's new car and smiled through the window at Deborah. The other woman responded with a slight nod before disappearing inside with her daughter.

Dan climbed back into the car with a grin. "That went well."

"It was lovely. I think you're making real progress."

At Christmas, Dan had asked Deborah if she needed anything for Bella and bought clothes and books as well as making a doll's house for his daughter. Margaret had invited them all to her house for a New Year's dinner, including Karen and her mother, and afterwards Deborah had agreed to let Dan have Bella for a few hours without her supervision. At first it was at Margaret's house and then she had agreed to let Dan and Karen take her to a soft-play park. This was their fourth trip out alone with Bella and a weekly routine had been established.

Karen added, "It won't be long before you even get a kiss with that hug when you drop her off."

As Dan drove out of Penryn he asked, "You definitely haven't given Deborah any money, have you?"

Karen couldn't help but smile. She'd spent time with Deborah to understand her concerns and talk about the benefit of a father's influence. They both grew up with single-parent mums. They had that in common and Karen used that to build on. Because Dan's business was booming he could pay a good level of child support. Even so, Deborah had been reticent about letting Dan take his daughter out for the day without her. Karen's promise to accompany him with Bella had been the persuading factor. Not money, not pressure, but another woman's presence.

Dan was a natural, a great dad. Although Bella had her awkward moments, over time Karen thought things would improve, especially when she started school.

Karen said, "We just talked, that's all." The truth was she'd told Deborah that she was back with Dan. It wasn't really true, but over the past few months they'd been good friends—best friends again. She'd got the job of head of communications for a major accountancy practice in Truro and lived at her mum's. She still woke at night with terror sweats and saw a therapist, but the nightmares were becoming less frequent and the therapist had suggested her next session might be the last.

Dan turned off the main road.

Karen looked over. "Why are we going this way?"

They passed the part of the farm now split off and renamed Gwidden Farm. Next to the post with the new name, the "for sale" sign had been changed to "under offer".

Karen stared. "My God, I can't believe it!"

"Me neither. I accepted quite a bit less than advertised, but a quick sale works for everyone. Looks like they'll be developing it for adventure days. Paintballing, off-road driving, that sort of thing."

Dan continued to the entrance to Searles Farm and turned in to the drive.

"Just wanted to see how things were progressing with the old house," he said. "Although I'm not sure I'll have success selling this half of the farm."

He drove through the arcade of trees and stopped before the front entrance. Two new lemon trees had been planted by the front door. Scaffolding had been constructed and it looked like the builders had begun dismantling the damaged roof.

Dan kept the engine running, and she was surprised when he set off again only seconds later. He didn't turn around but drove on past the barns onto the track towards the woods. His new 4x4 made easy work of the ruts, and when they reached the treeline he turned left, scooting around Lower Field. Since harvesting the sweetcorn, the field had been allowed to go fallow, peppered with white and blue flowers. Dan stopped on the track where he had on the first day back and recounted the story of boys he'd once rescued from the silt.

"You're a hero," she said.

"Not really."

They sat on a rug by the water's edge and watched the sea birds. Although the air had a hint of winter coolness, the spring sun warmed their faces and he wished he'd brought a bottle of wine.

For a long time they sat in comfortable silence before Karen said, "Odd about the cow's bones in the mine. Do you think we'll ever find out what had happened?"

Dan waited a beat. "I have my suspicions, though I'd never want to say. I found more in John Searle's second safe than just the fake love letter. There was also evidence of blackmail by Geoff Jenkin. Searles was the biggest beef, and a pretty large dairy, farm. The BSE crisis of the eighties would have wiped him out, so Jenkin was disposing of the infected cattle and doctoring the records. I think he used that to get the farm manager position."

"Dumping the carcasses in the mine?"

"That's what I think."

"Couldn't your father have reported him?" She continued to call John Searle his father and suspected one day Dan would revert to the same. The man had brought up his nephew, mostly alone and through hard times. Even if Dan didn't feel it, the old man had done his best. He had been a stoical God-fearing man and, although she knew what Dan was about to say, she didn't believe it.

Dan shrugged. "Jenkin couldn't have done it alone, and he wasn't the farm manager. So I don't get his motivation."

His motivation was *to be* the farm manager, she thought, but decided now was not the time to bring that all up again. Jenkin was a greedy man who saw an opportunity and exploited it.

Dan shrugged again. "Anyway, I don't want anyone to know my suspicions in case it comes back on John. I think it's best left and forgotten."

She watched a fish jump and cause large ripples in the mirrored surface of the river, as clear as the crisp blue sky. She thought about the news that Alan Croggan had been convicted of aggravated kidnapping and received a reduced ten-year sentence for his cooperation. Gary Collick had fully recovered from being shot, but the ex-detective sergeant would spend twenty years at Her Majesty's pleasure for his involvement.

After a minute Karen said, "You know you were lucky, don't you?"

"What do you mean?"

"If Agent Sisoko hadn't turned up at the farm in time... It was a hell of a gamble."

He shook his head, unwilling to think of what would have happened if Sisoko hadn't responded.

"It wasn't a gamble," he said. "I had no other choice. I thought Collick still had you and I had to try and save you—no matter what the cost."

"Told you, you were a hero." She wrapped an arm around him and they went back to watching the river before she felt the courage to say, "You know what you said before, that love wasn't about facing your greatest fear, but about not wanting to grow old without the one you love?"

"Did I say that?"

She looked at him seriously and couldn't tell if he was joking or not.

"Well I know what you meant." She took a breath. "I want you to know that you are the one person I can't live without."

"What about the issues? What about the reasons you left me? I wasn't ambitious enough. You wanted the bright lights and excitement."

"I've had enough excitement to last me a lifetime. But that's not the same. I know now that I was wrong. I want family and stability and the love of a good man... who just happens to be a white knight in a 4x4 charger."

Dan stared at the far bank and said nothing.

Karen let him think and then said, "I love you, Daniel Searle. If you won't have me back now, then I'll just have to wait until you come to your senses."

He stood slowly, pulled her to her feet and pointed along the foreshore. "This would make an excellent spot for decking. I always fancied a New England-style house. The walls would be here and here." He pointed as he walked. "And here would be the front porch."

She stood beside him, squinting, unsure what he was actually saying.

"The boatyard... I'm too busy to justify using the loft as a home. Plus there's too much history." He smiled. "And I've got planning permission for a house right here on this spot."

"What about Black Woods? You'd be very close, and they've always scared you."

Dan looked at the trees and the hard, dark edge where they met high tide. "There's nothing in there to scare me. There's certainly evil in this world, but it's not a spirit, a Buccaboo or a man, although I think it's in some men's hearts."

"And there's good too." She put her arm around him.

He smiled, "Yes there is. And, if there's a battle between the light and the dark—whatever people call them—then I reckon the light is winning."

"I think so too." Karen kissed his cheek and looked again at the area he had paced out. "It's a nice spot for a house."

"A New England house," he corrected, "with decking overlooking the creek. Perfect for sitting out on with a beer on a summer evening. But not on my own of course. With company. And such a house would need plenty of love... and a family. It'd be far too big for one person."

"Are you saying you'll have me back?"

He pulled her close and gave her a long kiss. "In a heartbeat, baby. In a heartbeat."

Acknowledgments

Most people only get to read a book when it's a final product. My wife gets to see it when it's far from finished and has to put up with hearing about it over and over again. So thank you, Kerry for being a great sounding board and for amazing me every day. Thanks to my parents for their edits and feedback on an early draft. Hopefully you'll approve of this final version. I'm also grateful for your constant enthusiasm and support. In addition, Pete Tonkin deserves my gratitude for his comments and reviews. And a final mention for Richard Sheehan, my extraordinary editor. I don't know how you do it. Of course, any remaining mistakes are my own.

murraybaileybooks.com

KEEP NO SECRETS... TELL NO LIES

HIDE THE TRUTH...

When Alex MacLure's friend and colleague dies he is determined to
carry on her research. He finds she has left him a coded message and
as he tries to make sense of it all, he discovers she was murdered.
And now the murderer needs to silence him.

...JUST STAY ALIVE

With only a few clues and a mysterious object Alex follows a trail from
London to Cairo. He must crack the code and expose a shocking and
inconceivable truth before the secret is buried for ever.

Available now in paperback and ebook